THE LIGHT
IN THE
DARKNESS

ELLEN FISHER

BANTAM BOOKS

NEW YORK TORONTO LONDON SYDNEY AUCKLAND

THE LIGHT IN THE DARKNESS

A Bantam Fanfare Book/October 1998

FANFARE and the portrayal of a boxed "ff" are trademarks of Bantam
Books, a division of Bantam Doubleday Dell Publishing Group, Inc.

ISBN 0-553-57922-3

Published simultaneously in the United States and Canada

Bantam Books are published by Bantam Books, a division of Bantam
Doubleday Dell Publishing Group, Inc. Its trademark, consisting of
the words "Bantam Books" and the portrayal of a rooster, is Regis-
tered in U.S. Patent and Trademark Office and in other countries.
Marca Registrada. Bantam Books, 1540 Broadway, New York, New
York 10036.

PRINTED IN THE UNITED STATES OF AMERICA

WCD   10   9   8   7   6   5   4   3   2   1

"SAY IT,"

he commanded softly, eyes gleaming with something more than hope. Jennifer saw the powerful emotion in his eyes, recognized it for what it was with feminine instinct, and helplessly responded to it.

"I want you," she whispered, less shyly now.

The expression of raw, elemental passion on his face left little doubt that he returned the sentiment in full. How he could want her so powerfully, so desperately, she could not fathom, but it was evident that he did. She was unable to bring herself to question fate. Slightly dazed at the direction events were taking, she repeated, "I want you."

The crystalline truth of those words shocked her. She had thought herself attracted to his younger self, a man with Grey's arrogance and charm, but with Edward's passion. Somehow that man was before her now. He came slowly to his feet, staring down at her with all the passion that was his nature etched on his handsome face.

And Jennifer felt the first passion of her life welling up in response. She did not struggle when his lips touched hers. Instead she responded eagerly, joyfully, wrapping her arms around his broad shoulders, reveling in the strangely delightful sensations his caressing hands and lips aroused. The taste of apple brandy was so intoxicating, his arms around her so warm and solid, that she wondered dizzily if she were dreaming.

It had to be a dream.

Reality had never been this wonderful.

Dedicated to the memory of my sister,
Karen Leigh Kraft

Truth will come to light; murder cannot be hid long.

—William Shakespeare

ONE

"I do not want a wife."

Edward Greyson enunciated each word with care. Gulping a mouthful of Madeira, he scowled darkly at his sister over the rim of his wineglass. "I have no need for a wife," he went on, warming to his subject. "No desire for a wife. And furthermore, I can scarcely conceive of a woman who would be foolish enough to voluntarily live under the same roof as myself, excepting, of course, you. To sum it up completely, therefore, I have no intentions of 'gracing Greyhaven with a bride,' as you so eloquently put it. *Ever.*" He poured himself another glass, sloshing some of the alcohol onto the thick Oriental carpet that adorned the floor of the parlor, and fixed his sister with a piercing silver glare. "Any questions?"

Catherine Greyson met his belligerent gaze without flinching. "Yes," she said coolly, without the least trace of humor on her elegant features. "When are you going to find a wife?"

Her brother's scowl darkened. "Either you are losing your hearing," he said with annoyance, "or your good sense. We have been through this repeatedly, and I see no reason to go over it yet again. Leave me alone." He turned his back on her, staring moodily at the broad expanse of the James River through the wavy glass of the window, but Catherine refused to be dismissed so summarily.

"My good sense?" she echoed angrily. "I am losing neither my sense nor my hearing, Grey, but I do believe that I am beginning to lose my sanity from living in the same house as you. You are enough to try the patience of Job!"

"My point exactly," Grey said, his gaze fixed on the river. "If a saint like yourself can scarcely bear the sight of me, how can you expect any ordinary woman to do so?"

"Damn it, Grey!" Catherine snapped, temper overcoming her wonted poise. "Despite your dissolute ways, every woman along the James has thrown herself at you, but you have scorned every last one. Some of them are far more saintly than I—"

"Surely not," Grey said in a tone of mocking disbelief that told her he was enjoying her outburst immensely.

"You don't need a saint," she said wearily, torn between sympathy and rage. "You simply need a woman who will make you happy. And since you will be in Princess Anne County for a month, won't you just *look* for such a woman?"

Grey turned on her abruptly, forgetting his feigned fascination with the view. "No woman on earth can make me happy," he said savagely. "I am going to Princess Anne County to visit my friend Kayne O'Neill, not to seek a wife."

"Promise me you'll look."

Grey smiled wryly at his sister's persistence. "You make it sound as simple as purchasing horseflesh."

"If you were to find a suitable woman, it could be."

"A suitable woman," Grey repeated. "And, pray tell, what sort of woman is suitable to be the wife of a drunkard?" His tone was sardonic, but she heard the self-loathing beneath it.

"A girl of good breeding, of impeccable manners," she clarified, ignoring his bitterness and the sympathy that stabbed her. "A lady worthy of the Greyson name."

Grey merely looked incredulous, and she shook her

head impatiently. "Grey, you simply must marry. Once the Greysons were one of the finest families in Virginia; now we are scorned by our own class and mocked by the common planters. And little wonder. You don't dice, you don't race your stallions against other gentlemen's stock, you don't participate in cockfights. And you have showered contempt on every eligible young lady who has had the misfortune to be introduced to you. We never have visitors anymore, for you've gone out of your way to alienate every family along the James. The entire county thinks you peculiar, if not outright mad."

"Surely," Grey said scathingly, "you don't believe that I give a damn about the opinion of my neighbors."

"I know you don't. It's scandalous, really, how little regard you have for what others think of you. What would Mother and Father have thought of your conduct these last years? They would have been horrified."

"As to that," Grey drawled with utter unconcern, "I cared even less for what our parents thought than I do for the opinions of our neighbors."

"What about children?" his sister continued. "Surely you want a son."

Grey shook his head slowly, glancing down at the nearly empty goblet he held in his hand. A slight, self-deprecating smile lifted the corners of his mouth as he said curtly, "Whether I want a son is not the question. Rather the question is, would I be a good father?" He raised the glass slightly. "I think not."

Instantly sensing that she had taken the wrong approach, Catherine attacked from another angle. "What about me?" she demanded. "Do you care nothing for my future? However do you expect me to find a husband when most of the young men in the county believe that you are demented?" She knew perfectly well that at three and twenty she was still unwed because she was lame, but she was willing to use any argument, no matter how unfair, if it would encourage him to seek a wife.

She was pleased to see faint concern replace the cold

indifference on Grey's lean face. "I did not realize you were in such dire need of a husband," he said slowly. In truth, he had thought little about Catherine's future, so engrossed had he been in his own problems these last years. Now, staring thoughtfully at her, he realized that she was indeed somewhat beyond the usual age for matrimony. Had she ever had so much as a single suitor? To his shame, he found that he had no idea.

Catherine's gaze found his. "Isn't that what all women want?"

"Perhaps. And yet I think that the woman who prefers my hand in marriage to spinsterhood is a fool. However . . ."

He hated the thought of marriage, despised it with a savage vehemence. And yet perhaps he did have some responsibility for his younger sister. It was a damned uncomfortable thought.

At any rate, he was bloody sick and tired of being nagged constantly about the subject. He took another long draught of Madeira, steeling himself. "If it will make you happy," he growled reluctantly, "I promise to search for a bride during my stay in Princess Anne County."

"Wonderful," Catherine breathed, smiling for the first time since their argument had begun. "If you'll only look, I'm certain that you can find a suitable woman."

Again that curious mocking smile crossed Grey's harsh features. "Very well," he conceded. "If I find a suitable woman, I promise you I will bring her to Greyhaven as my wife."

TWO

Jennifer Leigh Wilton found the dark man seated in the shadowy corner of the Pine Tree Ordinary extremely disturbing. She was accustomed to the lascivious stares of men, to their sneering laughter and coarse groping hands. But this man, with his hawklike features and elegant clothing, was far different from the usual patron of the tavern. He seemed to regard her, and all the noisy occupants of the smoke-clouded room, with a detached silver gaze that bespoke aristocratic distaste.

Her anxiety was not improved by the fact that the only person in Jenny's small world whom she considered a friend, Carey O'Neill, had left the tavern abruptly, leaving a nearly untouched tankard of ale. Carey, the only regular patron of the ordinary who had never attempted to pat her bottom or run a crude finger inside her neckline, had risen to his feet the moment the dark man entered the tavern and cast a look of cutting disdain at him as Carey stalked from the taproom. And Jenny had not missed the scornful glance the dark man had sent back. It was obvious that Carey O'Neill disliked the dark man for some reason, and Carey was the only person in the world whose opinion Jenny valued.

Despite her unease, however, Jenny maneuvered her way through the rough-hewn pine tables and the rowdy customers, all of whom were gulping ale and smoking clay pipes, to stand next to the dark man's table. It was lit only by a rushlight, a sliver of rush soaked in animal fat and held in a crude iron holder. But despite the dim light, disconcerting silver eyes snapped to her face and quickly surveyed her from her lank mouse-brown hair, topped with a simple white mobcap, to her worn leather shoes and too-small homespun gown. If possible, the look of revulsion on his aquiline features intensified.

Forcing herself to speak, Jenny stammered, "What—what may I get for ye, sir?"

She noted that he appeared vaguely amused by her all-too-apparent nervousness. He seemed to decide not to torment her further. "Ale," he said curtly, and looked away.

Realizing that she had been dismissed, Jenny turned away and shuffled back through the crowded taproom, deftly avoiding the regular customers who liked to pinch her bottom as she passed. " 'E wants ale," she reported.

Her uncle, a big, burly man with a sullen face and a worse disposition, poured a tankard of ale and handed it to her. "Ye make certain yer attentive enough to the gentleman, mistress," he admonished her. " 'Tis plain to see 'e thinks 'e's too good for the likes of this tavern, but being as 'e's deigning to drink our ale we shan't refuse him any. 'E 'as the look of a man who likes 'is liquor, 'e does. We could make a shilling or two on 'im tonight." His eyes dropped to the front of Jenny's outgrown gown, which stretched tightly across her small but firm young breasts, as if speculating exactly on how the maximum profit could be made, but Jenny did not notice. She had already turned away to deliver the ale.

Apprehension made her hands so unsteady that she almost spilled the ale. It was not that she was afraid of the dark man and his disapproving stare. Nothing could break into the calm stillness of her mind to frighten her, for terror had been beyond her for many years. But nonetheless she was conscious of a faint feeling of alarm, and her hands trembled slightly as she placed the pewter tankard on the pitted pine table before him. Once again he glanced up, and his eyes met hers squarely. They were a pale gray which seemed to glow in the light of the rushlight on the table and in the dying sunlight that filtered through the windows. And, she saw with surprise, his eyes were empty, as empty as hers must be.

He was, she realized, like her. He was beyond caring what life might hold. And the realization that there was someone like herself, indifferent, unfeeling, shocked her into a sudden reaction. She yanked her hand away too quickly, and the mug of ale fell onto his lap.

As the cold liquid cascaded across his long, muscular legs and fine woolen knee breeches, he slowly rose, looking down at her with an expression that was part amusement, part fury, and part utterly unreadable. Jenny discovered deep within herself a brief flash of fear, for he was a very tall man. The top of her head came nowhere near his shoulder. And though he was lean, the powerful muscles in his arms were clearly visible where he had carelessly pushed up his ruffled sleeves.

Jenny swallowed and raised her eyes to his, meeting his gaze levelly. In his silver eyes she saw a glint of approval, instantly extinguished. And then the world exploded.

"Clumsy bitch!"

Jenny found herself on the hard-packed earthen floor, her ears ringing. There was blood oozing from a cut on her cheekbone where a heavy fist had struck her. At first she thought that the dark man had hit her, and a curious disappointment seeped through her. But then she looked up and saw her uncle's angry form standing over her.

Of course, she thought with resignation. Her uncle had struck her in the past with far less reason. By spilling ale over the gentleman she had alienated a man who was likely to be a very lucrative customer. By her uncle's standards, she richly deserved a beating. She heard the first titters of amusement and struggled to her feet.

Once again, she realized dully, she was to be the evening's entertainment for the tavern customers.

Her uncle moved toward her, a murderous expression on his face, still bellowing expletives at her. Jenny did not cringe, only stood swaying with a pitifully patient expression, an expression that said clearly that this treatment was exactly what she expected. She could have run from her uncle's fists into the gray darkness outside, but there was nowhere to go. The ordinary was her only home, virtually her entire world, bounded by virgin forest on one side and Pine Tree Creek, the small body of water that spilled into the Lynnhaven River and from there into the great Chesapeake Bay, on the other. Here and there, carved from the forest, were plantations, small specks of civilization in a vast and savage country, but their owners were aristocrats who cared nothing for the well-being of a tavern wench. There was no one to help her. Besides, she had long ago concluded that she must merit this treatment. She waited silently for the next blow to fall.

And then the dark man stepped forward.

Jenny stared at him, wide-eyed. No one had ever come to her defense before. In this rural area of Virginia it was not unknown for disagreements to become vicious wrestling matches, with the contestants struggling to gouge each other's eyes out, or even to castrate each other. She had once seen a man after one of his eyes had been plucked from its socket, and the memory still made her want to retch despite the layers of callousness she had developed. Her uncle was a big, beefy man, and she had never thought anyone would dare to challenge him—certainly not for the sake of a mere tavern wench!

But the dark man moved so quickly that a wrestling match was out of the question. One moment he was glowering down at her uncle, and the next moment his opponent was sprawled on the floor, blood oozing from his split lip.

"I suggest," the dark man said in a low tone that nonetheless carried all the menace of a wolf's growl, "that you refrain from striking the girl again." His deep voice resounded in the suddenly quiet tavern as he turned back and

sat back down at the table. Stepping over her uncle's pros-
trate form, Jenny hastened to get her champion more ale.

Edward Greyson had already dismissed the incident
from his mind as he strode from the tavern into the gathering gloom and mounted his restless stallion in one easy
motion. He had no idea what had accounted for his sudden burst of chivalry, an impulse he believed had died
within him long ago, but he had drunk enough ale that he
was not inclined to be introspective. It was enough to assure himself that it would never happen again.

In point of fact, he had virtually forgotten the meek tavern wench with the huge eyes that had stirred him to such
unaccustomed pity. Inebriated as he was, his mind filled
with a different concern.

He had been in Princess Anne County for three weeks,
and as of yet he had not met a single woman he could envision marrying. He had not told his friend Kayne O'Neill of
his halfhearted attempt to seek a wife, yet the moment he
had arrived at Windward Plantation, every ambitious
mother in the county had descended on the plantation
with her unmarried daughter in tow. They acted like vul-
tures circling over a carcass, drawn irresistibly to his
wealth as well as to the scandal and mystery that had surrounded him for years.

And every last one of those daughters was an idiot.

The past three weeks had done nothing to alter his conviction that most women were vapid and foolish creatures
possessing no more brains than pigeons. For three weeks
he had been his usual rude self, sharp and cutting and callous, and the women had only fawned over him the more.
Today he had actually gone so far as to tell one young lady
that her display of flesh was more suitable to a courtesan
than to a lady—and the girl had been foolish enough to
take it as a compliment, giggling and slapping him lightly
on the arm with her fan.

Faced with such incredible stupidity, and slightly concerned lest he embarrass his friend and host by saying something even more appallingly rude, Grey had fled to this godforsaken little ordinary to drown his concerns in even more alcohol than usual.

He swore under his breath. He seemed to have two options. He could wed one of these simpering females and install her as mistress of Greyhaven. Or he could listen to Catherine's incessant harping on the subject for the rest of his life.

Neither option was particularly appealing.

Noticing at last that his stallion was dancing impatiently, he decided to ride back to Windward Plantation and give the matter more consideration there. Perhaps a glass or two of Kayne's excellent apple brandy would help him consider the situation more clearly. As he gathered the reins into his hands, however, a small sound startled him into whirling the stallion about.

The wench who had so ineptly served him ale had followed him out into the darkness. Now she stood staring up at him, a small slender figure with disheveled hair and huge eyes that appeared black in the dusk. She spoke quietly. "Please take me with ye."

Grey said nothing, only stared down at her. His gaze did not hold the slightest bit of interest, for she was less than nothing to him.

Even in the gloom, however, he could see the nascent hero worship shining in her dark, pleading eyes. Clearly she had decided he was some sort of hero. And obviously, just as any shrewd woman of her class might, she had decided to "reward" him for his heroic actions by offering her body in trade for security and protection. His repugnance increased at the thought. *The opportunistic little fool.*

Some of his revulsion faded, as she went on haltingly, "I'm a 'ard worker, sir. My uncle could tell ye that. Whatever ye might need—I can spin and cook—"

He relaxed slightly as he realized that she was offering

her limited skills as a servant, rather than her body, in exchange for his protection. Not that he had had the slightest intention of bedding her—her body was far too filthy to be attractive. Like most people of her class, she was unable to waste the time heating water to bathe in. Bathing was a luxury only the planter class could enjoy on a regular basis. She was in all likelihood louse ridden. No, her body held no attraction for him.

However, he had no need for a servant. After all, he owned over ninety slaves to spin and cook and to perform the other labors that kept a large plantation running. Not even deigning to answer, he started to turn the restive stallion away, and she actually dared to catch at his stirrup. "Please!" she murmured, and there was desperation in her voice.

It was not pity for her plight that made him glance back down. He knew that if he left her here he was damning her to a life of pain and degradation. He knew by the hopeless, empty expression in her dark eyes that she was beaten often. He did not care. What made him halt his stallion and look back down at her was the memory of his sister's nagging voice, raised in one of her interminable lectures.

He had promised to look for a suitable wife.

Looking down at this bedraggled, pathetic specimen of humanity, he almost smiled. This dirty, unattractive child was perfect for him. She would never expect love, compassion, or even respect. She had learned to expect nothing from the world, and that was precisely what he would give her.

And if he were to marry this child, this unattractive girl with the incredibly lower-class manners, polite Virginia society would be appalled and astounded. He would be the scandal of the colony—and not for the first time. He felt an irrepressible smile curving his lips at the amusing thought of how shocked his neighbors would be. Even his mistress would be scandalized by his actions.

Furthermore, he mused, if he installed this chit as mistress of Greyhaven, he would no longer have to tolerate the un-wanted advances of every unwed maid in the colony. (He did not object to the advances of married, experienced women, but starry-eyed virgins bored him.) If he wed the child, he would never feel obliged to spend time with her, or converse with her. Certainly he would never have to bed her.

In fact, he would have to make no alteration in his lifestyle whatsoever. If he were foolish enough to marry a lady of his own class, she would expect him to entertain her, to escort her to routs, and to leave the sanctuary of his study on occasion to converse with her—in short, she would make unacceptable demands on him, just as his sister did. His surly, selfish habits would have to change. This girl, on the other hand, would expect nothing from him at all. His life would change very little—except for one small but delightful detail.

Catherine would never dare nag him again.

Perhaps if he had not been so drunk, he would not have regarded the idea in the light of a joke. But once it occurred to him, it was all he could do to keep himself from laughing out loud.

He looked down at the earnest, solemn eyes peering at him from behind a tangle of brownish hair, and he smiled devilishly.

"I think," he said, "that I would like to speak with your uncle."

"Ye must be daft!"

Privately Grey agreed. Certainly he had been accused of being daft, or even outright mad, frequently enough. It was an image he cultivated the way other gentlemen culti-vated an aura of breeding and prosperity. Prosperity, Grey thought, was dull. Insanity was far more interesting.

He grinned inwardly at the thought but leveled a harsh stare at the innkeeper. "I beg your pardon?" he said coolly.

The man was clearly disconcerted. "I—I beg yer par-don, sir," he stammered. "I forgot my place, I did, just for a minute. 'Tisn't any concern of mine, sir, if ye think my niece is attractive, though I can't say I agree with ye. No, sir, I can't. She's been naught but trouble to me since the first day she—"

Recognizing the beginnings of a diatribe, Grey waved his hand carelessly, and the beefy man immediately cut his sentence off. He knew his betters, and was appropriately respectful, despite the fact that his better had provided him with an ugly bruise and a throbbing jaw earlier in the evening.

"I gather the girl's no favorite of yours," Grey interrupted. A vast understatement, he thought, recalling the girl's expression of hopeless resignation as her uncle struck her. "That's why I'm offering to take her off your hands."

The man seemed baffled. He knew full well that Grey had been lying when he spoke of marriage. Wealthy planters such as this one did not marry tavern wenches. The idea was utterly ludicrous. Yet the fellow did seem to have taken a fancy to his little niece. No doubt he'd use her body until he tired of it and then abandon her.

That did not concern him. All that concerned him was the best way to profit from the situation. He had planned on selling his niece to a local planter, Carey O'Neill, who had oftentimes expressed an interest in setting the girl up as his mistress, but this man appeared to be considerably wealthier—and, he thought shrewdly, might be inebriated enough to pay more than the girl was worth.

"She's been trouble, I grant ye," he said at last, choosing his words carefully, "but the girl's like a daughter to me, sir. I promised my sister I'd take care of the child and I 'ave. I couldn't let 'er just leave with a stranger, sir."

A sudden grin broke over Grey's impassive features. It was a disconcerting expression on his solemn face, reminding the innkeeper of a wolf. A ravenous wolf. "How much?"

" 'Ow—much, sir?"

"I'm taking the girl with me," Grey said. The grin

disappeared as suddenly as it had come, replaced by implacable determination. I know you're not so attached to her as you pretend. What do you want in exchange?"

"I'd be losing a good pair of 'ands, sir. 'Twould take a good sum of money to console me for the loss, if ye follow my meaning." Blatant avarice gleamed in his eyes as he added, "What're ye offering?"

Grey frowned. Few men, no matter how wealthy, carried more than a few coins with them, for money was scarce in Virginia. The true currency was tobacco. Transactions involving tobacco, however, necessarily took place on paper, due to the sheer impossibility of lugging thousand-pound hogsheads of tobacco around. Because Grey had left the O'Neills' house expecting to do little more than quaff a few ales, he did not have a tobacco warehouse receipt or much else of value on his person to offer in exchange for the girl. Then his expression lightened. "Come outside," he commanded.

The shorter man followed him into the darkness. He came to an abrupt halt when Grey put his hand on the arched neck of a magnificent black stallion. "The horse for the girl," Grey said simply.

The man stared at the horse for a few minutes, speechless. The stallion was beautiful, a shade over sixteen hands, long legged and deep chested. It was a horse such as few men could afford. And, if it were to be sold, it would bring an incredible amount of money.

"Done," he agreed.

Thus it was that Edward Greyson obtained a new wife for the price of one thoroughbred stallion. Had he been completely sober, he would have laughed at the idea of trading his best horse for a ragged girl. And later, in his sober moments, he would wish repeatedly that he could reverse the trade.

He was to find out that women cause far more trouble than do horses.

·　　·　　·

"You're going to what?"

Grey's expression was carefully neutral. "I'm going to be married," he repeated, adding with complete honesty, "I've finally found the perfect woman."

His friend regarded him through narrowed yellow eyes. Few people knew Edward Greyson as well as did Kayne O'Neill. The two men had known each other for a decade. Kayne knew better than anyone, save perhaps Catherine Greyson, how Grey despised the thought of marriage.

Now, studying the younger man intently, Kayne was certain that he saw a gleam of amusement in Grey's otherwise perfectly solemn eyes. Suspiciously, he asked, "Are you in love with her?"

The gleam vanished instantly, replaced first by indignation and then by a hard, shuttered expression. "Of course not," Grey snapped.

Kayne nodded, watching the play of emotions on his friend's face. Kayne was some twenty years older than Grey, yet he seemed younger. Peace and joy had left their marks on his face, just as grief and dissipation had marked Grey. Next to Grey, he was considered one of the most attractive men in the colony by the ladies of the upper class. It had long been a source of great despair among such ladies that Kayne was married—and worse yet, happily married.

The two men were seated in the study in Kayne's house, Windward Plantation. It was a red brick dwelling in the Dutch style that had been popular some years before, gambrel roofed and with its brick laid in the sturdy and attractive Flemish bond pattern. It was not half so large and grand as Greyhaven, nor was Kayne's land as extensive. Here along the Lynnhaven River in the southernmost part of Virginia, the colonists had settled early and relatively thickly. Tobacco, of course, was the lifeblood of the colony, but tobacco was a greedy master, destroying the soil rapidly and always demanding more. The planters along the James had on the whole more land, and were consequently more wealthy.

But what Windward Plantation lacked in elegance, it more than made up for in a comfortable atmosphere and a reputation for hospitality. Grey knew there were few people who would have been willing to put up with his surly presence for more than a week. Kayne had cheerfully tolerated him for three. All the O'Neills had been friendly, except the eldest son, Carey. Carey made it clear by his words and actions that he despised Grey and tolerated him only because he was a guest in their home. The two men had clashed for the first time seven years before, and over the years Grey had grown inured to the younger man's dislike. He thought Carey an idiotic young pup and decidedly preferred Kayne's company to his son's.

Just now, however, Kayne was determined to find out what lay at the bottom of Grey's unexpected declaration. "If you feel nothing for the lady," he inquired, "then what is 'perfect' about her?"

"Everything."

"Is she of good family? Is she beautiful?"

"She's a tavern wench," Grey said bluntly, delighting in the stunned expression that descended onto Kayne's features, "and she's louse ridden. And she is as far from beautiful as it is possible for a woman to be."

At this astounding answer Kayne could find no words. For a long moment his mouth hung open, then he closed it with a snap. "A tavern wench? Have you lost your mind?"

"You've been wed so long you've forgotten what it's like to be a wealthy unattached man," Grey said. "You can't recall, can you, how young ladies—girls, really—throw themselves at you, and try to trap you into compromising situations. Have you forgotten how mothers capture you in a corner and force you to listen to how clever their empty-headed little dears are, how talented they are—at playing the harpsichord, or useless needlework, or painting garish watercolors?" Grey scowled in a way that would have terrified most of the young maids he was describing in such uncomplimentary terms. "It wouldn't be so bad if I truly believed they were intrigued by my charming personality—but of course we both know I haven't one. It doesn't improve my opinion of women, I can tell you."

"I grieve for you," Kayne said dryly. He could almost have laughed at the disgusted expression on his friend's face, had he not been so concerned by his actions. "I suppose that this young, er, lady you have pledged your hand to is not so superficial and vapid as the ladies of our own class?"

Grey shrugged. "I don't doubt she would have been, had she been brought up properly. As it is, she knows nothing of money or luxuries. In fact, she knows little of anything. I have never seen a face so devoid of personality or self-respect."

"Then why—"

"If I marry this pathetic little creature," Grey explained, "I'll never again have to deal with women weeping on my shoulder and begging me to marry them. True, they'll still clamor for the privilege of being my mistress—but that nuisance can be borne."

Kayne almost smiled at the younger man's blatant misogyny, but he managed to keep his composure. He well knew how irritated Grey had been by the parade of simpering, eligible young women visiting Windward these past three weeks. But simple irritation was no reason for Grey to act so recklessly. It would surely ruin his life—and the girl's as well. "Damn it, Grey," he said, adopting the stern tone he used when his children were wayward, "that's hardly fair to the girl. Do you think she'll want to be shackled to a man who despises her for the rest of her life?"

Grey shrugged. "She'll be better off. Her uncle beats her—every day, from the looks of it. And an ordinary is hardly a wholesome environment. No doubt she's a doxy as well as a serving wench. She'll be happier at Greyhaven."

Kayne pushed a lock of silver-streaked red hair out of his eyes. He was becoming annoyed by the young man's callousness, even though he had grown to expect such an attitude from his friend these last years. Furthermore, he was certain that there was more to this situation than Grey was telling him. Possibly there was more to the situation than Grey was willing to admit, even to himself. "I don't doubt you'll get the French pox," he said sharply. "And it will be no less than you deserve."

"Good Lord, man, I have no intention of sharing a bed with her. Do you think I want a bedraggled, vermin-infested urchin cluttering up my bed?"

"Surely she is not so filthy that the dirt has become ingrained. At any rate, if you intend to marry her, bedding her is the accepted custom. But, Grey," Kayne added, "think what you are committing yourself to. What if you ever fall in love with another woman? You'll be trapped in this farce of a marriage."

"I will never fall in love," Grey stated flatly. There was a hard edge to his voice that said that this conversation was over, but Kayne ignored it.

"You can't know that," he persisted. "After all, you are only thirty—hardly in your dotage. Perhaps someday—"

"*Never,*" Grey said with absolute finality.

Inwardly, Grey knew Kayne was genuinely trying to help him see reason. Awakening this morning with a split-ting headache, and contemplating his impossibly rash actions of the night before in the clear light that streamed in through the window, he had wondered if perhaps he had not gone entirely mad. He recalled the pitiful crea-ture he had betrothed himself to, her thick lower-class accent, her greasy, stringy hair, her tattered, outgrown gown, and he had to suppress a shudder. His excesses had led him, not for the first time, into folly.

And yet he refused to go back on his word, for a number of reasons. The first was that his honor was at stake. He had already committed himself. No doubt the girl's uncle would be willing to forget the bargain as long as Grey per-mitted him to keep the stallion, but his word was his word. Once given, he could not go back on it. The second reason was the amusing thought of how outraged Catherine would be. That timid, filthy, uneducated child would be the mistress of Greyhaven. It would be worth the cost of his stallion just to see Catherine's fury. After all, she had goaded him into this.

He recalled the expression of fear, buried far beneath the surface, he had seen in the wench's eyes, but he suppressed the fleeting memory easily. He was certain that he was not motivated by pity. There was no room in his dark soul for such an emotion.

Annoyed by his friend's criticisms, as well as by his own self-doubt, he caught up the cut-glass decanter of apple brandy sitting on the open mahogany desk and poured himself another glass. Kayne eyed him with open distaste. "That's always your answer, isn't it?"

Grey lifted a questioning black eyebrow in a characteristic gesture and gulped a mouthful of the brandy. "My answer to what?"

"To everything. Whenever you want to forget, you drink." A moderate man by nature, Kayne could not approve of his friend's excesses. "And you want to forget every minute of every day."

Grey drank the rest of the brandy in a gulp and fixed the older man with an angry, almost savage look. "I can never forget," he growled. "I don't want to forget. Every minute of every day, I *remember*—"

He turned his head away and stared blindly at the wall. Kayne said gently, "Don't you think it's unfair to marry, feeling as you do? Perhaps it's true that she's unhappy in her current situation. But mightn't she be just as unhappy, married to a man who despises her because she can't be what he wants her to be?"

"Who I want her to be, you mean."

"Perhaps," Kayne agreed softly.

There was a silence in the room. Then Grey turned his head away from the wall and smiled at his friend. It was a genuinely warm smile, quite unlike his usual sardonic snarl, and it transformed his chiseled features to an astonishing degree. For a moment he looked like the contented young man Kayne had met ten years before, rather than the sullenly temperamental man he had become.

"I appreciate your concern," he said quietly. "Truly I do. But I've already made the arrangements. I imagine the girl's uncle has sold Tempest already."

Kayne blinked. "Am I to understand that you traded your horse for the girl? Good Lord, Grey, your callousness astounds even me. I cannot believe—"

"Furthermore," Grey went on calmly, ignoring his friend's outburst, "the banns have already been posted. The matter is settled. I will be married in three weeks."

At that moment the door to the study opened and a stunningly beautiful, ebony-haired woman entered. She crossed the chamber with quick, confident steps and stopped beside Kayne, placing a hand on his shoulder. He raised his hand to hers and squeezed it as though for support.

"Pray, gentlemen, do continue," she said merrily. "I believe I must be hearing things, for I could swear that I just heard Grey state that he was going to be married."

"You heard correctly," Kayne said through clenched teeth.

"Good heavens. Judgment Day must be at hand."

Grey grinned despite himself. Sapphira Carey O'Neill was still a beautiful woman, though she was over forty and had borne four children. Her midnight black hair was piled atop her head in a fashionable style, and the deep blue gown she wore showed clearly that her figure was still lovely. "It must be," he agreed. "Good morning, Sapphira."

"Practically afternoon," she corrected. "But no matter. Tell me how you came to propose to some fortunate young lady—if indeed you are not jesting with me." She smiled in his direction but her gorgeous blue eyes did not quite find him, for Sapphira was blind.

"I am not jesting. But I am not certain I want to explain the entire story again. Perhaps your husband will tell you about it." Grey placed his glass back on the desk and stood up, bowing in her direction even though he knew she could not see him. There was something about Sapphira that impelled him to be gentlemanly in her presence. "If you will excuse me, I believe I will go for a ride."

He strode from the room. Sapphira waited until the front door could be heard closing behind him, then squeezed her husband's hand. "Kayne, is he really going to be wed?"

Kayne looked across the room at the fire, blazing to drive away the January cold. "Yes. In a manner of speaking."

Sapphira looked exasperated. "Pray do not speak in riddles. Whom does he intend to marry?"

Sighing, Kayne explained the entire situation to her in as few words as possible. "I believe I've seen the girl at the Pine Tree Ordinary," he added. "Not only is she extraordinarily plain, I suspect she is simple. I still cannot believe Grey intends to go through with this farce."

"He cannot!" Sapphira said vehemently. Her blind eyes were filled with alarm. "Kayne, we must stop him. This arrangement is not fair to either of them."

Kayne groaned. "There is nothing we can do, Sapphira. You know as well as I do that when Grey is set on a course of action, nothing can turn him aside. We can only let him muddle through as best as he can."

"We are to stand by and watch him ruin his life?" Sapphira responded indignantly.

Kayne smiled sadly. "My beloved, we have stood by and watched him ruin his life these past seven years. There has been nothing we could do about it before." He bent his head in sorrow. "And there is nothing we can do about it now."

Carey O'Neill was as startled by the news as his father had been half an hour earlier. "You must be joking," he said incredulously.

He was seated in the Pine Tree Ordinary, with an ale before him, despite the fact that it was barely noon. Due to the hour, the taproom was virtually deserted, empty of acrid pipe smoke and ribald conversation, and Jenny was free to talk with him as she had not been last night. He looked up earnestly into her features. "Surely," he said with great intensity, "you are joking with me. Tell me you are jesting, Jenny."

Jenny stared down at him blankly, and he sighed. He should have known better. Jenny Wilton never joked. "Very well, obviously you are not joking." He shook his head, causing some of his dark russet hair to spring loose from its queue. "I cannot *believe* you are going to marry Edward Greyson, of all people."

Jenny looked at him shyly. "I understand," she said humbly. "I'm naught but a tavern wench, and 'e's . . . well . . ."

"It's not that," Carey said sharply. He had inherited the broad, amiable features of his father, along with his mother's merry blue eyes, but his face was neither merry nor amiable at this moment. "Your uncle and I had agreed—" He broke off whatever he had been about to say, looking irritated. "Well, that isn't relevant any longer, since your uncle has apparently struck a bargain with Greyson instead. The simple fact is that Greyson is very definitely not the sort of man you should marry."

Jenny smiled slightly—very slightly. She had known Carey O'Neill for years now, and as she grew into young womanhood he had begun speaking with her, actually *talking* to her—a novel thing in Jenny's experience. Most customers spoke to her only to demand ale or make crude comments. Her uncle's communications with her were generally limited to oath-laden reprimands and well-placed blows. Her aunt, a pale, timid woman, never spoke at all if she could avoid it.

Carey and Jenny had had numerous conversations in the ordinary over the past two or three years. A year ago she had even begun meeting him outside the ordinary, near the small creek that separated the ordinary grounds from O'Neill land, on those rare occasions when she had completed her duties and was able to slip away from her uncle's watchful eye. She knew perfectly well her uncle would have been infuriated were he to find out she had been meeting a man in the woods, yet Carey had always been a perfect gentleman, never so much as touching her or trying to kiss her, content only with her company and her conversations. He was virtually the only man in her life who had ever treated her as a human being. Of course, she thought, he had never prevented her uncle from striking her the way Edward Greyson had last night.

No man had ever protected her from her uncle's wrath before.

And yet Carey had always been kind to her, invariably taking care to thank her when she brought him ale, often-times regaling her with entertaining stories, so that she looked forward to their all-too-brief conversations. Nor did he ever join in the raucous laughter at her expense when her uncle punished her for some real or imagined failing. She thought of Carey as a friend, the only friend in her lonely existence, the nearest thing to a brother she had had since losing her own brother eight years before. Surely, with his obvious disquiet about her impending marriage, he was demonstrating more concern for her than her uncle ever had.

Of late, however, their relationship had changed some-how. There was something about Carey's expression when he looked at her, something that was not brotherly at all, something that filled her with a nameless apprehension. It puzzled her, but she was unable to determine exactly what was going through his mind these days.

Your uncle has apparently struck a bargain with Greyson instead. What in the world did he mean?

"I don't understand ye," she said calmly. "Ye left the tav-ern when 'e came in, and ye didn't see the fight. 'E struck my uncle and nearly broke his jaw, 'e did. 'E's a fine man, a good man."

Carey bit his lip as he placed his tankard of ale firmly onto the table. He had known Grey for years, and had never made any secret of the fact that he despised him. It infuriated him that Grey was permitted to visit at Wind-ward Plantation and was treated as an honored guest, rather than as the dog he was. And even more irritating was the fact that his father seemed to treat Grey more like a son than he treated Carey. No, he thought bitterly, Kayne treated Grey as an *equal*.

He struggled to keep the bitterness out of his voice as he spoke. "Jenny," he began carefully, "I don't know what accounted for his uncharacteristic behavior last night, but Greyson is *not* a good man. I don't wish to frighten you, but I can't let you go into this marriage unaware of what he is."

Jenny's unchanging features managed to take on a cast of stubbornness. Having decided that Greyson was a hero, she did not particularly want to hear him denigrated. "My aunt is waitin' for me," she reminded him. Jenny was incapable of engaging in an argument, and thus had become a master of avoiding conflict. "There be a passel o' dirty linen that needs a good washing."

Seeing that she did not want to listen to him, Carey caught her arm to prevent her from leaving the table. "Jenny," he said urgently, pulling her down so that she had no choice but to sit in the chair next to his. "Don't marry him. Please, you must believe me. You know nothing of Virginia society, and I have known Greyson for a very long time. He is a very bitter man. He's a rakehell. And—and— he's a murderer."

Jenny stared at him in blank surprise. "How d'ye know?"

"I don't know it for certain," Carey confessed. "It was never proven. But nearly everyone believes he was guilty. He murdered . . . well . . ." Carey paused, then burst out angrily, "I don't understand why my father continues to permit the man into his house. He treats him like a son, whereas I—"

Jenny gave him a sympathetic look. She was aware of the frequent conflicts Carey had with his father, for he spoke often about their disagreements. Into her mind, which was more astute than either Grey or Kayne realized, crept the suspicion that Carey was jealous of the friendship between Greyson and Kayne O'Neill. No doubt that served to explain why Carey had so often lately been at the tavern in the middle of the day, morosely sipping ale after ale, rather than at Windward Plantation. It also explained why Carey had stalked out of the tavern last night, scowling blackly, when Greyson walked in. "Never mind," she said gently. "It may be true, but I can do naught to stop it now anyway. 'Twas arranged between my uncle and Mr. Greyson last night. I will be wed in three weeks."

"Jenny, you *can't*."

Jenny lowered her eyes to the table and spoke so softly he could barely hear her. "I want to marry 'im, Carey."

She wanted Edward Greyson to take her away from the tavern and her empty, lonely life here, wanted it more desperately that she had ever dared to want anything. She remembered the way he had looked last night, staring down at her from the back of his massive black stallion, his cloak swirling about his shoulders in the cold January breeze, his features lean and predatory, like a hawk's, and as impassive and unyielding as if they had been carved from granite. He had looked every inch the hero he had acted. And then he had done the heroic thing in asking to marry her.

The only thing that had worried her was the look of disdain Carey had cast Greyson as he left the tavern. It had been more than evident that Carey disliked Edward Greyson, and she valued Carey's opinion. But now she felt she understood the reasons behind Carey's attitude, and her concern abated, leaving nothing but admiration for her hero in its place.

Apparently Carey saw she could not be swayed from this path, for an expression Jenny could not interpret crossed his broad face—an expression of loss, she thought. Perhaps even of envy. "I understand," he said. The anger that had filled his voice was gone, and he spoke in his customary gentle tone. "God knows Greyson is offering you more than I could—though perhaps not as much as you think." He paused, giving Jenny only a brief moment to contemplate that puzzling statement, then went on heavily, "If you find you need help, will you find a way to contact me?"

"Of course."

"If you ask for my help," Carey went on, "I will—I will take care of you. I promise. And if you must, you know how to use the knife."

Jenny nodded. When she and Carey had begun meeting at the creek, they had spent much of their time simply talking. But Carey had also invested some time in teaching her how to use a knife in self-defense, even showing her how to throw it accurately. She had become quite adept at it. He had taught her when her figure first began to take on the curves of womanhood, and at his insistence she always carried a knife in the pocket of her petticoat. For some reason she was unable to understand, he had wanted her to be able to protect herself. It had never occurred to her that he might have planned on keeping her for himself, for, with her utter lack of vanity, she was incapable of such a thought.

She knew, however, that she could never use the knife. Submission to the inexplicable rages of men had been beaten into her for too long. And surely she would never need to use it on her soon-to-be husband, the man who had saved her from her uncle's fury. She was calmly certain he would never hurt her.

"I 'ave to go and work now, or my uncle will be getting annoyed," she said. "And don't worry, Carey. I am doing the right thing. I'm certain."

She thought over what Carey had told her as she walked to the back of the ordinary. There an enormous cast-iron pot full of dirty sheets and boiling water was being stirred by her aunt, a quiet, withdrawn woman who had long ago been cowed into perpetual silence by her husband's rages.

Edward Greyson was no murderer, Jenny thought, remembering how he had protected her last night. He was an extraordinary and heroic man. Of that she had no doubt. It was inconceivable that he could be a murderer. Or was it?

Then she remembered the expression on his savage face when he struck her uncle, and suddenly she was not quite so sure.

THREE

Jennifer Wilton Greyson had never been so wretchedly miserable in her entire seventeen years of life. Even her uncle's beatings had been bearable compared to the endless agony she was suffering through now. Every muscle in her body ached from riding steadily for two days. She wondered, for the millionth time, why the stranger she had married had not simply sailed from his plantation to Princess Anne County. Virigina was riddled with creeks and rivers that made it painfully difficult to get from one point to another by land. Roads were rarely wide enough to accommodate coaches, except in larger settlements such as Williamsburg and Norfolk, and a rider frequently had to pay a ferryman to cross bodies of water, while his horses swam behind. Sensible people generally traveled by water if they were going any great distance.

But when she had diffidently asked Grey why he had ridden all this way, he had said only, "I like to ride."

His replies to her timid attempts at conversation had all been terse, almost angry, and she had long ago abandoned any effort at drawing him out. He was a strange, silent, brooding man, and she had been quickly intimidated into silence. She realized that she had very little to say to him anyway. They had virtually nothing in common. He came from a sophisticated, educated world, whereas her world was a backwater tavern.

And she was discovering now that it had not been such

a bad world. This outside world appeared to consist of nothing but endless forests sliced through by rivers and swamps. They rarely caught sight of cultivated fields as they rode down the narrow dirt path. There was virtually nothing to look at to distract her mind from her aching muscles, aside from the occasional egret lifting gracefully away from a creek bank, or more rarely, a fox slinking through the underbrush.

Her physical discomfort was bad enough, but her mental discomfort was worse. On the long ride, with little else besides her misgivings to occupy her mind, she had found herself wondering repeatedly why Edward Greyson had married her. He seemed to have no interest in her at all, never speaking to her voluntarily and rarely glancing in her direction. More puzzling was the fact that, although they had stopped at inns for the past two nights, they had slept in separate chambers.

Jenny was an innocent, much more so than Grey would have believed, but she knew enough of such matters (for the walls of the ordinary had been none too thick) to know that couples traveling together generally shared beds. And she knew that this was expected of married couples—though heaven knew she had seen few enough married couples at the ordinary. Most couples spending the night there had had a more improper and less permanent relationship.

She looked ruefully down at her gown. Although it, like her other two gowns, was woven of coarsely woven wool, called homespun, it had been dyed with indigo, a plant grown specifically for its blue dye. She had always thought it was the prettiest of her gowns. Accordingly, she had worn it to her wedding. But even at their wedding, she reflected, Grey had scarcely glanced at her. They had been wed in the Lynnhaven parish church, with only Kayne O'Neill and his wife, Sapphira, as witnesses. Kayne had watched the ceremony with an odd expression of pity on his handsome features, and after the ceremony Sapphira had pressed her hand, and whispered, "Good luck, my dear." But Grey had said nothing, had not even kissed her.

He had simply gone through the ceremony with the same expression of cool detachment that he wore now.

She risked another glance at his stern profile. He was uncommonly handsome, she thought. Or perhaps striking was a better word to describe his high cheekbones and sharply curving nose. His lips were chiseled and sensual, though they tended to be set in a rather sullen cast. Thick black eyebrows arched over rain-colored eyes. She noted that his long ebony hair was still pulled neatly back in its queue and that his well-cut clothes still looked immaculate. She knew that the indigo gown, and the rough woolen cloak she wore to ward off the January cold, were dreadfully wrinkled and stained with the dust of days of traveling. Not to mention that strands of her hair were escaping from the unfashionable knot at the back of her neck and straggling about her face.

He looked like an aristocrat. She looked like a tavern wench.

He seemed so far beyond her reach, so distant, and for a moment she almost smiled, pleased that this man had, for some reason known only to himself, wed her. He had not married a lady of his own class; he had chosen to wed her, despite her lowly origins. This knowledge made her feel very special and fortunate. He must feel something for her, she told herself firmly. After all, he had come to her defense in the ordinary, something no man had ever done before. And then he had asked her uncle for her hand in marriage. He must care something for her. He *must.*

Emboldened by the thought, she decided to risk another effort at conversation. "It must not be dreadful far now," she ventured.

Grey did not so much as glance in her direction. "No," he agreed. "It's not."

And that was all. No smile, no effort to be pleasant. He merely kept his pale eyes fixed firmly on the path before him. Jenny stared at his profile, bewildered. Why had he married her if he did not care to speak to her, or even to look at her?

She puzzled over her husband's eccentric behavior for a long time, but could come up with no explanation for it.

At long last the path began to show signs of constant travel, growing wide enough to accommodate a carriage. No longer could it properly be called a path; it had become a tree-lined avenue. Grey urged his horse, a magnificent dark bay stallion presented to him by Kayne as a wedding present, into a canter, and Jenny awkwardly urged her dappled gray mare to keep up, praying she would not disgrace herself by falling from the sidesaddle she was precariously perched upon.

The forest fell behind them as they swept past cultivated fields, delineated by the stacked split rails known as worm fences, and toward a house that, to Jenny's unsophisticated eyes, seemed a palace. Compared to the lesser houses of Princess Anne Country, it was truly magnificent. It had been designed in the Georgian style popularized by the governor's mansion in Williamsburg. With large one-and-a-half-story wings symmetrically placed on either side of the two-and-a-half-story main house, the enormous red-brick edifice was surrounded by lesser outbuildings—a smokehouse, lumber house, kitchen, poultry house, stable, and a quantity of slave quarters farther from the house. From a distance it appeared more like a small village than a house and dependencies. But even if it had stood alone the house would have been striking, fully two hundred feet long and with six chimneys rising high into the air above the dormered slate roof. Woodsmoke curled from the chimneys, permeating the cool air with its welcoming scent.

Beyond the house a formal garden with trimmed boxwood hedges and a lovely, velvet green lawn sloped gently down to the blue water of the James River. Jenny nearly fell off her mare with astonishment as they approached. She was to be mistress here! She, who had never lived in any structure more elegant than a whitewashed clapboard tavern, was to reside in this glorious house! She felt as though she were dreaming. But the magnificent structure was real, and so was the man who rode beside her, slowing his mount to a trot.

As they rode closer to the mansion, Jenny saw a woman emerging from the pedimented stone doorway. A tall, regal woman who, despite her obvious youth, walked with a limp, leaning heavily on a cane. She waved happily at Grey, who pulled his horse up, dismounted gracefully, and bowed. "Catherine," he greeted her, and the single word held more affection than Jenny had yet heard from him.

Jenny watched, forgotten and bewildered. Who was this woman her husband treated with such courtesy? He had not mentioned that he lived with any relatives. Surely her husband did not have a mistress installed in his house? And then the young woman looked up, her eyebrows swiftly drawing together in a frown at the sight of Jenny, clinging awkwardly to her saddle.

Catherine stared at the tattered and dust-covered girl for a moment, and then she turned to her brother. "Grey? Have you hired this girl as—a servant?" Her tone, and the disapproving pause that punctuated her sentence, made it clear that she thought Jenny to be a whore rather than a servant.

Jenny realized that she should dismount and be introduced, but her legs were tired and weak from the long ride, and her long skirt was tangled up in the sidesaddle abominably. She glanced pleadingly at her husband as her horse sidestepped nervously, but he made no move to help her dismount, merely raised one eyebrow sardonically and looked at her. The expression on his face, she noted in sudden burgeoning misery, was identical to that on the face of the woman—contempt, scorn, and distaste.

Recognizing at last that her husband was not going to help her, she tried to slip from the horse's back as Grey had done—smoothly, fluidly, in one easy motion. Unfortunately for what little dignity she possessed, her foot inadvertently dug into the mare's flank, and the animal, already made skittish by her inexpert riding, jumped sideways. Jenny fell in a graceless heap to the ground, embarrassment flooding through her as she looked up at the two people who were studying her as though she were a rare and repulsive variety of insect.

Grey smiled mockingly. "Jenny," he said, and in his voice there was a vicious humor, "this is my sister, Catherine Greyson." He gestured toward the filthy, bedraggled creature who sat in a cloud of dust, peering up forlornly. "Catherine, meet my wife."

The woman stared down at Jenny in horrified silence, then turned to confront the tall man beside her. "Good Lord, Grey," she demanded, "what have you done?"

FOUR

Jenny felt even more hideously awkward inside the great brick house than she had been sitting in the slowly settling dust. She had not imagined it was possible to feel this embarrassed. In the ordinary she had often been stared at, coarse remarks had been made about her anatomy, rough hands had groped rudely at her flesh, yet she had never been observed with such icy distaste. Perhaps it was because she had belonged in the ordinary. She did not belong in this house, in the midst of such splendor, and it was slowly beginning to dawn on her that she never would.

Grey had caught her arm and propelled her into the house as soon as she regained her feet. She stared at her surroundings with awe as the heavy paneled door swung shut behind her. Sweet-smelling beeswax candles in a brass chandelier of simple, graceful design lit the entrance hall. On either side of the door were stately ionic columns carved of wood, and elaborate dentil molding ornamented the fourteen-foot ceilings. The stairway was set off from the entrance hall by a wide elliptical arch of carved wood, and there was more ornate carving along the side of the stairway. Even the chair rails in the passage were ornamented with a wall-of-Troy molding.

And most surprising of all, the house slaves wore red-and-gold livery in the manner of English servants. Their clothing was by far finer than Jenny's.

Jenny had never seen such richness. Grey had firmly

steered his gaping bride into the parlor and started to guide her to a chair, but Catherine instantly objected.

"Grey, she'll dirty my upholstery. For heaven's sake, put her on the settee. She can't damage that."

Jenny had thought herself incapable of emotion, but now she felt so sick with humiliation that she could make no objection as her husband deposited her on the cherry-black leather upholstery of a settee before the fireplace. Shivering in front of the roaring fire, she warmed her numbed fingers and watched the Greysons argue. She felt that, to them, she was of no more value than the settee she sat upon. Perhaps even less.

"Oh, for God's sake, Catherine," Grey was saying now in tones of exasperation, "you make it sound as though I have committed a hanging offense. And to think how often you have exhorted me to find a wife."

"A *suitable* wife!" Catherine reiterated angrily. "Not this—this *creature*." Jenny recoiled, both from the callous words and the acerbic tone.

"On the contrary, what woman could be more suitable?" Grey inquired sweetly. Upon his entrance to the parlor, he had demanded brandy from one of the slaves. He was now gulping it greedily between sentences. "I don't want a wife who will expect me to fall in love with her, or even"—he glanced at Jenny and shuddered in fastidious distaste—"to bed her. This chit is perfect. She knows her place. She would never dare to criticize my, er, eccentric habits—"

"Your damned drinking!" Catherine flared. "You can't bear the thought of a woman trying to reform you."

"Quite right." Grey's manner, now that he had polished off one goblet of brandy and begun another, had transformed with dizzying swiftness from moody to cheerful. "A woman of our class would be horrified at my excesses. To this child, on the other hand, inebriation is the rule rather than the exception. She will not expect me to change, as a woman of breeding might."

They were speaking of her as though she were invisible, apparently completely unconcerned as to whether their discussion hurt her or not. Jenny cringed in an agony of embarrassment and humiliation, only to sit bolt upright at Catherine's next words.

"For heaven's sake, child, don't slouch in such a manner. Have some pride. After all, you are a Greyson now—however distasteful that may be to us." She turned hopefully to her brother as a thought occurred to her. "I don't suppose an annulment is possible? Surely you did not actually bed the filthy creature?"

"It is possible," Grey acknowledged, "but I will not obtain one. Marital relations are not necessary, not when there are so many other willing women about."

"You do not intend to have a son?"

Grey frowned slightly and studied his brandy. "As we discussed before, I would not make a suitable father."

"Nor do you make a suitable husband!" Catherine snapped.

"I agree." Grey's voice had turned glacial. "I was perfectly content to live in a fog of memories and alcohol, but you, my darling sister, persisted in pressuring me to find a wife. I at last decided to oblige you."

"I had hoped a wife would give you new interest in living."

"You were wrong."

Catherine stared at him a few moments longer, engaging in a silent battle of wills, then she bent her head in defeat. Turning to the girl, who sat nervously erect on the settee, she said harshly, "Well, what's done is done. Come along, child."

As Jenny rose obediently to her feet, Grey demanded, "What are you going to do?" He was alerted by the defiant expression on his sister's aristocratic features that she was, very definitely, up to something.

But the face Catherine turned to him was full of innocence. "Why, I'm going to make a lady of her, of course. What is there left for me to do?"

"A lady?" Grey repeated incredulously. His gray eyes swept over his wife's unadorned, too-small indigo gown, ludicrously out of place in such luxurious surroundings, and he gave a short contemptuous laugh. "This uneducated, uncultured child? Most likely she's illiterate. Jenny, can you read?"

Startled to be addressed directly, Jenny stared at him, struck dumb. At last she stammered, "N-No, sir."

"Simpleminded, unattractive, and filthy," Grey growled. "And *you* want to transform her into a lady."

"Damn it, Grey!" Catherine was visibly exasperated. "You brought her home. We have to do *something* with her."

"Put her to work in the cookhouse," Grey suggested helpfully. "She claims to be able to cook. You needn't teach her anything."

"And what will people say?"

Grey rolled his eyes. "I do not trouble myself about what others think."

"Because you are in an alcoholic haze most of the time," Catherine said tartly. "I'm not concerned about their opinions of you, Grey. Heaven knows most of them already believe you to be mad, and quite frankly I'm not certain they aren't correct."

Catherine paused for a moment and studied the pitiful young woman her brother had married, still staring at the chamber as if it were a castle filled with extraordinary treasures. The wide-eyed expression on the girl's face filled her with an unwonted sympathy, which she tried her best to ignore. God knew the girl really did belong in the cookhouse. But she was determined to outmaneuver Grey. He had married this simple, common child merely to spite her, and she was not going to let him get away with it. She would not let him get the upper hand.

"No," she said at last, "I'm concerned about this poor child. She must be terrified, for she knows full well she doesn't belong here. The least I can do is make her feel welcome."

Grey slanted her a look full of suspicion. "Just where were you thinking of installing her?"

"Diana's chamber would be appropriate," Catherine

began in her most reasonable voice, but Grey cut her off
angrily.

"Diana's chamber? Are you insane? The *stables* would
be more appropriate! Catherine, I absolutely will not
permit—"

"You are seriously suggesting that the lady of the house
sleep in the stables?"

"Well, why not?" Grey demanded. "Look at her. *Look* at
her! Does she not belong in the stables?"

Catherine studied the girl judiciously. "She could certainly do with a bath and some more suitable clothes. For
the time being, we can cut down some of Diana's—"

"Absolutely not!" Grey's shout of outrage was frenzied,
and Jenny shrank back, appalled and intimidated by his
fury. The man she had married no longer seemed handsome. His face was dark with the combined effects of anger and alcohol, his eyes glinted silver with rage, and his
mouth was compressed into a narrow slash across his face.

Catherine seemed unimpressed. "Don't be foolish, Grey.
No one has used that chamber in seven years. And the
gowns are in all likelihood motheaten anyway. You're being
maudlin."

"You will not use that chamber for a tavern wench,"
Grey ground out between gritted teeth.

Catherine smiled innocently. "Quite correct, dear. I will
use it for your wife." She gestured imperiously to Jenny,
and the girl scurried after her as she hobbled from the
chamber. As they began to ascend the broad treads of the
staircase, Jenny jumped nervously when she heard the unmistakable sound of glass shattering against a wall.

"Don't concern yourself about him." Catherine's manner was not exactly friendly, but it was less chilling than it
had been before. Catherine was beginning to realize she
had misjudged the girl. Originally she had thought Jenny a
fortune hunter who had somehow trapped Grey into marriage while he was inebriated. But during her argument
with Grey it had become evident that the child was only

here because Grey had deluded her in some way. No doubt he had thought it a capital joke. She shook her head at her brother's unbelievably crass behavior and went on, "He's angry a good eighty percent of the time. The other twenty percent he sulks. One simply has to ignore him and go on living."

Jenny swallowed nervously. In her experience, angry men demonstrated their anger in only one way—by striking the first person who got in their way. She found that her mouth was too dry to comment.

"You *can* speak?" her sister-in-law inquired acidly.

Jenny nodded shyly, then, realizing that some verbal response was required, stammered, "Yes, of course, but—"

Catherine interrupted. "We shall have to do something about that wretched accent of yours. And your smell! When did you last bathe?"

Jenny paused on the landing by an ornately carved mahogany tall case clock that stood nearly nine feet tall. Her brow furrowed in thought, and Catherine waved her hand impatiently. "Never mind. That answers my question quite well enough, thank you. As to your manners, we shall have to tutor you. A word of advice—Don't emulate Grey."

The girl nodded solemnly, and Catherine let out an exasperated sigh. The child could not so much as recognize an attempt at humor. Was there a personality anywhere in that small, fragile body?

Probably not, Catherine reflected. After all, a tavern maid could have had little opportunity for intellectual conversation, or any conversation at all, for that matter. Brought up in such an environment, the girl could hardly be expected to demonstrate intelligence. Jenny reminded her of a timid mouse who, foolishly venturing from its secure hole, was now paralyzed by its fear of the unknown surroundings. Like a mouse, she seemed to expect a cat to leap upon her and devour her at any moment.

At the top of the stairs, Catherine pushed open a door. Its hinges creaked as though it had not been opened for years. "This was Diana's chamber," she said, her voice hard once again. But Jenny sensed that the distaste in her voice was aimed at the unknown Diana, not at herself.

"Who—who was Diana?" she inquired shyly.

Catherine shot her a look of surprise. "Did he not tell you? Well, I suppose that is no surprise. He rarely speaks of her if he can avoid it." She stepped into the chamber and glanced around at the dust-covered surfaces.

"Diana," she said, "was his first wife."

FIVE

"Diana died seven years ago," Catherine explained as several slaves brought heated water up and poured it into a massive oaken tub in front of the fireplace, where a fire now roared. "He—well, you may as well know. He worshipped her. As you might have guessed from the fact that he has never allowed anyone into this chamber. Even he never comes in here. He sealed off this room from the rest of the house after she died. If only he could shut the door on his memories as easily as he did the door to this chamber, he would be happier. But he cannot seem to forget her, no matter how many years pass."

Jenny glanced around timidly. In the center of the chamber sat a small round table, the sort at which a lady might paint watercolors. She wondered if the unknown Diana had painted landscapes at that table. On one side of the room were two large windows with dark blue curtains and wood-slatted venetian blinds. Between them stood an immense mahogany clothespress, fully six and a half feet tall, and next to each window was a carved chair upholstered in the same dark blue damask-patterned wool. On the wide planks of the floor lay a brightly hued blue-and-red woven rug, called a list. Across the room stood a tall canopy bed with short, curving legs terminating in ball-and-claw feet. Near the bed was a linen-draped twilight, or dressing table. Atop the table a looking glass leaned against the wall, flanked by two silver candlesticks of ornate classical design. Nearby stood a stand that held a porcelain basin and jar for washing, and a walnut desk completed the furnishings in the chamber.

The chamber was far grander than the loft she had slept in at the tavern, and the wide mahogany bed with its wool covering and plump feather pillows looked infinitely more comfortable than the pallet and straw-filled mattress she was accustomed to, yet the dust and cobwebs that covered everything depressed her. Clearly nothing had been disturbed for many years, almost as though the ghost of Grey's first wife still haunted this room. Jenny felt that she might prefer the stables, after all.

In her quiet voice, she asked, " 'Ow did she die?"

"She was murdered," Catherine said flatly, and Jenny felt a tremor run through her as she remembered Carey's warnings. Her apprehension quieted somewhat as Catherine continued. "We never found out who the murderer was. It was a small loss, so far as I was concerned, but Grey was inconsolable. I think he wished he had died with her. It was then that he started to drink so heavily. Over the years, instead of letting her fade from his mind, he has built up her memory so that he recalls a goddess instead of a mortal woman."

"Ye did not like 'er," Jenny observed. It was a statement, not a question, and Catherine raised her eyebrows, both at the girl's unexpected perceptiveness and the fact that the child was actually daring to speak without stammering.

"No, I did not," she admitted. Jenny pulled her eyes away from the impressive furniture and looked at her, her dirty face implying the question she did not dare to ask, and Catherine shrugged.

"I suppose I was jealous," she volunteered. "Grey and I were very close then—we never argued then as we do now—and I suppose I resented how completely absorbed he was in another person. I was still very young, and he had become like a parent to me after our father and mother died. Furthermore—" She paused for a long moment. "I did not think she was good for him. She was haughty.

Caustic. I must admit, however, she returned my hostility in full. Perhaps I am somewhat haughty myself."

Jenny glanced at her somewhat nervously, wondering if Catherine would resent her as well. Probably not, she decided. Grey was hardly obsessed with her, as he had apparently been with his first wife. For that matter, it scarcely seemed that he cared whether she lived or died. Surely Catherine could not resent her presence at Greyhaven.

Catherine dismissed this history with a shrug. "Ah, well. That was long ago. If only Grey did not behave as though it were yesterday. . . ." She gestured to the girl. "Into the tub with you."

Jenny shot her a look of absolute horror, but Catherine was not someone accustomed to being disobeyed. "In your case, child, modesty is foolish. I can scarcely believe that several men, at the very least, have not sampled your charms. Take off those horrid clothes and get into that tub. *Now.*"

Slowly, with every outward evidence of reluctance, Jenny obeyed. She had never before been naked in the presence of another. She had always slept in a shift and, upon arising, had simply pulled one of her few gowns on over the shift. And now she was being forced to disrobe both in the presence of this steely-eyed aristocrat and a young black woman who held a cloth in one hand and an imposing amount of lye soap in the other.

"I am remaining," Catherine said in her elegantly cultured voice, "to ensure that you are entirely clean when what you so plainly perceive as an ordeal is completed. Step into the tub, please."

Though politely phrased, it was clearly an order rather than a request. Jenny obeyed meekly. The water was extremely hot, a most unusual sensation. Jenny had rarely bathed in her life, and then usually in cold water. She gingerly sat down in the tub.

At that moment the door slammed open, and to her horror Edward Greyson stormed into the chamber. Sinking chin-deep into the water, she stared at him helplessly with huge dark eyes. He returned her look coldly, then turned to address his sister.

"So." His voice was slurred, and Jenny realized that he had had a great deal to drink. But Catherine seemed completely unmoved by the anger on his aquiline features. "You have actually installed this—this *creature* in her room."

"It's a shame to let this lovely chamber go to waste," Catherine said mildly. "There's quite a good view of the James."

"I don't give a goddamned—" Grey began angrily, but Catherine cut him off.

"Really, Grey, you're a dreadful influence. The child must not be exposed to such language. At any rate, let me point out that *you* are the one who brought her here. I am merely trying to make the best of the impossible situation you have created. Accordingly, we are currently bathing her and making her presentable, as befits the wife of a Greyson. Good-bye, Grey," and to his surprise Grey found himself gently propelled into the hall and the door closed nearly on his nose. Fuming, but aware that he had been outmaneuvered for the time being, he raged back down the stairs.

Still flaming with embarrassment, Jenny found her hair being lathered with the lavender-scented soap, rinsed, and lathered again. Then the slave handed her the soap, indicating that she was to wash herself most thoroughly. Jenny thought to protest, but one glance at Catherine's implacable face silenced her.

Catherine Greyson was a handsome woman, she decided. She might have been beautiful but for the aquiline nose so like Grey's, which was far more suited to masculine features. Her eyes were a flinty gray, darker than her brother's; her mouth was wide and full but seemed humorless. Her chestnut hair was gathered in an unattractive but practical style at the nape of her neck, and she wore a high-necked, spinsterish gray woolen gown. All in all she was a woman Jenny found to be most intimidating. She scrubbed herself thoroughly under the scrutiny of those piercing eyes.

At long last clean, cleaner than she had ever been in her life, and being dried by the slave with a finely woven linen towel, Jenny dared to ask another question. "Why d'ye call 'im Grey instead of Edward?"

"Oh." Catherine shrugged. "He's been called that since he was a child. Partly because of his gray eyes, of course, but partly because he has always been so somber. So intense. It always seemed appropriate, somehow." She hesitated, then added a word of warning. "Diana was the only person to ever call him by his given name. I wouldn't advise you to do so."

Jenny nodded. The thought of calling her strange, remote husband by his first name had not even occurred to her. Nor would she feel comfortable referring to him by his nickname. If she were to call him anything at all, she decided, it would probably be Mr. Greyson.

The maid sat her down, though Jenny was still unclothed but for a silk wrapper, and began to untangle her dripping hair. Catherine studied her thoughtfully as she winced beneath the onslaught of the silver comb. "And now let me ask you something," she said. "Why did you marry Grey?"

Jenny's eyes met hers in the mirror. "I thought 'e was a 'ero," she murmured.

Catherine laughed shortly. "Grey's not a hero. He's a bastard."

Jenny had no reply to make to that statement. It seemed entirely too obvious to comment on. In the past hour it had become painfully evident that Grey had married her solely to spite his sister. Now she understood all too plainly why he had acted as though he could barely stand the sight of her. He had intended to make her sleep in the stables and work in the cookhouse, as though she were a slave. He found her pitiful and contemptible.

The memory of his angry voice slashed into her pathetic remnants of self-respect. *Simpleminded, unattractive, and filthy.* These painful words revolved endlessly in her mind.

While Jenny's long hair was being combed out, Catherine paced the floor of the chamber slowly, thinking out loud. "Grey does not have the respect he should have for you. Not surprisingly, as you were scarcely the sort of woman a man of our class would respect. Now that he has been foolish enough to wed you, however, you are a lady. We shall have to work hard to make you worthy of that designation.

"And then, perhaps, you can earn Grey's respect." At the brief flash of hope that illuminated Jenny's face, she snapped, "His respect, but not his love. Don't be foolishly romantic. It's normal enough for a girl your age to long for love, but love is not necessary in a marriage. Respect is. Eventually, if things continue as they are, you will grow to loathe the very sight of your husband, and while Grey probably deserves your hatred, I cannot in good conscience condemn a girl your age to such a life."

Jenny gave her a dubious look from beneath her tangled wet hair. She knew full well that she would never have the confidence and poise that the other woman exuded. She was nothing more than a tavern wench. She was nothing at all. But she wanted something more than his respect. She wanted love.

"If I could earn 'is respect, couldn't I earn 'is love someday?"

Catherine felt a flash of sorrow and pity for the girl, condemned forever to a loveless existence. She had probably never known love in her life, or even kindness, and from the expression on her face she wanted it desperately. But she ruthlessly suppressed her pity, and said sharply, "Grey has no love left for anyone. He's grown colder and more bitter with each passing year. Don't fool yourself into believing you can change him, for women cannot change men, no matter how much we might like to. Heaven knows I've tried . . . and you have seen the results of my efforts." She sighed, and added, "But since God—or Grey—has given you this opportunity to change yourself for the better, you should not pass it up. We can start with your name. Jenny is inappropriate for a lady. Is your full name Jennifer?"

The girl nodded.

"Then that is the name we will use. With your hair done up properly, and in a decent gown, you may perhaps be presentable. But appearances are not all that being a lady entails. You must be able to read and speak intelligently. You should be able to embroider, to paint, to play the harpsichord. . . ."

Jennifer glanced up, and for the first time interest gleamed in the dark depths of her eyes. "Th'arpsichord? I need ter learn somethin' about music?"

"That is part of being a lady, yes. And, perhaps most importantly, you must learn to comport yourself in company. We will start immediately. Tonight you will join Grey and myself at dinner."

"Oh," Jenny began, "I would rather—"

Catherine cut her off sharply. "What you want is irrelevant. You will do what I tell you to do. I fully intend to transform you into a credit to yourself and to the Greyson name—whether you like it or not."

A few hours later Jennifer's hair, long and thick though it was, had dried in front of the fire. Having found a dark green silk gown that could be pinned up hastily, Catherine laced Jennifer into it, using a long, slender, silver bodkin to lace the stays, then stood back and admired her handiwork.

" 'Tis too tight," Jennifer objected, the discomfort of having her stomach and ribs pressed in overcoming her normal reticence. She had never had to wear stays or hoops before, and they felt terribly confining.

"Ladies wear stays," Catherine replied in a voice that brooked no argument. She walked around the girl and nodded, looking pleased with herself. "Your hoops are too wide, of course, since narrower hoops have come into fashion since this gown was made. But no matter, we will get you new gowns. You will do very well, after all. You may have none of the appropriate social graces, but those can be learned, and I expect you to learn them. But you already have something that cannot be learned."

Jennifer seemed surprised to discover that she actually possessed something of value. "I do?"

Catherine nodded, and for the first time her stern features relaxed into a smile. "You do," she affirmed. "You have beauty."

She was startled when the girl turned her back and walked away. Following the girl to the window, she inquired, more gently than was her wont, "What is the matter?"

"Yer laughin' at me," Jennifer said. There was no bitterness in her voice, no rancor, only a flat statement of fact. It occurred to Catherine that she fully expected to be laughed at, that she accepted it as a normal part of life, and that it would never occur to her to resent it.

Nonetheless, she hastened to reassure the girl. "Of course I am not laughing at you, Jennifer. I'm laughing at Grey."

Now the girl turned, her eyebrows lifted questioningly. Knowing that she would not verbalize her curiosity, Catherine explained, "You must have realized by now that Grey brought you here only because you were the most inappropriate woman he could find to wed."

Jennifer nodded slowly, her cheeks flushing. She had come to understand Grey's motives over the past few hours, but to hear it stated so baldly was nevertheless humiliating.

"What Grey did not realize," Catherine went on, "was that underneath the dirt and homespun gown, you are actually quite lovely." At Jennifer's expression of disbelief, she pulled the younger woman across to the looking glass atop the twilight.

"Look at yourself," she commanded.

Jennifer stared at her reflection doubtfully. Certainly the gown improved her appearance, despite its poor fit.

The stays did a good deal to give her a semblance of a figure, and the low-cut, square neckline emphasized what little cleavage she had. But her face, although cleaner, seemed
much the same to her. She lifted her hands in a gesture of
confusion.

"How can you not see it?" Catherine said in exasperation. Scrubbed and coiffed and laced into a decent gown,
the girl was more than beautiful, she was stunning. Incredibly dark green eyes stared out from beneath arching
golden eyebrows. Her face was a perfect oval, and her nose
was small and straight, the nose that Catherine had always
dreamed of having. Her hair, a shimmering amber rather
than the mousy brown it had appeared when unwashed,
was arranged simply but elegantly. She was small and slender, but far from shapeless.

Jennifer gave her an apologetic look. "I am not pretty,
mistress." She smiled shyly, and added, "Not th' way ye
are."

If any other woman so lovely had made that statement,
Catherine would have dismissed it as false modesty. But
it was apparent that Jennifer had meant it quite honestly.
Evidently the girl had no self-regard whatsoever. Catherine wondered idly what such beauty paired with such astonishing lack of guile and vanity might do to the heart of
an unsuspecting man.

A man such as Edward Greyson.

Struck by the thought, she considered for the first time
the possibility that Grey's heart, frozen into ice on the day
of Diana's death, could be melted. What if Grey only
needed a companion, a young, lovely girl to lift him out of
the misery in which he had been mired for seven long
years? After all, Grey was only thirty. Like Jennifer, like
Catherine herself, like all humans everywhere, he must
sometimes long for love and happiness.

Perhaps, Catherine mused, she could use the girl to turn
the tables on Grey once again. Twice now he had dared to
supplant her as mistress of Greyhaven, the first time with

an arrogant, haughty woman who had despised her, the second time with an utterly unworthy child. She had resented the intrusion both times, for she and Grey had been close since childhood, and she despised having to share him. But she loved him unreservedly despite his infuriating ways. Catherine looked down at the frightened child.

A plan began to form in her mind. Perhaps she could mold this girl into something other than a credit to the Greyson name. Perhaps, using Jennifer's beauty as a weapon, they could bring Grey out of his morass of self-pity. She was devoted to her brother, despite the arguments they seemed to have constantly nowadays, and she was willing to try anything, anything at all, that might bring him happiness.

Of course, given a choice, she would not have brought the girl here. No matter how bad the girl's circumstances had been, they could hardly have been as miserable as life with a drunken stranger would be. But now that Jennifer was here, Catherine could see no reason not to use her startling beauty to tempt Grey into living again.

It didn't matter, she thought, whether or not the girl had the intelligence of a peahen. Diana had hardly been capable of adding two and two, yet Grey had adored her. Catherine knew from observation that men did not insist on intelligence in a beautiful woman. If only the girl could lose her timidity and be taught to flirt, to smile, to flutter her eyelashes . . .

Her plan fully formed, Catherine smiled as she considered Jennifer, who was still staring at her reflection, trying to see her own beauty. The girl, she thought, might turn out to be a blessing in disguise, after all.

Dinner was as dreadful as Jennifer had feared. Her husband sat at the opposite end of the mahogany gateleg table, glowering at her, quite obviously almost too drunk to stand, yet Catherine made small talk as calmly as though this were an everyday occurrence. Perhaps, Jennifer thought fearfully, it was. Perhaps she would have to face Grey, drunken and angry and bitter, across the dinner table every night for the rest of her life.

To take her mind off that disturbing thought, she looked around at her surroundings. The dining room was as opulently furnished as the rest of the house. The shining surface of the table was covered with a white linen tablecloth, and over it hung a brass chandelier. The flickering light from the candles illuminated the fine Chelsea porcelain, beautifully painted with flowers, birds, and butterflies. A portrait of a hawk-nosed man in a powdered wig, whom Jennifer assumed was Grey's father due to the unmistakably strong resemblance, hung over the fireplace. The gentleman depicted in the painting wore a dour expression that seemed common in this household.

Near the fireplace stood a marble-topped serving table. On it stood several silver columnar candlesticks bearing long thin tapers, which served to illuminate the chamber further. The beeswax candles produced less smoke and a less acrid scent than the tallow candles Jennifer was accustomed to. She had never imagined such profligate use of candles. After all, she had been responsible for making candles at the tavern, and it had taken her an entire day of hot and difficult labor to pour tallow into molds and make scarcely a month's supply.

The paneled walls of the dining chamber were painted a gold color, and the seats of the chairs were upholstered with golden wool to match. The chairs themselves were remarkable, being heavily carved in the Chippendale style. The arms of the chairs terminated in snarling dogs' heads, the mahogany faces of which reminded her uncomfortably of the savage, dark face of her husband.

Amidst all this splendor, Jennifer felt far out of her element, even clad as she was in the hastily pinned-up yet remarkably elegant silk gown. Lifting her eyes from the wonders that surrounded her, she found Grey's hard silver gaze slashing across her face like a blade. She winced under the impact of his stare.

"She has wretched table manners," Grey said to his sister with something like satisfaction. Jennifer's eyes leaped to Catherine in a mute appeal for help, as these were virtually the first words he had spoken all evening. She was painfully aware, even without Grey's cruel reminder, that she did not belong here, eating salty Virginia ham and succulent wild duck off china and silver. For an instant she wished that she were back in the ordinary, clad in her familiar homespun gown, eating plain fare from pewter plates and utensils, as she had been born to do.

Catherine glanced swiftly at the girl, and Jennifer thought she saw a trace of pity on the other woman's stern features. "Pay him no mind, Jennifer," she said gently. "We'll teach you better manners quickly enough. After all, no one is born knowing the correct way to hold a fork."

"She doesn't belong here," Grey grunted irritably. His oddly metallic eyes were still fixed on Jennifer, displaying a strange expression that made her exceedingly uncomfortable. "She should be in the stable, dining with the horses."

Catherine smiled slightly. Unlike Jennifer, she had no difficulty in reading the expression on Grey's face. He was bewildered—bewildered that the plain little caterpillar he had brought home had been transformed so easily into a butterfly. He had had no real idea what Jennifer's face and form might look like, hidden as they had been by grime and that shapeless homespun gown. And now, facing a lovely woman across the dinner table, his thoughts were all too obvious. Grey found Jennifer attractive, and this annoyed him.

Men, Catherine thought with amusement, were remarkably predictable. Her plan was going quite well so far. She had known that Grey could not be indifferent to Jennifer's beauty, even if he was indifferent to the girl herself. In an attempt to make him even more uncomfortably aware of Jennifer's charms, she said lightly, "I hope you agree that Jennifer looks every bit the lady. Emerald green is a lovely color on her, don't you agree?"

Grey did not answer. A muscle jumped in his taut jaw as

he continued his perusal of the girl. Catherine went on calmly, "I chose not to powder her hair. I thought its color too lovely to hide." She had never before seen hair of that particular shade, a dark blond the color of late afternoon sunlight. She had chosen to draw it up in a simple arrangement atop Jennifer's head, loosely plaiting it into a knot, which displayed the long graceful line of the girl's throat.

Grey's eyes lingered upon Jennifer a moment more, then, not without effort, he tore his gaze away and made his sister the object of his stare. "If you plan to turn her into a model of feminine deportment," he said coldly, "surely you should accustom her to pomading and powdering her hair. Otherwise she might be thought peculiar, as I am, simply because I prefer my own hair to someone else's. But then, I do not suppose you should concern yourself overmuch, for I imagine she will be considered odd anyway."

"I hope not," Catherine responded, unwilling to let him anger her. "For, you see, I do intend to turn her into a 'model of feminine deportment,' as you put it. I do not think the task will be too difficult."

Grey smiled derisively. "I think you're wrong."

But Catherine noted with satisfaction that his eyes strayed back to Jennifer repeatedly throughout the rest of the meal.

When at last the last course, a creamy and delicious dessert called syllabub, had been served and the ordeal of dinner was over, Jennifer fled up the stairs to her chamber, which had been dusted and aired out somewhat this afternoon. A slave helped her out of the green gown and banked the fire that had warmed the chilly air in the chamber. Clad only in her shift, she lay on the dark blue coverlet of the big mahogany bed and stared blindly at the canopy.

She was well aware that neither member of the household was pleased by her presence. Despite her kind words and sympathetic gestures, Catherine clearly resented the fact that she was here. She had quite pointedly treated Jennifer as a subordinate. Catherine was obviously determined to remain the mistress here, to maintain her control over the little world that was Greyhaven.

Jennifer was astute enough to realize that Catherine's apparent interest in transforming her into a lady was simply an attempt to turn the tables on Grey. Grey had begun a war by bringing home a tavern wench as his wife. He had won the first battle, shocking and scandalizing his sister. But Catherine, like a good general, had already engaged him in another skirmish by announcing her intention of transforming his wife into a lady. Jennifer was nothing more than a pawn in a family game for power and control. Catherine, she was certain, cared nothing for her well-being at all.

And Grey—Grey liked her even less than Catherine did.

She had never realized before that there are different kinds of abuse. Her uncle's physical abuse had been straightforward enough, and she had dreaded it, but the psychological torture Grey was inflicting upon her was a more insidious sort of abuse. She would almost rather have been beaten than face her husband's vicious remarks and cold stares every day. And she was beginning to realize that it would be a daily torment. Even if she could avoid him most of the time, she would still have to sit across the table from him each evening at dinner and be on the receiving end of his foul moods.

It was a disturbing thought, disturbing enough to cause her to toss and turn despite the unaccustomed softness of the feather mattress and the rope springs of the bed. At last, quite certain that she would get no sleep despite her exhausted and aching body, she rose quietly, drew on her old indigo gown—for she could not lace herself into that dreadful green gown without help—lit a candle with the tinderbox on the table next to her bed, and walked quietly down the stairs.

At the tavern, she had often sneaked outside at night and stared at the stars. It was the only time in her life of hard work and servitude when she ever had a few moments to herself. She found it very relaxing to lie on her back in the grass, looking at the brilliant points of light scattered thickly across the sky and listening to the music in her head. She never mentioned the music anymore. Once she had told her uncle that she heard music in her head, tunes that she had never before heard, melody and harmony weaving into a beautiful whole, and he had slapped her. "Bloody daft bitch," he'd said.

Since then she had told no one, not even Carey, for fear of being thought mad. But the music was beautiful, and she only heard it when she was at peace. There had been little enough peace in her life since her parents had died. Looking at the stars seemed to be the only thing that could quiet her mind and make her feel calm.

Walking silently toward the massive front door, she heard someone's voice. She hesitated, fearful of being caught. Then she recognized it as Grey's voice. Apparently he was talking to himself. Perhaps, she thought, he was as daft as she herself was.

Curiosity getting the better of her, she crept nearer the study door, from behind which his voice drifted. The door was ajar, and she peered cautiously around it. Her husband was slouched in a leather-upholstered easy chair, his tanned features deeply shadowed by the light of the guttering candle perched on the edge of his secretary desk. His empty eyes, black in the candlelight, were fixed on a portrait over the fireplace. And he appeared to be addressing it.

"I miss you," he said hoarsely. "I miss you so much." Though the words were blurred with drink, there was no mistaking the note of love and longing that shaded his voice. "I wish—that you could be here with me—"

And then he paused, apparently listening for a response.

Jennifer drew in her breath so sharply that she was afraid he would hear her, but his attention was focused completely on the portrait. He *was* mad, she realized dully, yet the realization did not bring horror, only pity. It mattered not one bit to her that her husband was insane, for she believed that she herself was none too sane. Who was to define sanity, in such a mad world? But the grief on his face was enough to make anyone pity him, even someone like Jennifer, who could feel so little.

Grey started murmuring again, too quietly for her to hear the words. She glanced quickly at the painting over the black-painted mantel. It depicted a lovely woman, with ice blue eyes and snow blond hair, clad in a pale blue satin gown with lavish ruffles of lace adorning the low neckline. In her bodice was a single pink rose. Jennifer stared from the portrait to Grey's ravaged face, and she understood.

Grey was talking to Diana.

Now Grey's voice grew louder, as though he were arguing. "I know I shouldn't have brought her here, beloved, but I only wed her so that I could be left alone. Alone with you." A pause. "Please don't be angry with me, love."

In his mind, Jennifer realized, Diana was angry with him for installing another woman in her place. Now he began to plead with her. "Please, dearest, I didn't mean any harm. Come back, beloved—please come back!"

And then he collapsed back into his chair and sank his head wearily into his hands, still murmuring, "Come back . . . come back. . . ."

Still peering anxiously around the door, Jennifer's eyes widened. Astonished, she watched as the cold, bitter man she had married wept like a child.

SIX

"Oh, God, Grey, I've missed you."

Grey regarded his mistress sardonically, no trace of affection discernible on his face "More to the point, I suspect," he drawled, "you've missed the amusement I provide."

To illustrate his point, he let his hand drift from her mahogany hair to her bare breasts, lightly brushing over nipples that were erect in the chilly January breeze. She moaned, protesting huskily, "Truly, Grey, I have missed you. As well as the amusement you provide."

Grey shrugged indifferently and turned away, much to her dismay. His body had been sated for now, and he no longer had any interest in her as she sprawled on the ground. Her body was lovely, voluptuous yet firm, but he had no use for her once she had satisfied his lust. He had not missed her in the least.

He buttoned his breeches and brushed away sundry bits of pine straw that were clinging to his elegant, if somewhat disheveled, clothing. Usually they made love in an abandoned, crumbling cabin that had formerly been slave quarters, but Grey, made more amorous than usual by his six weeks of abstinence, had been impatient. The cold weather of the past few weeks had given way to an unseasonably warm day, almost springlike, and they had made love in the forest atop his fine woolen cloak.

"A parting of more than a month should have given

you an opportunity to improve your relationship with your husband." He glanced at her, a dark, slashing brow quirked. "Or, perhaps, with another man."

"Grey!" she protested indignantly, golden brown eyes wide with feigned innocence. "You know there is no one else for me."

"Would that you could say those same words to your husband," Grey remarked dryly.

She propped herself up on one elbow, covering herself against the chilly breeze with the cloak they had lain on, and stared at him. "Are you feeling guilty, Grey?" She gave him a feline smile. "Could it be that you are developing a conscience?"

"God save me from that folly, Melissa. Why should I feel guilty for bedding a woman caught in a loveless marriage? If your husband doesn't have the good sense to make you happy, he should expect you to look elsewhere for your pleasure."

But he did not look in her direction. Melissa realized he did indeed feel guilty—not because of her, he never spared a thought for her—but rather because he felt that he was betraying Diana. During lovemaking he was invariably passionate and gentle, if somewhat detached, but afterward his face always took on an expression of self-disgust, as though he were repulsed by his lack of control.

But today he seemed even more distant than usual. "Something is disturbing you," she persisted, driven not by sympathy but by her prurient curiosity.

Grey shot her a level look. "I'm surprised you haven't heard," he said flatly. "I've married."

Melissa sat up abruptly, staring at him with something like shock. Had Grey somehow fallen in love in a short six weeks? Grey, who was so obsessed with his dead wife? Grey, whose heart had turned to stone so many years before?

And then she glanced down at her bare breasts, gleaming ivory in the midday sun that filtered through the pine trees, and almost laughed aloud at her absurd thoughts. Of course Grey had not fallen in love. Even Grey could not be callous enough to bring home a woman he loved and hurry to his mistress's arms the following day.

Nor was his dark, preoccupied face that of a man in love. She smiled, certain now what must have happened and so relieved that she dared to tease him. "Really, Grey, you should have been more careful. There are ways to avoid such unpleasant consequences, you know."

Much to her surprise, he burst out laughing. Rarely had she heard him laugh. At last he stopped, and said, still grinning sardonically, "I'm afraid you have the wrong idea. I haven't bedded the chit—I wouldn't bed her for a bloody fortune."

"Then why—"

"Catherine told me to find a wife, someone worthy of the Greyson name," Grey explained briefly. "I did so."

Melissa eyed him, wondering nervously if his new wife would be a rival for his attention. "Someone worthy of the Greyson name?"

"I should say so," Grey replied, resembling a wolf as he grinned. "I wed a tavern wench."

Melissa could not prevent herself from smiling in relief. "A tavern wench!" she repeated in amused shock. "Grey, how could you do such a thing? My God, what will people say?"

Grey grinned more widely at her shocked response. It was exactly the sort of reaction he enjoyed provoking. "What they always say, I daresay. That I am quite mad. And I suppose I am."

Such a woman as Grey described certainly could be no rival, and the scorn he felt for his new wife was evident in his tone. Melissa's concern, of course, had only been for herself; the self-loathing that had led Grey to marry someone so far beneath his social station concerned her not at all. Despite their long-term relationship, which had endured off and on for nearly seven years, she had little genuine fondness for Grey, for he was not a man who inspired affection. "As long as she will not cause you to forget me," she murmured seductively.

Grey looked at her shoulders and round, full breasts, glistening in the sunlight. "Small chance of that," he replied in a halfhearted attempt at gallantry, though she knew full well that he scarcely spared her a thought unless he wanted a woman to warm his bed. He added more seriously, "What puzzles me is why you ever wanted me to begin with."

Melissa hesitated. She had her own reasons for cuckolding her husband with Grey, reasons that she preferred he know nothing about. "You are very attractive," she said at last. "Every woman in Virginia wants you." That, at least, was true enough. Despite the rumors that he was mad—or perhaps because of the rumors—women were drawn irresistibly to him. Part of his attraction was his immense fortune, but that did not explain why married women pursued him almost as zealously as unwed girls.

Grey frowned, his heavy black eyebrows drawing together over pale silver eyes. "Your husband is handsome as well, more so than I am."

Melissa sighed. How could she explain the powerful magnetism that Grey exuded? True, he was not handsome in the traditional sense, but he radiated a strength that was extremely attractive, even when he was foxed, and his carved features were strikingly aristocratic. She did not reply, afraid that she might betray herself if the subject went further.

"If you were unwed," Grey pressed on with single-minded determination, "I would have suspected your interest was in my fortune. As it stands, however, I cannot imagine what it is about me that you find attractive." He was not modest; he was aware that women seemed to like to look at him. Generally, though, a few moments in his presence cured them of any notion that he was attractive in any way beyond his looks. Melissa, on the other hand, had been his mistress since shortly after Diana had died— though he had not restricted himself solely to her bed. Far from it.

"Does your wife find you attractive?" Melissa countered, uneasy with the direction the conversation had taken.

Grey turned away. An expression strangely foreign to his face, a look almost of embarrassment, was beginning to settle over his features, as though even he was appalled by what his callousness had done to the girl he had married. "I hardly think so. At the beginning I believe she saw me as a hero, a knight in shining armor, but—I took steps to correct that. I cannot bear to have her following me like an adoring puppy." He shrugged, "She is not bright, perhaps even a little simple-minded. I think she is afraid of me."

Not surprisingly, Melissa thought, studying his sharp profile, the curving nose and jutting cheekbones, and the harsh expression etched, apparently permanently, on his face. To her surprise she felt a brief stab of pity for the poor girl whom Grey had married. To be wed to such a cruelly indifferent man, to be ripped from familiar surroundings and thrown into a completely foreign environment—the child must be terrified. And Grey, typically enough, did not seem to give a damn.

Melissa suppressed her unwanted surge of pity. The girl's presence, she realized, was to her advantage. If Grey was no longer being pursued by every unwed ninny in the colony, she could continue to hold his attention. She alone would share his bed. And to further her aims, to obtain what she wanted most, that was necessary. The happiness of a mere tavern wench, she decided coldly, mattered not at all.

While her husband dallied with his mistress in the woods, Jennifer sat in the parlor learning to be worthy of him. So impressed was she with her attire that she barely listened when Catherine spoke. She regarded her wide hoops with a peculiar mixture of delight and distaste. As a lowly tavern wench, she had never before worn side hoops, or panniers. She knew that some members of the middle class, such as shopkeepers' wives, wore hoops fashioned of bent wood. But *she* was now wearing hoops made of bone! They made her green silk gown look elegant and fashionable, yet they were terribly awkward to walk in. The bone stays that made her already slender waist impossibly tiny were even less comfortable, laced as they were so tightly that she could barely draw a deep breath. But she was now a member of the Virginia aristocracy. She had to wear such things at all times.

"*At all times,*" Catherine stressed as she watched her pupil practice a slow, genteel walk. She sounded as though she suspected the girl of unladylike behavior already, and Jennifer quailed, thinking of how she had drawn on her indigo-dyed dress the night before.

Catherine groaned, thinking it would take weeks, years—perhaps forever—for the girl to learn to walk in a ladylike manner. Despite the fact that Catherine had carefully demonstrated a graceful walk as best she could, given her infirmity, the child seemed incapable of walking slowly, with her head held high. Her gait was best described as a scurry—she walked quickly with her head bent submissively, as though she expected to be struck violently by a fist at any moment. Catherine supposed that was only natural, given Jennifer's background.

"Very good, for your first day as a lady," she lied, smiling kindly. It was impossible not to feel pity for the girl. She gestured to one of the chairs. "Come sit and we'll have tea."

Jennifer stared at her blankly. "Tea?"

"Certainly. Have you never drunk tea before?"

The girl shook her head silently. Tea was imported from England, and was so expensive that it was usually kept in a locked box. Someone of her social station rarely had an opportunity to drink it. She seated herself on the ivory damask seat of a heavily carved chair and watched as Catherine prepared the tea on a mahogany Queen Anne tea table with legs so long and slender that it reminded Jennifer of a gawky colt. Valuable commodity that it was, the tea was kept in a canister in a locked chest, along with a larger sugar box and other tea accessories, such as sugar tongs and teaspoons.

Once the tea had steeped, Catherine poured it from a chased silver teapot into gorgeous botanical china cups of the same pattern Jennifer had seen the night before. She poured it through a strainer spoon, a special spoon with a pierced bowl, which prevented tea leaves from accumulating in the cup. "Do you want sugar?"

Wordlessly, Jennifer nodded.

Sugar, another item that, like tea, could not be produced in the colony, was shipped to Virginia in cones, which were then broken up in the kitchen. Catherine picked up a chunk of sugar using sugar tongs and presented the cup to Jennifer, who stirred it with a teaspoon, the back of which was stamped with the picture of a ship with its sails flying. She had never seen such a fine spoon, accustomed as she was to crude pewter tableware, and she admired the stunning workmanship for a few moments before remembering to sip her tea.

"Do not slurp your tea in that fashion," Catherine corrected her at once. "Sip it quietly."

Chastened, Jennifer tried to sip less noisily. It seemed that she could do nothing here without being criticized. Everything was so different! She had not realized what a ceremony the rich made of the simple act of drinking tea. The tea was delicious, sweet and warm, wonderfully pleasant on a day that was slightly chilly.

While she sipped her tea, she studied the parlor surreptitiously. Everything in the chamber bespoke the enormous wealth of the Greysons, from the superlative Oriental carpet that adorned the wide-planked floor, to the Kirckman harpsichord that stood in the corner with two silver branches of candles atop it. The matched pair of black walnut bookcases against the opposite wall had glass doors covered on the inside with curtains, as was customary to prevent light from fading the leather bindings of the valuable books within. Even to her unsophisticated eyes, it was evident that every piece of furniture in the room had been made by master craftsmen.

With surprise, she noted that the fireplace mantel was painted black, signifying that the family was in mourning. She recalled that the other mantels she had seen throughout the house had been black as well. Did Grey still consider himself to be in mourning for Diana after seven years?

Considering the scene she had witnessed last night, it seemed all too likely.

Her eyes were drawn to the portrait over the fireplace. A woman with unpowdered hair, black as a raven's wing, and piercing gray eyes stared out over the room. She was smiling, but it was not a pleasant smile. She was beautiful, yet she looked self-absorbed.

Seeing the girl's curiosity, Catherine said quietly, "It is acceptable to make small talk while one drinks tea."

"Who was she?" Jennifer nodded at the painting. Somehow she knew the woman portrayed was no longer alive. Everywhere she turned in this grand mansion there was a painting of a dead person. For the second time in two days it occurred to her that ghosts seemed to watch over the living at Greyhaven. The thought made her shudder.

"Our mother. And yes, she was as unkind as she looks. Father was cold, but she was intentionally vicious. Beautiful but cruel."

Then Grey takes after both his parents, both cold and *vicious.* Jennifer crushed the thought instantly. It was wrong, terribly wrong, to think such things about one's husband.

"I'm the one who insisted on hanging the portraits of our parents," Catherine added. "Grey despised Mother and Father both. He wanted to burn the paintings. I would not let him."

How dreadful, Jennifer thought, that he should hate both his parents so much that he would want to destroy their portraits. She wondered what they had done to provoke his hatred. "Why?"

"Why did I stop him from burning them?"

"No. Why did 'e 'ate them?"

Catherine frowned into her teacup. "It's hard to explain," she said slowly. "As I've said, Father was cold. Indifferent. He cared for no one but himself. And Mother—she antagonized him purposely. They were always fighting. Mother had a talent for provoking arguments. There was never a moment's peace in our house. I think that's why Grey built the new house when they died."

"Th' new 'ouse?"

"Greyhaven was built by Grey," Catherine explained. "When he inherited all of Father's land nine years ago he swore he'd never live in the old house again. He built the new house on the same piece of land—he owns land all up and down the James River, but this is the best land, and the nearest to Williamsburg—and he tore the old house down, brick by brick. When we lived here as children the plantation was named Edgewood. He renamed it. He even furnished the house with new furniture and silver. He wanted nothing whatsoever to remind him of our parents." She paused. "It's almost as though our parents never lived at all. That's why I insisted on keeping their portraits."

Jennifer nodded solemnly. She could understand that. "I 'ave naught ter remind me of my parents," she volunteered, surprising Catherine. "I don't even remember them."

"When did they die?" Catherine inquired.

"I was nine."

"And you don't remember them at all?"

Jennifer shook her head. What little she could remember of her life before she came to live with her uncle in the Pine Tree Ordinary she firmly suppressed. She did not want to remember. But she did wish that she had something of her mother's—a miniature, a piece of jewelry, something. Anything to remind her that she had once had a family that loved her.

How strange, Catherine thought. They actually had something in common. She, an aristocrat, a born-and-bred lady, had something in common with this pitiful and abused girl. They had both experienced the loss of their parents. For the first time she thought of Jennifer as a person, rather than as simply a pawn in her ongoing war with Grey.

"My parents died when I was thirteen," she said. "I remember them all too clearly. The screaming, the constant arguments . . . Even before they died, I thought of Grey as more of a parent than they ever were." She saw Jennifer's surprised glance, and added, "Grey was different then. More responsible. Kinder. Less self-absorbed. He was like a father to me, willing to fight my battles for me and to comfort me when I was hurting. I don't know how I would have gotten through my childhood without him. He was always there for me."

"There was no one there fer me," Jennifer said in a barely audible voice.

Catherine's eyes met hers squarely across the tea table. "There is now."

So far as Catherine was concerned, Jennifer was now a member of the Greyson family, with all the rights and privileges that entailed. She bent her efforts and her considerable will to making Jennifer into a lady, one that the family might be proud of. The two young women, along with several of the house slaves, spent a great deal of time sewing new gowns for Jennifer, using bolts of cloth Catherine had intended to use for her own clothes, and cutting down older gowns found in the massive mahogany clothespress into more fashionable styles. They used as their guide the little fashion dolls, called moppets, that were imported from England dressed in the current fashions.

Catherine also spent long, painful hours drilling Jennifer on her speech, trying to eradicate her lower-class accent. Later she would teach her to read and write, along with the other accomplishments so necessary to the education of a lady. Recognizing that she could not instantly erase every trace of Jennifer's origin, she focused her early efforts on simply transforming Jennifer's appearance.

The more ladylike Jennifer became, Catherine noticed, the more irritable Grey became at dinner. She took this as a good sign.

Two weeks after Jennifer's arrival at Greyhaven, on a sunny and unseasonably warm February day, Moses, the liveried butler, found Catherine in the garden and told her there was a visitor waiting in the parlor. At the mention of the woman's name, Catherine stared at him for a moment in disbelief, then limped to the parlor with unladylike haste.

"Mistress Lightfoot," she said in a decidedly uncivil tone. "What are you doing here?"

Melissa Lightfoot, seated on the settee, smiled at her without getting up. "Why, Catherine, dear," she said in a silky voice. "What an unfriendly greeting. Aren't you going to offer me refreshment?"

"No," Catherine said tersely. "I want you out of my parlor."

"*Your* parlor?" Melissa rose to her feet and looked stubbornly at Catherine, smiling sweetly but dangerously. "On the contrary, I believe Grey's wife is now the mistress of Greyhaven. Christopher and I have come to meet her and to extend her the courtesy of a visit."

"Indeed. And where, might I ask, is your husband?"

"He'll be here in just a moment. He's watching the slaves to make certain they tie the horses up properly. You do get so *few* guests here, after all."

Catherine forced her features to remain passive, but her hand gripped the silver head of her cane so tightly that her knuckles whitened.

"And since I am a, well, special friend of the family," Melissa went on, "I would like to meet Grey's wife. Jenny, isn't that her name?"

"Jennifer," Catherine quickly corrected, noting the

thinly disguised scorn in Melissa's voice. She stood looking at the other woman for a moment, her mind racing furiously as she tried to find a way out of this predicament. Of all the people for Jennifer to meet first! At last, seeing no alternative, she spoke courteously. "Of course I will let Jennifer know you and your husband are here to see her, Mistress Lightfoot. Won't you sit down? I'll have the slaves bring some refreshments."

Victorious, Melissa settled back onto the settee, arranging her topaz skirts around her artistically.

Catherine made her way up the stairs and knocked at Jennifer's door. "Jennifer," she said, a faint tinge of nervousness evident beneath her usual hauteur, "please come downstairs. There are—visitors—who would like to meet you." She wanted to warn Jennifer that Melissa was Grey's mistress, but she held her tongue, knowing that the knowledge would only distress Jennifer. Better that she tell Jennifer later.

Wondering at the anxiety in the other woman's voice, Jennifer rose to her feet in automatic response. She still felt herself to be a servant, and Catherine seemed to treat her as one. Although her requests were always phrased politely, there was invariably a trace of authority in her tone. Nonetheless, Jennifer's initial dislike for the woman had faded into a more charitable emotion.

The girl smoothed her new gown. It was of deep blue silk that emphasized the warm honey tone of her skin and her dark blond hair. The panniers were comparatively narrow, but hoops of any kind still felt strange. On the front of the bodice was a stomacher, a stiffened panel of triangular shape that was finely embroidered. The boned stomacher, as well as the still-unfamiliar stays, made it virtually impossible for Jennifer to slouch. She followed the other woman down the stairs, her head held high, hesitating at the parlor door but then stepping into the chamber.

Seated on the high-backed settee were a fashionably attired couple. Their eyes instantly riveted on Jennifer with avid curiosity. Somewhat taken aback by their stares, she paused and regarded them. The man was perhaps Grey's age, though he seemed younger, with an easy grin quite unlike Grey's habitual sullen expression. He was handsome, very handsome indeed, with features perhaps more regular but less striking than Grey's. His nose was straight and patrician, his mouth full and sensual. His dark blue eyes followed her every move with a strange intensity. Though he was undeniably, classically attractive, he lacked Grey's aura of strength and startling masculinity. Jennifer realized with dismay that she was comparing the man to Grey, to his detriment, and switched her attention to the woman.

The lady sat straight-backed on the settee. She was more strikingly attractive than the man, with deep brown hair contrasting stunningly with perfect, pale skin. A shocking expanse of creamy flesh swelled above the low-cut, square neckline of her topaz gown. Dark brows arched over golden brown eyes the color of fine sherry, which stared at Jennifer assessingly.

Apparently recalling his manners, the man jumped to his feet and regarded Jennifer with open admiration. She saw that he was rather short, especially when compared to Grey. "Remarkable," he said softly, as though to himself.

The woman stood gracefully, smiling at Jennifer in a manner that could be interpreted as either friendly or condescending. Jennifer was inclined to believe the latter. "We'd heard Grey married," she said coolly, "and we just had to come see for ourselves. How lovely you are, my dear. I can't imagine a more *suitable* addition to the Greyson family."

From the slight stiffening of Catherine's body, Jennifer realized that the apparent compliment was an insult. She faintly understood the veiled insult—a drunkard, a cripple, and a tavern wench. But anger, or emotion of any kind, was foreign to her nature. She said nothing, as was her way, only regarded the other woman with clear green eyes. Catherine stepped in.

"Jennifer," she said, and her voice was as calm and polite

as though the insult to her family had completely escaped her, "this is Christopher Lightfoot, and his wife, Melissa. They live on the neighboring plantation, which is known as the Cove."

Observing her sister-in-law's poise, Jennifer concluded that a lady must politely disregard insults. Clearly this creature with the golden brown eyes was no lady, despite her low-cut gown and elegant coiffure. Far better that she model her behavior after Catherine's. "Pleased t'meet ye," she murmured, executing an extremely clumsy curtsy and mentally cursing whoever had invented side hoops.

Melissa's smile took on a decidedly unfriendly cast. "Such a charmingly quaint accent you have, Mistress Greyson," she said with savage sarcasm, uttering a trilling and patently artificial laugh. "Is it foreign, perhaps?"

"Now, now," her husband broke in before Jennifer could formulate an answer, "plainly the lady is not from this area." Jennifer exhaled a deep sigh of relief, grateful for his intercession, but her gratitude fled abruptly at his next words. "Tell me, Mistress Greyson, how did you meet your husband?"

Jennifer sent a pleading look in Catherine's direction, but it was evident from the expression on Catherine's features that she had no more idea how to deal with the situation than Jennifer did. She had hoped that this situation would not come up so quickly. Due to Grey's reclusive behavior, they rarely had visitors these days. And Jennifer had not yet had to attend church or any other sort of social function where she might have met their neighbors.

But of course, Catherine reflected sourly, news traveled quickly in Virginia. And their neighbors were bound to visit, to stare at Jennifer and to mock her accent and manners, under the guise of welcoming her to the area. She was struggling to teach Jennifer how to speak and act like a lady, but it was a long and torturous process. In the meantime the neighbors would gawk. She bit her lip, unable to determine the best way to satiate the Lightfoots' curiosity without revealing too much.

Before she could open her mouth, however, a deep voice rumbled behind her. "She swept me off my feet," Grey said.

Catherine turned and saw her brother leaning negligently on the doorjamb. A wave of relief swept through her, followed promptly by a sensation of fear. Who knew what Grey might take it into his head to say? He might have come into the parlor to save Jennifer from the wolves, or to throw her to them. She prayed he would not humiliate them all.

Turning, Jennifer saw him lounging in the doorway, positively radiating raw power. He was clad for riding, wearing only a linen shirt with ruffles at the throat, the clean white stock contrasting oddly with his tanned skin, and buff knee breeches that clung to his muscled thighs. His calves were encased in riding boots of soft leather turned down at the top below the knee. Under his arm he carried a beaverskin tricorne trimmed with the metal braid known as point d'Espagne. His ebony hair was not confined, falling in loose waves to his shoulders.

Clearly he had just returned from his daily ride. Protocol, of course, demanded that he change before seeing his guests. It was unthinkable that a man entertain visitors without a coat and waistcoat, and without his unruly hair confined beneath a wig, or at least tied neatly in a queue. Jennifer did not care how scandalous his appearance was. She stared at him, noticing only the way the linen of his shirt, wet with sweat, clung to his broad chest and shoulders. Realizing the direction her thoughts were taking, she looked away hastily, shocked at her wanton reaction to her husband. Never before had she been so drawn to a man. Then again, she had never before known a man who was so blatantly, powerfully masculine.

Grey grinned and stepped into the room. Completely disregarding his appearance, and the fact that he reeked of stables and perspiration, he seated himself on the ivory damask-covered seat of one of Catherine's prized chairs. Catherine sent him an indignant look but said nothing.

Resting a booted foot on one knee, Grey faced his guests. "She swept me off my feet," he repeated, nodding toward his wife. "I knew that no matter how long I looked I would never find a woman more perfect for me in any way. Isn't that so, darling?" He smiled lazily at his wife.

Jennifer stood frozen. Despite the careless use of the endearment, she realized wretchedly that he was making fun of her again—and worse, that their guests realized it. She noticed the amused looks that passed between Melissa and Grey. And too, she noticed that the lovely dark-haired Melissa was eyeing Grey in much the same fashion she herself had been a few moments ago, with an almost predatory gaze, as though the woman was far more affected by the aura of virile strength he radiated than she had any right to be.

She wanted to flee the chamber, to run from her husband's mocking smile. She wished, desperately, that she had never asked Grey to take her with him that night weeks ago. There was a saying, "Better the devil you know." She had married a devil, and her life was no better now than it had ever been. She was as alone as ever.

She barely noticed the rest of the conversation, for it was not directed at her. She might as well have been a piece of furniture. Grey sat and answered the Lightfoots' constant stream of questions, casting apparent looks of devotion at Jennifer until she wanted to burst into tears. It was all too obvious that their guests knew the truth, that Grey had only married her to embarrass his sister and scorn society.

When at last the Lightfoots had left, and Grey had gone upstairs to change without another word to his wife, Catherine smiled grimly at Jennifer.

"What a vulture that woman is. And her husband is little better."

Jennifer sighed, partly in relief and partly to relieve the choking feeling in her throat. She had never been so close to tears in the past nine years as she was now. Getting her voice under control, she decided to finally speak. "They did not seem t'take ter me."

At that astonishing understatement, Catherine turned and glared at her. "And you have no idea why, do you?"

" 'Tis obvious," Jennifer objected, somewhat offended that Catherine thought her to be such a ninny. "I'm not of th' same class. I don't belong, and I never will."

"That isn't all." When Jennifer only stared at her blankly, Catherine clarified, "Melissa is Grey's mistress."

The room seemed to whirl around Jennifer. Tears threatened again. No wonder Grey regarded her with such contempt, she thought miserably. She could not hope to compete with such a lovely and sophisticated woman. She remembered the topaz silk gown the other woman had worn, her beautiful brown eyes and shining mahogany hair, and she felt hopelessly, completely inadequate.

"That's how she knew all about you," Catherine was explaining. "No doubt he told her everything. To Grey, your marriage is only a joke, nothing more."

Jennifer felt as though she were crumbling inside, but her face remained as still and calm as always. Studying the girl's features for traces of emotion, Catherine could find none. If Jennifer was affected by the news that her husband thought of her in the light of a joke and laughed about her with his mistress, she gave no sign of it.

Catherine could not know that when Jennifer went upstairs, she locked the door to her chamber and wept into her pillow for a quarter of an hour. They were the first tears she had shed in nearly nine years.

And while Jennifer cried upstairs, Catherine sat in the parlor and stared thoughtfully into the fire. Damn Grey, she thought savagely. Damn him to hell.

Her plan was not going well at all.

SEVEN

"In . . . the . . . be-beginning . . . was the Word. . . ."
Catherine nodded approvingly. "Very good," she said
with uncharacteristic enthusiasm. She had been delighted with her pupil's progress. Jennifer had learned the
sounds of the alphabet and had progressed into reading,
however poorly, within three months. The girl was considerably more intelligent than Catherine had expected.

Even more surprising than her intelligence was her vigi-
lant desire to learn. Perhaps it sprang from her desire to
transform herself from a common tavern wench into a
suitable planter's wife, or perhaps it was an innate quality,
but Jennifer seemed determined to memorize and analyze
every bit of knowledge that came her way. Usually it was
Catherine who grew tired of the lessons and called a halt to
the learning for the day. Jennifer seemed tireless, almost
relentless, in her search for more knowledge.

After the lessons were over for the day, the two young
women talked. Though neither would have admitted it,
they were fast becoming close friends. In the evenings,
while Grey sulked in his study, Catherine and Jennifer
played backgammon, draughts, and whist. Jennifer had
never before had a woman friend, and the experience was
slowly encouraging her to emerge from her shell. Catherine was too stiff to admit even to herself how she enjoyed
talking with the other woman, but the truth was that their

friendship filled a void in her life. Since Grey was considered mad by most of the planters along the James, they all too rarely had visitors. Catherine had been denied the chance to make friends for many years now.

"And the light shineth in darkness, and . . . and the darkness comprehended it not. . . ."

Recalled to the present, Catherine reached out and took the Bible from the other girl's hands. Grey's library, like the library of any well-educated gentleman in the colony, included a vast quantity of classic works, by authors as diverse as Homer, Shakespeare, and Chaucer, as well as more practical works, such as *Tull's Horse-Hoeing Husbandry*, but Catherine had wisely decided to teach Jennifer to read using a book she was somewhat familiar with. "I think that's enough for now." To forestall the inevitable look of disappointment on Jennifer's face, she said thoughtfully, "You know, Jen, I still don't feel as though I know you very well. What was your life like before you came to Greyhaven?"

Jennifer shrugged. "It was not much of a life," she said, reticent as ever.

"Were you happy?"

Jennifer shook her head.

"Why not?"

At last Jennifer was coaxed to speak. "I did not care for my uncle," she said honestly. "You know that he beat me, for any reason or for no reason. And my aunt was a timid woman who did not dare to stop him. I scarcely knew her at all, even though I lived with her for nine years. She never spoke."

"So your uncle punished you for no reason whatsoever?" Catherine said. Her parents had never punished her; in fact, they had rarely paid any attention to her at all. She wondered now if perhaps she had not been lucky in that regard. "That doesn't seem very fair."

Jennifer remained silent, and Catherine frowned. "You don't expect life to be fair, do you?"

"My life 'as never been fair," Jennifer said with a complete lack of bitterness. Despite her words, there was no self-pity in her tone. She seemed to be merely stating a fact.

Poor girl, Catherine thought. These days Jennifer only saw Grey at meals, where he maintained an icy silence. The rest of the time he seemed to go out of his way to avoid her. The entire situation was intolerable, yet Jennifer bore it without complaining.

To cover the sympathy she was certain showed on her face, Catherine said irritably, "For heaven's sake, pronounce your aitches, Jennifer." Jennifer's lower-class accent, while fading noticeably, always annoyed her, perhaps because it seemed so at odds with the young woman's upper-class appearance. Today she wore a rose-colored open robe gown, with the bodice and overskirt joined together, but with the skirt open in front to reveal an ivory petticoat. Masking the extremely low, round neckline was a filmy kerchief. Her waist appeared impossibly tiny, owing to the tight stays, and Catherine thought with satisfaction that no one could have guessed by looking at her that three months before she had been little better than a slave. Unfortunately, most of the changes were superficial. But considering the girl's startling level of intelligence, Catherine was confident that she would very shortly be a lady in every way.

"There was another thing," Jennifer remarked idly, surprising Catherine, who had never known her to speak without prodding. "My uncle believed that I was mad. He used to beat me for that reason, every now and then."

"I can't imagine why he would think that," Catherine said honestly. Despite the unpleasantness of her childhood, Jennifer seemed relatively normal, if reserved. Certainly she was the sanest member of this household!

Wide green eyes, the color of pine needles in the summer sun, glanced gravely at her as if deciding whether to disclose a momentous secret. At last Jennifer said, "Because I hear music." At Catherine's puzzled expression, she clarified, "In my head. Every now and then a traveler would take out a fiddle and play a tune in the tavern. I can hear those tunes whenever I want to. But I also hear other tunes, tunes I've never heard before."

"Melodies you made up yourself?"

Jennifer considered this with her customary solemnity. "I suppose so," she agreed at last, "though I never thought about them. They just came into my head." There was a slight, embarrassed pause, and then she burst out, "You said I could learn to play the harpsichord. When?"

Startled by the girl's enthusiasm, Catherine said, "Well, I thought learning to read was most important." At the girl's crestfallen expression, she added, "However . . . I suppose other accomplishments are important, too. If it means that much to you we can start on the harpsichord today, if you like."

Jennifer smiled, actually smiled, and the radiance of it spread across her face like the rays of a sunrise spreading across the sky. Leaping to her feet, she lifted her skirts and ran down the stairs with childlike glee. Catherine followed more slowly, leaning on her walking stick.

"I know I can learn to play," Jennifer was saying excitedly from the bottom of the staircase as Catherine limped down the steps. "I know I can! I've dreamed about playing the tunes in my head. And new tunes, ones I've never heard of or imagined. I never thought I'd have the opportunity—" She broke off, suddenly aware of Catherine's surprised stare at her uncharacteristic burst of words. Once again her quiet self, she followed the other woman meekly into the parlor.

As Catherine had expected, Jennifer was full of questions about music, her enthusiasm for the subject overcoming her reticence. At first, puzzled, she inquired why the scale only went up to G rather than to Z. When her curiosity regarding that enigma was satisfied, she demanded an explanation as to why there was no black key between B and C. Her questions might have gone on forever had not Catherine demonstrated the scale. Jennifer ran through the C-major scale, clearly delighted to actually be touching the instrument, then, to Catherine's utter astonishment, she picked out a melody, with surprisingly few mistakes.

"I understood you to say you had never played the harpsichord before," Catherine said in surprise.

"I haven't."

"Then where did you learn to play that melody?"

Jennifer gave her an apologetic half smile. "I heard it once."

"And you can play it? Just like that?"

Jennifer nodded and played the melody again, perfectly this time.

The girl had an innate grasp of intervals, Catherine realized. Teaching her how to play might be easier than she expected.

She ran into an unexpected snag, however, almost immediately. Once she had given Jennifer a rudimentary explanation of fingering techniques, she tried to show the girl how to read music. Jennifer became perplexed, then frustrated.

"I don't understand," she protested, unhappy that she was a poor student, but simply unable to grasp the concept. "You say that the little blob on the parchment is C. How could it be? This"—and she struck a key—"is C."

Catherine sighed mentally and started over. "The notes on the paper represent the notes that you play," she explained with praiseworthy patience. "When you see that note on the paper, you know that you are supposed to play C."

Jennifer's brow was still furrowed, so Catherine added, "It's somewhat like reading out loud. The letter A stands for a specific sound, or a limited number of sounds. The letter A has no innate meaning—it's a symbol that represents a sound. These notes are like letters. They represent the sounds you make when you strike the keys."

Jennifer nodded slowly. "I think I see," she said, then added, "but why bother to write it down at all?"

"So you can remember it, of course."

"How could you forget it?"

Irritably, Catherine started to snap at the girl for asking foolish questions, but she caught herself. It was evident from the guileless expression on Jennifer's face that she had meant the question quite seriously. Perhaps, having once heard a piece of music, she was incapable of forgetting it.

Intrigued by the notion, Catherine began to test her hypothesis. "Play this," she said, playing a simple melody.

Jennifer listened carefully, her head tilted to one side, her eyes half-shut in pleasure. "That is beautiful," she breathed when Catherine finished. "Did you compose it?"

"Hardly," Catherine said, in awe of Jennifer's reaction. She had never seen Jennifer show so much delight in anything. For that matter, she had rarely seen Jennifer show any emotion at all. Clearly the girl had a genuine love for music. "I am not a composer. It was written by a man named Corelli."

Jennifer played the tune haltingly, then played it a second time with perfect accuracy, obviously entranced by the melody. "How lovely," she whispered. "I wish I could write something like that."

"Perhaps you can," Catherine said, "when you know more about music. But I have never heard of a woman composer."

Jennifer looked at her in surprise. "Never?"

"Never that I've heard of. It is considered a ladylike accomplishment to play the harpsichord, but not to write music." She remembered Jennifer's enthusiastic description of the tunes she heard in her mind, her longing to create new tunes. "However," she added kindly, "perhaps you will be an exception to that rule."

"Perhaps. After all, I am not a lady."

Catherine looked at her and smiled. "Not yet."

And perhaps not ever, Jennifer thought. But, not wanting to distress Catherine, she did not say it aloud.

A few hours later, Jennifer walked slowly along the winding dirt path that sliced through the woods on the

Greyson property. At the Pine Tree Ordinary, she had scurried along on whatever errand she had as rapidly as possible, so as to avoid her uncle's wrath. At times she still found herself almost running from sheer habit. But today she walked slowly, head held high, partly because Catherine had taught her that ladies never looked as though they were in a hurry, and partly because her voluminous skirts tended to prevent running anyway. Her rose overskirt and ivory petticoat were draped over whalebone-and-canvas panniers, and the front of the skirt was flattened by a system of cords. If she forgot herself and tried to walk too hastily in such a gown, she would tumble to the ground in a graceless heap.

She had left the house because Catherine had tired of the lessons. Jennifer would have happily plunked at the keys of the harpsichord all day, but at last Catherine had driven her from the parlor, and Jennifer had decided to come for a walk. Due to the unseasonably warm May weather, it was cooler in the shade of the tall pines and oaks that graced the forest than it was inside the great brick house.

For months Catherine had tried in vain to impress upon her that a lady should take her constitutional in the formal gardens that spread out behind the great house. But Jennifer did not like the formal gardens. The oyster-shell-strewn paths were edged by English boxwood, forced to put down roots in this foreign soil and then trimmed into artificially geometrical shapes. Jennifer did not care for the boxwood, which seemed out of place in this wild land. Nor did she care for the bell-shaped, multihued flowers, imported at great cost from someplace called Holland, that bloomed so profusely among the hedges.

Jennifer preferred the small kitchen garden nestled close behind the cookhouse. There grew more modest but more charming plants such as lavender, which was already starting to extend purple, sweet-smelling flowers toward the sky; rosemary, with its pungent, spicy aroma; and the descriptively named, fuzzy-leafed plant called lamb's ear.

But most of all, despite all of Catherine's lectures to the contrary, Jennifer preferred the forest. Here grew the great oaks, never disturbed by man, that stretched out their massive limbs in all directions and seemed to almost reach the sky. Here also were maples and tall green pines. Smaller trees known as dogwood dotted the forest with their white, four-petaled blooms in the spring. In the winter the forest was adorned with the brilliant scarlet berries of the wild holly. And all year round the forest rang with the songs of a million birds, from the shrill-voiced blue jay to the sweetly trilling red-winged blackbird.

Jennifer felt much more at home in the woods. The formal gardens made her uncomfortable, serving to remind her that she was as superficial as its imported beauties, and as out of place. She felt like the boxwood, forced to grow in this alien land, being trimmed into a shape that was alien to her.

Strange, how she still felt like an interloper here. Whenever she walked through this forest, she had to remind herself that she was a Greyson. No one would run her off the property. But despite that knowledge, she could not seem to rid herself of the uneasy sensation that she was a trespasser. Perhaps it was because she knew in her heart that she was no lady, despite the silk gown and her new affected upper-class accent. Or perhaps it was because her husband seemed to have forgotten her very existence. Each night at dinner he glowered at her across the table, but he never spent time with her otherwise. If they happened to pass in the wide central hall he never spoke, or even favored her with a glance. It was easy to forget that she was a married woman.

Thus, when she saw a riderless bay stallion trotting toward her, it took her a few seconds to associate the animal with her husband. Staring at the horse, she recalled her nightmarish trip from the ordinary to her new home. This was the same stallion, no doubt, for there were no other horses so magnificent in the stable. And Grey was too fine a horseman to have been thrown.

Suddenly concerned, she stepped forward. At her sudden movement, the stallion slid to a stop and eyed her warily. Cautiously, for the stallion was no better tempered than his master, Jennifer spoke gently to the beast. His ears flickered forward. Encouraged, she gathered his reins in her hands, turned him about, and led him back down the path. She would not have dared to attempt to ride him, even in her old indigo gown, for she had never ridden before or since the trip to Greyhaven. In a full hoop skirt it would be impossible even for an excellent horsewoman—which, heaven knew, she was not.

In a few moments she saw her husband's still form lying on the path, and sudden apprehension filled her. Somehow, despite his skill as a rider, Grey had been thrown, and he might be badly hurt. Tangling the reins around a branch, she rushed forward, only to stop abruptly.

Near Grey was coiled a black snake.

Its body was thick and long. Jennifer was too far away to identify it positively, but she was morbidly certain it must be a water moccasin, a poisonous snake very common this near the river. No doubt the snake's presence had caused the horse to spook.

The question was, had the snake bitten her husband?

Slowly, so as not to startle the snake into striking at Grey's outflung hand, she reached beneath her overskirt for the knife she always carried in her pocket. She had never used it in her own defense. Once, in her fifteenth year, a man had caught her outside in the dark as she had made her way back from the necessary house and pressed her up against the clapboard wall of the ordinary, his hands tugging up her skirt and reaching down into her bodice. She had never even thought of the knife, merely submitting quietly, passively, to his advances. She would have been raped had her uncle not happened upon the scene and slapped her for what he termed slatternly behavior.

But then only her honor had been threatened. Now a man's life was in danger. No matter how strange and remote he seemed, Grey *was* her husband. She drew the knife from her pocket and threw it as Carey had taught her. Sailing end over end, it neatly sliced through the snake's head, pinning it to the ground despite the efforts of the writhing body. She strode over to the snake, pinned its head with the heel of her leather shoe, and cut the head off.

When she straightened up, she found Grey sitting up and observing her with a rather bemused expression.

"An excellent throw," he remarked dryly.

She stared down at him. "Your neck is not broken?"

"Apparently not," Grey said wryly, "although I am not certain the same can be said for my head." He rubbed a bruise that marred his forehead and scowled. "I was not paying proper attention when my horse shied. I was careless."

"More likely you were reckless," Jennifer said in an uncharacteristically tart tone, recalling the countless times she'd seen him galloping the bay at breakneck speed away from the stable. "And if the fall didn't kill you, the snake might have."

At her outburst, Grey threw back his head and laughed. She looked at him in astonishment, having never heard him laugh before. His tanned face suddenly looked much younger, as though the laughter washed away the lines of grief on his features. Abruptly, as if aware of her puzzlement, his laughter stopped, but he was still grinning as he pointed to the snake's severed head and inquired, "And how would it have done that?"

Jennifer gazed at him, bemused. With the sternness momentarily erased from his face, she realized, he was excessively handsome. His gray eyes shone silver with merriment; his long, onyx black hair had escaped from its queue and fell carelessly around his aquiline features. She felt that same inexplicable tug of attraction for him she had felt before.

With an effort, she tore her gaze away from him and looked at the snake. Its head did not have the characteristic squat triangular shape of a poisonous snake.

"Oh," she said in a small voice. "I thought it was a water moccasin."

"Hardly," Grey said, still chuckling. "It was an entirely harmless water snake."

"Oh," Jennifer said again. She could think of nothing more to say. She felt deflated and rather absurd. She turned away, deciding to beat a hasty retreat and walk back to the house.

"Just a minute." His hand caught her elbow, and turning back she saw that he had effortlessly regained his feet. Clearly he was not badly hurt. He was very tall, she thought, gazing at his broad chest, not daring to look up into those laughing eyes. "How is it that you were here to save me from the snake?"

Aware that she was being teased, Jennifer nonetheless answered awkwardly, "I—I like to walk." Suddenly she realized how it might look to him, as if she had been following him about as a duckling follows its mother, and she flushed. "I walk through these woods every day," she added with a trace of defiance.

"A long walk," Grey observed, "especially in this heat. What if you fainted?"

"I 'ave—I have never fainted."

Of course. She was not one of the pampered women of his own class. Virginia had been the frontier until recently, and women of all classes had worked hard, in the fields as well as in the kitchen. But within the past fifty years the rich had acquired enough slaves so that their women could supervise rather than do the work themselves.

Jenny—Jennifer, as his sister had christened her—on the other hand, was accustomed to backbreakingly hard work, whether in Virginia's humid summers or in the freezing cold. Of course a simple walk did not cause her to faint! Nonetheless, he reflected, the constricting clothing she now had to wear must make it difficult for her to breathe, let alone exercise. Surreptitiously eyeing her narrow waist, he wondered briefly what it would be like to wear stays. He himself would probably faint before he took two steps, he concluded.

"Why don't you ride, if you like to amble through the woods?"

Surprised that he seemed to be taking an interest in her, she lifted her eyes to his. "I cannot ride, sir."

Grey noted for the first time, almost absently, how big her eyes were. Her skin was still a light golden color, due to her enthusiasm for sunshine and fresh air, and against the gold her eyes shone like jade. He had never seen such dark eyes. "You rode all the way from Princess Anne County," he pointed out, admiring the way her long, unbound hair streamed like honey down her back.

"I had to," she said simply.

"If you cannot ride," he said, trying to ignore the brief flare of respect he felt for her courage, and the shock of another emotion that surged through him when her beautiful eyes looked up into his face, "then your education as a lady has been sadly neglected."

"Catherine cannot ride. No one can doubt that *she* is a lady," Jennifer pointed out, instantly defensive of her friend. She glanced away, finding that meeting his steady gray gaze made her inexplicably nervous.

"She can ride," Grey said, relieved yet at the same time sorry that she had dropped her gaze from his, "though it is somewhat awkward for her to mount and dismount. The simple fact is that she is afraid of horses."

At this slight upon her mentor, the woman she regarded as the epitome of all ladylike graces, Jennifer actually dared to contradict him. "She isn't afraid of anything."

Grey laughed out loud again. "You are damned loyal," he said admiringly. "Or do you really perceive her that way? My sister is a strong woman, I'll admit—too strong, some might say—but the fact is that she is terrified of horses. She was thrown from a horse when she was younger, you know, and her leg failed to heal properly, despite the best efforts of the doctor. She will not go near the stable."

He paused and considered her appraisingly for a long moment. "Perhaps I can teach you to ride."

Jennifer was by now so nervous under his steady, unwavering gaze that she retorted without thinking. "I am not certain I care to be taught by a man who cannot keep his seat, sir."

Grey scowled blackly for a moment, then, reluctantly, smiled. "You may have a point there." He turned away as though her acerbic comment had broken some sort of spell, walked to his stallion, and untied the beast. "Come. I'll walk you home."

She quailed at the idea of actually walking all that distance in her husband's terribly unnerving company, but she had little choice. Timidly she walked beside him as he led the great bay stallion back down the path.

Grey was silent for a time, and Jennifer, characteristically, did not speak. At last he said musingly, "I don't know what I am to do with you."

At her questioning glance he went on, "I had no business marrying you. As young and pretty as you are, you should not be tied to a—a drunkard. To a man who cares nothing for you. Yet there is no way out of this predicament. Divorce is not possible in Virginia. Annulment is a possibility, but having pulled a weed from the mud and transformed it into a flower, I find myself strangely reluctant to cast it back into the mud."

"I am not a flower yet," Jennifer said, uncertain whether to be flattered or offended by this curious speech.

"Not yet, perhaps. But I doubt you would be content were you to return to the ordinary. You are not the same simple girl I met there. Your horizons have expanded. Catherine tells me that you love to learn, and that you are, in fact, quite intelligent." He sighed. "Having brought you here, I cannot send you away. To do so would be unfair to you. You are, after all, my wife."

"For better or for worse," Jennifer agreed, as solemnly as ever.

"Probably for worse," Grey said, smiling in that sardonic way he had. "At least you appear to harbor no romantic notions about loving me. Quite rightly, I suppose, for I am anything but lovable. I—I regret bringing you here, Jennifer. I am trying, however feebly, to apologize."

Jennifer glanced up quickly, and he thought again how lovely and how very young she was. She did not belong here, with nothing but a crippled woman and a madman for her family. "Apologize?" she repeated. "You have naught to apologize for, sir."

"For God's sake, stop calling me sir," Grey snapped, unaccountably irritated by the word. "You make me feel like your grandfather. Call me Grey. Everyone else does."

Shying away from such familiarity, Jennifer repeated faintly, "There is no need for you to apologize."

Grey scowled more blackly than before. "Ah, but there is. True, I've given you more opportunity to learn and grow than would ever have been yours had you remained in Princess Anne County. But there you did not know what you were missing. And by bringing you here I have trapped you in a parody of a marriage."

He paused, as if hesitant to disclose something, then added with brutal frankness, "I have a mistress, you know."

Jennifer did not break stride. "Yes, I know," she said calmly. "What I don't understand is why. I thought you were devoted to the memory of—" Suddenly appalled by what she had almost blurted out, she came to a halt and fell silent.

A bitter smile twisted Grey's mouth. "In mind and soul, I am. In body—well, I am still a young man. I cannot live the life of a monk. But I assure you I shall not force my attentions on you. You deserve better than a man whose heart is in the grave."

"And your mistress doesn't?"

The words escaped her lips before she could stop them. She could have cursed herself for daring to speak so. Grey, however, did not seem angered. He considered her question calmly.

"She does not appear to object," he said at last. "She is,

after all, married. Therefore, falling in love with me would be futile. I assure you, Jennifer, that she does not cherish any romantic notions regarding me. She knows all too well that I can never love again."

Jennifer recovered herself and started down the path rapidly. She said nothing, but her thoughts were so clearly written upon the delicate planes of her face that Grey, who never explained his actions to anyone, felt oddly compelled to explain further. He said almost gently, "It isn't so bad as all that, Jennifer. She is, quite frankly, a beautiful, amoral bitch. I have no admiration for her mind or her character—nothing but her body attracts me. And as crass as that sounds, I believe she feels much the same way about me. As long as we both understand that our relationship is based purely on physical pleasure, no one can possibly be hurt."

"What of her husband?"

Grey shrugged with complete unconcern. "Either he was a fool to marry Melissa in the erroneous belief that she was a lady, or he cares nothing for her. Either way, he is no concern of mine." He added a little anxiously, "I hope you do not care that I have a mistress because you are harboring any feelings for me?" He did not want the puppyish adoration of a child. He wanted sex and he wanted his memories, and more than anything he wanted to be left alone.

She turned, amber brows arched questioningly. "How could I have any feelings for you? Today is the first day we have ever had a conversation."

Something—guilt, perhaps—flickered briefly in the granite depths of his eyes, but he covered it by drawling coolly, "I have really had no desire to speak to you until now. You must be aware, after all, that when I first brought you to Greyhaven you were a less than fascinating conversationalist."

Aware that he was intentionally insulting her, Jennifer bit off the sharp retort that sprang to her lips and looked away. She was still unable to express anger. Even knowing full well that no one would strike her for saying what she thought, she felt compelled to bury her emotions. Hence she said nothing at all, and the walk back to Greyhaven was completed in bitter silence.

EIGHT

Jennifer sat in her chamber the next day, idly practicing writing her name upon parchment. Writing was not as easy as Catherine made it appear. Catherine's handwriting was elegant and graceful, whereas Jennifer's writing looked like spiders crawling across the page, their legs sprawling in all directions. Even worse, her quill kept blotting the ivory page, even though it was the feather of a heron, which Catherine had assured her made the best quill. The best quill did not seem to be good enough to compensate for her poor writing skills. At last, annoyed by her failure to print "Jennifer Wilton Greyson" successfully even once, she threw the quill down in exasperation.

As always, her active mind leaped forward to other thoughts. She found herself wondering if Diana had frequently used this desk. No doubt she had sat here and written notes in a graceful, ladylike hand. Doubtless she had never sat in this chair struggling to write her own name.

The thought only made Jennifer feel more like an interloper than ever. From the snatches of slaves' gossip she had overheard, she had come to realize that Diana had been much admired. The only person who had not seemed to wholeheartedly idolize Diana was Catherine, and even Catherine had implied that Diana was a "model of feminine deportment." Catherine had respected Diana, even if her jealousy had made it impossible for her to like the woman. Diana's ghost seemed to hang over Greyhaven, making it impossible for Jennifer to ever feel comfortable in these elegant surroundings.

Though she was as yet unable to fully express her emotions, her ability to acknowledge her feelings to herself had improved. Staring absently at the burl walnut prospect door in the desk, she admitted to herself that she was frustrated, perhaps even envious. Everyone here—well, almost everyone—seemed to believe that Diana had been a perfect angel, a lady born and bred. Jennifer was acutely aware that *she* was neither a lady nor an angel, and she felt keenly unworthy.

Surely, she thought, Diana could not have been so perfect as she appeared. After long years of observing the inebriated and rowdy men who congregated at the ordinary, Jennifer had understandably developed a rather cynical view of human behavior. She had become certain that no one was perfect. Everyone had some flaws, and most people had a great many.

What had Diana really been like?

Catherine was the only person who had intimated that Diana was less than perfect, yet she had also admitted that she had been jealous of her. Perhaps, if the years had improved Grey's memories of his first wife, they had also tarnished Catherine's memories.

Jennifer could not be certain.

Her idle gaze fell upon the papers filed neatly in the pigeonholes of the desk. Perhaps, she mused, the answers were here. She reached a slender hand impulsively toward the desk, but pulled it back almost instantly.

The papers within the desk, she told herself firmly, were none of her business. It appeared that they had been undisturbed since Diana's death. No doubt no one had thought to remove them from this chamber, since she had been unable to read when she had first arrived. Or perhaps Grey was not even aware of their existence. She knew that the door to this chamber had been closed since the day of Diana's death, as though Grey had been unable to face the empty room. And when she had first come to Greyhaven, the desk had been closed and thickly spread with dust. No one had read those papers for a long, long time.

Tentatively, glancing guiltily toward the closed door, though she knew full well that no one would enter without knocking—no one had done so since that first day, when Grey had burst in—she took out a pile of parchment.

The first sheet was written in a bold, masculine hand. Grey's hand, she realized, her breath catching oddly in her throat. She read:

"My beloved—"

It was too personal. She had no business reading this. She knew it. And yet she stumbled on.

It was a love letter, written by Grey for the only woman he had ever loved. Though many of the words were incomprehensible to her untutored eyes, the tone was unmistakable—the tone of a man desperately, irrevocably in love. The sort of love that nothing, not even death, could shatter. Reading the letter, she felt another pang of envy toward Diana, who had been capable of inspiring such undying love. Jennifer longed for love and affection, and she was painfully aware that she could never obtain it. She struggled through the letter, yearning for a vicarious knowledge of the emotion that she herself would never know.

The letter was full of glowing descriptions of Diana's youthful beauty and wondrous soul, as devoid of real content as love letters usually are, except for the last line. It was curiously wistful, almost sad, and it read:

"Please, darling, don't ever leave me, for if you did I could not bear to live. My life without you would be empty."

Jennifer studied this line curiously. Grey had known, even eight or nine years ago, what Diana had meant to him. He had foreseen how empty his life would be without her. He must have loved her very much, she thought, and wished hopelessly that she herself could experience that sort of love.

But it was a foolish wish, and she knew it.

Carefully placing the letter back in the desk, she stood and rubbed the back of her neck, grown stiff from sitting still overlong. Puzzling out the letter had taken a good hour. Plainly, if she was going to search through the letters in search of some knowledge about Diana, it would take a very long time.

"My dear Mistress Lancaster . . ."

The date indicated that this was the first letter Grey had ever written to Diana. Jennifer hoped the letter would give her some idea of how they had met, as well as a glimpse into Grey's personality before he had become so embittered. It was odd to think that the curt, savagely temperamental man she knew had once been capable of writing such a formally courteous letter. She read on, "I cannot tell you how delighted I was to have the opportunity to speak with you at your uncle's house. It is rare that one meets a young woman of your beauty and kindness. . . ."

Edward Greyson leaned against the split-rail fence and stared admiringly at the enormous black stallion that grazed in the field. "He's gorgeous," he said enthusiastically.

Kayne O'Neill grinned at the young man's enthusiasm. Like most young blades, it seemed, Grey was interested in two things—horses and women. Not necessarily in that order, he reminded himself. "He's a descendant of my first horse, Crimson," he said. "Crimson was the best horse my father ever bred. Hurricane there is the best horse I have ever bred."

Grey nodded thoughtfully, studying the stallion as he lifted his finely shaped head to gaze at the onlookers, and then galloped across the field in an astonishing display of speed, almost as though showing off for his audience. The first thoroughbred to be imported to Virginia, a son of the Darley Arabian named Bulle Rock, had arrived in 1730, and almost since that very day the O'Neills had bred thoroughbreds. Hurricane, Grey knew, was the latest and finest in a long and distinguished line. "God knows I need some good horses," he said. His words were directed at Kayne, but his eyes did not leave the stallion. "When my father died three months ago, I decided that the first thing I should do with his money was to buy some better stock. The horses in our stables are appalling. Nags, every last one of them. I was told you breed the best horses in the colony."

"Quite true," Kayne said without any display of false modesty. "I've won every race I've entered with that stallion. He's made me a great deal of coin over the years. There are always some fools who don't mind losing money by betting against me."

"Would you be willing to sell him?"

"Hardly. Not for all the tobacco on your plantation. But I do have a colt by him you might be interested in. He's black as sin, too. I think he'll be the spitting image of his sire, and I hope he'll be as fast."

"I'd like to see him," Grey decided. At twenty-one, he considered himself an excellent judge of horseflesh. His mind on horses, he turned around and nearly collided with a young lady. "I—I beg your pardon," he stammered.

The young lady smiled politely. "Quite all right, sir. Uncle Kayne, Aunt Sapphira sent me out to inquire if you wanted to invite your visitor in for tea. She said to tell you it was quite horribly rude of you to take Mr. Greyson out to the field without offering him refreshment first, after he's ridden all that way."

Kayne looked annoyed. "Mr. Greyson insisted on seeing Hurricane first. He said he was more interested in horses than refreshment. Kindly tell your aunt—"

"Actually, Kayne," Grey broke in, "I find that I am in need of refreshment. I believe tea would be quite welcome, indeed."

Kayne almost inquired sardonically what had caused this sudden change of heart, but he caught himself in time, observing that Grey's attention had suddenly been transferred from the stallion to his niece. Well, that was hardly a surprise. Diana was outstandingly beautiful. She had been visiting them for the past fortnight and in that short time they had already had more visitors than they had had in the past year.

Edward Greyson, however, with his newly inherited wealth, was a better catch than any other young man who had yet come calling. Furthermore, Kayne liked him. Hastily he made introductions. "Grey, this is my niece, Diana Lancaster. Diana, Edward Greyson."

"A pleasure to meet you, Mr. Greyson," she said politely, dimpling as he took her hand.

"Please, call me Grey. Everyone does."

"Grey?" she repeated. "I like Edward better."

"Then, by all means, call me Edward. And may I have the honor of calling you Diana?"

"Certainly." Her manner was reserved and ladylike, and yet Grey was attracted more strongly than if she had behaved seductively or wantonly. She was lovely, her silver-and-snow beauty emphasized by the shell pink gown she wore. Her hair was icy blond, her skin luminously pale. As she turned toward the gambrel-roofed house he saw that her patrician profile was elegant and pure, her delicate coloring reminding him of a cameo come to life.

She was everything he wanted in a wife, he mused as they walked back toward the house. Greyson was a man who made decisions quickly. Within five minutes of his first glimpse of her he had already decided to offer for her. But she deserved better than Edgewood, the house where his parents had fought, where he had grown up in the center of the storm that was his parents' relationship. The house that was forever tainted by his memories of his childhood. At that moment he decided he would build her a new house, a house to surpass any in the colony. A house that would even rival the governor's mansion in Williamsburg. A house that would set off her beauty like the setting for a precious jewel.

Jennifer put the letter down on the desk and sat back in her chair thoughtfully. Even though this was quite plainly the first letter Grey had written to Diana, it had been more than obvious that he already loved her. Beneath the politely worded courtesies had been a passion that was evident even to Jennifer.

She sighed. The young man who had written that note—Edward, as he had signed it—had been passionate, loving, and full of life. The man she was married to, Grey, was distant, cold, and imprisoned by his grief.

For just a moment, she allowed herself to indulge in the fantasy of being married to Edward. He would be courteous, holding her chair for her at the dining table and engaging her in animated conversation. Affectionate, spending time with her in the afternoons. Passionate, kissing her in the evenings in his chamber . . .

She shook her head, aware that she was being ridiculous. Edward was gone. Only Grey remained.

Closing the desk, she left the chamber. It was time for the day's harpsichord lesson.

That afternoon Catherine emerged from the parlor, where she and Jennifer had been playing the harpsichord, and knocked hesitantly on Grey's study door.

"What the hell do you want?"

Catherine shook her head in frustration. It was still early in the afternoon, but her brother was obviously even more drunk than usual, judging from the faint slur to the words. Nonetheless, gritting her teeth, she pushed the door open.

"Grey," she said imperiously, "you must come hear this."

"Hear what?" Grey said, obviously annoyed. "A beginner at the harpsichord struggling to pick out a tune? Don't be absurd. You wanted to educate the chit. It is your responsibility. I'll have nothing to do with it."

"I wouldn't call you out of the important work you're so engrossed in," Catherine retorted, casting a scornful glance at the decanter of Madeira that sat open on the secretary, "if I did not believe you would wish to hear this. Get up."

"I do not wish to get up," Grey said between bared teeth. Despite himself, he found that he was interested in whatever had Catherine so fascinated, but he certainly wasn't going to admit it to her. Besides, he resented her authoritarian tone. After all, he was the head of this household. He crossed his arms in a stubborn gesture that indicated he had no intention of leaving his chair.

Catherine promptly switched tactics. "Slovenly creature," she said. "No wonder you're fat."

Grey emitted a sound much like a snarl and came to his feet—six foot three inches of whipcord-lean, solidly muscled, and extremely irritated man. "This had better be interesting," he warned.

Having won the battle, Catherine smiled sweetly. "I think you will find it so."

She led the way into the parlor. Jennifer, seated at the harpsichord, glanced up with a hesitant smile, which instantly withered beneath the crushing impact of Grey's scowl. He flung himself down in a corner chair, and growled, "Very well. Now that you have successfully disturbed my peace and quiet, pray show me what you find to be so intriguing."

Catherine leaned over Jennifer and pointed at the sheet music. "Play that, my dear. Just the melody."

Jennifer shot her an imploring look and said quietly, "In front of *him*?" Catherine nodded implacably, and Jennifer, squinting obediently at the page, picked out the notes stumblingly. She hit several painfully wrong notes despite the slow tempo, as was quite usual for beginner keyboard students.

When she had finished, she stared dully at the music, not daring to glance into Grey's face. But the sardonic amusement was clear enough in his voice as he drawled, "Remarkable, truly remarkable. If I didn't know better, I'd have thought she had six years of lessons."

Rather than seeming dismayed by her student's

mediocre performance, Catherine appeared almost as amused as her brother. "Now, Grey," she instructed, "come over here and play something. A simple melody, please." Her brother eyed her lazily, and she said sharply, "For heaven's sake, you can bear to get out of that chair for a moment or two. Humor me."

Grey, stood up, crossed the room in two long, if slightly unsteady, strides, reached over Jennifer's shoulder, and played a brief dance tune with his right hand. He had just begun to turn away when the sound of the same melody, flawlessly played, arrested him.

He turned back slowly and regarded Jennifer with something akin to disbelief. "Do that again."

Obligingly, Jennifer played the tune once again.

Grey regarded her, heavy black eyebrows gathering like storm clouds over his eyes. Thoughtfully he reached across her and played a fragment of a tune, using both harmony and melody. "Try that."

"I haven't yet taught her about chords," Catherine began defensively, but her words were cut off as Jennifer played exactly what Grey had played an instant earlier.

Grey was still watching her with an intent expression. "Now play the first melody I played." She complied.

He stared at her a moment longer, then crossed the chamber and plucked a book from one of the black walnut bookshelves that stood against the wall. Briefly flipping through the pages, he settled on a relatively simple passage and thrust it curtly under her nose. "Read this out loud."

Jennifer did not resent this authoritarian tone, for she was incapable of doing so, but she could not see what the book had to do with her harpsichord lesson. Puzzled, she looked up doubtfully into his silver eyes. "Read it," he repeated implacably.

It happened to be the Bible, opened to Ecclesiastes, a book that Grey read frequently. Though he was a poor Christian indeed, there was something about the gloomy passages of Ecclesiastes which echoed in his soul.

Beginning where his finger indicated, Jennifer read obediently, "To everything there is a season—"

She went on well enough, stumbling every now and then. At last Grey slammed the book shut and returned it to the shelf.

"Very well," he said curtly, crossing the room once again and looking down upon her from his great height. "Repeat what you just read."

Jennifer saw nothing particularly odd about the request, though the way he stared at her made her nervous. She recited what she had read, word for word, some thirteen verses, not making a single error despite the repetitive nature of the passage.

When she had finished, Grey studied her in silence, then turned to his sister. Catherine looked bewildered. "How on earth did she—"

"A perfect memory, obviously," Grey said. "Or as close to perfect as the human memory can be." Some of the shadow had faded from his eyes, to be replaced by alert interest. He had not been so intrigued by something in years. "Small wonder that she learned to read so quickly."

He shot Jennifer a quick, assessing glance. "Quite remarkable," he said softly, as though speaking to himself. "It appears that when I married the child I got more than I bargained for. Much, much more."

N I N E

Jennifer found herself lying awake in the darkness that night, completely unable to sleep. Her husband had finally noticed her, had even looked at her with something resembling newfound respect and admiration. Why he should admire her for a quirk in her character over which she had no control she could not fathom, but it had been evident from the expression in his eyes that he did.

And now that he had noticed her, now that she had earned his attention, possibly, just possibly, he might begin to feel some sort of affection for her. The words she had read this afternoon came back to her with perfect clarity. There was a time to mourn, but there was also a time to love. Perhaps the time for Grey to mourn was finally over. Perhaps, at long last, it was once again time for him to love.

With those hopeful thoughts racing in her mind, she could not sleep. The music of the stars was calling to her. Slipping from her bed and pulling on a loose linsey-woolsey gown that did not require stays, she glided silently downstairs, only to pause at the sight of flickering candlelight in Grey's study.

"Grey?"

She moved closer to the door, seeing that his head was buried in his hands, his shoulders shaking. The words he had written to Diana darted through her mind, and she felt a stab of pity for her husband, so lost by himself but so completely unable to ask others for guidance.

Last time she had discovered Grey thus, she had only dared to peer around the edge of the door. This time, moved by an impulse she could not explain, she crossed the chamber swiftly and placed a hand on his shoulder. "Grey!" she whispered urgently. "It's all right. I'm here now."

Slowly he lifted his head, raking her face with his gaze. What she saw in his stormy gray eyes caught at her heart. Defeated, haunted, they were the eyes of a dying man.

"Don't cry," she murmured, brushing the tears from his haggard face as though he were a child. Strange, she thought, how he could be so arrogant and remote by day, yet so terribly vulnerable by night. "Don't."

"I can't help it," Grey muttered in a voice clogged to hoarseness by tears. As if embarrassed by her clear, level gaze, he lowered his face into his hands once more.

Jennifer had no idea how to deal with his emotions, or with anyone's emotions, for that matter. She had cried only once in the last eight years. Until she had come to Greyhaven she had not even felt the need for tears. And now, faced with someone else's grief, she found herself at a complete loss.

She stroked the thick black hair as he bowed his head in abject misery, wishing she could do more to ease his pain. "You mustn't feel this way," she said softly, aware that her words were woefully inadequate in the face of his agony. "Please . . ."

Grey looked up at her through red-rimmed eyes. "Ah, God," he said tiredly. "You're right. I should feel nothing, but I'm too full of emotion. All I can feel is love and sorrow and grief, churned together and swirling inside of me until I choke on it." He clutched her hand to his cheek in a gesture so childlike that a lump came to her throat.

In a moment some of his pain seemed to fade. He looked up in a way that was almost shy and studied her features in the candlelight. She thought there was something strange about the way he looked at her; his expression was intent but oddly blank, as though he were looking through her somehow. "You're very beautiful," he said at last. "Did you know that?"

Startled and shocked by his sudden mercurial change of emotions, Jennifer flushed a brilliant red and started to back away, but he caught her arms in a surprisingly strong grip. "Don't go," he pleaded in a desperate, low voice. The agony had faded from his features, replaced by something even more elemental. "I need you. You are so beautiful. . . ."

She sensed that he was dreadfully drunk, but she could not pull away. His long fingers held her arms so tightly and his hopeful silver eyes held her pinned. "Grey," she said in what she hoped was a reproving tone. "Let go of me."

"I can't," Grey whispered. One of his hands released her arm and reached up to stroke the smooth curve of her jaw. Jennifer froze at the peculiar sensation of his strong, calloused fingers caressing her soft skin. "I've tried, but I can't. I can never let go of you. Oh, God, I want you. And you want me too. Please tell me so."

She could not look into those brilliant silver eyes and lie. "I do," she admitted faintly. Heaven help her, it was true. There was something so blatantly masculine about him, clad as he was in a ruffled linen shirt that was open at the neck, exposing part of the solidly muscled expanse of his chest. There was something terribly compelling about his sharply chiseled features, thrown into sharper relief than ever by the faint light of the candle. Grey was more than attractive, more than handsome. He was irresistible.

"Say it," he commanded softly, eyes gleaming with something more than hope. Jennifer saw the powerful emotion in his eyes, recognized it for what it was with feminine instinct, and helplessly responded to it.

"I want you," she whispered, less shyly now.

The expression of raw, elemental passion on his face left little doubt that he returned the sentiment in full. How he could want her so powerfully, so desperately, when he had rarely even acknowledged her presence in the past she could not fathom, but it was evident that he did. She was unable to bring herself to question fate. Slightly dazed at the direction events were taking, she repeated, "I want you."

The crystalline truth of those words shocked her. She had thought herself attracted to his younger self, a man with Grey's arrogance and charm, but with Edward's passion. Somehow that man was before her now. He came slowly to his feet, staring down at her with all the passion that was his nature etched clearly on his handsome face.

And Jennifer felt the first passion of her life welling up in response. She did not struggle when his lips touched hers. The thought of struggle never occurred to her. Instead she responded eagerly, joyfully, wrapping her arms ardently around his broad shoulders, reveling in the strangely delightful sensations his caressing hands and lips aroused. Even when his lips opened and his tongue delicately stroked hers, she did not recoil in shock, only pressed herself closer to him. The taste of apple brandy on his lips was so intoxicating, his arms around her so warm and solid, that she wondered dizzily if she were dreaming. It had to be a dream. Reality had never been this wonderful.

It was no dream. His questing hand on her breast, his mouth moving caressingly down the sensitive flesh of her throat, all were real. The emotions she had kept bottled inside for so long flooded powerfully through her body and her mind, destroying all conscious thought and volition. She could only moan in helpless pleasure and press her soft body closer to his hard one.

Even when he pulled her down onto the Oriental carpet she made no protest. She could not have formulated an objection had she wanted to. This was what she wanted, this was all that mattered. Every dream she had ever had was fulfilled as he kissed her with ever greater ardor. The weight of his body pressed her into the soft carpet, and she reveled in the sensation. She was helping to ease his grief, and she knew joy for the first time in a very long time.

His hands slid gently over her skin, pushing aside the voluminous folds of her gown and boldly investigating the silken warmth of her calves and thighs, sliding up further to the wet warmth between the golden curls at the junction of her legs. Jennifer bit her lip to keep from crying out at the extraordinary sensation. Her hips began to move in an insistent rhythm that was foreign to her. When at last he pushed her skirts up, his heated flesh seeking hers eagerly, she moaned and wrapped her arms tightly around his waist. "Grey," she whispered into his ear, wishing she could tell him how much the sensations he was evoking meant to her, how much she loved being close to him, how much closer she wanted to be to him. He shuddered as her warm lips brushed against his ear.

"Oh, God, Diana," he moaned. "I love you so much."

Diana.

Jennifer stiffened involuntarily in shock and horror, but it was too late. His body forced its way into hers, ripping her apart. She cried out in sharp agony, wounded in body and spirit. Above her Grey's eyes snapped open and he stared at her with bewildered confusion, as if awakening from a dream. He could not stop himself, but finished in three quick thrusts, then withdrew hastily.

The instant his weight lifted from her body, Jennifer curled into a defensive ball on the floor. She wanted to get up and run from the chamber, but her legs would not obey her commands. Her passion had dried into dust the moment he had moaned out Diana's name. The sudden, humiliating realization that he had imagined he was making love to Diana sent embarrassment flooding through her, making her stomach tighten with nausea. She had never felt so ill in her life. Ruthlessly she cut off her emotion and buried it, deeply, where she would never feel it again.

If this was what emotion felt like, she wanted no part of it. No passion. No love. Nothing. The empty barrenness she had felt before she met Grey was so much safer. The recollection of Grey's voice calling out for his dead wife slashed through her brain, and she realized bitterly that she had been a naive fool.

Grey was resting his head on his hands as he sat beside her on the carpet, but this time he was not crying. "I'm sorry," he said softly. "I had no idea you were a virgin. You just—you seemed so willing—and it was so easy to pretend you were Diana—" He shook his head. "I used you. I'm sorry."

He got to his feet and hastily left the room. Jennifer lay curled on the carpet for a long time, feeling the blood seeping slowly from between her legs as though her soul were bleeding. At last she got up, rearranged her clothing with shaking fingers, and sat down at the desk to stare dully at the candle flame until at last it flickered out.

Grey did not return to the study.

Grey could not seem to dismiss the incident from his mind the following morning. An unfamiliar but extremely unpleasant sensation of guilt dogged him as he sat in the gloom of his study, glowering darkly at the green paneled walls.

He had not intended to harm his wife. True, he admitted, he rarely concerned himself with other's feelings, but he had never wanted to cause such hurt as had been evident in Jennifer's huge dark eyes before her face lost all expression.

The entire event was a blur in his mind, blurred not only by alcohol but by his intense longing for a woman he wanted desperately and could never have again. At first, deep in his memories, he had actually believed that Jennifer was part of his dreams. Her hair, though darker than Diana's, was blond, her face beautiful, and he had been seduced by her soft voice and even softer body. By the time he realized she was no dream he had been unwilling to let her go. And he had no idea that she was still a virgin.

To himself he admitted he'd known she was not Diana long before she'd stiffened in his arms and cried out in anguish. Her skin was golden, her flesh smooth and muscular. True, she was beautiful and blond, yet her body was entirely unlike Diana's pale, soft, voluptuous figure. She was strong in a way no woman of his class could ever be, made powerful by years of backbreaking work. And oddly enough, he had found her strength, her smoothly taut body, to be incredibly attractive. He had not been able to stop himself.

No, he corrected himself with vicious honesty, he had not *wanted* to stop himself.

He remembered her soft voice consoling him, her hands stroking his hair, and a wave of self-disgust shook him. She had only been trying to help him, to comfort him, and he had rewarded her by causing her mental and physical pain. The more he concentrated, the more blurred his memories became. Irritated though he was by his inability to separate dream from reality, he nevertheless recalled that she had been warm and passionate and loving. And he had taken advantage of her innocent, open response and hurt her, badly.

At last, self-recrimination gnawing at him in a most unusual way, he leaped to his feet and stalked into the parlor, where Jennifer sat at the keyboard. Engrossed in working out some prettily complex composition of her own on the harpsichord, she did not hear him until he cleared his throat. At the sound she spun around, eyes wide.

He welcomed her show of fear, for it was preferable to the emptiness that had filled her haunted eyes last night. And yet he felt that he should reassure her, if possible.

An apology would have been the logical place to start. But Grey, being male, did not apologize easily. Instead he cleared his throat again, almost nervously, and said gruffly, "I've been thinking."

Jennifer said nothing, only averted her gaze and stared intently at the ornate silver buckles that adorned his shoes as though they were the most fascinating things in the world.

"A few days ago," Grey said hesitantly, "I promised to teach you to ride. Why don't we start today?"

Her large eyes flew to his face.

"Please," he added.

Jennifer was stunned. She had never heard Grey ask for anything before. Uncomfortable though his presence made her, she knew an apology when she heard one.

"All—all right," she stammered.

Grey's stern face relaxed visibly. "Good. Change into a habit and come along. I'll be at the stables finding a suitable mount for you." And turning, he strode from the chamber.

That first day, Grey helped her mount and showed her how to sit in the sidesaddle so that she could ride without constantly fearing that she would fall from the horse's back. Despite her initial, obviously uncomfortable reaction to his hands touching her, she allowed him to gently help her into the saddle. Soon she stopped recoiling from his touch and forced herself to pay attention to what he was saying.

Then he began to lead the docile gray mare in a circle. After a few terse commands—"Sit straight in the saddle. And don't saw on the horse's mouth that way, damn it—" Jennifer began to relax and found herself sitting more easily on the horse's back. Then Grey had her walk the horse across the pasture and studied her.

She was a natural horsewoman, he mused. Straight carriage—no doubt due to Catherine's schooling—gentle hands, a reassuring voice. The little mare appeared to trust her rider. And then Jennifer turned the horse back toward him, and he saw that she was smiling openly, clearly happy with her accomplishment, and his breath caught in his throat.

She was beautiful.

He had never before realized it so clearly as he did in that moment. She was wearing a scarlet habit of camlet, a coarse worsted mixed with silk, which was styled in the fashion of men's clothing, having a separate, high-necked bodice over a waistcoat. The habit had sleeves that covered her arms to the wrists, in contrast to her usual gowns, nearly all of which ended in cascades of lace at her elbows. Atop her amber hair she wore a black tricorne adorned with a feather. The outfit flattered her, even while it concealed more of her slim figure than did the fashionably low-cut gowns she usually wore. The color emphasized her vivid coloring and bright hair. And the smile lit up her entire face in a way he had never seen before.

He realized that she rarely smiled, and he resolved that he would make her smile more frequently.

When she rode back across the pasture and looked down at him for approval, he nodded. "Very good," he said briskly, ignoring the curious emotion that was slowly seeping through him in response to her youthful beauty. "In a month you'll be riding as if you were born on a horse."

She smiled again, more hesitantly this time. Grey did not tell her how beautiful she was, but he thought it, and found that it was difficult to tear his eyes away from her.

By the end of the week, she and Grey embarked on a ride through the forest. Grey rode his bay stallion, and the delicate gray mare cantered easily by his side. Despite the time they had spent together this week, and despite Grey's curiously social mood, Jennifer still found herself quite uncomfortable in his presence. It was difficult to look at him without remembering that awful night when he had seduced her.

"You're very quiet," Grey observed at length. It was odd, after all these years of resenting company, that he should be the one trying to draw her out. A scant week ago he would have discouraged all attempts at conversation. But a week ago he had not been so painfully conscious of his own depravity.

"I'm concentrating."

Grey glanced over at her. Her lovely face was, indeed, set

thoughtfully. "Don't try so hard," he advised. "You're doing fine."

Jennifer glanced at him, found his gray eyes intent on hers, and looked away hastily.

Grey sighed. His efforts to get to know the girl he'd married and brutally used were, so far, fruitless. Which was, of course, no more than he deserved. He struggled valiantly to keep the conversation going. "Do you like Greyhaven?"

"It's lovely."

It seemed impossible to get more than three words out of her. Grey sighed again and racked his brain for other subjects.

"You have adjusted remarkably well to life as a member of the gentry," he remarked at last. "I am . . . impressed by your capacity to learn."

The moment he made the inane remark he realized how incredibly condescending it sounded. But at least it did provoke a response. Jennifer lifted her head and met his gaze, her green eyes rapidly darkening with a contemptuous expression that suggested his opinion was of no interest to her whatsoever. "Indeed."

"Truly," Grey said, realizing with embarrassment that he had offended her and that he should try to make amends. Consequently, for the first time in his adult life he permitted his tongue to leap forward without the guidance of his brain. "It seems remarkable that any woman could learn so readily, let alone a woman of—" He stumbled to a halt, suddenly aware of the insulting nature of what he had been about to say and of the frigid expression that was slowly settling over her features. "Of your, er, few opportunities. That is—"

"In other words," Jennifer said, as dispassionately as ever despite the angry sparkle in her eyes. "I am not as hopelessly moronic as you originally believed me to be."

That was, quite bluntly, so apt a condensation of what he had been about to say that Grey almost burst out laughing.

He restrained his humor, realizing that Jennifer was blazingly angry. She had been calm, too calm, ever since that night a week ago. Perhaps anger would be good for her. At any rate, it was better than the complete lack of expression that she had worn all too often this past week. Anger, he thought, was better than nothing. And he knew that he deserved it.

Deliberately, he provoked her further.

"Precisely," he said, ruthlessly suppressing his urge to grin. "In fact, when I first met you I supposed you to be simple-minded. It was only later that I came to admire you for your intellect."

"Indeed," Jennifer said in a voice that was actually beginning to quiver with fury. "How curious. My impressions of you have been the reverse. I once believed you were intelligent. It is only recently that I have come to believe that you are simple-minded."

At that insult—an insult that Grey would readily have strangled anyone else for—he gave vent to his amusement, throwing back his head and shouting with laughter. Jennifer watched him warily out of the corner of her eye, wondering about the sanity of a man who seemed cold and unyielding whenever she tried to make polite conversation, but who laughed when she was shockingly rude.

Grey wiped his eyes and shook his head, still chuckling. "Jennifer," he said in a voice that still trembled with humor, "you are a remarkable young woman, as far from simple-minded as it is possible to be. I'm ashamed of my lack of perception whenever I remember how badly I misjudged you at the ordinary. Your mind is amazingly quick."

Jennifer bit her lip, then accepted his words as the apology they were evidently intended to be. "Thanks to you," she said honestly, "and the opportunities you've given me to learn. I can't tell you how grateful I am—"

"Christ!" Grey swore, and to her utter surprise every trace of laughter disappeared from his features. "Don't ever speak of gratitude to me again, damn you. *Gratitude!* What have you to be grateful for?"

Jennifer stared at the expression of self-loathing that had instantly replaced the amusement on his face, and she had the sudden shocking impression that he felt guilty about the night he had seduced her. That was why he had spent the last week teaching her to ride, trying in his awkward way to make conversation. And that was why he could not accept her gratitude.

Grey, she realized with surprise, actually had a conscience.

She found that she did not want him to continue berating himself for his actions. That night had been as much her fault as his. Led into romantic folly by the letters she had been reading, she had made a singularly idiotic assumption in thinking that he might actually be attracted to her. She had been a fool.

She decided to try to turn his mind away from his guilt, to try to keep the conversation going. Accordingly, she glanced down at the fine cloth of her scarlet habit, so different from the coarse prickly cloth she had worn at the ordinary. "Fine clothing?" she suggested practically.

Grey looked surprised at her light suggestion, then his habitual scowl returned. "You are not foolish or superficial enough to believe that clothing makes a particle of difference. Are you?"

"Those," Jennifer observed in her best tutorial tone, a perfect imitation of Catherine's teaching voice, "are the words of someone who has never worn homespun. It is not warm enough in the winter, and in the summertime it *itches*." The grimace she made was eloquent.

Grey glanced down ruefully at the Holland linen of his shirt and the finely woven wool of his biscuit-colored knee breeches. "You have a point," he acknowledged. "I've always worn fine clothing, and never thought twice about it. Money," he added sourly, "has never been my family's problem."

"Then your childhood should have been a happy one," she said softly.

He heard the unmistakable note of longing in her voice and stared at her intently. She sounded as though she'd never experienced happiness, and as though she wished for it desperately. "It was not," he admitted finally.

She seemed puzzled, as though unable to envision a family both wealthy and unhappy. "That is what Catherine said as well. You were both unhappy, then. Why?"

"Money does not confer happiness," Grey responded harshly. "It may help you stay warm in the winter, but there is very little else it's good for. After all"—he gestured expansively at the vast forest they rode through—"I am wealthy. Am I happy?"

"You don't seem so."

"You're very astute, my dear. I am miserable. Money—material things—none of it has anything to do with happiness. At twenty-one I became betrothed to a woman, a woman I loved very much, and in order to please her, I utilized a small portion of the money my father left me in order to build her a house as beautiful as any in the colony, as grand as the governor's mansion. I hired artisans and bought the best local furniture and had the best silver imported from England. And then—" He paused, then burst out, "Six months after I carried her over the threshold she died, and I was left with a spectacular, empty house, an enormous fortune—and nothing. Absolutely nothing. All the gold in the world is not worth one strand of her beautiful hair."

Hearing the frustrated longing and passion in his voice, Jennifer was reminded once again of the young man who had written the letters she had read, a man who had designed and built a castle for his wife, a man who had given his heart once and who could never give it again. Edward Greyson, filled with poetry and fire. And once again she wished she could inspire that sort of enduring love. There was something very compelling about Grey when he spoke that way, something that she found irresistibly attractive.

Remembering what had befallen her the last time she had been swept away by the passion in his voice, she said coolly, "Nonetheless, money is a wonderful thing to have."

"Wonderful," Grey repeated in scornful disgust. The torrent of emotion flooding his voice had been dammed up, and the bitter, distant man she had married was back. "That is what my father would have said—what he did say, more times than I could count."

"Your father liked money?"

"Liked it, worshipped it, was mad about it. He cared nothing for Catherine and myself; he and Mother cared only for money. He married her to get his hands on her fortune, and he got exactly what he wanted—her money, but not her. Neither of them cared a fig for the other, but so long as they had money they were happy. At least, they thought they were happy."

Jennifer's mind painted a vivid picture of an ebony-haired little boy, growing up in a household where money was the only thing that mattered, the only way to purchase affection. A little boy who had grown into a man who tried to purchase his wife's love with a grand house and furnishings. Fighting back her sympathy, she said slowly, "It seems to me that people of your class have no financial problems, so they have to manufacture their own troubles. Perhaps some people have a need to be miserable."

Grey reined the bay stallion to an abrupt halt and stared balefully at her. "Are you suggesting that *I* have created my own problems?"

Jennifer brought her mare to a stop and looked at him thoughtfully. It was not in her nature to express her thoughts, but she saw in Grey a man who was suffering needlessly—a man she could not bear to see suffering. Gathering her courage, she said frankly, "Yes, I think perhaps you have."

Grey shook his head, as if denying her words. "God, don't you think I—I would have saved her if I could have?"

"Not that," Jennifer said, realizing he was referring to Diana. "That was beyond your control. Death always is. But . . . Grey, it has been over seven years. People have to mourn, but someday you have to get over the grief. You have to move on."

A muscle jumped in Grey's rigid jaw. "I don't want to move on, damn it. Not without her."

"My point exactly," Jennifer persisted. "You may not want to move on, but you have no choice. Life doesn't stop simply because the people you love die. You have to keep going. And you're being held back, and controlled, by your drinking."

Grey scowled darkly. "I drink because I want to," he growled. "I can remember her more clearly—"

"Perhaps you used to drink because you wanted to," Jennifer snapped, "but now you drink because you have to. It's been so long that she's fading from your memory, and you are trying desperately to hold on to her. You are creating your own problems, just as I said—so terrified of joy, so afraid of the slightest possibility of happiness, that you're fighting to hold on to your misery."

Grey abruptly urged his stallion into a canter. "What do *you* know about grief?" he snarled over his shoulder as she cantered after him. "Have you ever lost anyone you loved?"

Jennifer was silent for a moment, then decided to answer the question. "Yes. My family. When I was nine."

Grey did not slow his horse as she came up beside him. "How did they die?"

Jennifer refused to look at him. "I do not wish to talk about it," she said evenly.

"Indeed," Grey responded coldly. "Then perhaps you can understand that I do not wish to speak of Diana's death."

Jennifer accepted the rebuke and said nothing more. It was impossible to get past Grey's defenses. He wore anger and bitterness like a suit of armor. He did not care that she was concerned for him; he cared little for anything.

The only thing he had ever cared for was Diana. And Diana was gone forever.

·   ·   ·

"My dearest Diana . . ."

That afternoon, Jennifer found herself at her desk, reading the faded letters in Diana's desk once again. Why she should torment herself so, she had no idea. The folded pieces of parchment told a love story—the only love story of Grey's life. Perhaps she read them to remind herself of what Grey had suffered, and of what he had been like before he had lost his first wife.

Or perhaps she was seeking to learn more about her husband—a man who laughed warmly one moment, then became cold the next.

"I cannot tell you how happy you have made me," she continued reading, pushing her misgivings away, "by agreeing to be my wife. I only regret that so much time must pass before I make you mine. . . ."

Grey knelt on one knee in the Lancasters' parlor before his beloved. He had come to see Diana at her merchant father's well-appointed Williamsburg home, bringing along his best friend, Christopher Lightfoot, who had been appropriately impressed by Diana's beauty and charm. Grey had been pleased by his friend's reaction. This angelically beautiful creature was going to be his . . . assuming, of course, that she accepted his suit.

"Of course I will marry you, Edward," Diana said softly.

Grey kissed her hand several times, rather carried away by her answer, before rising to his feet and looking down into her face. He felt an utterly boyish smile of joy cross his countenance but could do nothing to prevent it.

"You may kiss me," she told him.

He bent and kissed her. His kiss was full of ardor, the kiss of a young man who loves a woman for the first time, and who feels loved in return. Her kiss was restrained, almost cold, the chaste kiss of a properly brought-up young lady. Vaguely, in the back of his mind, he wondered if he would want to be kissed like that for the next fifty years, but he suppressed the thought quickly. He should not be disappointed by her restraint; ladies could not be expected to kiss like whores.

"I am going to build you the most spectacular house in the colony," he told her enthusiastically, sitting down on the settee and drawing her down next to him. She permitted him to hold her hand as they talked. "I have already drawn up the plans, based on *Palladio Londinensis,* or *The London Art of Building,* as well as some other English books I was able to obtain at the Virginia Gazette *printing office here in Williamsburg. It will be a large and impressive house—a suitable foil for your beauty, my dear."*

Diana smiled politely at the compliment as he went on with the enthusiasm of youth, "It will even make the governor's mansion look shabby by comparison!"

Having seen her father's house, he was even more pleased with his decision to build a larger and finer mansion. The Lancaster dwelling was a brick cube in the Georgian style, with two enormous chimneys rising above its hipped roof. It was a lavish home inside and out. Clearly Diana was accustomed to every luxury. He was determined to give her all that she was accustomed to—and more.

Jennifer placed the letter back into the desk, staring blankly into space. Then, as if moved by a sudden irresistible impulse, she snatched up the quill that lay on the desk, dipped it into her silver inkpot, and began laboriously scribbling on a piece of parchment.

There was so much she wanted to say to her husband, words that she could never dare speak, but could write. She would pour out her feelings for Grey onto parchment, then hide the letters away in the desk forever, just as she had learned to conceal her feelings behind her calm and unemotional facade.

She had so *much* to tell him.

Yet, after a few awkward sentences, she threw the quill down in disgust. She simply did not know enough words to describe her feelings accurately. It was utterly impossible for her to express what she felt, for her vocabulary was inadequate to the task.

She had no way, no way at all, to express what she felt for Grey.

But for the first time in many long years, she felt a great deal.

TEN

As the summer progressed, Jennifer continued to study reading and the harpsichord, as well as the intricacies of how a lady managed a large plantation. At the ordinary, she had done all the menial labor, such as spinning, sewing, cooking, and washing clothes. As the wife of a wealthy planter, however, she was not expected to do the work, simply to supervise. She learned how to plan meals, how to determine when a hog needed to be butchered to replenish the smokehouse, and when new cloth should be woven. (Homespun cloth was used at Greyhaven to clothe the field hands, and it was also shipped to England and sold there.) She had to decide when the scuppernong grapes should be harvested and made into wine, and when the peaches should be made into preserves and peach brandy. There was a remarkable amount to learn and remember.

She learned, for example, that no tobacco was produced at Greyhaven, although the other properties, known as quarters, that Grey had along the James River did plant and sell tobacco. Instead, the crops included corn and wheat, and cider from the apples in the orchards was produced and sold as well. Grey also sent slaves to Williamsburg once a week to sell firewood and fodder to the town residents on the market green. Many residents of the town also ground grain at the plantation mill, located on a mill pond that had been created by damming a small creek.

Despite her studies, and her duties as mistress of this

plantation, her life was remarkably pleasant and easy whenever she compared it to her long years as a tavern wench. Grey and Catherine, born as they had been to the planter class, seemed to be completely unaware of how fortunate they were. This land gave abundantly of its riches, such as wild turkey, duck, and venison, and the river produced delicacies such as oysters in the winter, crabs in the summer, and delicious varieties of fish all year round. Jennifer had never eaten so well in her life. And although she had to supervise the cooking and the other work done on the plantation, she no longer had to do the work herself.

Whenever she had free time from her studies, Jennifer spent her spare time rifling through the letters stored in the walnut desk in her chamber. She found herself moved by the romance she had uncovered—a romance long dead, yet still vividly alive on the parchment stored in the desk's pigeonholes. She managed to suppress her vague feelings of guilt, telling herself that if reading the letters could teach her something about her enigmatic, distant husband, it was well worth it.

Some of the letters were written in a graceful, sloping feminine hand—letters Diana had written to Grey that had not been completed or sent for some reason. These letters, though affectionate, seemed slightly distant and cool when compared with the violently passionate sentiments expressed in Grey's letters. Had Diana not returned Grey's love in full, or had she simply been reserved, as befitted a lady? Jennifer was unable to decide.

At last she had sorted laboriously through nearly all the letters. Apparently Grey had wooed Diana mostly through letters, since Diana had lived in Williamsburg, nine miles away. This seemed rather romantic in Jennifer's eyes. She certainly would have preferred it to being sold in exchange for a horse!

Perhaps it was not surprising that Jennifer, who had known no love since the death of her family long years before, found herself strangely moved by the love exposed so plainly by Grey's letters. Coupled with the normal human desire for love, her immense imagination made it easy to fantasize that the letters had been written to herself, rather than to a woman who had been dead for years. The letters were so passionate, so alive, it was hard to believe the sentiments they described belonged in the past. It was all too easy to imagine that those sentiments were directed at herself.

And consequently, starved for love and affection as she was, Jennifer fell headfirst into love with her husband.

She was not aware of it at first, of course. In the beginning, she was only aware of admiration for his passion for life, so evident in the letters, so different from her own passive resignation to the realities of existence. As the weeks passed, however, she found that she began to feel more than admiration.

When at last she recognized her sentiment for what it was, she also recognized the futility of her love. She was not in love with the surly, embittered man who was her husband, but rather with the man who, so many years ago, had been capable of passion and intense joy. The Edward who had existed nine years before was so different from the man she had married that they might as well have been two different people. Only rarely did she catch glimpses of Edward beneath Grey's sullen demeanor, when Grey laughed, or when his memories brought out a shadow of the passion that had once been his nature. Grey, she realized bleakly, was all that was left. Edward was dead.

Ironically enough, she had fallen into the same trap as her husband. She was in love with someone who no longer existed.

"My beloved . . ."

It was the last letter Grey had ever written to Diana, and Jennifer began reading it as reverently as if it were holy writ. She had read all the letters; she had imagined herself in Diana's place; and now her vicarious romance was coming to an end. She read on.

"I can scarcely bear to wait a fortnight," Grey had written in his scrawling hand, "to make you mine. After two long years of designing and building Greyhaven, it is all but impossible for me to imagine that you will soon join me here. I certainly hope you find our house to your liking. . . ."

A black carriage drawn by matched chestnuts came up the curving drive, its iron-rimmed wheels rolling smoothly over the road. Edward Greyson was bringing his new wife home from Williamsburg. Diana sat on the leather-upholstered cushions, her skirts spread gracefully around her, as she stared eagerly out the window.

"Oh, Edward," she sighed as she caught sight of the vast building. "It's so beautiful. I love it!"

Grey smiled, pleased that his wife liked the building he'd worked on for so long. The house itself had cost him very little, since the bricks had been made on the property from the Virginia clay and the timber had been cut from the forest. Only the windows had been shipped from England. He had paid the building supervisor a mere one hundred and fifty pounds, and the actual construction of the dwelling, which had taken a full two years, had of course been carried out by slaves. The interior of the house had cost him far more, filled as it was with excellent furniture made by Williamsburg artisans, and with fine silver imported from England at great expense.

He cared nothing for the expense, however. It was more than worth it to see the expression of delight on his wife's face. "I'm pleased that you like it," he said. It occurred to him that she had never told him she loved him. But at least, he thought with satisfaction, she freely admitted to loving the house.

She was always the reserved and proper lady.

The carriage pulled up in front of the massive stone-pedimented doorway, and Grey swept his wife out of the

*carriage and carried her across the threshold of their house.
Their life together was beginning.*

Jennifer placed the letter back into the pigeonhole. Just
as Grey had once told her, he had designed this entire
mansion for Diana. Once again, she felt a twinge of sorrow
for the young man who had learned from his parents during his lonely childhood that love had to be bought. Surely,
she thought, Diana would have been content with a lesser
dwelling. Surely Diana must have loved him. How could
she not?

As she sat there, staring vacantly at the letters stacked
neatly in their pigeonholes, her eyes fell upon the prospect
door, a small, keyholed door of burled walnut in the center
of the desk. Idly she wondered what was behind the door.
Perhaps, she thought hopefully, there were more letters
from Grey hidden there. Perhaps her vicarious romance
did not have to end yet. She attempted to pry the door
open with her fingernails, but found that it was locked.
The attempt won her nothing but a broken thumbnail.

Recalling that she had found a key on her twilight, she
stood up and crossed to the dressing table. She brought the
key across to the desk and tried it in the keyhole. It fit.

Behind the prospect door was a small cache of letters,
written in an unfamiliar masculine hand. Jennifer began
to glance through them idly, then stiffened in sudden
shock. Hastily she shoved the letters back into the desk,
slamming and locking the prospect door. Grey, she thought
with horror, must never see those letters.

They would destroy him.

ELEVEN

That summer was even more blazingly hot and humid than Virginia summers usually were. The colonists' clothes were modeled on the fashions from England, a much cooler climate. Jennifer had to suffer the oppressive heat in silk and linsey-woolsey gowns that would have been far more appropriate in England, and the tight stays and undergarments that held her skirts out over her hoops only added to her misery. More than once she wished for her old homespun gowns back.

However, now that she was a member of the aristocracy, she had no choice but to suffer. The front and back doors of Greyhaven were thrown open at all times, to encourage the cool breezes from the James to circulate through the wide central passage. All the windows were wide open as well, allowing air into the great house, and mosquitoes as well. On the worst days of July there was no breeze at all, and Jennifer and Catherine did very little all day except sit in the parlor, perspiring and praying for a stray breeze from the river.

Grey, of course, being male, suffered less, for around the house and grounds he had no need to wear anything but a linen shirt, carelessly open at the neck and with ruffled sleeves pushed up over his elbows, and knee breeches and stockings. Jennifer concluded cynically that men must have designed women's clothing, while reserving the comfortable clothing for themselves. Certainly no sensible woman could have designed the gowns she had to wear!

The nights in July were only barely more tolerable. The heat of the day abated somewhat when the sun went down, but the humidity continued. No rain came to cool the parched land. One particularly brutal night Jennifer lay sweltering in her feather bed with her perspiring skin pressed uncomfortably against the linen sheets for what seemed like hours. Far away she could hear the faint rumblings of thunder, but she knew there would be no rain. It seemed sometimes as if it would never rain again. Finally, realizing that sleep was going to elude her, she got up, laced herself into the simplest of her gowns, and walked barefoot down the stairs and out into the night.

Owing to the heat, Grey had also found himself unable to sleep that night. He sat in the green-paneled study, reading Ecclesiastes and brooding. He had been busy looking over his tobacco crop on another quarter some miles from Greyhaven today, and had just arrived home an hour or two before. As a consequence, for once in his life he had had very little to drink. As he sat in the gloom, he heard the faint creak of a stair. Moments later, someone padded barefoot past the study toward the door that faced the James.

Jennifer, he deduced quickly. Jennifer did not walk with Catherine's halting gait, and moreover, Catherine was a proper lady who never would have stepped outside her chamber without wearing shoes, no matter how scorching the weather. At any rate, he knew that Jennifer liked to wander out at night. He had heard her walk quietly past his study a number of times. Ordinarily he was far too wrapped up in his private grief to care where she was going. Tonight, in his unusually sober state, he wondered just what she was up to.

Rising from his chair in front of the walnut secretary, he strode after her with the silent tread of an Indian.

Unaware that she was being followed, Jennifer made her way through the oyster-shell-strewn paths of the for-

mal garden, across the wide brown lawn discolored by the
heat and lack of rain, and toward the James River. The
sounds of the night seemed to be calling to her—the river
quietly lapping against the reeds and the sand, the frogs
singing in a vast chorus. As she drew nearer the river, the
air grew cooler, and a faint breeze seemed to caress her
cheeks. She paused at the water's edge, looking at the
beauty of the river in the moonlight, enjoying the feel of
the sand shifting under her feet as she wiggled her toes.

If one did not turn around and see the vast bulk of
Greyhaven, stretching two hundred feet from end to end,
with its formal gardens spreading out in front of it with
geometric precision, it was easy to imagine that Virginia
was still a wild land, untouched by Englishmen. The James
River, she thought, was too beautiful to be used for fishing
and shipping and the other purposes men put it to. It was
an entity in itself, calm and wide, proud and beautiful.

Her eyes on the river, Jennifer began to step out of her
gown.

Behind her, Grey stiffened in shock. He had stood behind her quietly for some time, wondering exactly what
was going through her mind as she stared fixedly at the water. Now he knew what had drawn her to the water's edge.
It *was* bloody hot, he acknowledged to himself, and he admired her intelligence and ingenuity in thinking of a way
to fend off the Virginia heat.

Jennifer might look like a lady on the surface, he
thought with a grin, but despite her silk gowns and her
vastly improved accent, her actions tonight proved all too
clearly that she hadn't taken Catherine's lessons to heart.
He guessed that she had been in the habit of cooling off in
the Lynnhaven River at her home. No *lady* would walk
down to the river in the dark and go swimming, but apparently tavern wenches did.

His grin faded rapidly as she peeled off her shift and
stood naked in the moonlight.

All amusement fled, to be replaced by pure masculine
hunger. He stared at her slender, softly rounded body,

illuminated by the moonlight. She was turned partly toward him, and he could discern the elegant shape of a breast, high and round, the womanly curve of her hips, and the long slim columns of her legs. She reached up and unpinned her hair, and it tumbled down around her shoulders, a long dark golden mass gilded by the moonlight, hanging nearly to her waist.

Grey stood transfixed. He was vaguely aware he should turn away, but he could not have taken his eyes off her if his life depended on it. His gaze was riveted to her as she stepped into the gentle waves, like Venus returning to her shell. His eyes widened as she walked into the water, only to disappear under the surface of the river.

A moment later she reemerged and paddled about the water for some time, her hair floating around her. At last she stood up, waist-deep in the water, and glanced in the direction of the house. She gave a little shriek of surprise as she finally noticed Grey.

She could not see his face, but she knew from his rigidly alert posture that he was avidly watching her. Even though she could not see his eyes in the moonlit darkness, she could feel them devouring her body. He took a reluctant step forward, as though unwilling to come to her but dragged to her by forces beyond his control. Jennifer wanted to dive back under the water and swim to safety, yet her legs would not move. She stared at him, compelled to look as he had moments earlier, as he deliberately stripped off his clothes and stood naked on the beach. His state of arousal was obvious, yet even that sight, which should have frightened her, could not make her eyes waver from him. He was beautiful, beautiful and incredibly masculine.

Grey slowly moved across the sand and walked into the water, pausing in front of her so close that she could feel his breath against her forehead. She stared up at his face, her eyes wide with alarm and with another emotion she could not identify, and saw passion and anguish warring together in his features. It was obvious that he wanted her, that he was drawn to her against his will, yet that he despised himself for his weakness.

He put his arms around her and bent to kiss her, tasting the water of the James on her lips.

Her arms encircled his neck and she returned his kiss, opening her lips to let her tongue meet his.

The water eddied around them, the waves lapping at their bodies, as they moved closer together.

And then Grey broke away. "No," he said hoarsely. "I won't do this to you a second time."

Jennifer blinked as tears sprang to her eyes at his rejection. "I—I don't understand," she whispered.

"I hurt you before," Grey said tightly. "I used you. I swore I wouldn't do it again."

"I thought—" Jennifer broke off, realizing how foolish her thoughts had been. For a fleeting moment she had believed he wanted her, not Diana, not a memory. For a brief, wonderful moment it had seemed that there were no obstacles between them.

Her thoughts were written clearly on her face, and Grey hated himself. He did want her, violently, and he could not deny it, even to himself. But Jennifer wanted more than sex. She was very young and very fragile, and like all very young girls, she would want love. Love was beyond his capacity to give.

He deliberately crushed her hopes.

"I don't want you," he said. "After what happened between us last time, you ought to know better. Why would I want someone like you, when I could have virtually any woman in the colony?"

Something about his words rang hollow to her. She lifted her eyes and studied his features. Despite the harsh words, his eyes were still fixed on her nipples, which peeked out between the wet strands of her long hair. Jennifer smiled faintly as she realized her feminine power for the first time.

He wanted her, and he was unable to entirely disguise his desire.

"You're lying," she said calmly but with absolute certainty. "You do want me, but you don't *want* to want me. Look at me, Grey." She raised her arms, lifting her dripping hair so that it no longer fig-leafed her upper body, so that her breasts and erect nipples were raised as well. She heard his sharp intake of breath. "You want me, not Diana. *I am not Diana.*"

Grey swallowed convulsively and took a step toward her as if drawn by an irresistible force. Jennifer shivered with joy and anticipation as he bent down and whispered into her ear. "Jennifer," he murmured.

"Yes," she whispered.

"Go to hell."

Jennifer stood frozen on the bank of the river, watching in blank amazement and baffled hurt as he stalked, dripping wet, from the river and strode stark naked toward the house, carrying his clothes over his arm.

TWELVE

They rode through the woods the next day, though by tacit consent they refrained from mentioning the incident at the river. The truth was that Jennifer could think of little else, but she did not have the courage to bring up the subject, and Grey never alluded to it. Neither of them wanted to disturb the fragile balance of their relationship by bringing up unpleasantly awkward subjects.

The daily rides had become a custom, something both Jennifer and Grey looked forward to, although either would have died before admitting it to the other. Jennifer enjoyed her husband's presence. It was pleasant to know that he had come to consider her a real person, an entity with thoughts and feelings of her own, thoughts that he sometimes displayed interest in. When he had first brought her to Greyhaven and sneered at her as she sat in the dust, she would have sworn the day would never arrive when her husband would treat her as a human being.

Oddly enough, Grey had only begun to show an interest in her after that dreadful night when he had seduced her. She was certain that her original impression had been correct, that he must feel remorse for what he had done. There seemed to be no other likely explanation for the sudden alteration of his behavior.

Though she spent an hour or two with him almost every day, she still felt that she knew very little of the man she had married. When they spoke at all, they spoke of mundane topics, such as the weather, or the horses that they rode. Jennifer longed to start a real conversation, but she had absolutely no idea how to go about it.

The heat continued unabated. The sky was a hazy blue, untouched by clouds, and the green branches of the oaks and maples stretched out above the path, providing a cool refuge from the sun. Jennifer's dappled mare trotted placidly along beside Grey's bay stallion. She rode easily now, almost expertly, Grey noticed, feeling a small stab of pride that he ruthlessly suppressed. The weed he had plucked from the muck of the tavern had grown into a flower so quickly and effortlessly that it was easy to believe that she had been a flower all along.

Of course, he did not voice his thoughts to Jennifer. He almost never spoke his thoughts directly, but she sensed that he no longer held her in contempt. He did make an effort to speak to her every now and then; at times he even attempted to be kind. (These occasions were generally a miserable failure, but she appreciated the effort.) But she wanted more than a husband who discussed the likelihood of rain with her. She wanted a husband who told her his innermost thoughts, who shared his feelings and hopes and dreams with her.

She wanted Edward. She was married to Grey.

Out of the silence, she said abruptly, "What was Diana like?"

The silence went on.

At last Grey spoke, in a harsh voice as stony as his features. "Why do you ask?"

Jennifer swallowed nervously. "She ... she meant a great deal to you. I only wanted to know why."

"I loved her. Why else?"

"Why did you love her?"

Startled by the simplicity of the question, he turned in the saddle to face her. "I've never thought about it," he responded honestly. "Why does any person love someone else? All I know is that to me she was all that was perfect."

He thought Diana was perfect, Jennifer thought with

some annoyance, *and only recently has he decided I'm human.* Her curiosity getting the better of her, she asked, "How did she die?"

The muscles along Grey's jaw tightened reflexively. "I'm certain Catherine has told you the story."

"I know she was murdered," Jennifer conceded cautiously. "But beyond that, no one has told me anything about it."

"For the good reason," Grey said tonelessly, "that it is an ugly story. She was beaten viciously . . . her throat was cut. . . ."

"Oh, God," Jennifer breathed. "I'm so sorry. I shouldn't have—"

"She was also raped," Grey went on as though he hadn't heard. His tone was wooden. "I—I was the one who found her body. She was lying in red mud. Her blood had soaked into the soil, and all her beautiful hair was caked with it. I still remember sitting next to her body, in the red mud—"

"Shh," Jennifer interrupted, reaching across the distance that separated them and laying her fingers gently on the taut muscles of his arm. He was breathing heavily, his face distorted with pain and horror as he relived that long-ago scene. "I didn't mean to bring up such an awful subject, Grey. I'm so sorry." Privately she thought that if Grey were mad, as so many people seemed to believe, there was little wonder. If she had found someone she loved mangled and destroyed in such a hideous way, she would certainly have gone mad herself.

Grey looked at her concerned face, and the raw pain in his silver eyes vanished almost instantly, to be replaced by the harsh indifference that he wore like a garment. "Don't concern yourself about me, Jennifer," he grated. "I'm all right."

"Sometimes I think you're never all right," Jennifer said honestly. A wave of horror and embarrassment washed over her. Dear God in heaven, what had possessed her to say such a thing? To prevent Grey's inevitable angry rejoinder, she went on hastily, "But what was Diana like?"

Grey eyed her narrowly for a few moments, apparently unable to decide whether he should do battle with her or not over her last remark. Evidently he decided on the more peaceful alternative, for he merely shrugged, saying mildly, "I told you already."

"You said she was perfect," Jennifer persisted. "Forgive me, Grey, but that tells me very little. What did she like to do? What were her interests?"

"Well . . ." Grey's forehead wrinkled. "She was a very accomplished lady," he said at last, sounding oddly hesitant, as though something were puzzling him. "She painted excellent watercolors . . . and she played the harpsichord well enough, I suppose. . . ."

"What did she truly love to do?"

Grey began to look annoyed. "I told you. She was a perfect lady. She excelled in everything. *Everything*."

Recognizing the veiled menace in his tone, Jennifer subsided into silence. Grey rode quietly alongside of her, thinking. For the life of him he could not remember what Diana had really enjoyed doing in her spare time. As he had told Jennifer, she had excelled in all ladylike pursuits, but he could not recall that she had particularly enjoyed any one of them. Unlike Diana, Jennifer pounded with enthusiasm at the keys of the harpsichord until Grey, closed in his study, sometimes thought he would have to take an ax to the damned instrument. Jennifer was still a student of the harpsichord, not a master, yet she obviously delighted in playing music.

Jennifer also enjoyed riding, he reflected, glancing again at her perfect seat and the easy way in which she controlled her mare. Diana, on the other hand, had not particularly cared for any pursuit that might have exposed her to the sun's rays. As a consequence, Diana's skin had been as white as newfallen snow, in sharp contrast to the golden hue of Jennifer's skin. Jennifer enjoyed walking through the forest and breathing its clean, fresh air as much as he himself did.

He stopped that line of thought abruptly, recognizing

that he was engaging in comparisons between Diana and Jennifer . . . and that he did not like some of the conclusions he was drawing. Of course Diana had preferred the indoors, he thought. Diana had been a lady born and bred, not a tavern wench masquerading as a planter's wife. And if he could not think of any outstanding features she had possessed besides her beauty—well, over seven years had passed. Despite his best efforts his memories had grown clouded with time. But no matter how dull she might sound when he tried to describe her to Jennifer, she had been a paragon, a woman beyond compare. There had been nothing dull about her. She had been exciting, vivacious, lovely. . . .

It was a relief for Grey to see the house as they emerged from the forest. Soon Madeira would help him suppress his disloyal thoughts, and his uncomfortable, growing awareness that Jennifer was as beautiful and exciting as Diana had ever been. He did not want to think about Jennifer. He wanted to concentrate on the only thing that mattered—

Diana.

As they rode toward the house, however, Jennifer reined in her mare abruptly. "What in the world is going on?"

Grey heard the sound too. Sighing, he brought his stallion to a pawing stop. "It sounds as though one of the slaves is being whipped," he said with no hint of concern in his voice.

"Whipped?" Jennifer turned and stared at him with sharp disapproval. "Catherine told me that the slaves are never whipped."

"They are only whipped for serious transgressions, such as stealing or attempting to run away," Grey explained, thinking longingly of his Madeira. He started his stallion toward the house, but to his annoyance, Jennifer turned her horse toward the slave quarters. He had little choice but to follow.

A young black man knelt on the ground. He had obviously just been whipped, for blood oozed from his back.

Jennifer dismounted and walked across to confront the overseer. "Why are you whipping this man?" she demanded.

"I caught 'im stealin' from the smokehouse, I did," the overseer told her. He glanced up at Grey, still mounted on his stallion, and his aggressive tone immediately altered into an unctuous whine. "I only gave 'im ten lashes, sir."

"You see?" Grey ignored the overseer and spoke impatiently to Jennifer. "Stealing is a serious crime. At some other plantations this man might get a far worse punishment. Some planters administer up to sixty lashes for stealing."

"You can hardly blame him for stealing food," Jennifer snapped angrily, "given what you feed your slaves."

Grey stared blankly at her, as if she had suddenly begun speaking in tongues. "What do you mean, madam? I make certain every slave gets generous portions of cornmeal and salt pork. That is, after all, what slaves typically get to eat."

"How would you like to live off corn bread and salt pork?" Jennifer retorted scathingly.

Grey scowled. She had a way of making him consider things from different perspectives. It was a knack she had that particularly annoyed him. For the thirty years of his existence, first at the old house and now at Greyhaven, slaves had gotten the same treatment and lived on the same diet. This was how it had always been.

And yet, faced with her angry green eyes, he felt a peculiar compulsion to defend his actions.

"They are permitted to garden," he started again. "They can supplement their rations of cornmeal and salt pork with whatever they grow. I don't think—"

"For heaven's sake, Grey," Jennifer interrupted sharply. "They work from dawn to dusk. How much spare time do they have to garden? I ate better than they do at the ordinary. And I ate very poorly indeed, compared to how you eat."

"Are you suggesting I feed my slaves at my dinner table?"

"I am suggesting," Jennifer said, oblivious to the fact that she was committing the unforgivable sin of challenging his authority before servants and slaves, "that you feed your slaves decently. And that you not permit them to be whipped." She gestured angrily at the bloody welts that marred the young man's brown skin. "How is this different from permitting my uncle to beat me?"

"Your uncle beat you for no reason at all. I only permit my slaves to be whipped for a good reason."

"Such as stealing to supplement their meager diet?"

Belatedly, she became aware that his eyes were blazing with rage. He managed to restrain himself, however, saying very calmly indeed, "I will think about it, Jennifer."

"Will you feed them better?"

"I said," he repeated slowly, "I will think about it."

Jennifer looked at his face and wisely decided not to press the issue further at the moment. She inclined her head coolly. Feeling that she had dismissed him as if he were a servant, rather than the master of Greyhaven, Grey whirled his stallion about and galloped toward the stable.

It was, he mused, one of the very few times he had ever seen her angry. Despite her fury—or perhaps because of it—she had looked more beautiful than ever. Her image was burned into his mind. He remembered the way her features had been animated with irritation as she spoke, of the way her green eyes had blazed, and he cursed under his breath.

He really needed a glass or two of Madeira.

"Hello."

The soft, musical voice startled Jennifer out of her reverie. She had walked a very long way this afternoon, her mind occupied with thoughts of the fight she and Grey had had this morning, and had finally sat down to rest before returning to the house. Blinking, she glanced up and found herself staring into the brilliant eyes of her husband's mistress.

"Good afternoon," she replied warily, uncertain of proper etiquette. Was one required to be polite to the light-skirts of one's husband? She was quite positive Catherine had never mentioned the correct way to handle such a situation!

The other woman said nothing in reply, only studied her intently. Feeling at a distinct disadvantage, Jennifer came to her feet and stared back as insolently as she could manage.

The sight was not reassuring. Melissa was as beautiful as she remembered, unpowdered mahogany hair piled elegantly on her head, topped by a flat, wide-brimmed silk hat. She wore a dark blue gown that emphasized the pale perfection of her skin. Jennifer felt gauche and unattractive in her presence.

Melissa felt much the same way about Jennifer. She saw a graceful young woman, so small and delicate that Melissa felt plump and awkwardly tall by comparison, with amber hair falling free over her shoulders, and a vibrant, golden complexion. Incredibly dark green eyes regarded her intently, yet the girl did not speak. At last, oppressed by the awkward silence, Melissa felt obliged to say something.

"You are beautiful," she admitted grudgingly. "I wonder that Grey doesn't see it."

One of Jennifer's eyebrows flew upward at this unexpected statement. She had hardly expected to be complimented by the woman. "I do not think beauty matters to Grey," she said frankly.

"Perhaps not," Melissa said. "And yet all the women he has been involved with have been beautiful. Diana, you—and myself."

The stunned reaction she had hoped for was not forthcoming. Jennifer's expression betrayed no emotion whatsoever. "If you think to horrify me by disclosing that you are his mistress," she said calmly, "it won't work. I already know."

"He *told* you?"

Jennifer shrugged. "He told me he had a mistress. Catherine advised me as to who the woman was."

Melissa seemed oddly disturbed by this piece of information. "I cannot believe he told you."

"I will not tell anyone else, if that is your concern," Jennifer offered, thinking that the woman was afraid of discovery by her husband.

Melissa smiled acerbically. "Half the county knows. They call me Melissa Lightskirts. Even my husband knows, although he doesn't seem to care. That wasn't what concerned me. I know better than anyone just how callous Grey can be, but you must have been taken utterly by surprise. Grey told me of your, er, background. When you came to Greyhaven you must have been frightened enough already, without the added pain of discovering that your husband had a mistress he had no intentions of giving up."

Puzzled by the other woman's odd mixture of sympathy and hostility, Jennifer stared at her. A faint sense of loyalty to her husband made her explain, "Grey is so wrapped up in his own pain that he has no idea that others can be hurt."

"He doesn't *care* that others can be hurt," Melissa said coolly. "And you would do well to remember that, and not to make excuses for his dreadful behavior. The only way to get along with Grey is to ignore him when he is in a rage— a good ninety percent of the time, I should think."

Jennifer felt a peculiar flash of resentment. It was as though the other woman knew Grey better than she did, and wanted her to know it. She decided not to let this conversation go further. Assuming that the other woman had been heading toward Greyhaven, she said coldly, "May I walk with you to the house?"

Melissa looked at her in astonishment, then burst out laughing. Her unwonted sympathy was gone, replaced by her amusement at Jennifer's naïveté. "Are you offering me a bed?"

"What do you mean?"

Melissa pulled a piece of parchment from her pocket and handed it to her, still laughing. "I really do think it would be the height of bad taste for me to make love to your husband in your house, but if you insist, Grey's nice wide bed would be more comfortable than the tumble-down shack we usually use."

Puzzled by the other woman's mirth, Jennifer unfolded the parchment. It said only, "Come see me this afternoon. Two o'clock. Grey."

The parchment dropped from her nerveless fingers as she stared at the woman.

"I see," Melissa said merrily, "that it has at last dawned on you why I am on your property."

Jennifer stared a few moments longer, then tried to speak. Anger, still a new emotion to her, rose in her chest, rendering her incoherent. "Do you mean that you—are you saying that he—in the middle of the *afternoon*?"

Melissa shrugged elegantly. "It's much easier to sneak out of the house in the afternoon than at night, my dear." She smiled saucily. "Would you like to come watch and see how it's done?"

Jennifer barely restrained the urge to slap the other woman. "And you called *him* callous," she said savagely.

Melissa smiled back at her innocently as she turned away, heading for her tryst in the forest. "Perhaps," she called back over her shoulder, "Grey and I deserve each other."

"I rather think you do," Jennifer agreed, her eyes glittering with fury.

When the other woman had disappeared in the forest, Jennifer sat back down and stared dully at the gleaming expanse of the James River, visible through the trees. Grey had asked his mistress to meet him so that he could put his hands on her, kiss her, do all the intimate things he had done to Jennifer that night so long ago.

How could he spend the morning with her, riding, then spend the afternoon with his mistress? It was incomprehensible, bewildering, and utterly infuriating. For the first time in her life, Jennifer felt jealousy. Jealousy and anger. She wanted to kill Mistress Lightfoot, and she wanted to kill Grey . . . not necessarily in that order.

"Do you wish to go for a ride today?"

Jennifer looked around in surprise, seeing Grey leaning casually on the parlor doorjamb. She wondered how long he had been standing there watching her. They rode together every day, but today she had lost track of the time somehow. She felt odd, unfocused, and fuzzy-headed. Although she'd been plunking at the harpsichord for some time she had accomplished very little. Perhaps, she thought, she was still upset by her encounter with her husband's mistress yesterday.

"I don't think so," she said at last.

Grey frowned at her. It had taken her a long time to reply, as though her mind was not working as quickly as usual. Or perhaps, he thought, she was angry. Of course, he realized, that was it. They had clashed yesterday for the first time, and she was still annoyed with him.

"Are you angry with me?" he inquired, wandering into the chamber.

Jennifer turned to look at him. He looked irresistibly handsome, clad for riding in his usual simple outfit, a shirt of fine Holland linen with a fall of lace down the front and steel gray knee breeches. The riding boots he wore covered his calves, drawing attention to the powerful muscles in his thighs.

Oddly enough, though, she did not feel the little pull of attraction for him that always quivered in her stomach when she looked at him. She felt too hot and uncomfortable to care how he looked. She realized that she had lost the thread of conversation.

"What?"

Now Grey looked at her very curiously indeed. "I said, are you angry with me?"

Jennifer stared at the floor. For some reason it was difficult to frame a response. "I don't think so," she said vaguely.

Grey looked irritated. He had never thought that she was the type to play games, but it seemed he had been wrong. "Rot. You *are* angry. Well, Jennifer, you are not going to win this argument by ignoring me. I don't care a fig for your company, damn it. Don't fool yourself into believing otherwise."

He stormed from the chamber, telling himself that he did not care whether she rode with him or not. On the contrary, a ride by himself through the woods would be an enjoyable change. After all, hadn't he been riding alone for years?

A half hour later, he returned irritably to the house, still telling himself that he had enjoyed his solitary ride. True, he admitted grudgingly, he usually rode for far longer. But he had not missed Jennifer's company. Not at all.

As he entered the wide central passage, he was surprised to see several of the house slaves bustling about. Catherine stood on the landing next to the enormous tall clock, calling down instructions. Standing in the hall, Grey fixed her with a look of annoyance. "What the hell do you mean by this disturbance?"

"Jennifer is ill," Catherine said distractedly. "She—" She got no further before Grey dashed past her, leaping up the wide steps three at a time. The expression on his face had changed with almost comical swiftness from irritation to anxiety. She recovered from her surprise as he put a hand on the doorknob to Jennifer's chamber. "Grey! What do you think you are doing?"

Grey turned his head and regarded her as though she were simple-minded. "I'm going to take care of her," he said, as though it should be perfectly obvious.

"Nonsense. She has a high fever. I should be the one to nurse her."

"She is my wife," Grey said in a tone that suggested it would be unwise to argue. He did not understand the knot of dread that had coiled itself in his stomach when Catherine had told him that Jennifer was ill, but he knew he could not wait patiently in his study while she suffered. He had to do something to help. The thought of waiting downstairs to find out whether his wife lived or died was intolerable.

"What do you know about illnesses?"

"I took care of you when you had the ague at least three times when you were younger," Grey pointed out in tones of utter reasonableness. He added briskly, "Don't argue with me, Catherine. We'll both look after her."

"Very well."

Grey looked at her thoughtfully. "Bring up some of that hot drink made of marigold petals so that we can bring her fever down. And bring cold cloths. And for God's sake, try to be more quiet." He disappeared into the chamber.

THIRTEEN

Jennifer was indeed very ill. Suffering from a very high fever, she drifted in and out of consciousness for three days. Once she thought she heard a deep voice talking to her softly and a callused hand holding her own, but it might have been delirium. At other times she was vaguely aware of an ice-cold cloth bathing her body, cooling her fevered skin, and a gentle hand forcing a vile-tasting liquid down her throat. She suffered through many hallucinations, murmuring the names of people she thought she saw. On the fourth day she opened her eyes.

Sunlight was streaming in through the two tall windows in her chamber, illuminating a slouched figure, asleep in a mahogany armchair with his long legs sprawled out before him. Squinting through blurry eyes, she saw to her surprise that it was Grey. His jaw was covered with dark stubble, and his clothes were wrinkled, as though he had been sleeping in them for days.

"Grey?"

Her voice was only a faint croak, but Grey stirred instantly. "Jennifer!" he burst out. "You're awake." He nodded to a slave who sat across the chamber, and she got to her feet and left the room hurriedly.

Jennifer tried to nod and failed utterly. "Thirsty," she whispered pitifully.

"Of course you are," Grey said comfortingly, pouring her a glass of water and lifting her head so that she could drink it. "You had a high fever, but it broke last night. We were very worried about you, Jennifer."

"We certainly were," Catherine said as she limped into the chamber, having been summoned by the slave. Jennifer observed that she did not look any fresher than Grey. Her normally impeccably coiffed chestnut hair was in disarray, and her gown was rumpled. "I wanted to summon the leech to come see you, but Grey would not permit it."

"The doctor would have bled her," Grey said tiredly, in the voice of one who has been through this argument a hundred times, "and she could not have borne being weakened further."

"How fortunate for Jennifer that you know more about medicine than doctors do," Catherine retorted in her most acerbic tone.

Grey shot her a quenching look and stood up, stretching luxuriously. "Now that you are awake," he said to Jennifer, "I am going to leave you in Catherine's capable hands. I need a bath. And a shave."

"And some clean clothes," Catherine added, sniffing fastidiously.

Grey grinned, looking more cheerful than he had in days. "I'll be back in an hour or so," he told Jennifer. She was too exhausted to make any reply, but her eyes followed him as he strode from the room.

Catherine sat down in the blue damask-upholstered chair that Grey had vacated. "How are you feeling?"

"All right," Jennifer murmured feebly.

"Liar," Catherine retorted. "But don't worry, you will be feeling better soon. I believe the worst is over."

Jennifer's eyes were still on the door. Catherine smiled at her. "He *does* need a meal and a bath, you know. He hasn't left you for three days, Jennifer."

"Really?"

"Really," Catherine confirmed. "He was out riding when I found you unconscious in the parlor, but he has been by your side since he returned." At Jennifer's skeptical look, she added, "No one was more surprised than I. He *insisted* on taking care of you. He was the one who sponged you off and kept you cool. He made you drink water, even in the worst of your delirium, and forced medicine down your throat. If not for his care, you might well have died. And who knows, perhaps he was right about not summoning the doctor."

Jennifer was grateful that she had not been bled, but she was unable to say so. She found that she was already too exhausted to talk. Catherine understood her expression. "Go back to sleep. I'll see you when you wake up again, and then you can have some broth."

But Jennifer was already asleep.

Grey strode back into the chamber less than an hour later, freshly shaven and wearing clean clothing. He glanced at Jennifer, then turned to his sister. "Did she have anything to eat?"

Catherine shook her head. "She was too tired. Perhaps the next time she wakes up."

"She needs to eat."

"She needs to sleep more," Catherine countered. She watched Grey as he walked across the chamber and stood staring down at the frail figure in the bed, his forehead wrinkled with concern. The anxiety that had been in his eyes for three days was still evident, and she felt a sisterly need to offer consolation.

"Grey . . ." she began.

Her brother turned to look at her, his slashing brows lifted questioningly.

"She'll be all right."

She watched as it slowly dawned on him that he had shown far too much concern over the past days for a woman he professed to care nothing about. The expression of anxiety on his face faded to be replaced by the indifference he usually wore. Perhaps, she mused, he really cared nothing for Jennifer at all.

But if that were the case, then why had he been by her side for three days?

"Of course she'll be all right," he replied carelessly. "Little doubt of that now, I suppose. No need for me to remain up here now. You'll let me know if there's any change?"

"Of course," Catherine said quietly, sorry that her reassuring comment had caused her brother to withdraw back into his self-absorption. The last three days had been a welcome reminder that Grey was in fact capable of human emotion.

Grey nodded to her curtly and disappeared out the door. She heard his footsteps as they echoed down the stairway. Grey, she realized, was going to his study to have a drink.

For the first time it occurred to her that Grey hadn't had a drink in three days. She smiled. There could be no doubt. His indifference had indeed only been a mask.

To her disappointment, Jennifer did not see Grey again for another two days. She drank broth on the first day, then solid food, and grew stronger, but she wished desperately that Grey would come to visit her. She clung to the memory of Grey, bedraggled and unshaven, sleeping in the uncomfortable chair next to her bed. She clung to Catherine's words: *He hasn't left you for three days.* He had cared for her like a child. Surely she must mean *something* to him.

But if she did, then why did he not come to visit her?

She was contemplating this question morosely when the door creaked open and Grey walked quietly into the chamber. She turned her head. "Ah," he said. "You're awake."

Jennifer nodded, conscious of a foolish rush of joy at the sight of him. She could barely restrain her smile.

"Are you feeling better?" he inquired, settling down in the chair next to her bed.

"Much, thank you."

There was an awkward silence. Then, feeling that something should be said, Jennifer ventured, "Catherine told me you took care of me while I was ill. It was—very kind of you."

"It was no difficulty," Grey replied politely, as if she had thanked him for a common courtesy, such as holding a door open for her. "Sickrooms are no novelty to me. I nursed Catherine through fevers several times while she was growing up. My mother did not have the constitution or the patience to take care of sick children."

"My mother took care of me while I was sick," Jennifer said absently.

"Yes, I know. You spoke of her while you were ill."

"I did?"

"Yes." Grey paused. "You begged her not to leave you. Jennifer, perhaps this is none of my business, but how did your parents die?"

Jennifer's eyes jumped to his, and he saw a flash of panic fill them. She tried to hide her reaction by shrugging and giving him a rueful smile. "I don't really remember them."

"I don't believe you," Grey said bluntly. "For one thing, you asked for them constantly while you were ill. Also, how old were you when they died? Nine?" When she nodded, he went on, "You have a perfect memory, Jennifer. I can't believe you could forget what happened only eight or nine years ago."

Aware that he was watching her closely with alert silver eyes, Jennifer looked down and said coolly, "Nevertheless, it is true."

"Hmmmm," Grey mused, and after a moment's pause he attacked the problem from another angle. "Who was Robert?"

Jennifer glanced up in alarm. In that brief moment of silence, she had thought he was dropping the subject. Realizing that he was determined to pry the answer from her, she said reluctantly, "My brother."

"Your only sibling?' She nodded. "Older or younger?"

Her eyes flashed in a rare show of anger. "Younger."

Grey was not so obtuse he could not sense her reluctance to talk about her family, but that only made him more curious about the subject. "Is he dead, also?"

"I don't want to talk about it, damn you!" Jennifer exploded. "Leave me alone!"

Grey sighed. As usual, he thought, he had behaved like the very embodiment of tact and sensitivity. In his clumsy attempts to pry the story out of her, he had only succeeded in upsetting her. He knew better than anyone that she should not be upset while recuperating. An apology was in order.

"Jennifer," he said without any trace of contriteness whatsoever in his voice, "I'm sorry if I caused you distress."

Jennifer gave him a disbelieving stare. "You are not."

Grey grinned but did not deny her words. Apologies were very definitely not his strong suit. "I heard you talking about your family while you were ill," he explained coaxingly, "but I could not piece together what happened to them. I just want to find out more about you."

"It is a very dull story," she said defensively. "We . . . we were poor. You wouldn't find it interesting."

"I'm willing to risk the boredom," he said with a teasing smile.

She sensed that he was not going to give up until she had told him the story. At any rate, if she gave in and told him how her family had died, he would remain at her side until she was finished. And that, she admitted glumly, was what she wanted. "Very well," she said reluctantly. "I'll tell you what I remember."

Jenny opened her eyes. Her eyelids felt as though they were weighted down with lead, but by sheer willpower she forced them open and stared into the darkness with blurry eyes. The room in which she lay was lit only by a rushlight. She could vaguely make out her mother's figure, face hidden in her hands, shoulders shaking. Her mother was crying.

"Mother?" Her voice was a dry rasp, barely audible, but her mother turned eagerly, hopefully, and caught at her hand.

"Jenny!" she exclaimed, then lowered her voice. "Ye're awake," she said in a thankful whisper. "At last, ye're awake."

Jenny stared vacantly around the chamber. The white walls, coated with a plaster made from coarsely ground oyster shells, seemed to flicker in the uncertain glow of the rushlight, and the rough-hewn table where the family ate sat with reassuring solidity before the fireplace. It was the same house she'd lived in all her life, but it seemed different somehow. Peculiarly empty. Alarmingly quiet. At last it dawned on her befuddled mind what was disturbing her.

"Where is Robert?" she asked, her voice cracking.

Her mother glanced away, her lips trembling. Jenny had never seen her strong mother look so helpless and fragile, and she felt a spurt of terror. Something was wrong, terribly wrong.

Her suspicion was confirmed when her mother spoke again. "Robert—is dead," she said, too exhausted and grief-stricken to try to couch the hard truth in gentleness. "So is yer father. They died of th' ague. I thought—ye were goin' ter die too—" She clutched her daughter's frail hand and her voice trailed off into pitiful silence.

Jenny stared at her, bewildered and frightened. Princess Anne County, riddled as it was with creeks and marshes, was not a particularly healthy environment. Everyone caught fevers, carried unbeknownst to the colonists by the ubiquitous mosquitoes, and all too many died of them. But her father? And Robert? How could they be dead?

She could hardly believe it. But her mother's head was bowed in sorrow, and tears were running unchecked down her cheeks. It must be true. She had never seen her mother cry before.

A new fear seized her. "Are ye sick?"

Her mother shook her head. "No, dear," she said gently. "Ye were all terribly ill, but I—I was fine. The fever did not affect me." Though she spoke softly, her voice was bitter, and Jenny could not understand why. At nine, she was too young to understand her mother's irrational feelings of guilt. Her mother had remained perfectly healthy while watching her family suffer and die before her eyes, and she hated herself for it.

"Darlin'," her mother said at last, "I want ye ter promise me something. If anything—if anything should 'appen ter me, promise me that ye'll go ter yer uncle at once. 'E'll take ye in."

Jenny wrinkled her small nose. She had met her uncle but rarely, and had never cared overmuch for him. It was impossible to imagine living with him. "Ye said ye weren't sick," she objected. "Nothin' will 'appen ter ye, will it?"

"Promise me," her mother insisted implacably, a very stern expression on her gentle features. She had already lost a husband and a son. If she were to die, she was grimly determined that her daughter would survive. "Just in case somethin' 'appens, ye must be taken care of."

"I promise," Jenny said solemnly.

Her mother laid a hand gently on her bright hair. "Such a good daughter ye are," she murmured. Then she straightened and said briskly, " 'Tis well that ye're better, darlin'. I will go straight ter bed, and when I awaken I must go see ter th' tobacco."

Jenny looked puzzled. "Ye've never seen ter th' tobacco before, Mother."

Her mother bit her lip. "Yer father is gone, darlin', and we shall need every worker we 'ave. I shall 'ave ter work in the fields alongside th' slaves if we're ter eat." The tobacco was their only source of income, and like many small planters, they barely eked out a living from the plant. It was a harsh crop, requiring attention the year round, and destroying what little land they possessed quickly. She had no idea how she was to manage, but she was determined that she would find a way.

"Can I 'elp?" Jenny's face brightened at the thought of helping. If only she could do something to contribute, perhaps she could wipe the misery and hopelessness from her mother's face.

"Shush, darlin'. Ye just rest."

In the next week, Jenny found that her illness had left her too tired to work in the fields—because of her inexperience, she probably would have been in the way anyway—but she struggled to sit up long enough to spin and do her other chores, despite the terrible dizziness that lasted well after her fever had left completely.

Her mother struggled every day, along with their two slaves, to do what needed to be done to the tobacco, but it was terribly hard work. Summer was the busiest time of year for the tobacco planter. In June the small plants had been planted in the fields. In July the plants were cut, in order to limit the number of leaves each plant grew and make the leaves that did grow larger. Now, in August, the lower leaves had to be removed. In September the plants would be cut and hung in the curing house to dry, then packed into the enormous casks called hogsheads and shipped to a public warehouse on double-hulled barges. It was an enormous amount of work for three people, one of whom was a woman who had never before worked in the fields.

One afternoon her mother staggered into the house, wearing an expression of mingled terror and fury. Jenny stumbled to her feet hurriedly. "Mother, what is it? What's wrong?"

"A storm," her mother answered dully. "There's goin' ter be a storm. A bad 'un."

Jenny made her way to the window and looked outside. The clouds were black and fierce as they scudded across the sky, and already the trees were beginning to bend in the wind. There could be no doubt—a hurricane was coming. Jenny was old enough to know what this would mean for the tobacco crop. Most likely it would be washed away entirely.

It was a terrible stroke of misfortune. In three more weeks the tobacco would have been safely hanging in the curing house.

As dusk drew nearer she sat in her bed, listening to the shrieking wail of the wind, and the angry force of the rain pelting against the windowpanes. It sounded like thunder.

"Mother?" she whispered faintly at last, frightened and needing the security of her mother's embrace. But her mother sat motionless, staring blankly at the walls. At last she turned, and the little girl was terrified by the vacant expression on her features.

"It's all right, love," she said, though it quite obviously was not. "Into th' fireplace with ye now."

Jenny looked at the gaping mouth of the cold fireplace uncomprehendingly.

"Th' fireplace is th' only safe place in th'ouse," her mother explained. "Th' roof may not stand up against th' hurricane."

Bundling Jenny in blankets, she urged her into the massive fireplace, thanking God as she did so that her husband had built the fireplace out of good solid brick, rather than of wood coated on the inside with clay, as so many of the poorer planters were forced to do. There was every chance that the fireplace would survive the gale, even if the roof were blown off. Her little girl was going to survive this night.

She straightened. "Ye stay there," she instructed fiercely. "No matter what 'appens, ye stay there. And in th' mornin' go ter yer uncle's 'ouse. 'E'll take ye in."

She turned the massive oak table onto its side and placed it in front of the fireplace to protect her daughter from flying debris. "I love ye," she whispered. Jenny stared over the top of the table timidly as her mother walked toward the door. Suddenly she realized just what it was her mother intended to do. "Mother, no!" she shrieked. "Mother!"

Her mother forced the door open against the screaming wind and stepped out into the wild storm.

Despite her mother's instructions, Jenny shoved the table away, her ague-weakened muscles made stronger by fear, and ran toward the door, mindlessly wailing for her mother. She clung to the doorjamb and the doorknob, fighting not to be ripped from the comparative safety of the house despite the awful wind.

"Mother, come back!" she screamed, but the wind whipped her words away before they were out of her throat. There was no chance that her mother could hear her above the storm, and little chance that she would listen anyway. She had already made her decision.

Jenny watched in helpless horror as a large branch struck the ground right next to her mother.

Her mother kept walking, staggering against the tremendous force of the wind, directly toward the little creek, which was raging far over its banks from the heavy rain and the exaggerated high tide. Jenny knew that her mother could not swim—not that an experienced swimmer could have kept her head above water in the torrent. As her mother stumbled into the roiling black water of the creek, she fell and was lost to view.

Sobbing hysterically, Jenny managed to slam the door shut and stagger back across the chamber. Pulling the table back against the fireplace and the blankets over her head, she huddled pitifully in the big fireplace, trying to shut out the dreadful howling of the storm, and trying to forget the horrid vision of her mother's suicide. She tried to sleep, but her few moments of rest were disrupted by nightmares in which wolves with slavering jaws stalked her, or in which a dark thundering river swept her from the house. All night the gale raged. Only toward dawn did it abate, and then Jenny dropped off into a haunted sleep.

When she woke up the sun was shining through an enormous hole in the roof where a pine tree had fallen onto the house, crushing it. Jenny managed to climb out of the house and searched for the slaves. They had vanished, very probably taking advantage of the opportunity to run away.

With no possessions other than the ragged gown she wore, knowing that she was now alone in the world, without parents or brother, Jenny embarked on the journey to her uncle's tavern.

As she finished her story in a quavering voice, Jennifer found that her cheeks were wet with tears. Grey was staring at her with horror and pity written plainly across his aquiline features. Now he took her hand gently into his.

"Don't cry, darling," he murmured, using the endearment that her mother had always used. Jennifer felt her throat constrict painfully at his use of the word, and she glanced away, embarrassed that the memories of her family, which she had thought securely locked away, could buffet her so.

"I was always alone after that," she confessed in a hoarse whisper. "I had no one, no one at all. Once I brought home a puppy I found in the woods—I had always wanted a dog—and my uncle drowned him. He said he wouldn't waste coin on yet another mouth to feed."

"I am very sorry," Grey whispered gently, stroking her hand. "I should not have asked you to tell me the story, but I had no idea . . . and now I've caused you distress at a time when you need your rest. I'm so sorry, Jennifer."

Jennifer dashed the tears away with her free hand. "I am all right," she said in a surprisingly level voice. "It all happened so long ago. I had forgotten. . . ." She paused. "How *could* I have forgotten them? I miss them so much. I miss them. . . ." Her voice broke abruptly, and Grey, to his own great surprise, pulled her into his arms and let her sob against the solidity and warmth of his chest, stroking her long golden hair and making the soothing noises one makes to comfort a lost child.

She looked up again at last, her eyes widening at the sight of his face so close to her own. But his face seemed less forbidding than usual, softened by unwonted sympathy and compassion. For a moment he seemed to be the same gentle man who had cared for her while she was ill, who had stayed by her side for three days and slept in a chair while she lay in a fever-induced stupor.

"I should not cry," she said, voice steady and eyes calm, if red rimmed, as they met his own. "My mother was sweet and good, but what happened occurred long ago. It is not good to dwell overmuch on the past."

Grey sensed a reproach to himself in her words, and the kind, gentle man he had been for a brief moment vanished, to be replaced in an instant by the surly husband she was accustomed to.

"Your mother's last act," he said with brutal frankness, "was not the act of a good, sweet woman, but of a selfish one."

Jennifer was still acutely aware of his muscled arms, casually imprisoning her against him, and the contrast between his affectionate stance and his harsh words bewildered her. She looked indignant. "My mother was *not* selfish."

"Self-absorbed, then," Grey said implacably. "She abandoned a terrified young girl in a hurricane. She left you to the tender mercies of her brother, even though she must have known he was abusive. It is true that she had gone through a great deal, but nothing can justify or excuse such behavior."

"She loved my father and brother dearly," Jennifer retorted rather sharply. "She was inconsolable after their deaths."

"She was selfish," Grey argued vehemently. "When she lost them she thought of no one but herself. She could not see your pain for her own."

Her dark eyes stared directly into his while she considered his statement. "You may be right," she conceded at last. "She had no thought for anyone but herself and how empty her life had become. That is not love—it is merely loneliness."

Grey flushed at her words, realizing that her words could be applied to himself as well as to her mother. "Are you implying that I did not love Diana?" he asked in a low, savage growl.

"I did not mention Diana," Jennifer countered cautiously, aware of the fury beginning to burn like molten silver in his eyes.

"Didn't you?"

"If you want to know the truth," Jennifer said, as tactfully as possible, "I believe that you once loved Diana. But now . . . now you love nothing more than a memory. It seems to me that love must change and grow, or it is not love."

Grey fought the impulse to drop his arms from around her, leap to his feet, and stalk from the chamber in high dudgeon. For once, he forced himself to listen to what she had to say.

Though he longed to deny it, brutal self-honesty forced him to admit that much of what she said was true. His love for Diana, the ardent and earthy love of a young man for a beautiful woman, had somehow altered over the years into a kind of reverence, as if Diana had been a creature of light and poetry rather than a flesh-and-blood human being. Intellectually, if not emotionally, he knew she had been no goddess, but merely a mortal woman.

Diana's ghost could not hope to compare to the girl in his arms.

Jennifer was solid, warm, and delicate, almost fragile, in his embrace, one of her firm young breasts pressing against his chest. Her hair, which Catherine had managed to comb into a semblance of order that morning, cascaded down her back, brushing lightly over his arm. A powerful, aching surge of desire swept him.

It was peculiar to actually desire someone besides the memory that had haunted him for years. He had made love to other women solely to relieve the demands of his body, but desire—the longings of the mind and the heart—had not been involved. For the first time, he realized that he desired Jennifer. Not just her figure, which had held such attraction for him that night he had seen her swimming in the river, but all of her—her lithe but gently rounded body, her lovely face, her quick and agile mind. He wanted to hear the music that she heard, and most of all he yearned to make her desire him as he desired her.

Jennifer was real. And Diana was not. Not any longer.

He was aware of a sudden, overpowering impulse to tilt up her chin and press his lips against her soft, yielding mouth, to push her back against the pillows and make love to her until she cried out with pleasure. Incredibly erotic images exploded in his brain as he held her against his chest.

But Jennifer was fragile, still recovering from a week of

illness. With an enormous exertion of willpower he dropped his arms from around her and stood up. She looked up at him in confusion, bewildered by his long thoughtful silence.

"You may have a point," he said curtly. "However, I do not believe I wish to discuss it further. I have matters I must attend to. If you will excuse me?" Nodding to her coolly, he strode from the chamber rapidly.

After an hour's hard and exhausting ride on his bay stallion, he convinced himself that what he felt for Jennifer was no different than what he felt for any other young and attractive woman. He had been sitting on her bed, with her virtually curled up in his lap—of course he had been aroused by her nearness!

He did not return to Jennifer's chamber to visit her. Within a week, she had recovered from the illness with the resilience of youth. Grey took care not to be alone in her chamber with her again.

He visited his mistress every day for a week. But for some reason, the sex was remarkably unfulfilling.

Grey could not imagine why.

FOURTEEN

August was as hot and humid as July had been, the intense heat unbroken by any rain. It seemed to Jennifer that it would never rain again. As she regained her health, she and Grey resumed their daily rides, though they never spoke of her illness, or of what had happened between them at the river. Sometimes Jennifer glimpsed an odd expression in Grey's metallic eyes when she turned and met his gaze, but he always dropped his eyes hastily and looked away.

Nothing had changed.

They rode through the forest one afternoon, far from Greyhaven. "We are nearly on Lightfoot land here," Grey remarked, startling Jennifer, for it was virtually the first thing he had said to her all day. He was more silent and remote than ever these days. "We should turn and go back."

Jennifer nodded. They turned their horses and cantered back down the path. A sudden rumble startled her, and she looked up. The green canopy of trees overhead could not hide the black clouds that hung ominously low in the sky. "I do believe it's going to rain," she said.

"God knows we could use it," Grey responded with a planter's sincerity. Drought meant ruined crops. Rain meant the salvation of his crops—and cool weather. He felt a cool breeze and realized that the rain was nearly upon them. He should have been paying more attention to the weather.

It had become impossible for him to concentrate on anything when Jennifer was near.

A cold drop of water fell onto his hand. They needed to find shelter. "This way," he called, turning his stallion down a little-used path.

Jennifer, who had never been down that particular path, looked at him warily. "Is this a shortcut?"

"No," Grey said shortly, "but there is an old cabin down this way. We won't be able to get back to the house before the rain comes, and I don't want you to get drenched. You've just recovered from an illness, after all."

The thought that he cared for her well-being filled her with warmth, and she followed him without further questions.

A loud clap of thunder startled her mare, and the horse reared suddenly. Certain that she was going to fall, Jennifer caught at the horse's mane frantically, dropping the reins in her panic. Without guidance or control, the mare jumped forward at a gallop. Grey quickly maneuvered his stallion into the mare's path, cutting off her escape and letting the enormous beast shoulder her to a halt. Catching the frantic animal by the bridle, he spoke softly to her until her eyes stopped rolling. Jennifer sent him a look of gratitude, all too aware that she would have been unseated had the mare bolted, and he smiled with a rare show of sympathy.

"We're almost there," he said soothingly. Whether he was soothing the mare or Jennifer, she could not be certain.

They pulled up their horses in front of an old, weather-beaten cabin of rough-hewn boards that had once been whitewashed. Most of the paint had long ago blistered off. It had probably once been slave quarters, Jennifer speculated, and realized that the house Grey and Catherine had grown up in must have been in this vicinity.

Dismounting, they dashed into the cabin just as the rain began falling in earnest. Looking around the dingy cabin, Jennifer saw that her supposition had been correct.

Along the walls stood the roughly constructed furnishings that were characteristic of slave quarters—a bed and two chairs. In the corner she saw a dust-covered stringed instrument, similar to the ones that the Greyhaven slaves often played in the evenings. Curious, she brushed away some of the cobwebs and picked it up to examine it.

"It's called a banjar," Grey told her, settling into a crudely built chair.

Jennifer plucked experimentally at the strings, but the instrument was far out of tune. Cringing at the discordant notes, she put the banjar back down on the floor and glanced around curiously.

It was beginning to strike her as peculiar that there was only one bed in the cabin. Slaves did not have the luxury of having chambers to themselves. There must have been many beds lining the walls of this building at one point in time. Someone had removed all but one cot. Walking across the room, she sat on the mattress. It was soft, filled with goose down, just as her bed at Greyhaven was.

Slaves did not sleep on feather beds.

Melissa's voice echoed in her mind: *Grey's nice wide bed would be much more comfortable than the tumble-down shack we usually use.*

At last it dawned on her that Grey had taken her to the cabin where he met his mistress.

She looked at Grey accusingly, but he was sitting in the chair and idly studying the silver buckles on his shoes, being careful not to meet her eyes. It occurred to her that he was embarrassed.

And yet he had had very little choice but to bring her here. Had they had to ride all the way back to Greyhaven, she would have been drenched in the downpour, and then she might very well have had a relapse.

What else could he have done?

Her lips twitched as she began to see the humor in the situation. Here she sat, on the edge of the bed where her husband dallied with another woman. Little wonder Grey was embarrassed. No doubt, when he had made the hasty

decision to bring her here, he had hoped she wouldn't realize exactly what purposes he used this shack for.

"How fortunate that you knew that this cabin was still
here," she remarked, suppressing her laughter with an effort.

Grey glanced up at her laughing tone and saw the light
of amusement dancing in her eyes. Damn her, he thought
in sudden annoyance, she was laughing at him!

"I've had occasion to stop in here before," he said coolly.

"Yes, quite recently, from the looks of it," she said, nodding toward the distinct tracks his boots had made in the
dust that covered the floorboards, and the smaller prints
made by a lady's shoes. It was all too evident he had been in
here quite a bit recently, and that he had had company. She
was no longer able to repress her smile. "It must have been
raining more frequently than I thought this past week or
two."

Reluctantly, Grey grinned. She knew as well as he did
that it had not rained for weeks. He was a little shocked by
her attitude. Any other woman would have taken a riding
crop to his back for daring to bring her to the cabin where
he trysted with his mistress. But then again, Jennifer was
not like any other woman he knew.

Any other woman would have been jealous.

He wished that she were jealous.

He pushed the thought aside hastily, bewildered by his
own foolishness. Ridiculous! Why would he want a jealous
wife?

He knew the answer to that: because he wanted her.
And he wanted her to want him. Trapped alone with her,
with no distractions, his mind was drawn irresistibly to
thoughts of kissing her, and his eyes dropped to her lips.

Jennifer saw his gaze drop and interpreted his change of
mood correctly. She had seen that heavy-lidded, sensual
expression before. Nervously, she got up and walked across
to the small window, making the first inane remark that
occurred to her. "I don't think it's going to stop for a
while," she observed, seeing the sheets of rain driven by the
gusting wind and hearing thunder rolling overhead.

Behind her, she heard Grey's footsteps. His arms encircled her, pulling her against him, and he brushed his lips against her hair. The golden strands smelled of lavender, and he breathed the scent in deeply, closing his eyes in helpless pleasure.

"I don't mind," he whispered.

Jennifer stiffened against him. "Grey," she objected faintly. Ignoring her protest, he turned her in his arms so that she was facing him and pressed his lips to hers hungrily.

She kissed him back, warm, passionate, and loving.

When he lifted his lips from hers she placed both hands on his shoulders and shoved hard.

Caught off balance, Grey staggered backward and sat down hard on the floor, causing a cloud of dust to rise around him. He regained his feet with the smooth, rapid motion of a panther and stood looking down at her with a dangerous expression. All his desire had ebbed away rapidly. "What the hell was that for?" he demanded.

Jennifer's eyes were blazing in a very uncharacteristic fashion. "How dare you," she said softly. "It's bad enough that you would bring me to—to this place, but I understand that you had no choice. But then—how dare you try to seduce me here, of all places? Simply because your mistress isn't here, did you think you could avail yourself of my body instead?"

"I didn't—" Grey began, but she was not finished.

"I am sick and tired of you using me to replace some other woman," she said, her voice rising in fury. "If you cannot touch me without pretending I am another woman, then I don't want you to touch me at all. Do you understand me?"

There was no point in trying to explain to her that he had not intended to use her as a substitute for Melissa, or even for Diana. No point in trying to explain that she was the only woman he had thought of for days. No point in telling her how she haunted his nights and his dreams. He could not admit that he wanted her—even to himself.

"I apologize," he said coldly. "It won't happen again."

"I forgive you," Jennifer said, adding with a flash of humor, "but only if you forgive me for pushing you."

"I imagine I deserved it."

Jennifer nodded slowly. "Yes. You did." She walked back across the room and sat in one of the chairs, feeling oddly deflated.

If only, she thought miserably, he had wanted her for herself. If only she did not have the feeling that he wanted nothing more than sex, and that any willing woman would satisfy him.

If only he were not so damned attractive.

If only she did not love him.

For the next hour rain hammered on the roof of the shack, the wind howled, and thunder rumbled.

But inside the shack there was only silence.

Jennifer managed to stay away from the abandoned slave quarters for several days. She did not want to know how often Grey met his mistress there. It was beneath her dignity, she told herself repeatedly, to spy on her husband.

Yet one day that week she found herself riding her gray mare down the narrow path that led to the old shack.

The drought had at last broken. The humid days were often relieved by afternoon thunderstorms, and today looked as though it would be no exception. As she approached the cabin, Jennifer kept a cautious eye on the dark clouds that had already begun to rise ominously against the sky.

She reined in her mare abruptly as she saw Grey's bay stallion tied outside the cabin.

Firmly, she told herself that what Grey did was none of her business. Most husbands sought affection outside the marriage bed, and Grey was certainly no exception. Men, she knew, had certain needs, and since she did not share his bed, she could hardly expect him to remain celibate for all his days.

Despite her good intentions, however, she rode nearer to the cabin.

She heard muffled creaking sounds, soft masculine groans, a woman's cries of ecstatic delight.

Grey was making love to his mistress.

Jennifer hesitated only a moment before making a decision. She hastily untied Grey's stallion and led the fractious beast back toward Greyhaven.

The first cool drops of rain were beginning to fall as she arrived back at the main house. Jennifer smiled to herself as she gave the horses to the black stableboy to walk and rub down. It was a very long walk back from the cabin.

She hoped it rained all afternoon.

That evening, Jennifer knocked on Grey's study door. At his surly acknowledgment, she walked into his study.

"What do you want?"

Ignoring his less than courteous tone, Jennifer studied him thoughtfully. She had heard him cursing lividly in the entrance hall as he dashed in from a torrential downpour a few minutes earlier. He had changed out of his wet clothes, but his black hair was still dripping wet, plastered to his neck and shoulders. Delighted though she was that he had been caught in the storm, she nevertheless managed to keep her features impassive. It would not do for her to laugh at Grey when she had a favor to ask.

"I made up a menu that I think would be appropriate for the slaves," she said hesitantly, thrusting a piece of parchment toward him. "I hoped you would take a look at it."

"No."

Jennifer felt herself becoming irritated by his curt refusal. Was he going to refuse to compromise on this issue solely because he suspected she had forced him to walk home in the rain? It occurred to her belatedly that she had chosen a poor time to try to speak reasonably with him. But was there ever a good time to speak reasonably where Grey was concerned?

"Why not?"

"I don't need to look at it. I trust you to make decisions such as these without consulting me."

At his words, so different from what she had expected, Jennifer's mouth fell open. "Really?" she squeaked at last.

Grey lifted an eyebrow. "Of course. After all, you are the mistress of Greyhaven." He turned back to his desk. "Now, if you will excuse me."

Realizing she had been dismissed, Jennifer turned and walked toward the door. She paused, glancing back over her shoulder, as a thought occurred to her. There was one other important matter which needed to be discussed. "Grey . . ." she began hesitantly.

Grey glanced up, irritation plain on his lean face. "Yes?"

Jennifer gulped at the ominous gleam in his eyes, but stammered out her question anyway. "Will you—will you continue to permit the slaves to be whipped?"

Her husband's features darkened. "That is *my* decision," he said in a tone of soft warning, "not yours."

"But—" Jennifer broke off at the deepening expression of annoyance on his face. Marshaling her courage, she went on haltingly, "The field hands are afraid, Grey. They never know when they might be whipped. It's terrible to live in fear of a beating. I—" Her voice dropped to a whisper. "I know how they feel," she finished softly.

Grey studied her for a moment. Some of his irritation drained away as he considered what she had said. She never talked about her life in the tavern, and he knew what it had cost her to mention it. Her distress was all too obvious. He had never seen her so pale.

Unbidden, a memory flashed into his mind. A picture of her swaying in front of a stocky, powerful man, waiting with pitiful patience to be beaten, while around her rowdy men laughed and cheered.

He had only seen one night of her uncle's violence.

For her, the violence had gone on for years.

"Actually," he said coolly, "I have already made that decision. Slaves will no longer be whipped at Greyhaven, regardless of the offense. Also, you might be interested to know that I have fired the overseer. It occurred to me rather belatedly that it seemed my slaves were being whipped rather often. I interviewed some of the slaves, and I could find no evidence that the young man we saw being whipped actually stole anything. I suspect the overseer was simply possessed of a bad temper and looking for excuses to take it out on my slaves."

"He ought to have been whipped himself!" Jennifer said indignantly.

A small smile played around Grey's mouth. "I took care of him," he said, thinking of the black eye and split lip he had given the man before ordering him off the premises. Grey was not in the habit of permitting his valuable property to be damaged by fools.

Jennifer had left the study before she realized Grey had said nothing about the fact that she had taken his horse. Surely he must have realized she was the culprit once he returned to the house and found his stallion already in the stable. Evidently, she mused, he was none too angry with her. She supposed she was relieved . . . and yet it would have been nice to make him furious. God knew he deserved it.

Recalling the virulent oaths she'd overheard as he dashed into the house from the pouring rain, she realized that he had in fact been furious. He had simply not wanted her to know it.

She smiled to herself as she made her way across the wet lawn to talk to the slaves in the cookhouse about the new menu. For the first time, she did not seek input from Catherine in implementing a new idea.

After all, *she* was the mistress of Greyhaven.

FIFTEEN

Fall came to Virginia at last, splashing the forest with vivid shades of crimson and topaz. The wild geese began to fly overhead, and Grey began to take a fowling piece out with him every few days and bring home a plump goose for dinner. The geese were lovely, their black heads contrasting beautifully with their gray bodies, and Jennifer hated to see them killed, but they were delicious, and their feathers were useful for stuffing mattresses and pillows.

Other migrating birds passed through: the descriptively named canvasbacks, small ducks with long bills known as shovelers, and the green-headed mallards. Sometimes the ducks also found their way onto the Greysons' dining table. As the days grew colder, however, and the leaves fell from the trees, many of the birds flew further south.

Grey groaned inwardly as someone knocked on the door of his study one gloomy winter afternoon. Life with two females, he thought with irritation, was deucedly annoying. It seemed that he was never left alone in peace and quiet any more. Even his study, which had once been his refuge, was no longer sacrosanct. All too often nowadays his quiet afternoons were disturbed by Jennifer practicing the harpsichord in the parlor, which was across from the study, or by Catherine tapping on his door like a damned woodpecker.

Today he particularly wanted to be left alone. This morning the first winter storm of the year had arrived bringing icy, stinging, rain. The ground turned slick and dangerous, making it impossible for Grey and Jennifer to take their customary ride. He had to admit grudgingly to himself that he missed her. For the first time, he was becoming painfully aware of how much he enjoyed her company.

He was even more irritated because he had spent most of the day moping and fighting the insane impulse to walk into the parlor and suggest to his wife that they pass the time playing draughts or chess. She, on the other hand, had spent the morning constructively, practicing the harpsichord. It was more than evident, he thought with annoyance, that *she* did not miss their daily ride at all. *She* did not miss his company.

With these thoughts circulating through his mind, he ignored the knock at the door, hoping whoever it was would go away. The knock came again, more loudly this time, and Grey sighed.

"What the hell do you want?" he demanded.

The door opened, and Catherine, clad in an unfashionably high-necked dark gray gown, came in. "I'll take that as an invitation to enter," she said calmly, smiling at him. Grey did not return the smile. Whenever Catherine smiled at him there was trouble in the offing.

"What is so important," he said tightly, "that you must disturb me?"

Catherine sat down in one of the leather-upholstered chairs and faced him. "I have had a brilliant idea," she began. "More than brilliant. Astonishing, extraordinary—"

"Oh, for Christ's sake, get on with it," Grey growled.

Catherine looked slightly wounded. "Very well. It seems to me that I should consider finding another place to reside. I do not want to become your spinster sister who depends upon you for support for the rest of my years, especially now that you are married. I should really consider looking for a husband so that I can marry and get out of your way."

Grey turned to face her, lifting his eyebrows in surprise.

"Don't be ridiculous, Catherine. You've never been in the way. In fact, you've been invaluable in teaching Jennifer how to be a lady."

"I'm glad you feel that way," Catherine went on smoothly, never missing a beat. "Because my idea has to do with Jennifer as well."

Grey's eyes narrowed suspiciously. "Just exactly what is your idea?"

"A rout!"

Astounded, Grey stared at her for a long moment. "You must be joking," he said at last. "A rout? Are you suggesting that we give a rout here? In *my* house?"

"Yes!" Catherine said happily. "For Twelfth Night. It would be the ideal setting both to introduce Jennifer to society and to begin my search for a husband. After all, we have that lovely ballroom in the east wing that has hardly ever been used. It would be the event of the season!"

Twelfth Night, Grey knew, was the most celebrated holiday in the colony, even more so than Christmas. The planter class frequently threw lavish celebrations. A rout at Greyhaven would certainly be a popular event. And Twelfth Night was little more than a month away. If he agreed to this mad scheme, people would invade his house in a month, laughing and talking and in general making bloody nuisances of themselves. His peace would be shattered entirely. It would be perfectly appalling.

And yet . . . Catherine did need a husband.

Before he could mount any sort of coherent defense, Catherine got to her feet. "Good!" she said brightly. "I'm so glad you agree. Jennifer and I will start work on the guest list right away. And of course we'll have to sew new ball gowns."

Grey's head snapped up. The thought of Jennifer in a ball gown made his body tighten. The attraction he felt for her ordinarily was bad enough. Gowned and coiffed like a princess, she would be gorgeous. He would probably go mad.

But Catherine did need a husband.

"Fine, Catherine. You do that."

Catherine smiled at him like a queen granting favors to her subject. "There's just one other thing."

Grey lifted a dark brow. He knew Catherine well enough to know that she would casually try to pass off her most unpalatable suggestion as if it were of no significance whatsoever. What could be worse than the notion of holding a rout at Greyhaven, he had no idea. Nevertheless, he mentally braced himself as he waited. "Yes?"

"Jennifer needs to learn to dance, since we will of course have dancing. I cannot dance, due to my infirmity, so you—"

Grey jumped to his feet and scowled down on her from his imposing height. "No," he said sharply. "Absolutely, positively, definitely not. I will not teach her to dance. It is utterly, totally, and completely out of the question."

"Why not?" Catherine inquired in her most innocent and reasonable tone. Grey knew that tone all too well. She wielded it like a weapon whenever she was trying to make him feel like a loutish, unmannered boor.

"I hate dancing," he snarled.

"Oh, really, Grey. Would you prefer that all of Virginia laugh at your wife because she has no idea how to dance the minuet?"

Yes, I would, he thought, but he did not dare to say it aloud. Because then Catherine would see his weakness and strike. He could not admit that he was afraid of holding his own wife in his arms, afraid of what he felt every time he touched her. He had promised Jennifer he would not kiss her again. He had told himself over and over that he did not want her. But none of it was true. He did want her, and if he was forced to touch her he would surely kiss her. And then he would make love to her. . . .

"I will not waste my time teaching her to dance," he said firmly, trying to suppress the images he had conjured up of holding Jennifer, clad in a low-cut ball gown, against his body. "I care nothing for what society thinks. If it matters so much to you, I suggest you hire a tutor."

"A tutor?" Catherine echoed in dismay. "But Grey, tutors teach children the social graces, not adults."

"I daresay they can teach adults as well as children," Grey said. The corners of his mouth quirked upward in amusement as he watched Catherine try to mount another offense. Clearly she had not expected him to suggest a tutor, and she seemed to be floundering. "I believe the Madisons have an excellent dancing master," he suggested politely, sitting back down in his easy chair. "Perhaps you could hire him to give Jennifer lessons."

"But—"

Grey waved a careless hand. "If another tutor would suit you better, that is perfectly acceptable," he said magnanimously. "I'll leave the details to you. Hire whomever you please. Now, Catherine, I do have some work to do. If you would excuse me . . ."

Outmaneuvered, but not beaten, Catherine frowned as she left him in his study. She had managed to get Grey to agree to a rout, and for that she was profoundly grateful. She was not blind to the growing attraction between Grey and Jennifer, but her foolish brother was so stubborn that he needed some sort of added impetus. Her original goal in making Jennifer into a lady had been simply to show Grey that he had not succeeded in outmaneuvering her. But due to her growing friendship with Jennifer, her intentions had changed. Over the past year, she had grown nearly as fond of Jennifer as she was of her own brother, and she wanted to see them both happy. Her purpose was not to snare a husband at all. Rather her purpose was to bring Grey and Jennifer closer together. And this time, she decided with determination, it was going to work.

It was unfortunate that Grey had rebelled at the notion of teaching Jennifer to dance. She had hoped to force them into each other's arms, literally as well as figuratively. But if Grey would not teach Jennifer to dance, he would surely dance with her at the rout. She smiled to herself.

We'll just see, she mused, *how he reacts when he sees Jennifer in the ball gown I have planned.*

Grey didn't have a chance.

Caught up as they were in preparations for the rout, Catherine and Jennifer spent a great deal of time together planning the menu and the festivities and sewing their ball gowns. They giggled together like little girls as they decorated the house inside and out with fruits, green garlands, and kissing balls studded with sprigs of mistletoe. Neither of them could remember such a happy Christmas.

Grey, on the other hand, was miserable. Grey detested the twelve days of Christmas. He detested the gaiety and the social whirl, the smiling faces and the giving of gifts. He detested the good cheer that seemed to emanate from everyone like a particularly loathsome disease. Most especially, he detested this particular Christmas, when he was being forced not simply to attend a rout but actually host one. Consequently he was in an exceptionally vile mood when his wife actually dared to tap softly on the partially open door of his study.

Berating himself for not shutting and locking the damned door, Grey glowered at her in annoyance. "What do you want?" he drawled in a tone that implied whatever she had to say could not possibly be of interest to him.

Jennifer faltered a bit at his angry gray eyes, which seemed darker than usual, but she persevered. "It—it's Christmas day," she began.

Grey greeted this absurdly obvious statement with incredulity. "Indeed it is," he agreed at last, in a gentle tone that one might use to an imbecile. "I do thank you for informing me of that fact. Why, in spite of the garlands and holly you and Catherine have strung all over the house, I do believe I was on the verge of forgetting. Christmas, you say? How singular!"

"I am well aware you know that it is Christmas, Grey."

"Then why remind me of that regrettably unalterable fact?"

Jennifer paused under the onslaught of his gray eyes, wishing she had not intruded on her husband today. Clearly Christmas affected him badly, for he was obviously in an even more dreadful mood than usual. And yet this matter could not wait. Screwing up her courage, she finally managed to explain hesitantly, "I—have a present for you."

Grey's eyebrows shot up as he gaped at her, dumbstruck. All the anger and impatience drained from him as he stared at her. Of all the things he had expected her to say, that had not been one. A present? The child had gotten him a present after his churlish behavior over the past few weeks?

It was impossible. And yet there was no doubting the sincerity on her lovely face. Jennifer had, for some obscure reason known only to herself, gotten him a present.

"A present?" he repeated, as though the idea were completely foreign to him. It had been so long since anyone had given him anything. Or, for that matter, since he had admitted to himself that he wanted anything.

Her thoughtfulness touched him deeply. For an instant, it seemed as though she cared something for his happiness, and he was profoundly grateful. Unfortunately, her next words shattered his gratitude like glass.

"Of course," Jennifer said, and, lest he realize just how much he meant to her, added hastily, with an attempt at airiness, "It is the expected thing. It *is* Christmas, and you *are* my husband."

Grey's mouth snapped shut quickly. For a moment he had believed that she was making a peace offering, or better yet, a gesture of friendship despite their differences. And he had been astonished by the warm pleasure that had suddenly washed over him a minute ago, only to be abruptly cut off by her final cool words.

So the chit had gotten him a present because it was the "expected thing," had she? Of course, she had never been to Williamsburg, or anywhere else for that matter, so what could she possibly have gotten him that would be worth having? She could have bought nothing that he would want on the limited allowance he'd given her, anyway. A moment ago he would have accepted the gift with all the tact he could muster, but now, angered anew by her chilly words, he decided not to humor her. His old bitterness and hatred of Christmastime and its related festivities were back, more strongly than ever.

"A generous thought, I'm sure," he said in a tone that was distinctly bored, "but I'm afraid you have wasted your effort. I have everything I could possibly desire, except for that which is beyond my grasp. There is nothing you can give me that I would want. So, you see, your gift would be entirely superfluous."

Jennifer blinked hard, feeling tears stinging her eyelids, but she was unwilling to let him see them. Only Grey could reduce her to tears. And he did it so often! But she had worked so hard on his gift that she could not simply give up and walk out of the study. She blinked back the tears.

Struggling to hold her voice steady, she said levelly, "Perhaps you do have everything you need, Grey. But there are certain things that are not necessary but that are pleasant to possess."

Her husband gave her an insolent grin that did not touch his cold eyes. "Perhaps. But obtaining *pleasure* has rarely been difficult for me."

The intentionally cruel reference to his mistress hit her almost like a physical blow. *Why is he acting this way?* she wondered in mounting anguish. Perhaps she had only imagined the flash of hope and delight she thought she'd seen on his features when she had first mentioned a gift. "At any rate," Grey went on coldly, "anything that you could afford would be of no interest to me."

"You cannot be certain of that until you have seen my gift," Jennifer countered, struggling valiantly to maintain a bantering tone so as to conceal her hurt. She could not bear to let him see how much his callous indifference wounded her.

Grey raised his eyes to the ceiling in silent supplication, then evidently tired of the game and scowled at his wife. "Very well. What is it?"

Relieved that curiosity had gotten the better of him, Jennifer almost smiled. "You will have to come into the parlor," she told him airily.

Grey frowned even more at being forced to leave the refuge of his study, but he reluctantly rose and followed her into the parlor. Glancing about with a fine show of disinterest, he said coldly, "I don't see it. Where is it?"

"Such impatience," Jennifer teased gently, trying desperately to conceal her terror that he would turn on his heel and stalk back to the solitude of his study. "Why don't you sit down?"

Grey went to the settee, stretched out on his back with his legs dangling over the edge, and threw his arms over his face. "I'm ready," he said in a muffled voice. "Hurry, or I'll be tempted to take a nap."

Hardly encouraging words, but Jennifer realized that her infuriatingly contrary husband was as enthusiastic now as he would ever be. Her footsteps were muffled by the heavy Oriental carpet as she crossed the room.

Grey lay sprawled on the settee, wondering impatiently when he could get back to his study and have a drink. And then he heard his gift.

It was like nothing he had ever heard. A melody, simple yet strangely plaintive, rang out from the harpsichord. In a moment the melody was joined by another, and then another, all interweaving like threads in a vivid tapestry to create a startlingly lovely whole.

Grey sat up slowly and stared in stunned surprise at his wife. Her back was to him, presenting him with a view of little except the long, dark gold hair falling free to her waist. But in her posture he saw passion, animation, violent emotions as her hands flashed lightly across the boxwood keys. And he realized for the first time that Jennifer did express her emotions, but always privately.

At last, she was voluntarily sharing her emotions with him.

The music went on, intimate as a caress, falling delicately on the ears of the one rapt listener. Something in the pathos of the music struck an answering chord deep within him. It expressed his loneliness and sorrow so plainly that he could not move, could do nothing but sit and listen, entranced.

Then, slowly, it changed. The tragedy of the melody slowly metamorphosed into a major key, the tempo accelerated until Jennifer's fingers were leaping across the keyboard like deer across a meadow. It concluded with a series of gloriously joyful chords.

And then there was silence. Jennifer did not turn to look at him, only stared in dumb misery at the keyboard, feeling that all the effort she had poured into the composition of her piece had been wasted. Grey no doubt felt only contempt for the gift on which she had worked so long and so hard. She heard nothing from the settee. Most likely, she thought wretchedly, he was asleep.

And then a hand came down gently on her shoulder. Looking up in surprise, Jennifer saw her husband, and sudden hope lit within her at the sight of his warm expression.

"I apologize for what I said earlier," Grey said simply, staring down into her face as though he had never seen it before. In her music he had caught a glimpse of her soul, and he was surprised to realize what he had not known before, that the beauty of her face came not from the regularity of her features, but from what was inside her. Whatever it was that had created that music. "That was the loveliest gift anyone has ever given me."

Overwhelmed and astonished that her music had wrought such a dramatic alteration in his behavior, Jennifer gave him a brilliant, spontaneous smile. "You liked it?"

"Jennifer, it was—" Grey searched futilely for words vivid enough to express the inexpressible. He knelt beside her and looked up into her face with something akin to reverence. "I did not know you were capable of creating such a lovely thing," he told her honestly. "More and more I wonder at my own stupidity at failing to see how extraordinary you are now and before, when first we met."

Made uncomfortable by the reference to the awkward circumstances surrounding their wedding, Jennifer adroitly changed the subject by handing him a piece of parchment. On it were a profusion of notes.

"I wrote it out," she explained in response to his puzzled expression, "in case you couldn't remember it all." Honesty compelled her to add, "Actually, Catherine helped me write it out, but *I* composed it." There was evident pride in her voice.

Grey took the parchment from her as carefully as if it were a treasure and smiled up at her gently. "It was wonderful. The first part—it sounded like I feel, all too often. Alone and angry."

"I was thinking of you when I first played it," she admitted. "And the second part, the happy part, I wrote for you as well. I hope—I hope that someday you can be happy, Grey."

Her genuine hope for his happiness, after all he had done to mire her in the same misery in which he was trapped, touched him deeply. Almost without volition, he raised a hand to her face, gently curving it against her cheek, and kissed her. He had intended it to be a brief kiss of thanks, to express how much her gift had meant to him, but the moment her soft lips touched his, a violent shock of ecstasy and overwhelming desire jolted through him and he knew he could not kiss her chastely. His hand curved around the nape of her neck, pulling her head down, and he kissed her urgently, demanding a response.

To his surprise, she gave him one. Her lips parted and she kissed him warmly. She was as warm and passionate as her music, he thought. His fingers entwined in the thick hair at the nape of her neck, asking for more, and she gave it to him without reservation. Despite her degrading and painful first experience with sex, despite the fact that he had fully expected her to slap him and run from the chamber in fear and loathing, she only wrapped her arms around his neck and returned the kiss as passionately as he gave it.

Fighting the urge to pull her from her chair onto the carpet, Grey pulled away. For an instant her eyes looked into his with disappointment, then she dropped her gaze. Grey's silver eyes did not leave her face as he stared at her in bewilderment.

"Jennifer," he said at last, softly, "you are in love with me. Aren't you?"

First her music, and then her shameless response to his kiss, had betrayed her. He knew how she felt. Jennifer nodded shakily, feeling her cheeks stain a bright red. "Yes. I am."

"Unbelievable," Grey said gently. It was tragic, he thought, that such a young and beautiful woman should be in love with a man such as himself, dissolute and far older than he should be. "After all I've done to you, and knowing as you must that I can never love you in return, it's difficult to believe that you could love me." He paused and then went on slowly, "That must be true love."

Jennifer's eyes met his for an instant and she smiled sorrowfully.

"No, Grey," she told him. "It's stupidity."

And before he could stop her his wife ran swiftly from the room.

SIXTEEN

It was Jennifer's first rout, and she was acutely nervous despite the fact that it was being held in the familiar surroundings of Greyhaven. Although Greyhaven seemed more familiar to her now, almost like home, she sometimes found herself staring in awe at the grandeur around her exactly as she had the first time she had walked into the parlor. Despite the spacious chambers, the shining silver candlesticks, the magnificent Oriental rugs, she was slowly beginning to believe that someday she might fit into these surroundings.

It helped that she was clad in a ball gown more glorious than any gown she had ever imagined. She and Catherine had sewn their gowns together, with help from the house slaves, and Jennifer was delighted with the result. Her gown was of a forest green satin, the exact color of her eyes, shot through with gold threads, and its stomacher was covered with the small bows known as *echelles*. The skirt parted in the front to reveal a ruffled gold petticoat, and the elbow-length sleeves terminated in cascades of golden lace. The gown was so low-cut that Jennifer had at first objected, wanting to mask her exposed cleavage with a filmy handkerchief, but Catherine had overruled her protests.

Catherine's gown was nearly as revealing. It was of gray satin, but not a spinsterish gray such as Catherine all too often wore. It shimmered and glowed in the light, clinging to her torso and then billowing out over her side hoops.

Her petticoat was a lighter silvery gray. With her hair piled in an elaborate style on top of her head, pomaded, and powdered with white rice flour, and wearing white lead powder and rouge on her face, she looked surprisingly attractive.

Catherine had refused to powder Jennifer's hair, and had only lightly applied the white powder to her face. "Your complexion is too beautiful to cover," she explained as Jennifer surveyed herself in the looking glass. "Most women have to wear a great deal of the powder, or even wax, to conceal pockmarks and the like. You don't. And your hair is far too striking a shade to powder."

Jennifer looked at her doubtfully. "Won't I seem odd if I don't powder my hair for a rout?"

Her sister-in-law smiled mysteriously. "Don't think of it as being odd. Think of it as setting a fashion."

The real reason, of course, that she did not want to powder Jennifer's hair was because she knew Grey liked its color. Grey had never cared overmuch for hair powder and wigs anyway. But she could hardly tell Jennifer that. She would have left Jennifer's hair down, falling in a heavy golden cascade to her waist, if she had dared, but that would have been entirely too peculiar. Instead, she had arranged Jennifer's hair atop her head, combing it over horsehair pads in order to create a fashionably high-piled coiffure, and leaving a few wisps to curl winsomely in front of her ears.

Jennifer was still considering her hair in the looking glass. Her expression was vaguely mutinous and, afraid that the girl would insist on having her hair pomaded and powdered, Catherine tried to distract her. "After all," she pointed out, "you will be wearing the most beautiful gown at the rout."

Turning away from the glass, Jennifer smiled at her friend despite her nerves. "Besides yours, you mean."

"All the ladies will envy us," Catherine agreed lightly. She frowned slightly. "I wonder if the punch was made to my exact recipe? Perhaps I had better go down and make certain."

"Catherine," Jennifer said patiently, "you gave Moses your recipe four separate times. Three jugs of beer, three jugs of brandy, three pounds of sugar, and cinnamon and nutmeg. I'm sure he will make it just fine. I believe that you are as nervous as I am."

"Perhaps I am," Catherine admitted. "It has been eight years since we had any sort of rout here, and then I was very young. At sixteen I thought of a rout only as a chance to dance and obtain a husband. I had very romantic notions, at that age."

"Perhaps you will be less nervous if you think of tonight as a chance to dance and obtain a husband," Jennifer suggested.

"Heavens, Jen, I can't dance anymore."

Jennifer had momentarily forgotten her friend's infirmity, so graceful did Catherine look in her ball gown. "Well . . . perhaps not. But you can flirt and talk. No doubt you will enrapture every man in the ballroom."

Catherine did not answer. In her mind she was remembering the last rout she had attended, the one celebrating Grey and Diana's marriage. She had been young and she had enjoyed joining in the country dances. She had been partnered with several handsome young men who had showered her with flowery compliments.

A few days after that, her leg had been broken, and now she would never dance again.

She shrugged off her memories, recalling that her true purpose was not to gain a husband but to bring Grey and Jennifer closer together. It mattered very little whether or not she could dance. Somehow she had to get Jennifer and Grey to dance together, and that might be difficult.

Then again, she thought, glancing once more at Jennifer's lovely gown and youthful beauty, it might not be. It all depended on whether Grey intended to conduct himself like a proper host or if he was in one of his freakish moods.

She closed her eyes in a silent prayer. Everything depended on Grey. And Grey was not in the least dependable.

• • •

A half hour later Catherine and Jennifer stood downstairs, greeting the first guests as they arrived. The rout was being held in the east wing of Greyhaven, which, unlike most plantation houses, had a separate ballroom. Routs elsewhere were usually held in the parlor or even in the entrance hall, which was wide and large enough to be used for a number of purposes in most homes. However, when Grey designed Greyhaven he had added two wings to the typical Georgian plan. One of these wings was a magnificent ballroom, modeled after the ballroom of the governor's mansion. It was a long room with a fireplace at each end. Overhead, four glittering cut-glass chandeliers, known as lusters, were alight with candles. The middle part of the room was bereft of furniture, to permit dancing, but ornately carved Chippendale chairs with ivory damask seats stood along the walls for tired guests to rest their sore feet.

Jennifer's newfound confidence rapidly ebbed as the guests arrived. The men all seemed to be leering at her. The ladies, clad in brilliantly colored satins and brocades with square-cut or round low necklines that all but revealed their nipples, stared at her with a strange mixture of contempt and avid curiosity. Jennifer understood their attitude better now. As a class, the Virginia aristocracy had only recently acquired the money to build grand houses. The women of the planter class were now able to supervise the spinning and dyeing and cooking, rather than doing the hard labor themselves. And consequently, the aristocracy guarded its position zealously. Like English society, Virginia society had become strongly segregated by class. Though an English lord would have thought otherwise, the Virginia planters of the Tidewater firmly believed themselves to be every bit as important as the nobility. It was crucial to maintain their status in society. They were educated, clothed, and married toward that end.

What Grey had done by marrying her, then, had been a slap in the face of every planter in the area. Grey, with his glorious home and his endless acres of fine land stretching along the James River, had not seen fit to wed one of the simpering females of his own class. Instead he had wed an illiterate and uncultured woman, and, she recalled, his original plan had been to keep her exactly as he had found her, clad in a rough homespun gown, filthy and uneducated. He had planned to flaunt an utterly unworthy woman as his wife. She imagined herself standing here greeting her guests in her patched indigo gown and worn leather shoes, her hair greasy and her body filthy, and she shuddered slightly at the thought. How they would have stared at her then!

She had to admit that it would actually have been amusing in a bitter and hateful way, but it would have been horribly cruel to her. She had to wonder if perhaps she was not a little mad to have fallen in love with such an uncaring man.

As though her thoughts had conjured him up, she glanced up from greeting a scornful young lady in a floral-patterned cream brocade gown and saw Grey heading in her direction, coming from the main part of the house. Her breath caught in her throat as she realized all over again how handsome he was. Unlike the other men, attired in pastels like ice blue and lime green, Grey was wearing a gunmetal gray satin coat and waistcoat and black satin knee breeches. His clothes were completely unadorned with the braid, embroidery, or ruffles that the other gentlemen sported. His only adornment was the fine Flemish lace that covered his shirtfront, contrasting strongly with the bronzed skin of his face. He had disdained to wear a wig, or even to powder his hair, and his ebony tresses were gathered into a neat queue at the nape of his neck and secured with a black silk ribbon. His hands were clad in pearl gray gloves, and rather than wearing his tricorne he carried it beneath his arm, as was fashionable on formal occasions. She watched him for a moment, transfixed, staring as though he were the only other person in the room. He was so handsome that it took her breath away. And then he glanced up and saw her, and to her surprise, he stopped short and returned her stare.

God, but she was lovely, he thought, looking at her hungrily. Her gown emphasized the deep green color of her eyes, and the sparkling gold sheen of the fabric glittered in the light from the lusters exactly as her hair did. The light dusting of white lead powder she wore on her face served only to emphasize the golden shade of her complexion. He felt a burst of pride and possessiveness. Clad in satin and lace, she looked like she belonged here, like she had always belonged here. She was beautiful and graceful and everything a planter's wife should be.

Suddenly becoming aware that he had stopped dead in the hall, and that guests were giving him curious looks as they eddied around him, he regained control of himself and stepped forward. He could not believe the strong emotional reactions she provoked.

Damn it, but this attraction he had to her was most annoying.

With these hostile thoughts running through his head, he stopped by her side. Jennifer looked up at him, expecting a compliment on her appearance or at least a civil greeting. Instead, he said in a cool undertone, "For God's sake, smile. No one here knows that such solemnity is your usual expression. They all must think you're suffering from the headache." And with that bit of helpful advice he made his way through the crowd toward the punch bowl, leaving Jennifer staring after him in dismay.

Beside her, Catherine groaned inwardly. She had seen the stunned look in Grey's eyes when he stopped and stared at his wife. Obviously he found her more attractive than ever, and it was all too evident he didn't care for it. And being Grey, he was going to drown his concerns in punch. She was not surprised, only very disappointed.

Hiding her anxiety, she smiled at Jennifer as brightly as though Grey had been civil. "Don't forget that you and Grey are to lead off the minuet," she reminded the girl.

Jennifer nodded, but she did not look as though the

prospect of dancing with Grey pleased her. In fact she hated the thought of it. The only way Grey could stand to touch her, after all, was if he pretended she was Diana. They would dance together, and he would pretend she was another woman. . . .

The thought made her want to run from the mocking eyes and sneering smiles that surrounded her. She felt as though every person in the ballroom knew that Grey despised her, and that they were all laughing at her. Remembering Grey's pointed advice, however, she smiled woodenly at her guests, but it seemed to do little good. Apparently the gentry were determined to be polite only to their social equals. As a finely dressed tavern wench, she rated nothing more than a hostile stare. Even when she began to mingle, the groups she approached ignored her or actually turned satin-clad shoulders upon her, shutting her out.

At long last the music started, the stately strains of the minuet being played on the harpsichord, which had been moved into the ballroom for this event. As Jennifer began to make her way across the room, she was conscious that all eyes were upon her, and everyone seemed to be smirking. She was certain she was not imagining things. They *were* all laughing at her. No doubt, she decided, they knew she'd only recently learned to dance, and they expected to see her make a fool of herself.

Gallantly she squared her shoulders. She would show them that she could dance the minuet as gracefully as any woman in the room.

Then she came to a stunned halt, abruptly realizing why they were all laughing at her. Grey had already stepped into the middle of the floor to lead off the first dance. And Melissa was clinging to his arm.

Jennifer had not seen Melissa Lightfoot and her husband come in. Catherine had invited them, stating that it would appear odd if they were not invited, but she had added that it was highly unlikely that Melissa would dare to come. Yet there she was, dancing with Grey.

Melissa and Grey looked as though they were made for each other, Jennifer realized in an agony of jealousy and humiliation. Both were tall, graceful, and stunningly attractive. And both were cold and utterly heartless.

Feeling as though she had been struck by a bolt of lightning, Jennifer turned and made her way blindly across the floor, heading for the gardens. It was bad enough that all their neighbors were sneering at her, but now her husband was intentionally and deliberately insulting her. She could not tolerate the situation for another minute. Just as she reached the door, however, Catherine materialized next to her, catching her arm.

"Jennifer!" she said urgently.

Jennifer fixed her with a baleful glare. "I'm leaving," she snapped.

"No, you're not." Catherine held her arm more tightly. "They're all watching you to see what you do, Jen. Do you want them to laugh at you?"

"They're already laughing."

"They'll laugh harder. Don't leave, Jennifer. If you do, they'll never accept you. Never."

"I don't care!"

"Do you care what Grey thinks?" Catherine shot back. "Because he's watching you too. He's watching to see if he's won. Please don't let him win, Jennifer. You have the advantage over him, I know you do. He's afraid of you. He's afraid of having you in his arms, or he wouldn't have insulted you so badly. Even Grey has never been this inconsiderate, this outrageously rude, before."

"I am delighted," Jennifer retorted, "that I have inspired him to new levels of rudeness. Now let me go."

"Jennifer—"

"This is all your fault!" Jennifer hissed. Tears burned her eyes, but she refused to let them fall. She was tired of crying over Grey. He simply wasn't worth the trouble. "This was all your idea. Didn't you realize how Grey would treat me?"

"No," Catherine confessed, her eyes full of remorse. "I

thought—I thought perhaps if he realized just how beautiful you are he would fall in love with you."

Jennifer looked up suddenly and met her gaze. Suddenly, unexpectedly, despite the tears scorching her eyes, she smiled, realizing that she had been wrong to snap at Catherine. Her friend had her best interests at heart.

"I see. That's why you insisted on my ball gown being so low-cut. You hoped I would sweep him off his feet, is that it?"

Relieved and heartened at her friend's sudden lightening of mood, Catherine smiled back. "You do look beautiful, Jennifer. If Grey had any sense at all—"

"He doesn't." Jennifer was no longer in a hurry to get outside. She was determined to turn this situation to her advantage. Catherine was right; she could not let Grey win. Not when his behavior was so outrageously vile. "But perhaps . . . How do you think I can get his attention?"

"I would have thought that ball gown would have gotten his attention."

"It did, for a moment." Jennifer thought briefly. "Perhaps I could make him jealous."

Catherine bit her lip. "Perhaps you could," she said cautiously, "except for one thing. The men are not exactly queuing up to ask you to dance."

"No, they're not, are they?" Clearly, she thought, trying to make Grey jealous would be impossible. Perhaps she could attract him instead. "Well . . . perhaps I should flirt with Grey."

Catherine looked even more dubious. "I don't know, Jen. . . ."

Jennifer shrugged. "I might as well try." She was well aware that she might appear even more ludicrous to the avid onlookers, a pitiful wife seeking the attention of her disinterested husband, but she had to try.

The music stopped, and the dancers bowed and curtsied to their partners. Without stopping to think—for had she thought, she surely would have lost her nerve—Jennifer walked across the room to her husband's side, forcing a smile onto her lips. "Are you having a good time?" she inquired, batting her eyelashes as she had seen Melissa do. It was a ridiculous question, she knew, since Grey went out of his way to never enjoy himself. But she had to say something, and it was indicative of how superficial her relationship with her husband was that she could only mouth platitudes.

Grey looked faintly surprised, then pasted a patently artificial smile onto his face. "Of course," he replied, sarcasm dripping from every word. "Mistress Lightfoot and I were just discussing what a charming rout it is."

Horrified, humiliated beyond bearing, Jennifer tore her eyes away from her husband and discovered that he had been in the midst of a conversation with his mistress—most likely an intimate conversation, she realized. She had assumed that Melissa would return to her husband's side after dancing with Grey. Obviously she had been wrong.

Melissa looked beautiful and sophisticated, clad in a midnight blue velvet gown that emphasized the porcelain quality of her complexion and had a neckline so low cut that it would have caused almost any man under ninety to stare. She was a picture of the perfect lady, from her hair, powdered gray and frizzed in the French *tête-de-mouton* style, to the blue silk slippers that peeped out from beneath the hem of her petticoat. Jennifer stared dumbly at the other woman, who looked back with amused contempt.

Rather than following her first impulse and running headlong into the anonymity of the crowd, away from the mocking smiles of her husband and his mistress, Jennifer somehow managed to turn to Melissa and inclined her head slightly. "Mistress Lightfoot," she said with all the courtesy she could muster. "So good to see you again." She turned regally back to her husband and added, "However, I did not intend to interrupt your conversation. If you will excuse me—"

Grey's eyes had watched her with admiring amusement as she discovered her error but covered her mistake with aplomb. Now those silver eyes took on a mischievous sparkle as his hand caught her arm in a grip that looked husbandly but was in fact unbreakable.

"Not at all, my love," he said in a silky voice. "You were not interrupting in the least. Stay a moment and honor us with your presence. I have seen too little of you this past hour."

Appalled, Jennifer realized that his arm was around her shoulders, and the entire room seemed to be staring at them curiously. Judging from the shocked expressions settling onto faces all across the chamber, everyone there knew Melissa was Grey's mistress. And Grey's actions put Melissa on display as surely as they did Jennifer.

Helpless, trapped by her husband's powerful arm, Jennifer stole a glance at Melissa and saw anger and humiliation written clearly on the beautiful face.

Which one of us is he trying to humiliate? she wondered desperately. *And why?*

Grey went on cheerfully, and, it seemed to Jennifer, unnecessarily loudly, "Mistress Lightfoot is the epitome of social graces, my dear. If you wish to emulate a gentlewoman, let it be her. Her manners are impeccable, her behavior irreproachable. She is, in all ways, a perfect example of a lady."

This lecture, delivered with a sardonic smile, caused Melissa's eyes to glitter suspiciously. Of course, Jennifer realized with an unwanted pang of pity, Grey was poking fun at her. From the looks of derision and the outright snickers she could hear from around the room, the relationship between Melissa and Grey was obviously common knowledge.

"And Jennifer, of course," Grey proclaimed into the midst of the mounting silence, "is the perfect wife. She never chatters about nonsensical subjects such as fashion—indeed, she rarely speaks at all. She exists only to serve me. I could not have asked for a better wife."

The muted giggles chopped off abruptly and a horrible quiet settled over the crowd like a shroud. Once again Grey had reminded the gentry that he had chosen a tavern wench, a nobody, over their charming and eligible daughters. Jennifer wanted to faint, simply to escape from the staring eyes, but instead, gathering her courage, she turned to her husband and smiled. In a voice that she somehow kept from shaking she spoke into the silence.

"It is excessively kind of you to say so, sir," she said, smiling while she longed to kick him in the shin—or perhaps higher. Definitely higher. "Nor could I have dreamed of a husband as wonderful as yourself. Not everyone is as fortunate as I was, to wed such a model of gentlemanly behavior." Wrenching her arm from his grasp, she left Grey standing in the middle of the room, a little dumbstruck and a great deal amused by the way she had retaliated.

Trying to avoid giving the avid watchers the impression that she was running away, she crossed the room slowly, with all the dignity she could muster, and paused by the punch bowl, as if to check that the amount of punch left was still sufficient. Only then did she permit herself to open the paneled door that led to the garden and escape from the onlookers. She sincerely hoped she appeared to be a good hostess, rather than a woman on the verge of tears.

In the garden, she found a bench and sat down, shaking, not because of the low temperature, but from distress. Once again she had been reminded of how cruel Grey could be, how willing he was to make her an object of derision among their neighbors solely to amuse himself. She shuddered, remembering the watchful eyes, the ghastly silence, and Grey's hateful, sardonic grin.

And then she heard sobs. Curiosity compelled her to get up and wander quietly down the path that passed through the formal gardens. Not far away she found Mistress Lightfoot huddled on a bench, head in hands, sobbing as though her heart would break.

"Mistress Lightfoot?" she whispered.

"Go away," the woman snapped, trying to sound like her usual haughty self, but her voice broke on a sob.

Jennifer ignored the sharp rebuke and sat next to her. Grey had selfishly humiliated both of them, and now Jennifer found herself in the ironic situation of trying to comfort her husband's mistress. "It's all right," she murmured, laying a gentle hand on Melissa's shoulder. "Don't cry. He isn't worth your tears."

"I'm not crying because of him," Melissa snuffled pathetically. "It was the others, watching. They were all staring. I couldn't—I was so embarrassed—"

"So was I," Jennifer confessed. "But you must stop crying, or when you go back inside, every one of those people will know that you were upset. And that will be an admission of guilt, of a sort."

"You're right, of course." Melissa dabbed ineffectually at her reddened eyes with her fingertips, looked up, and gave a watery smile. "But why are you concerning yourself about me? You must hate me. Especially after he led off the dancing with me instead of you."

"I don't hate you."

"You should. After what I said to you the last time we met—"

"Quite frankly," Jennifer interrupted dryly, "I don't care if you're making love to Grey every afternoon, and twice on Sundays. If you want him, have him and welcome. I have struggled to make friends with the man, to get behind that cold facade of his, and I've slowly come to the conclusion that it isn't worth the effort. Tonight was the last straw. Nothing could be worth that much trouble."

"I don't believe there is anything beneath that facade," Melissa said tightly, swallowing hard as fresh tears fell. "No emotions of any kind. Just stone."

"No, there is something there," Jennifer said, thinking of the letters she had read and reread so many times. "But it's buried so deeply it might as well not exist. And I'm tired of trying to find it. At times I just despise him."

Melissa wiped at her eyes again. "So do I," she admitted in a harsh whisper. "You don't know how much I've regretted becoming his mistress. I only became involved with him because my husband had bedded—" She hesitated, looking straight into Jennifer's eyes, then glancing guiltily away. "Had bedded so many other women, and I wanted to make him jealous. But it never worked. I kept hoping Christopher would notice and become angry, but he never has. He simply doesn't care. And now . . . it's been so many years, I suppose I'm simply used to Grey. But I would so much rather have my husband. . . ."

"Is it too late to make amends with your husband?" Jennifer inquired gently. She did feel sorry for the other woman, trapped in relationships with two cold and indifferent men, but sympathy aside, she saw a chance to part Grey from his mistress. And with true feminine instinct, she struck.

"The whole county knows I'm Grey's mistress," Melissa said bitterly. "It's too late."

"What if we could convince them you weren't?" Jennifer was suddenly struck by an inspiration. Her eyes lit up with a mischievous glow totally foreign to her solemn features. "And revenge ourselves on Grey at the same time?"

She had never sought revenge before in all her life, always accepting whatever happened to her as inevitable. But she was tired of taking mistreatment meekly. For the first time in as long as she could remember, she was not willing to take abuse anymore. She was infuriated. Grey had intentionally and coldly humiliated both of the women in his life, just to amuse himself.

Jennifer was not amused.

Quickly, she outlined her plan to Melissa. Giggling, the two women walked back toward the house.

Every eye turned in their direction when Jennifer and Melissa walked together into the ballroom, smiling like the best of friends. A wave of whispered speculation surged through the chamber as they drifted through the crowd, parting to speak briefly with friends and guests, then meeting again at the enormous silver punch bowl.

Jennifer noted with some relief that Grey was not in the room. Probably he had gone to get something stronger than punch, she decided. The minuets had ended, and slaves were now playing the fiddle and banjar as accompaniment for the more cheerful Virginia reel. She suspected that Grey, with his hatred of gaiety, must certainly despise the reel. Therefore, he had probably beaten a hasty retreat.

Most couples in the room were joining in the dance that had just begun. Some older people, however, stood around the edges of the room watching the merriment. Near the punch bowl sat old Mistress Gordon, whom Melissa had told Jennifer was the worst old gossip in the county. Despite her advanced years, Mistress Gordon had the sharpest ears in the area—not to mention the sharpest tongue. Melissa had assured Jennifer that whatever words she uttered in Mistress Gordon's presence would be spread all over the county in a matter of days.

Jennifer intended to give her a great deal to gossip about.

The two young ladies, drinking glasses of punch, chattered inanities for a few moments while Mistress Gordon appeared to snooze in her chair. Then Melissa said brightly, on cue, "My dear girl, you do look well, indeed. But when are you going to present your husband with a son?"

Jennifer regarded the other woman with a look of sham surprise. "Don't tell me you didn't know!" she exclaimed in a stage whisper she was certain would be audible to the old lady, whose eyes had snapped open.

"Know what?" Melissa inquired innocently.

"My dear, my husband is incapable of siring a child. More than that," she added in a dire tone, stifling her laughter at the avid expression on the shocked old gossip's face, "he is incapable of performing his, er, marital duties, due to a riding accident some years ago. Why, I should have thought everyone knew."

"Heavens, how dreadful for you!" Melissa exclaimed, keeping a straight face only with the greatest difficulty.

"On the contrary, I find it to be a relief. So many women die in childbirth, I was delighted to find myself wed to a man who is unable to get me with child. And it is pleasant to think I will not have to lose my figure," she added, glancing smugly down at her slender waist. "No doubt," she added, "Grey's first wife knew of it too. I understand she had many suitors, but Grey was the one she chose to marry. I imagine she chose him for his, well, inability to become amorous."

Having cast these aspersions on Grey's manhood, the two ladies allowed their conversation to drift to other topics. And when Mistress Gordon hobbled away from her chair and began whispering into ears with a scandalized look on her face, they parted, smiling.

A half hour later, Grey returned to the ballroom, but he did not seek Jennifer out or even glance in her direction. Jennifer drank another glass of punch hastily. It had belatedly occurred to her exactly what Grey was likely to do to her once he discovered the rumor she had spread, assuming he connected the rumor with her—and she was wretchedly certain he would. This time, she realized with a tremor of fear, he would not stop at public humiliation.

Rather abruptly, she decided she needed a breath of fresh air. Leaving the hostess duties to Catherine for the moment, she fled out the door to the garden for the second time that evening.

As she walked down the path between the neatly trimmed boxwoods, she felt her heart, which had inexplicably been pounding, slow to a more normal speed. If only she could stay out here forever, away from Grey and away from the people who scorned her because of her origins. . . .

"Good evening."

Jennifer yelped in a very unladylike fashion and spun about to see Christopher Lightfoot standing just behind her. At the sound of his deep voice, her guilty conscience had imagined Grey had come after her. She gulped a few breaths of the cold air, trying to calm herself. "Good evening," she said politely when her voice was steady.

Christopher Lightfoot looked at her contemplatively. He was dressed elegantly, in a light green striped satin coat, trimmed with large quantities of gold point d'Espagne, and a heavily embroidered waistcoat. He wore a mountainous gray-powdered wig, and on his feet were the light, low-heeled shoes known as pumps. It was evident that he was something of a dandy.

His dark blue eyes narrowed slightly as he remarked idly, "You've certainly been spending a good deal of time in the garden this evening. Can it be that you don't care for the rout?"

"Not at all," Jennifer said. "I simply needed . . . some fresh air. I am enjoying myself immensely."

"Indeed," Christopher said in a voice that indicated he was not fooled. "And yet so few people in that ballroom seem willing to speak to you. So few people . . . except my wife."

Jennifer stared at him in sudden apprehension as he went on, "I must applaud your ingenuity, my dear."

"Ingenuity?" she repeated faintly.

"Absolutely. In one master stroke you revenged yourself on your husband for his unforgivably crass actions and got rid of his mistress. You are a remarkable young woman, just as I suspected when we first met."

"Mistress?"

"Come now," Christopher said with impatience. "You are perfectly capable of speaking in sentences longer than one word. Yes, your husband's mistress. My wife."

Jennifer looked up into his blue eyes and decided that honesty was called for in this situation. "We talked for quite some time," she told him. "She loves you very much."

"She has a peculiar way of showing it," Christopher said dryly.

"Nevertheless, it is true," Jennifer persisted. "I believe—" She hesitated, for what she wanted to say was unforgivably personal, then went on in a rush, "I believe she has merely been trying to get your attention. She feels that you do not love her."

"Small wonder. I do not." At her look of surprise, he said cruelly, "Oh, come now, Mistress Greyson. Are you so naive as to believe that most of us marry for love? On the contrary, most planter marriages are made for land and money. After all, do you love your husband?"

Jennifer paused, intending to give a glib, light reply, but the expression on her face gave her away. "I see that you do fancy yourself in love with him," Christopher went on. "Take my advice. Don't fall in love with him. He is not worthy of your admiration."

"What do you know about my husband?" Jennifer snapped haughtily, in the best imitation of Catherine she could manage.

"A great deal. He and I were once the closest of friends. In fact, we grew up together."

Jennifer's mouth fell open. Friends? Grey had been dallying with the wife of a man who had once counted him as a close friend? "Indeed," she said at last, her brain whirling madly. "Did he—I mean, did—"

"No," Christopher interrupted. He appeared amused by her consternation. "He did not bed my wife while he considered himself my friend. On the contrary, I broke off my friendship with him eight or nine years ago. I—"

He broke off and looked helplessly embarrassed. "Go on," Jennifer prodded. "Why did you stop considering him a friend?"

"I caught him in what I considered to be a cruelty," Christopher confessed. "He was forcing one of the house slaves to, well—"

"I don't believe you!" Jennifer burst out before he could finish. It was all too evident from his hesitation and from his embarrassed expression what he was suggesting. "I have known Grey for most of a year, and I do not believe that he would do such a thing. It is impossible!"

"Grey is capable of a great many things," Christopher continued implacably. The embarrassment that had tinged his features seemed to be gone now. "I think I should warn you that many people believe he murdered—"

"I have heard the rumors," Jennifer interrupted sharply. She remembered Grey's grief-stricken expression as he described how he had found Diana's body. Regardless of what others thought, it was more than obvious to her that Grey was no murderer. "I do not believe them. And if you intend to continue slandering my husband, then I will bid you good night." She turned her back on him and stalked back into the ballroom.

Christopher Lightfoot watched her go, an admiring light in his eyes. "She doesn't believe it," he said to the empty garden. "She doesn't believe it—but she will."

When Jennifer returned to the ballroom, she noticed immediately that the people who had previously snubbed her now seemed more willing to talk to her. Some even waved her over with friendly gestures. From the avid questions they plied her with, she quickly realized that the story of Grey's "infirmity" was sweeping the ballroom and that his neighbors were eager to obtain additional information.

Jennifer was more than happy to help. She cheerfully elaborated on the story, spinning more involved explanations, and suppressing her amusement with an effort.

To her surprise two or three men asked her for the next dance. Choosing a short, portly gentleman for her partner, she made her way easily through the elaborate steps of the quadrille, mentally thanking Catherine for hiring an excellent tutor who had managed to teach her the steps to all the common dances in a short month. At the thought of Catherine she glanced around to see how her sister-in-law was faring, nearly missing a step when she spotted Catherine in the midst of a knot of young men. She wondered if they were interested in her friend or if they were merely seeking more gossip. For Catherine's sake, she hoped it was the former.

When the dance was over and her partner had brought

her a silver cup laden to the brim with punch, Jennifer
courteously declined a dance from another man and stood
briefly by herself, watching the festivities. She was discovering that her high-heeled silk slippers hurt her feet when
she danced.

To her surprise, Melissa Lightfoot approached her, smiling almost shyly. "I believe it is going well," she remarked.
"Virtually everyone in the room seems to be whispering
and looking askance at Grey."

"Good," Jennifer said briefly. Perhaps Grey would discover what humiliation felt like.

Melissa looked across the room. A more stately minuet
was beginning to the strains of the harpsichord. "You have
a very fine harpsichord."

Jennifer's head snapped around at the note of envy in
the other's voice. "Do you play the harpsichord?"

"I love to play."

"So do I," Jennifer admitted, surprised to find that she
and Melissa had something in common. Perhaps, she
mused, they were not as different as she had believed. "In
fact," she confessed, "it is the only ladylike accomplishment I have mastered."

"Do you not care for watercolors?"

Jennifer sighed. Watercolors were definitely not one of
her accomplishments. "The paints always run together. All
my paintings look, well, muddled."

To her surprise, Melissa smiled. "Don't tell anyone . . .
but so do mine."

Before long, they were embroiled in an enthusiastic discussion about the relative merits of Handel and Corelli.
After a few minutes they were approached by several other
young women, who joined the discussion. The conversation was interrupted by the approach of a thin, long-
limbed young man, who asked Jennifer to dance.

She accepted, smiling. The evening had turned out
quite well after all.

•   •   •

Jennifer was seated at the twilight, brushing her long amber hair, when the door to her chamber suddenly burst open. Startled, she turned to see Grey stalking into the chamber.

"Good evening, Grey," she said coolly, as though her husband exploded into her chamber with a deadly look of rage on his features every evening. She took a deep, calming breath and hoped desperately he could not see the fear she felt.

Grey stopped just inches from her and stared down at her wordlessly, his silver eyes icy with fury. Feeling herself to be at a disadvantage, she quickly stood, but he still towered over her. Staring at his satin-clad shoulder, she felt very small and very helpless.

"Do you need something?" she asked brightly, struggling to hide her cowardice. She had hoped against hope that Grey would not find out about the rumor she had started tonight, but all too evidently he had.

Grey glared at her a moment longer, then crossed the room and sat down on the edge of the dark blue coverlet on the mahogany bed. In a low voice which nonetheless shook with rage, he said, "I found myself to be the recipient of a great many peculiar looks this evening. Perhaps you can tell me why."

Jennifer lifted an eyebrow. "Perhaps our guests were curious as to why you chose to humiliate both your wife and your mistress publicly. I know *I* was."

"It was an excessively dull rout."

"And that justified embarrassing us in such a fashion?"

Grey jumped to his feet and advanced on her angrily. "How did you dare spread that groundless rumor about me?"

Jennifer suppressed the urge to back up against the wall. She stood her ground and said haughtily, "Melissa told me in the garden that she regretted ever becoming your mistress. We could only think of one way to extricate her from the situation."

"And to humiliate me in the process!"

"I thought you did not care what your neighbors thought," Jennifer snapped. "Or is it that you are concerned only with what your *female* neighbors think?"

Unexpectedly Grey's taut features relaxed into a grin. With absolute confidence, he retorted, "Our female neighbors will not believe that absurd story."

"Then you have nothing to be angry about, do you?"

Her dark eyes were glinting with humor now, and Grey stared at her in surprise. The little minx looked unbearably pleased with herself!

"Perhaps," he admitted a little reluctantly, warmed more than he cared to admit by her amusement, "I did deserve to be publicly humiliated for my behavior."

"You deserved to be publicly *flogged*," Jennifer told him, but she was unable to entirely suppress her smile.

"Madam," Grey said with mock severity, "have a care. The least you could do is accept my apology."

"What apology?"

"I just said—" Grey paused and mentally reviewed their conversation. He grinned sheepishly. "Well, perhaps you're right. I had intended to apologize, at any rate. But admitting that I should have been humiliated is as close as I can come to an apology. To be honest, I believe it's been some time since I've apologized for my actions. To anyone."

"No doubt," Jennifer said dryly, "your behavior is ordinarily so far above reproach that you have fallen out of the habit."

Grey suddenly burst out laughing. He laughed so hard that he had to sit down on the bed. Jennifer wondered if he was perhaps having some sort of fit. She had never seen him laugh so heartily before.

"Jennifer," he said at last, wiping his watering eyes, "have I told you lately how amazing you are?" He looked up to see her bewildered expression. "No, I imagine I've never told you such a thing at all. I'm a fool, Jennifer. To have humiliated you the way I did tonight—it's a wonder you'll speak to me at all. And I've just realized what a tragedy it would be if I didn't have you to talk to sometimes."

Jennifer realized that he had risen from the bed and was walking slowly toward her, like a wolf stalking its prey. This time, the expression in his eyes did cause her to take a step backward. "What—what are you doing?" she said in a gasp as she found herself against the wall, pinned there by two strong arms and a long, muscular body.

"Why, what do you think, Jennifer?" Grey's response was little more than a whisper. "I'm apologizing to you, my dear."

Before Jennifer had time to do more than take a desperate gulp of air, his lips had found hers. He kissed her, not with the flaring passion of their last encounter, but gently, as though she were something very rare and delicate. Dreamily she felt his arms slide around her waist, and her arms encircled his shoulders in an instinctive response. Her lips parted, her tongue sought his, and she felt in his response a shadow of the passion she knew he was capable of. Yearning to feel that passion directed at herself—not at Diana—she pressed her body against his. Even through the layers of fabric that separated them she could feel his violent reaction. And his kiss deepened, forcing her head backward as he drank his fill of her.

At last he pulled his mouth away from hers, but he did not release his hold on her. She was so damned beautiful, still clad in her gorgeous ball gown but with her dark gold hair tumbling in wanton abandon about her shoulders and down to her waist, that he wanted to hold her against him like this forever. She pressed her face into his shoulder as his arms tightened around her slender waist. "Christ!" he swore under his breath. "Jennifer, don't you know you're playing with fire?"

Jennifer lifted her head and looked deep into his stormy gray eyes. What she saw there made her want to weep with joy. She had affected this cold, angry man. She, and she alone, had made him respond. For the brief moments that he had held her in his arms and kissed her, there had been no ghosts and no other women standing between them. It was written clearly in his face. He wanted *her*, and only her.

"I'm not afraid of you," she whispered gently.

Grey's arms dropped from her waist. "You should be," he said coldly, and left the chamber. Jennifer stared after him as the door to her chamber slammed shut and the sound of his footsteps disappeared down the stairs.

He was going, she realized bleakly, to his study. To be with Diana.

SEVENTEEN

Jennifer awakened the next morning to the sound of hooves on the road outside. Jumping from the damask-draped bed, she ran to the window and peered through the wooden slats of the venetian blinds just in time to see Grey's bay stallion disappearing behind the trees. She frowned slightly. Grey did love to ride—it was really the only activity he had any enthusiasm for, except drinking—but rarely did he ride so early in the day, and generally he waited for her to join him.

Still frowning, Jennifer summoned the young black girl who served as her maid. Once hooked into a topaz-colored woolen gown, she ran from her chamber and down the stairs in a most unladylike fashion.

Catherine was still eating breakfast in the dining chamber when Jennifer appeared. Seating herself at the table, Jennifer nodded good morning to her. "Has Grey gone somewhere?" she inquired, trying to sound casual, as though the answer was really of no interest to her whatsoever.

Catherine lifted her eyebrows in her characteristic gesture of surprise. "Didn't he tell you? He's gone to Williamsburg. He thought he'd be gone a few days."

"Williamsburg?" Jennifer repeated. "I thought he rarely left Greyhaven."

The older woman shrugged. "True. But he does go to Williamsburg sometimes, to—"

"To do what?"

"Never mind," Catherine said faintly.

"Catherine," Jennifer said in annoyance. "What does he do when he is in Williamsburg?"

It was a measure of how far their relationship had progressed that Jennifer should dare to demand an explanation. When she had first arrived here she would not have dared to even ask. But she no longer felt herself to be Catherine's inferior. They were friends. Catherine swallowed and looked across the table at her, clearly embarrassed.

"Grey usually says he's, er, going to visit friends."

"Oh," Jennifer said in relief. "Is that all?"

"Jennifer . . ." Catherine sighed. "Grey doesn't have any friends. Not in Williamsburg, at any rate."

Jennifer looked at her blankly, then suddenly went scarlet. "Do you mean to tell me—"

"Grey goes to Williamsburg when he's grown tired of his mistress," Catherine clarified bluntly, her cheeks turning pink with embarrassment.

Thanks to her actions last night, Grey no longer had a mistress, and Jennifer had assumed that state of things would continue. But evidently Grey did not agree. The memory of Grey's mouth against hers flashed into her mind, and she realized suddenly that he had not gone to Williamsburg because he was bored. He had run away. She knew as surely as she knew her own name that their kiss had affected him, despite the cold way he had left the chamber. That kiss had meant something to him. She *knew*.

And she knew, too, that Grey's first response to emotions of any kind was always to run away.

"Damnation," she said out loud. "He is a fool."

Catherine looked at her strangely. She had rarely heard Jennifer express disapproval of anyone before, let alone utter a curse. "I'll admit," she said slowly, wondering exactly why Grey's departure should provoke such a strong response, "that he should have told you that he was leaving—"

"He should never have gone," Jennifer said sharply.

The chestnut eyebrows lifted, then Catherine suddenly grinned. "I should think you'd be glad to be rid of his sulky presence for a few days."

"Are you suggesting that I should be glad that my husband finds me so unsuitable that he seeks—*friendship* elsewhere?" Jennifer demanded icily.

"You've never been overly concerned by his 'friendship' with Melissa," Catherine pointed out, her smile fading somewhat as she realized that Jennifer was genuinely, and uncharacteristically, angry. After the way Grey had humiliated her last night—and after Jennifer had humiliated him in return—she could not imagine why Jennifer was not happy to see him leave. At times even she herself was glad to see the back of her brother's heels for a few days. Sisterly love had its limits, which Grey pushed all too frequently.

"That was—" Jennifer pushed the porcelain plate piled with ham and eggs away and stood up, stalking restlessly to the window. Staring out at the green expanse of lawn, she went on, "Oh, I don't know. That seemed to be established somehow. And I don't think Melissa will be a problem anymore, for we worked out our differences last night. And now, just as soon as I get rid of her, what does Grey do but—oh, I could just kill him!"

This outburst was so unlike placid, peaceful Jennifer that Catherine gaped at her for a few minutes before any words could emerge. "Jennifer! Are you saying that you want a *real* marriage with him?"

Jennifer glanced over her shoulder in annoyance, her green eyes dark with anger. "Why not? Is there something I should know? Does my husband have the French pox?"

"I certainly hope not! But—but Grey is hardly the most approachable—"

"Other women seem to find him approachable enough," Jennifer said irritably. "I'm beginning to think that every woman in the colony has shared his bed. Every woman except me, that is. And I am getting bloody tired of it!"

Alarmed by her sister-in-law's vehement tone, Catherine tried to calm her. "Jen," she said evenly, "there's nothing you can do about it, so you may as well resign yourself to the facts. You know that all husbands seek out, well, companionship. Um, variety. Whatever it is that men want just can't be fulfilled by one woman. A wife's first duty is to provide heirs and secondly, to ignore any little—"

"Grey won't let me fulfill the first duty," Jennifer interrupted scathingly, "so I don't see why I should have to fulfill the second. Why should I stand idly by and watch him—"

"I'm not suggesting that you watch him!" Catherine said, and unexpectedly her shoulders began to rock with laughter. "I'm sure whatever he plans to do in Williamsburg he plans to do in private."

Jennifer turned to face her, and Catherine saw a faint smile appear on her lips. "You're probably right," she agreed. "Grey intends to have his fun privately. I doubt he'd enjoy an audience at all."

Hearing the mischievous tone in the other's voice, Catherine suddenly choked in horror. "Jennifer, I didn't mean—oh, Jen, you wouldn't!"

Jennifer's smile widened, and she looked positively feline, like a cat about to catch a particularly tasty bird. "Grey would be furious if I were to follow him to Williamsburg," she mused.

"He would be outraged," Catherine agreed readily. "He would probably kill you."

"Oh, I doubt that," Jennifer said sweetly. "He was very angry last night, and he didn't kill me. In fact, he kissed me."

Catherine's gray eyes went wide. "He kissed you?"

Jennifer nodded.

"Grey kissed you? My brother? Your husband? The same Grey who sulks in the study all day, every day? *That* Grey kissed you?"

"It may be hard to believe, but it's true. Grey kissed me. And I liked it. I would like to encourage more behavior of that sort in the future. But it's a certainty that Grey won't be kissing me if he's already kissing someone else. Which leaves me with only one alternative—to make certain he doesn't get involved with another woman."

"But Jennifer—" Catherine paused, trying frantically to formulate some sort of objection. "He'll most likely be frequenting his usual haunts, where the gentlemen play at dice and drink ale together. You can't walk into a chamber full of men. You *can't*. It would be scandalous."

"I have a plan."

"But—" Catherine began again, then stopped at the stubborn look on her friend's face. "Never mind," she said with resignation. "If you're that determined to go, there's nothing I can do to stop you."

Jennifer smiled. "Then let's get packed."

Catherine shot her a look of absolute horror and stood up. "Are you suggesting that I should go with you?"

"Of course," Jennifer said reasonably. "I'd get lost if I were to go by myself. Besides, it would be dangerous to go alone."

"No more dangerous than it would be for two women alone!"

"We'll take slaves. Please, Catherine, I don't want to go without you."

The look Jennifer fixed on her was so appealing that Catherine felt her resolve weakening. "I would like to, Jen, but—I can't ride. I'm lame."

"We'll take the carriage," Jennifer said promptly. "The roads are wide enough to accommodate a carriage between here and Williamsburg, are they not?"

"It isn't wise to take a carriage this time of year," Catherine objected. "It rains too frequently. The wheels are likely to become bogged down."

"Then we'll ride," Jennifer decided. "Grey said you were injured when you were thrown from a horse. He also said you were perfectly capable of riding a horse, but that you were afraid to."

Catherine's eyes flashed with fury, just as Jennifer had known they would. "That's not true! I'm not afraid of anything, and you know it."

Jennifer tossed down the challenge lightly, knowing that Catherine would accept it. The Greysons were so predictably proud. "Then prove it," she said, "and ride to Williamsburg with me."

If the truth were to be told, Grey's assessment had been absolutely correct. Catherine was deathly afraid of horses. But her friendship with Jennifer had come to mean a great deal to her. And she realized, perhaps more so than Jennifer did, how angry Grey was likely to be when he found that his wife had followed him to Williamsburg. She could not leave Jennifer alone to face his wrath.

Thus it was that two tired and dusty women, along with a small entourage of three slaves, rode into the capital of Williamsburg four hours later. Jennifer glanced around with ever-growing interest. "It's so big!" she marveled.

In truth, by English standards Williamsburg was a very small town. Its population was only about a thousand, including slaves, who composed almost half of the population. At public times twice a year, when the courts were in session, the town's population temporarily doubled, so there were many vacant houses. Also, many of the planters kept a town house here for occasional use. Consequently, the town looked considerably larger than it actually was.

In the last century, Williamsburg, built on the high ground between the James and the York rivers, had been a tiny settlement known as Middle Plantation. However, when it became evident that Jamestown, located as it was on a swampy and ague-infested island, was an inappropriate and unhealthy place for the capital of the colony, the capital was moved to Middle Plantation and the town renamed in honor of the king.

The tiny procession rode slowly down the main street, which was a mile long. (After a rainstorm, the street became so muddy that some Virginians joked that it was also a mile deep.) At the west end of the street stood the main building of the College of William and Mary, which was a divinity school. Most of the planters' sons were also educated here, although few remained in school long enough to obtain a degree. Most simply got the minimal amount of education deemed necessary to be cultured gentlemen and then returned to their plantations. At the far end of the street stood the Capitol. Along both sides of the street were small clapboard houses, most painted a neat white, and larger brick houses—though none, Jennifer noted proudly, were as fine or as large as Greyhaven. Every house sat upon a fenced lot of at least one half acre, as required by the town law.

As they rode along toward the Capitol she became aware of the stench that seemed to rise from the street and permeate the air. Having lived in the country all her life, she had never considered how the refuse of a thousand people and their horses would smell. She wrinkled her nose, seeing—and smelling—large piles of manure everywhere. In a house just ahead of them a window opened and a mob-capped slave dumped the contents of a chamber pot onto the street.

Jennifer made a mental note not to walk under the windows in town.

Catherine saw her expression and smiled. "It is quite noisome, isn't it? I never cared much for town. But at least the smell is bearable in the winter. You can just imagine how malodorous it is in July."

Jennifer breathed a silent prayer of thanks that it was still January. Then her attention was arrested by a structure to her left. She reined in her horse and stared. "Catherine, look!"

To their left was a wide green dotted with grazing sheep. But it was not the bucolic beauty of the scene that caught her attention. Beyond the green loomed tall brick-and-iron gates, marking the entrance to the most striking home Jennifer had ever seen. It was even more spectacularly beautiful than Greyhaven. "Who lives there?" she demanded.

"That's the governor's mansion," Catherine explained.

"It looks like a palace," Jennifer breathed in awe.

"Some people call it that." Unimpressed, for she had seen the two-and-a-half-story edifice a score of times,

Catherine sent her mount forward. Jennifer tore her attention away from the magnificent house and followed her.

They passed another green filled with bustling activity. Here people seemed to be engaged in the selling and buying of all sorts of commodities, from firewood to produce. She had never seen so many people in one place in her life. As they rode on, she noted that there were shops and taverns interspersed with the houses that lined the street. No doubt Grey was staying at one of the myriad taverns. But which one? She voiced the question to Catherine.

Catherine shrugged. "I think he usually stays at the Raleigh, up toward the Capitol. Grey doesn't tell me these things; I've assumed it from things he's said. He likes to quote a motto he says is over the mantel in one of the rooms there—'Hilaritas sapientiae et bonae vitae proles.'"

"What does that mean?" Jennifer inquired. Only recently literate in English, she naturally had no knowledge at all of Latin. Nor was an understanding of Latin required to be a lady. Needlepoint was a much more important accomplishment.

" 'Jollity, the offspring of wisdom and good living.' "

"Singularly inappropriate in Grey's case," Jennifer commented dryly.

As they rode down the main street, Jennifer continued to exclaim over the town. The main road was actually wide enough to accommodate two carriages side by side—a thing unheard of in her experience. Rarely had she seen a road wide enough for two horses to ride side by side. Williamsburg, she decided, was a remarkable town. She wished a little plaintively that Grey had brought her here voluntarily, then pushed the thought aside. She was here now. And she would make what she could of the opportunity.

Catherine reined in her mount in front of a long, story-and-a-half structure with white clapboard walls. "I gather you want to stay at the Raleigh?" she said, trying to conceal her relief that she would soon be off the back of her horse and safely on her own two feet again.

"No," Jennifer said decisively. "I don't want Grey to know I'm here yet."

"I don't understand. Why would you want to go to all the trouble of coming to Williamsburg and not let Grey know you're here?"

"I'll explain later," Jennifer said firmly. She did not care to tell Catherine her plan until the time had come to implement it, for she knew perfectly well that Catherine would object. "Where is another respectable ordinary where we could stay? Would that one be acceptable?" She pointed across the street to another white-painted building. The sign read Wetherburn's Tavern.

"I suppose so," Catherine agreed. "Even though Henry Wetherburn died a few years ago, it's well thought of—if not as fine as the Raleigh." She turned her horse toward the other building and dismounted with ill-concealed gratitude.

When dusk fell over the town, Jennifer explained the details of her plan to Catherine, and the older woman was just as appalled as Jennifer had expected. "Have you gone mad?" she demanded. "I told you that you cannot simply walk into the Apollo Room. Don't you think Grey will be infuriated when he sees you?"

"No," Jennifer said calmly. "Because he won't recognize me." She gestured down at the clothes she wore.

Catherine stared at her, caught between disapproval and admiration for her friend's courage and ingenuity. Jennifer had found a cache of old clothing from Grey's youth in a clothespress at Greyhaven. Now she stood arrayed in a young man's finery—dove gray knee breeches and bottle green coat and waistcoat. The waistcoat was embroidered with gold thread, and the coat was trimmed with braid. Her slender calves were encased in white stockings, and she wore a pair of old-fashioned, square-toed black shoes with silver buckles.

"How could he recognize me?" she asked reasonably.

Catherine studied her friend. The girl's breasts, which she had bound with a long strip of linen, were hidden fairly well by the loose-fitting coat, as well as by the ruffles that covered her shirtfront. The breeches clung indecently to her hips, but that was concealed well enough by the long coat, which fell almost to her knees. Only the slender curve of her calves was obviously female. "From the neck down," she admitted reluctantly, "you do look like a youth of sixteen or so. But Jennifer, what are you going to do about your hair? You can't just pull it into a queue. No man wears his hair *that* long. And besides, Grey would recognize its color instantly."

"I thought of that already," Jennifer said. Turning, she caught up a mound of black hair from the bed and put it over her bound hair. "I found this bobwig." Bobwigs were an informal wig that did not require powdering. Over the wig she placed a tricorne, then turned to Catherine expectantly. "Well?"

"I don't think he'll recognize you," Catherine had to admit. "But what exactly are you going to do?"

Jennifer's bright smile faded slightly. "I'm not sure," she admitted. "But if he *is* looking for a mistress, I plan to do everything I can to prevent his finding one."

A few moments later, Jennifer stepped out of the tavern into the darkened town. Golden candlelight streamed from the windows of homes and ordinaries, and rowdy groups of men tramped down the street, carrying tin lanthorns punched with holes that cast wavering shadows. There was enough light to make her way easily over to the Raleigh. She concentrated on walking quickly and purposefully, like a man, rather than taking slow, tiny steps as Catherine had drilled into her for so many months.

Entering the Raleigh, she made her way to the Apollo Room, guided by the sound of male voices raised in cheerful discussion and the smell of Virginia tobacco. She entered the room and crossed to sit at a table in the dimly lit corner, where she took the opportunity to survey her surroundings.

The atmosphere in the room reminded her of her uncle's

tavern, with its noisy tables of men and smoke-filled atmosphere, but it was clearly a much more prosperous ordinary. Its paneled walls were painted blue, and there was
dentil crown molding along the ceiling. The unvarnished
pine-planked floors were marred by the passage of many
booted feet, and the sturdy oak tables had been scarred by
dice boxes and innumerable tankards of ale. It was evident
that this was a popular gathering place for men. Above the
mantel she saw the gilded words Catherine had quoted,
Hilaritas sapientiae et bonae vitae proles.

She glanced around the crowded room, looking for
Grey, and spotted him easily at a table in the center of the
room. Despite Catherine's assertion that he had no friends
in Williamsburg, he was sitting with a crowd of men, all
drinking from pewter tankards and engaged in boister-
ously vulgar conversation. At least, she thought in relief, he
was not with a woman at this moment.

So relieved was she to see him alone that she allowed
herself to indulge in the luxury of staring at him, admiring
every detail of his handsome face. As though he felt her
stare, he turned and looked in her direction. A tiny frown
creased his forehead, an expression that suggested that she
seemed familiar but that he was unable to place her. Jennifer looked away hastily. To complete her disguise, she
took a foot-long clay pipe such as gentlemen smoked from
her pocket, filled it with tobacco, and lit it from the candle
on her table. The blue smoke curled in front of her face,
obscuring her from his vision. Grey looked away, apparently concluding that he did not know the young boy staring at him from the dimly lit table.

The scent of the acrid smoke made her want to cough,
although she was wise enough not to try to inhale through
the pipe. She took the pipe from her mouth and held it,
straining to hear the conversation at Grey's table above the
general babble of voices.

"Tom," one of the men was saying to a redheaded young
man who sat next to Grey, "don't try to keep up with Grey
here. He can drink you under the table."

"I want another ale," the young man insisted. He did, Jennifer thought, look a trifle woozy. Obviously he did not need another tankard of ale.

"Now, Tom," another man said, grinning jovially, "why don't you have something a little more suited to your age? Apple juice, perhaps?"

"Ale," the redheaded youth insisted.

"Young Mr. Jefferson here is studying law with George Wythe in town," the first man explained to Grey. "He studies all day and thinks he should revel all night. He'll have a devil of a head in the morning, though, if he keeps on this way."

Grey grinned at the young man. "Let him have his ale," he said. "You can't tell these young pups anything; they have to learn from experience. Tomorrow, when he's bent over the chamber pot all day, perhaps he'll learn the wisdom of not overindulging. Or perhaps not. After all," he added, quoting the motto over the fireplace, " 'jollity is the offspring of wisdom.' Perhaps it's the father of wisdom as well."

"Well said, old fellow," Thomas Jefferson said blearily. "Let's have another ale."

Jennifer's attention was jerked away from the men's conversation by the approach of a serving wench. Clad in a mob cap and a homespun gown colored a bright yellow with the dye made from Queen Anne's lace, the girl smiled down at Jennifer. "What'll ye 'ave, lad?"

Jennifer stared at her, caught in a web of memories. It was as though she were staring at herself a year ago. The girl was unwashed, uneducated, and clad no better than a slave. And unlike Jennifer, she would never have the opportunity to wear silk gowns and to play the harpsichord, or to pursue whatever dreams she might have. She would be a tavern maid until she married, or until she died. As Jennifer should have been.

Tearing her gaze away from the girl, she said hastily, in an artificially low voice, "Ale, if you please."

The girl, however, had noticed her fascinated stare.

"Anything else I can get ye, darlin'?" she inquired huskily, leaning over so that Jennifer had a better view of her cleavage. Jennifer choked back a horrified giggle. Catherine was right. She should not have come here. She was sitting in a roomful of rowdy men, spying on her husband, and rebuffing a pass from a tavern wench. This was not a situation a true lady would have gotten herself into.

"Just the ale," she said curtly.

The girl shrugged and walked away, her hips swaying in a blatantly sexual motion. Jennifer wondered if she herself would have been reduced to selling her sexual favors for cash if Grey had not married her. Certainly her uncle would not have passed up any opportunity to make money for long. At seventeen, she had been relatively innocent. Now, at eighteen, she knew what sex was and just how much men enjoyed it. And she also knew they were sometimes willing to pay for it.

Turning her attention back to the men, and putting down the pipe, which had gone out, she saw that the conversation had turned to politics. To her surprise, Grey was speaking. She had never thought he cared a whit for political issues.

"The Crown cares nothing for our well-being," he drawled, apparently in answer to another man's comment. "England limits us to producing nothing but raw materials and prohibits us from shipping our tobacco in any but English vessels. How many of us shipped with the Dutch until recently?"

There was a grumble of assent around the table.

"And now they have levied taxes on us, simply because England's coffers were depleted during the late war with France. I say England does not have the right."

"Treason, man. Treason!" objected one of the other men.

"Is it treason to object to taxation without any sort of representation?" Grey asked in a reasonable tone. "I don't believe so. England cares nothing for the well-being of Virginia planters. If she did—"

He broke off abruptly as the door to the room opened

and an older man, perhaps forty-five or fifty, walked swiftly in. He had silver-gray hair, and rather strange light blue eyes. Despite his age he was decidedly handsome. He stopped short as he passed Grey's table, and Jennifer looked around in confusion as the chamber suddenly became nearly silent.

"Greyson," he snarled. "What the hell are you doing here?"

Grey glanced up at him. Knowing her husband as she did, Jennifer rather expected him to leap to his feet and confront the man for his rude tone. Instead Grey remained seated, and his attitude and expression were strangely respectful.

"Good evening, Trev," he said calmly.

"I've told you before," the other man said in an aggressive tone, "to stay the hell out of Williamsburg."

Grey shrugged. "You don't own Williamsburg, Trev," he said in a politely regretful voice.

"Get out of here."

"I fear I cannot," Grey said without any change of expression. "I'm discussing business with my friends here. Would you care to join us for an ale?"

"I'd sooner rot in hell," the man he had called Trev growled.

"I'm sorry you feel that way," Grey said softly.

Jennifer watched from the corner, bewildered. She had never seen Grey take such abuse from someone so calmly. In her experience, Grey had always been willing to fight, with words if not with fists. His cool acceptance of the other man's ugly words was more than surprising, it was downright unprecedented.

Grey turned his attention back to his drink, apparently hoping the other man would pass the table and go away, but he did not. "You bloody bastard," he said viciously, and Jennifer began to suspect that he had had some ale prior to coming here. In her experience men did not ordinarily act so aggressively unless they were drunk. "You goddamned inebriated fool. I want you out of here *now*."

Jennifer saw Grey's jaw tighten at the insults, but he did not stand to confront Trev, nor did he leave. He simply took another swig of his ale. The men at his table were beginning to look embarrassed, possibly because he was so unwilling to fight. The insults the other man had vented should have provoked any man, except the most cowardly, into a rage.

Jennifer did not think Grey was a coward. No, there was something else going on here, some undercurrent of which she was not yet aware. She watched the drama that was unfolding with fascination.

"Now, Trev," one of the other men at the table said. "Why don't you join us for a drink and forget everything you've said? Grey has as much right to be here as you do."

The older man suddenly reached down and caught Grey by the front of his coat, hauling him upright. Due to Grey's great size, it took a good deal of strength to perform such a feat. Obviously the older man was still in excellent condition, despite his age. He was tall, although it was evident that Grey stood two or three inches taller. The two men stood nose to nose, staring at each other. On Trev's face was an expression of belligerence. Grey wore an expression of resignation.

"Now, Trev—" the man at the table began again, just before Trev's fist slammed into Grey's cheekbone.

Jennifer suppressed a yelp of shock and horror as Grey's head was snapped to the side by the force of the other man's blow. He staggered but did not fall. Looking into the other man's eyes, he said patiently, as if explaining something to a small child, "Trev, I won't fight you. *I won't.*"

The second blow knocked him sprawling backward. He fell toward Jennifer's table, collapsing in a heap nearly at her feet. Jennifer looked at the men, all of whom looked unbearably embarrassed, and she realized none of them was going to come to Grey's defense. They all wore the uncomfortable expressions of men who were friends of both combatants and who could not choose sides.

But *she* could choose sides.

As Trev stepped forward, she came to her feet and strode past her husband, who was sitting up woozily and beginning to struggle to his feet. She stood in front of Trev and stared at him coolly. "Leave him alone," she commanded.

Trev looked down at her with amusement. She was some nine inches shorter than he was, and the men's clothing she wore did not disguise the fact that she was slender and not particularly well muscled. It was all too obvious that she was no threat to him. "Out of my way, stripling," he said, pushing her aside.

Jennifer caught his arm with all her strength and managed to shove him off balance. He staggered back, facing her, and his amused expression faded. Instead he looked irritated by what he must have thought was a fifteen- or sixteen-year-old boy interfering in a tavern fight. He stepped forward, a menacing expression on his face.

She really had no choice. She was not going to permit this man to hone his fighting skills on her husband. Pulling her knife from her pocket, she held it easily in front of her. "I said leave him alone," she said quietly.

Trev stared at her, and at the knife held expertly in her hand, in startled disbelief. Then he looked over her head at something behind her.

"Hiding behind children again, I see, Greyson," he snarled contemptuously. "I'm not afraid of your little bodyguard, but you—you simply aren't worth the trouble, you son of a bitch." He turned his back on them both, the arrogant set of his shoulders eloquently conveying the scorn he felt, and strode out the door.

Jennifer turned to see that Grey had regained his feet and was towering over her, looking down at her in puzzlement. "Have we met?" he inquired.

She dared to glance up into his face, seeing the beginnings of a bruise on his left cheekbone and an eye that would become black shortly, then averted her eyes hastily, lest he recognize her. "I'll explain later," she said shortly.

"Right now we're going to leave." She strode off across the room, and Grey followed her, more out of curiosity than because he felt any need to obey her commands.

"Are you staying here at the Raleigh?" she inquired, taking care to keep her voice in an artificially low register, as they stepped out of the room together.

Grey nodded.

"Good. Then take me to your chamber. That bruise should be taken care of at once."

Slightly amused by the way this slim youth was daring to command him, he led her up the narrow stairs. When traveling, most men slept in common chambers that they shared with several other men. Grey, however, preferred a private room. He had paid the innkeeper sufficient coin to guarantee that he would not have to listen to another man's snoring.

"Sit down," she commanded once they were inside his room and he had lit a candle.

Grey eyed her with amusement in the flickering light and did not sit down. "Who are you?" he repeated. "You look familiar somehow, but I don't recall that we've met."

"We've met," she said curtly.

"Indeed. What is your name?"

Jennifer wet a cloth with the pitcher of water on the washstand. "I don't wish to tell you. Sit down so that I can tend to your bruises."

Grey stubbornly refused to sit. He did not take orders from fifteen-year-old boys. "You have already admitted that we've met. What possible harm could it do to remind me of your name, so that I can thank you for what you did in there?"

"I don't see why you should thank me," she said sharply. "You were perfectly capable of defending yourself against that man. Truly, I don't understand why you didn't."

"I couldn't. He was once my friend. And my father-in-law."

Jennifer turned around and stared at him, so startled by this revelation that she forgot to keep her eyes averted. That vitriolic, angry man had been Diana's father. That explained why his odd blue eyes had looked so familiar. Jennifer had looked at the portrait of Diana frequently enough to remember that she had ice blue eyes.

"You seem surprised," Grey observed, seeing the way her eyes widened in shock. He could not see the color of the youth's eyes in the dim light, yet something about those wide, dark eyes was strangely familiar. It only reinforced his earlier certainty that he had met this boy before.

Jennifer swallowed. At this point, if he realized who she was he was likely to kill her, just as Catherine had predicted. She wished that she had listened to Catherine and never embarked upon this ridiculous adventure.

"I have to go," she said faintly, dropping the cloth and hastening toward the door.

Grey caught her arm easily. "I want to know your name before you go."

"Let go of me!" she protested, trying to wrench loose from his grasp.

Suddenly Grey's expression darkened. She was not strong enough to be male. Her impotent efforts to escape made that quite clear. And her voice had drifted up into a higher register with anger. To confirm his impossible suspicion, he caught her chin between his fingers and cruelly forced her head up.

A pair of unmistakable green eyes, blazing with fury, glared up into his own.

He yanked off her tricorne and the bobwig, revealing her dark golden hair. His expression was slowly becoming murderous, just as Jennifer had feared. "What the hell are *you* doing here?" he bit out, still holding her wrist to prevent escape.

Desperate to get away from him, Jennifer aimed a kick at his shin. Grey yelped as her leather-clad toe made contact with his leg, but he did not let go, only tightened his grip with fury. "Sit down!" he snapped, pushing her down into a chair. Spinning on his heel, he bolted the door.

When he turned back his expression was still that of a snarling wolf. "And now," he said in a cool voice that belied the fury burning in his eyes, "you are going to explain to me exactly what you are doing in Williamsburg. And why you are dressed like a boy. And exactly what the hell you were doing in the Apollo Room, of all places."

Jennifer swallowed nervously, then raised her eyes to his and confessed the truth. "I was looking for you."

"Why?"

His tone was not in the least encouraging, but Jennifer stumbled on. "Well, Catherine said—that is, she thought—well, we understood that you were here to look for a—a lightskirts, if you will—"

"You thought I came to Williamsburg to look for a mistress?"

Jennifer nodded miserably. "And I was going to stop you."

Grey ignored the odd sensation he felt at the realization that she cared whether or not he had a mistress. His anger drained away abruptly. "And how," he drawled with sardonic amusement, "did you plan to do that?"

"I thought I would follow you—"

"Spy on me, you mean."

"That . . . is one way of looking at it," Jennifer admitted. "And then, if you picked out a mistress, I would stop you."

"How?" Grey inquired. "By pulling a knife on her?"

The thought was so absurd that Jennifer had to suppress her smile. "I suppose that might have worked. Actually," she admitted in embarrassment, "I didn't have a specific plan."

Grey looked at her down-bent head. She had been jealous, jealous enough to make her follow him to Williamsburg, and for some reason the thought filled him with pleasure. She cared enough about him to be distressed at the notion that he was looking for a mistress. No one had cared about him that much for a long time. He knew he should be angry with her, but he could not bring himself to be so much as annoyed. She *cared* about him.

"Jennifer," he said at last, in an unusually gentle tone, "I was not here to look for a mistress."

Her head snapped up. "Really?"

"Really," he confirmed. I can see why Catherine made that assumption, because the fact is that I have come here before for purposes of, er, diversion, but the truth is simply that I . . ."

He broke off and managed to look embarrassed. "I came to Williamsburg to find you a Christmas present," he told her.

"A what?" Jennifer uttered, looking at him as though he had gone mad.

"You went to a lot of trouble to write that piece of music for me," Grey explained in a rush, "and I decided I should get you something. I haven't been able to get to Williamsburg before now, since you ladies have been so wrapped up in the plans for that damned rout. But this morning I decided I should come here and find you your present." He looked unbearably embarrassed. It was obvious that he hated being caught in a kindness. Jennifer almost laughed at his expression.

"That was . . . very kind of you," she managed at last.

"And naturally," Grey went on in his most sardonic tone, "just when I was trying to do something nice for a change, you and Catherine decided I was up to something evil and underhanded, and you had to come after me to find out what it was."

At his disgruntled tone Jennifer could not restrain her laughter anymore. "Well, Grey," she protested, giggling, "you could not possibly have expected me to imagine you came to Williamsburg for such a noble purpose!"

Grey grinned back at her, the honest grin of amusement that made him look ten years younger. "I suppose not," he conceded graciously, delighted by her laughter. He had never seen her laugh so freely before. His grin widened, and he winced, having forgotten the bruise that marred his cheekbone.

"Oh, I forgot!" Jennifer said in sudden alarm at his pained expression. "Sit down. We should have applied cold water to your bruises at once."

Grey meekly sat on the edge of the bed and permitted her to press the cloth against his face. "A bruise or two won't kill me, Jen," he told her, amused by her feminine horror. Trust a woman to get upset over a black eye, he thought wryly.

Jennifer blinked, slightly startled at the casual way he had shortened her name. Catherine called her Jen sometimes, but from Grey it sounded almost like . . . an endearment. She looked into his one good eye.

"By the way," Grey added, and his voice sounded huskier somehow. "I want to thank you for coming to my defense."

"I owed that to you," Jennifer said softly, thinking of the long-ago night he had struck her uncle and saved her from a merciless beating. "But tell me—why was that man so angry to see you? I gather he was Diana's father, but—"

Grey's lips tightened. He did not particularly want to discuss the matter, but he supposed Jennifer was entitled to an explanation. "His name is Trevelyan Lancaster," he said shortly. "He was Diana's father. He is a wealthy merchant, originally from Norfolk, who lives in a very beautiful brick house on the village green, near the governor's mansion. And by the way, he is Kayne O'Neill's brother-in-law. He and Kayne married sisters."

"Then he's Carey's uncle," Jennifer said softly, without thinking.

"That's right," Grey agreed, wondering how the hell she knew Carey O'Neill. He was too absorbed in explaining his relationship to Trev, however, to let the matter concern him overmuch. "Trev gave me permission to wed his daughter, and he approved of me then. But—" He paused and took a deep breath. "He thinks I killed Diana."

Jennifer said nothing, only stared at him with stunned green eyes.

"At the time," Grey went on with obvious difficulty, "I was a suspect. Everyone was, really. But we . . . we never found out who the killer was. I had had an argument with

Diana that day, and at the time I was such a hotheaded young fool, a lot of people assumed I had killed her. Trev thinks so. And he's never stopped believing it."

Carey, Jennifer remembered, believed it too. No doubt Trevelyan Lancaster had convinced him of it. But Kayne O'Neill clearly did not believe it, or he would not continue to count Grey among his friends.

"Someone apparently told him I was in Williamsburg," Grey went on uncomfortably, "and he came to the Apollo Room to punish me for—for killing his daughter. He's come after me before. He hates me. But I don't hate him, and I can't bring myself to strike him, or even to argue with him."

"He's a fool," Jennifer said softly, hating the tormented expression in his silver eyes. "Only a fool could believe that you could murder anyone."

Grey took her hand blindly and clutched it tightly, as though clinging to her for support. "Thank you for that," he whispered raggedly. "Thank you for believing in me when no one else does."

Jennifer threaded her fingers through his, trying to convey wordlessly that she did believe in him. She sat down beside him on the bed, her arm sliding around his shoulders in a comforting gesture. They sat that way for a few quiet moments. Then Grey opened his eyes and looked down at their entwined hands.

He could not remember the last time he had held a woman's hand. Even Diana had been too remote to permit such a casual yet intimate gesture of affection. And he had certainly never felt enough affection for Melissa, or any other woman whose body he had used, to hold her hand, either during sex or afterward. Slowly he lifted Jennifer's hand to his lips and kissed it.

His kiss sent an odd shiver of sensation through her. Nervous, because the expression in his eyes had changed from wounded vulnerability to something inexpressibly, dangerously sensual, she tried to pull her hand away. "It's late," she said in an artificially bright voice. "I had best be going, or Catherine will worry that something has happened to me."

Grey did not let go of her hand. His free arm slid around her waist. "I don't think you should go just yet," he said in a husky voice.

She could tell by the expression in his glittering eyes that he was going to kiss her. She remembered her words to Catherine: *I would like to encourage more behavior of that nature in the future.* With a sudden burst of self-understanding, she realized that she had followed Grey here in order to try to seduce him.

She knew nothing about seduction. But somehow her nearness seemed to work on him like an aphrodisiac. She had no way of knowing that he found her irresistibly attractive, even clad in cast-off men's clothing. Perhaps even especially clad in men's clothing. There was something outrageously alluring about the way the gray knee breeches clung to her thighs and the silk stockings outlined the curves of her calves. Men's clothing, he thought, suited her. She was as stunningly beautiful in breeches as she had been in her green and gold ball gown. He bent slowly and touched his lips to hers.

This time he kissed her gently, restraining his violently physical response to her beauty as best he could. He did not want to frighten her. He dropped her hand and let his hand slide down her soft thigh. Jennifer shivered and slipped her hand around the nape of his neck, pulling him closer.

He let her deepen the kiss. She tentatively explored his lips and tongue with her mouth, then gently disengaged her mouth from his and let her lips trail across his jaw and down his throat. Grey tilted his head back and moaned softly as some of his self-possession shattered.

Jennifer stopped at his low moan. "Grey?" she whispered tentatively. "Did I do something wrong?"

"No," he grated hoarsely. "God, no." He captured her lips with his and kissed her harder, almost violently, and his hands sought the gold braid frogs of her coat.

He had never wanted a woman this desperately, he thought as he pushed off her coat and waistcoat, impatiently shoving them to the floor to get them out of the way. He had not intended to make love to her at all, but she was so damned gorgeous. He knew he was taking advantage of the fact that she was in love with him, but he could not seem to stop himself. Just this once, he promised himself. Once he slept with her one more time, once he slaked his desire in her beautiful body, this incredible, overwhelming attraction would fade. It was impossible that he could continue to want her so violently.

He was in the process of pushing off her breeches when he felt her sudden resistance. "Grey," she said faintly.

With a valiant effort at self-control, he propped himself up on his hands and looked down at her. He had pressed her backward on the bed and had been lying on top of her, kissing her as though he would devour her. She was clad in nothing more than the long shirt she had worn beneath her coat and waistcoat—and her shoes and stockings, which he had forgotten to take off—and he realized that he was still fully dressed. He managed a smile. "I'm sorry, Jen. I didn't mean to rush you so badly."

She seemed to find his smile reassuring, for she placed a hand against his cheek and her tense expression vanished. "It's all right," she whispered. "It's just that—well, aren't you going to take your clothes off too?"

Grey smothered a laugh. He could imagine that she felt rather vulnerable and exposed, lying there with very little on while he was fully clothed. Exerting every bit of self-control he possessed to pull away from her, he stood up and methodically began to strip off his clothing. Jennifer sat up and peeled off her stockings and shoes, which seemed to her practical mind rather superfluous at this point. When she looked up from her task, her eyes widened and she gave a startled gasp.

Grey had taken her at her word and divested himself of every stitch of clothing. His elegant clothes lay in a heap on the floor, and he stood before her naked without any show of modesty, his long, muscled body gleaming like bronze in the light of the single candle. Her eyes wandered admiringly over his broad chest and down his flat stomach, but then she averted them shyly at the sight of his straining arousal.

"It's all right, Jennifer." Grey spoke softly, aware that she might panic at any moment. He sat beside her on the bed, putting both arms around her and pulling her reassuringly to his chest. "Don't be afraid of me. Please don't."

"I'm not afraid of you," she whispered tremulously.

"Then why are you shaking?" he teased gently.

Jennifer pressed her face against his bare chest and spoke in a muffled voice. "It's just that—last time it hurt. A great deal."

Grey cursed himself, not for the first time, for behaving like a rutting beast and taking her virginity with such brutally casual indifference. "I know," he breathed into her hair. "But I promise it won't hurt this time. I promise."

He kissed her again, passionately yet tenderly, as though she were delicate, fragile, and infinitely precious to him. When at last he had pulled off her shirt, and the strip of linen that had bound her breasts, and lay atop her, caressing her silken body gently, he sensed that she was no longer afraid. She trusted him when he told her there would be no pain. *She trusted him.*

She opened to him like a flower unfolding in the sunshine. It took every bit of his self-control to enter her slowly, to show her that it did not hurt, to show her how good it felt. After long moments of indescribably gentle intimacy she cried out and her body clenched around him. He shuddered and pushed more deeply into her and lost himself within her.

Afterward she pressed contentedly up against his chest and went to sleep almost immediately. Grey, however, did not fall asleep right away. He held her against him and breathed the fragrance of her hair, thinking.

It had meant a great deal to him that she had trusted him enough to let him make love to her, after he had done so much to alienate her. For most of eight years, people had looked at him with suspicion. He had been very young when his first wife had died, and he had learned to conceal his youthful vulnerability behind a mask of bitterness and anger. Somehow Jennifer could see behind his mask. She knew him for what he was, a vulnerable and lonely man. And consequently she was not afraid of him.

If anyone was afraid, it was Grey. Jennifer could strip him of his defenses so easily it was frightening. He knew that she loved him, and that should give him the advantage in their relationship.

But somehow . . . it didn't.

He fell asleep with his arms still wrapped protectively around her.

When Jennifer awakened the next morning, sunshine was streaming in through the venetian blinds of the room. She blinked sleepily and looked around. The plain, sturdy oaken furnishings reminded her that she was in a tavern, not at Greyhaven. And that reminded her that she and Grey had shared startling intimacies in this bed. She sat up quickly and then clutched the linen sheet to her breasts modestly as she saw Grey sitting in the chair next to the bed, watching her.

She smiled tentatively, but her smile faded quickly as his expression did not change. "Good morning," she said politely, uncertain how to begin a conversation. She remembered exactly what he had done to her last night, and how she had responded, and her cheeks flamed.

Grey said nothing, only looked at her impassively. Jennifer realized with burgeoning misery that he was staring at her as he had when she was a tavern wench—as though she were entirely beneath his notice. But surely he couldn't feel that way after last night. "Did you sleep well?" she asked, trying desperately to provoke some sort of reaction.

At last he spoke. "No."

Jennifer stared at him, startled by his cold tone.

"I want to apologize for what happened last night," he went on. His voice sounded incredibly remote, as though the intimacies they had shared had meant less than nothing to him. "I know you are in love with me, and I took advantage of it and used you." Bewildered and confused, Jennifer blinked back tears at his impassive tone. "I don't know what you expected to happen this morning, but I want to make it clear to you that I do not wish to continue sharing your bed. Not now and not ever."

Jennifer somehow managed to restrain the tears that burned in her eyes.

Grey smiled slightly—a jaded and cynical smile. "I am accustomed," he drawled, "to sophistication in bed. I've lost count of how many women I've bedded since Diana died, but every last one of them has been experienced and willing and bold. After sleeping with so many experienced women, I'm afraid that anything less than that is simply— too dull."

He stood up. "I'll leave you alone while you dress," he said coldly, managing to make it sound as though he did not want to have to look at her naked body again. "Once you've returned to the tavern you and Catherine are staying at, I suggest you put a decent gown on and go back to Greyhaven. I will return in a few days."

As his hand touched the brass doorknob, he paused and looked back over his shoulder at his wife. "I just want you to realize," he emphasized, "that nothing has changed. *Nothing.* Do you understand?" When she nodded shakily, he turned the doorknob and strode from the room.

As Grey walked blindly down the stairs, he struggled unsuccessfully to blot out the memory of their lovemaking last night. It had been the most fulfilling sexual experience of his life. And despite what he had told himself last night, he wanted her more than ever this morning. Making love to her had not erased the attraction he felt for her, but had only made it stronger and more powerfully compelling.

This morning, when he had awakened and found her

sleeping in his arms, curled warmly and confidingly against his chest, he had realized bleakly that he could not trust himself to stay away from her. He was too drawn to her beauty and her innocent passion. Therefore, he had decided coolly, the only alternative was to make her hate him so much she would not come near him.

As he strode up the bustling main street of Williamsburg, away from his wife and away from the ecstatic and joyous night they had shared, he wondered why the hurt expression on her face should have torn so at his heart. After all, she meant nothing to him. He should not care that he had hurt her feelings. Yet, for some reason, he did. He cared a great deal.

It was utterly bewildering.

"Jennifer!" Catherine exclaimed as her friend walked into their chamber at Wetherburn's, still clad in breeches and coat. "Where have you been? I've been so worried—"

"I'm sorry," Jennifer interrupted, placing a hand on Catherine's arm. At least Catherine cared something for her, she thought bitterly. "I know I shouldn't have stayed out all night, but . . ."

Her voice faded out, and Catherine looked at her sympathetically. "I take it you found Grey."

Jennifer nodded. She did not trust herself to speak.

"Are we staying in Williamsburg?"

At last Jennifer spoke. "No," she said hoarsely. "But he is."

Catherine sighed. She had hoped, when Jennifer did not return, that she and Grey had worked out their difficulties. But Jennifer's expression made it eloquently clear that the situation between them was worse than ever.

To her surprise, she saw that Jennifer was crying. "Jen," she said in horror, "what did he do to you?"

Jennifer only shook her head dumbly, tears streaming down her cheeks, wrenching sobs shaking her shoulders.

For the first time, Catherine put her arms around her

friend and hugged her. "Damn Grey to hell," she said fiercely. "I'm so sorry, Jen. I tried to warn you. I was afraid—I was afraid this would happen."

"You were right," Jennifer choked.

"I always am where Grey is concerned, but I would give a great deal to be wrong, once or twice." Catherine sighed. "Perhaps someday I will be."

Jennifer sat in the parlor at Greyhaven, listlessly tapping at the keys of the harpsichord. There was no music in her mind today, nor had there been since Grey had stalked out of the tavern yesterday morning. She and Catherine had ridden back to Greyhaven yesterday afternoon. All day today she had sat in the parlor, wondering when Grey would return from Williamsburg and trying to convince herself that she did not care. But it wasn't true. She cared dreadfully.

Why, she wondered bleakly, did Grey have to be so mercurial? Why did he have to be so kind and loving one moment, and viciously cruel the next? If only he would ignore her, she would be able to forget him. But when he made love to her tenderly, as though she were the most precious thing in the world, then leaped at her throat with fangs bared like a starving wolf the next morning, she had no idea what to make of it. Sometimes she thought Grey enjoyed reducing her to tears. She suspected his motives were more complex than simple cruelty, but she could not imagine what those motives might be.

Her hands stilled on the keyboard as she heard the front door slam and booted heels clacking on the floorboards of the entranceway. Grey. Home at last. She suppressed her wild desire to race from the parlor and throw herself at him, begging to know what she had done to anger him. Dignity forbade it. She forced her hands to continue playing the melody she had been fiddling with, but it sounded harsh and atonal. Completely wrong.

She had expected Grey to go straight to his study and

his decanter of whisky. Therefore she was startled when the door to the parlor opened and Grey strode in briskly, closing the door behind him. The music broke off in a discordant clash and Jennifer turned to stare at him.

"Good afternoon," he said politely.

Jennifer said nothing, only stared at him harder. How could he be so rude one day and so civil the next? Perhaps he really was mad. It was difficult to believe a sane person could behave so.

Painfully aware of her confusion and the reason behind it, Grey paused awkwardly, then pressed on. "I've brought you your present."

"There is nothing you could give me that I would want," Jennifer said shortly, echoing back his own words with unmistakable hostility.

Grey cloaked his hurt with a sardonic grin. After all, he reminded himself, he had wanted her to hate him and had provoked her on purpose. He had no reason to feel hurt by her attitude. After his decision yesterday morning to distance himself from her, however, he was uncomfortably aware of his inconsistency in bringing her a present anyway. He wished he understood his own motives, but perhaps they were best left unexamined. "Odd," he drawled coolly. "You seemed to want what I gave you in Williamsburg."

Jennifer surged to her feet in rage. "How dare you remind me of that, you—"

"Before you feel compelled to say something unladylike," he interrupted, "let me present you with your gift." He opened the parlor door, and a spaniel puppy, perhaps six months old, trotted in. Its long silky coat was buff and white, and it looked fearlessly around at its strange new surroundings. When it spotted Jennifer, it began to wag its stub of a tail until its hindquarters wiggled frantically, and trotted across the room to her feet.

"Oh, Grey!" Jennifer knelt on the floor and gathered the puppy into her arms. It licked her face with enthusiasm. "He's gorgeous! Wherever did you find him?"

"I went to Williamsburg to purchase a dog for you, since you once told me you had always wanted one. Unfortunately, no one had a litter of pups available. As I was riding up the main street, this little fellow darted out in front of my horse. I was nearly thrown. It was quite evident he had no regard for hooves or carriage wheels. I feared he might be run over, so I picked him up and made inquiries. Since no one claimed him, I decided he would make an excellent pet. He seems friendly enough."

That was an understatement. Unable to keep the puppy from licking her face, Jennifer placed him back on the floor and stood up. Instantly the spaniel caught the hem of her petticoat between his sharp puppy teeth and tugged at it, growling with mock ferocity. Jennifer smiled in delight.

"Thank you so much," she said softly, at a loss for anything else to say. She was still angry with him after what had happened yesterday, yet it was difficult to maintain her hurt and annoyance in the face of his unexpected generosity. She was startled to realize he had remembered her offhand remark that she had always wanted a dog. The realization made her soften involuntarily and curbed the bitter words that might otherwise have risen to her lips.

Grey hesitated. It had taken him most of the day to cover the nine miles from Williamsburg, with the squirming puppy held firmly in his lap with one hand, and the reins of his nervously dancing stallion in the other. Yet he had been unable to determine his motives in bringing the pup home.

Yesterday he had intentionally alienated Jennifer and told himself that he was better off if she hated him. Today he was trying to win back her friendship. It was perplexing. He decided to try for a facade of cool indifference. "After all," he said in a chilly voice, "I did promise you a present."

Jennifer smiled uncertainly at him. Although she still hadn't forgiven him for his ugly behavior yesterday, she was reasonably certain he had intended the puppy as a peace offering, and she was willing to consider a truce. And yet his tone was as cold and indifferent as it had been yesterday morning. Perhaps, she concluded unhappily, he had simply brought the puppy because he thought she would be expecting it.

"He's a wonderful present," she said, averting her eyes from his face when he did not answer her tentative smile with one of his own. Picking up the puppy and cuddling him against her chest, she added thoughtfully, "What do you suppose a good name would be?"

"How about Nuisance?" Grey suggested.

She ignored the remark. "Let's see. Since you found him in Williamsburg, I believe I'll call him William."

"Quite a dignified name. Rather too dignified for the likes of him, I should think."

"Oh, I think he'll grow up to be dignified," Jennifer replied, putting the puppy back down on the Oriental carpet, where he promptly urinated.

"I shouldn't like to bet on it," Grey said dryly.

EIGHTEEN

Jennifer lay in bed, her eyes shut tightly. The world seemed to be spinning around her, and she had the irrational conviction that she was going to fall off her bed. Due to the hard work she had endured in her lifetime, she was generally healthy and far less prone to the vapors or other womanish illnesses than most other women were. In fact, she had only been ill once in the past nine years. But there was no denying that she was sick this morning. She knew that if she moved an inch she would be horribly and tumultuously ill.

The door opened. The young black maid, alarmed by Jennifer's greenish color, had summoned Catherine, who tiptoed across the chamber to the bed.

"Jennifer?" she whispered. "Are you all right?"

Jennifer wanted to smile at the concern in the other's voice, but smiling seemed like entirely too much effort. In a very small voice, she said, "I don't feel well."

Catherine laid a hand on her forehead. "You don't seem to have a fever," she said dubiously.

"Perhaps not," Jennifer said, her eyes still screwed tightly shut. "But the fact remains that I am dying." It was a mistake to have uttered such a long sentence. She suddenly leaped from beneath the covers and staggered across the room, vomiting violently into the silver chamber pot.

Catherine sympathetically averted her eyes. When Jennifer straightened, she said, "Better now?"

"Perhaps a bit," Jennifer admitted, leaning weakly against the wall. She no longer felt certain that she was going to die. The thought occurred to her, however, that living might be a less preferable alternative if her body insisted on feeling this way.

"You won't feel entirely well for a while," Catherine remarked calmly. "Seven or eight months or so, I should imagine."

Jennifer frowned at her, trying to imagine what sort of plague might last so many months. Abruptly her eyes lit up. "Are you saying I'm with child?" she demanded in wonder.

"I should say it's a likely possibility. When did you last have your monthly courses?"

Jennifer concentrated. "About two months ago, I think. Not since—" She broke off and burst into a radiant smile. "A baby! I'm going to have a baby!" Grey's baby, she thought joyfully. Perhaps it would be a boy, a child on which she could lavish all the love and attention she longed to lavish on Grey. A boy, with dark hair and silver eyes and a sharply curving nose . . .

"Where's Grey?" she demanded abruptly.

"Surely you aren't going to tell him."

Jennifer stared across the chamber at her sister-in-law, aghast. "Whatever do you mean? Of course I'm going to tell him."

"Are you certain Grey wants a child?"

"Of course," Jennifer said automatically. "How could he not want a child?" Even as she spoke, her mind questioned the assumption. How did she know Grey wanted a child? Certainly he had made very little effort to produce one. Perhaps, even with a son in the house, he would still barricade himself in the study, day after day, emerging only to sullenly eat dinner. . . .

"It has dawned on you, I think," Catherine remarked dryly, "that Grey would not make an ideal father."

Jennifer stared at her, wide-eyed. "He has no choice," she protested. "It's too late to debate whether or not he will make a good father. He's going to *be* a father, like it or not."

"Perhaps it would be wise not to tell him immediately," Catherine suggested.

"Why do you say that?"

Because I don't want to see you hurt, Catherine thought. *Because when he finds out, Grey is likely to become colder and more vitriolic than ever. Because I know for a fact that Grey does not want children.* "Grey has told me more than once that he would make a poor father," she said hesitantly, trying to explain in a way that would not unduly distress Jennifer. "He has indicated that he has no intention of fathering a child. In fact, when you first came to Greyhaven he specifically stated that he did not want children. I think I know when you became pregnant, and I don't think he intended—that is, I did not think that you and he were still—"

"Only once," Jennifer said briefly. She did not count the first time, the time Grey had carelessly taken her virginity on the floor. As far as she was concerned, they had only made love once. "In Williamsburg, just as I'm certain you suspected. It was a terrible mistake. At least," she added softly, resting her hand on her flat stomach protectively, "up until now I thought it was a mistake. Perhaps I was wrong."

Catherine nodded. It was exactly as she had thought. Apparently they had succumbed to passion—or, more likely, insanity—for only one night. Which meant that Grey felt nothing at all for Jennifer, and had regretted his actions afterward. Probably a reminder of that night, in the form of a son or daughter, would not be welcome.

Jennifer was still considering Catherine's last words. "Do you think Grey will be angry?"

"He had as much to do with it as you did," Catherine pointed out reassuringly. "It would be most irrational of him to be angry."

"Which means it's a likely reaction."

"Probably," Catherine admitted. "Why don't you wait for a while before you tell him? After all, it will eventually become obvious."

"I wish I could," Jennifer said after a pause, during which she did battle with her more cowardly impulses. "But it's Grey's child too. He has a right to know. And when the baby is born, perhaps he'll make more of an effort to be a good father. Who knows? Perhaps he'll even grow to love the baby."

"Perhaps," Catherine agreed dubiously. She could not imagine Grey holding a baby in his lap as it spat up on his clothes, or patiently cuddling a child, trying to stop it from screaming while it had the colic. The thought was ludicrous. After Diana's death, Grey had become incapable of love, affection, or gentleness.

It was on the tip of her tongue to say so, but Jennifer had already left the room in search of her husband.

She found Grey in the study, slumped in his chair with his habitual glass of Madeira on the desk beside him. "Grey?" she said softly.

Grey sat up abruptly and stared at her. Since he had presented her with William, there had been an uneasy truce between them. They had continued to ride together each morning, but their conversations had become more and more stilted. Of late they seemed to have nothing to say to each other at all. He wondered if she had forgiven him for his callously heartless words the morning after they had made love . . . or if she ever could.

And yet, for the first time since they had made love, she had sought him out in his study. For some reason his pulse beat faster. He had been lonelier than ever the last two months. "Yes?"

Jennifer noticed that his expression was not quite as black as usual, and she took it as a good sign. "I have some news," she began hesitantly. She could have sworn she saw hope in his eyes. Ridiculous, she chided herself, and added, "Rather good news, in fact. I'm—I'm going to have a baby."

Grey stood up slowly and looked across the room at her. A thousand emotions warred in his mind. A baby. A daughter as beautiful as she was, a girl he could indulge and lavish with dolls and clothes. Or a son, a boy he could teach to ride and hunt—

Then he looked down at the goblet of Madeira, and a wave of self-disgust shook him. He was not fit to be a father. He was dissolute and self-absorbed and his children would grow to hate him as he had hated his own father.

He crossed the yards of Oriental carpet that separated them and looked down into her hopeful, beautiful, upturned face. "Are you certain?"

"Yes," she whispered, unable to read the expression on his shuttered features. "I think so."

"Indeed," Grey said, the mockingly sardonic grin he all too often wore crossing his face. "And who, may I ask, is the father?" His voice was coldly and deliberately insulting. Jennifer stared at him in horrified shock, appalled by the unexpectedly ugly words.

"What?"

"Am I the father," Grey clarified, "or is some other man?"

He had intended to infuriate her, to drive her further away from him, but he was unprepared for the violence of her response. The palm of her hand struck him across his cheek with all the force she could muster, snapping his head to the side. Staggering slightly, he turned back to her and stared at her with a surprised expression that, under other circumstances, would have been comical.

"You bastard," she said in a low, savage voice. "You know there hasn't been another man. I wish there had been. I wish I could say my baby had been conceived in an act of love, rather than in a meaningless, sordid act with a hateful drunkard. But I can't."

Her words were even harder and more cruel than his had been, and they slashed through the layers of callousness that surrounded his heart and lacerated his emotions like knives. "Jennifer—" he protested softly, half extending his hand to her. It pained him to hear their night together described as sordid. It hadn't been sordid, but exquisite beyond imagining. "I didn't—"

"Don't touch me!" she snapped. "You are a disgusting, dissolute degenerate, and I despise you. I wish to God I'd never spent the night with you, but I felt so sorry for you. . . ."

The realization that she found him pitiful was almost too painful to bear. Grey flinched, turning pale underneath his tanned skin, and she saw his reaction and went on viciously, "That's right. I *pitied* you. And fool that I was, I thought perhaps I could help you somehow. I swear to you that I didn't enjoy it. It was meaningless and dull."

"I don't believe you," Grey said in a strangled voice. "You enjoyed it. I know you did." That night had meant everything to him. He had to believe it had meant a great deal to her as well. He had to believe it, or he would go mad. "Jennifer, please—" He stepped forward, reaching for her as if to embrace her, and she pulled away, her eyes blazing.

"Don't touch me," she warned again. "Or I'll strike you again. I mean it."

She could not let him touch her, or he would realize instantly that she was lying. She knew all too clearly she had made love to him that night because she loved him and because she found him irresistibly attractive, not because she pitied him. But he had hurt her when he mocked her for her lack of experience, and again when he cast doubt on her baby's parentage, and she was bitterly determined to exact revenge. The wounded, defenseless expression on his face told her she had been successful. He stepped back, obviously confused and hurt, and did not try to touch her again.

"Please tell me you don't pity me," he said softly.

"I do pity you," she said in a clear voice. "And when your child is old enough to understand you, he will pity you as well. You're a drunken fool, and I despise you more than you can imagine."

Casting a last scornful glance in his direction, she turned and strode from the study, her head held regally high. Grey stared after her for a long time. The thought of having a child frightened him, and he had foolishly allowed his fear to drive yet another wedge between himself and his wife. He realized that her opinion meant a great deal to him, more so than he had realized. When he had first met her, he had thought she was pitiful. But now he realized with painful clarity that she was strong and intelligent and courageous. Jennifer was right. *He* was the pitiful one.

Absently, he picked up his glass of Madeira and drained it.

"I cannot believe you said that to him, Jen," Catherine said anxiously when Jennifer furiously related the story to her that afternoon. Her ivory skin seemed paler than usual, and Jennifer looked at her in surprised annoyance.

"I would have said a great deal more," she retorted sharply, "had I not been almost too infuriated to speak. How dare he accuse me of—he deserved everything I said to him! Everything!"

"Perhaps he did. But Jen, you mustn't make him angry. You don't—you don't know what he's capable of."

"Of course I know what he's capable of," Jennifer snapped acidly. "He tore me away from everything that I was familiar with, mocked and humiliated me for being myself, took advantage of me, and now he has the gall to accuse me of adultery! Believe me, I *know* what he's capable of!"

"No. You don't." Catherine lowered her voice and spoke with deliberate calm. "Jennifer, I must tell you something. I should have told you before, but I had this foolish idea that you might . . . change Grey, somehow. But it's obvious Grey will never change, and you have the right to know. You need to know, under the circumstances. But please don't tell anyone what I'm about to tell you. Not for Grey's sake, but for your child's sake."

She took a deep breath. "When you first came here," she began hesitantly, "I told you that no one knew who murdered Diana. I lied.

"Grey killed Diana."

NINETEEN

"I don't believe it," Jennifer said, her eyes wide with shock. More forcefully, she repeated, "I *don't* believe it. Grey is capable of many things, but murder is not among them."

"We've both seen Grey become utterly irrational when he drinks," Catherine retorted. "Do you really believe there is *anything* he is incapable of?"

It was a telling point, and Jennifer was silent. She, of all people, knew just how irrational Grey could be. Suddenly she heard Carey's voice. *He's a murderer. Don't marry him, Jenny.*

"I am not telling you rumor or innuendo," Catherine went on heavily. "I was there. I know what happened. Everyone on this plantation knows they had a violent quarrel that afternoon. I don't know what they were arguing about, but everyone in the house could hear them screaming at each other in the parlor. It was a disgraceful display, especially since we happened to have company, Kayne and Sapphira O'Neill and their children. Kayne was Diana's uncle," she added informatively but unnecessarily.

That explained why Carey had been so certain that Grey was the murderer, Jennifer realized dully. He had been a witness. Fear began to seep through her, the appalling, sickening fear that she had fallen in love with a killer. Grey had admitted to her that he and Diana had quarreled that day. Could it be true?

She had read his letters to Diana; she had seen his soul. How on earth could she have misjudged him so badly?

"Diana stalked upstairs in high dudgeon," Catherine went on, haltingly, "and Grey went to his study and—"

"And got drunk," Jennifer finished bitterly.

"It was the first time. He'd never drunk before, at least not heavily. Just the occasional glass of ale with friends. He never drank as much as most gentlemen do. You see, our father and our grandfather drank to excess. Grey had a terror of ending up like them. He was always careful to maintain iron control of himself . . . until that night."

She paused. It was evident that the memories were cutting her like knives. "I happened to be in the parlor and saw Diana go out of the house a few hours later. Grey saw her go too. By that time he was as foxed as a man can be and still be on his feet. He lurched out the door after her, but I don't think she knew he was following her.

"That was the last time I saw Diana alive."

"That's hardly proof that he killed her."

"I'm not finished. In the morning, when they were both discovered to be missing, we all set out to find them. Everyone searched for them—myself, the slaves, and the O'Neills, excepting Sapphira, who is blind. Thank God I found them first.

"I found Diana in the woods near the river. There was blood everywhere, covering the pine needles she lay upon. She had been beaten badly, and her throat had been slashed. I found Grey not ten yards away, lying on the ground in a drunken stupor. He had obviously staggered away after he killed her but then collapsed before he got very far. There were bruises and scrapes over one side of his face. It was obvious that Diana had fought him, but she was not strong enough to save herself. Grey is a very powerful man, even when he is inebriated.

"When I found Grey I was terrified. I slapped his face until he woke up. When his eyes opened he stood up and staggered over to where Diana's mutilated body lay. He knelt beside her on the ground and cried, and I'll never forget his words. Over and over again, he sobbed, 'I've killed her. It's all my fault. Oh, God, I've killed her.' "

Catherine paused to draw a deep breath. Glancing up, she found Jennifer watching her with an intent, horrified expression.

"There isn't much else to tell," she went on wearily. "I managed to tear Grey away from her body before anyone else got there. I took him back to the house, washed his scratches, and tried to get him sobered up. When the others got back—Carey O'Neill found Diana's body—I swore that I'd found Grey collapsed in the stable, and that he had obviously been there all night."

With a jolt, Jennifer remembered the contemptuous words Trev had spoken as she stood in front of Grey, protecting him from the other man's fists. *Hiding behind children again, I see, Greyson.*

Trev, she realized, had known that the sixteen-year-old Catherine had lied to protect her brother.

"What about the bruises?" she asked in a trembling voice.

"I said that he'd fallen from his horse while riding the previous afternoon. Fortunately, no one had seen him that afternoon except a few of the slaves. The slaves had loved Diana, but they were more loyal to Grey, so they confirmed my story—though a slave's testimony is inadmissible in court anyway." She paused. "If I hadn't lied to protect him, Grey would have been sent to gaol—and hanged."

Jennifer thought of the gaol in Williamsburg, and a shudder ran through her at the thought of Grey locked up in a dark, dank cell, awaiting a trial, and being hanged. "Why did you decide to protect him?"

"I had to," Catherine said simply. "I was only sixteen at the time. Since my parents died, he had been my only guardian. Even before my parents died he was like a father to me, far more so than my real father ever was. We were always very close. I couldn't let him go to gaol. I couldn't let him die."

"And Grey let you lie for him?"

"I think Grey was in shock. He told me later that he has no memory of that evening, and I believe him. Alcohol frequently has that effect, you know. When he sobered up he couldn't even remember that he had killed Diana. He could remember nothing at all about that night. So he let me lie to protect him. But for the last eight years he has punished himself for killing Diana, and he's punished himself for not going to gaol. In effect, he's created his own gaol. That study is his prison, and alcohol is the bars that keep him inside."

Jennifer shuddered. "I wish you hadn't told me all this."

"I had no choice. I'm afraid that it's all happening again."

"What do you mean?"

"I mean," Catherine said levelly, "I'm afraid Grey may kill you. And I can't let it happen to you. You're my friend."

Jennifer stared in blank horror. "Why would Grey kill me?"

"Think, Jennifer. The situation is virtually the same. Grey is obsessed with you, and you and he have had a very ugly argument."

"We've argued before," Jennifer said tiredly, "more times than I could count. Besides, Grey is not obsessed with me. He hates me!"

"He *is* obsessed with you," Catherine insisted. "You may not be aware of it, but it is true. Trust me. Perhaps he doesn't love you, but he watches you constantly. It's painfully obvious that he is attracted to you. I noticed it the first night you came to Greyhaven. I'm afraid that somehow he may confuse you with Diana and make you pay for her imagined sins. I still have no idea what they fought over, but he must have been utterly infuriated with her, or he wouldn't have killed her. And is it so hard to believe he might make you pay for whatever she did? After all, he did attack you, accuse you of infidelity, simply because you're pregnant. You did nothing to deserve it. Isn't that right?"

"Yes, but—" Jennifer broke off. She could hardly tell Catherine that Grey had confused her with Diana once before. She had never told Catherine the full story about the terrible night she had lost her virginity, and she certainly could not tell her now. It would only worry her friend further.

But she knew something that Catherine did not.

"He's confusing you with Diana, Jennifer. I'm certain of it. And that means that you could suffer Diana's fate. It's my fault, Jen. If only I hadn't encouraged him to take another wife—"

Jennifer broke into her friend's self-recrimination. "Catherine, Diana was not the saint everyone thinks she was."

"I know that. I, for one, did not care for her."

"You were jealous of her relationship with Grey," Jennifer prompted, probing for more information.

"It was not merely that," Catherine said slowly. "I despised her."

"Why?"

Catherine hesitated. "I've never told you this, Jen. I've never told anyone, least of all Grey. But perhaps I should tell you."

Jennifer leaned forward with sudden interest, her eyes narrowed. Perhaps Catherine knew something that would help her clear up this mystery. "Please tell me."

Catherine took a deep breath. "It's Diana's fault I'm lame."

Seeing Jennifer's look of surprised disbelief, she went on, a little defensively, "It's true! I was riding Tempest, Grey's big black stallion, just a few days after Grey and Diana were married. Diana caught me as I was coming out of the stable and caught the horse's bridle. She told me that she was tired of having me underfoot and that she wanted Grey to herself for a while. She announced that she was going to pack me off to visit relatives. I told her I was going to talk to Grey, for I did not particularly want to go anywhere. After all, this plantation was my home. *She* was the interloper. As I was dismounting, she struck Tempest a blow with the crop she was carrying. He reared, and I fell to the ground and broke my leg. It was all her fault. I hated her!"

Startled by the older woman's vehemence, Jennifer blinked. "Wasn't Grey furious with her?"

"He never knew," Catherine said angrily. "Diana told him I fell, and he believed her story, damn him. I didn't dare try to contradict her. He was so infatuated with her that I knew he wouldn't believe me."

"I'm not surprised," Jennifer said slowly. "I've learned a good deal about Diana since I've been here, and I've become certain she was not the angel Grey thought she was. If she hadn't died, I don't doubt they would have been arguing frequently."

Catherine looked at her oddly. "What exactly have you found out about her?"

Jennifer sighed. "Diana was cuckolding Grey."

"Ridiculous," Catherine said at once. "Impossible."

"I have proof. Letters from the man she was having an affair with. They are upstairs, in my desk. I found them a long time ago."

Catherine looked dumbstruck. "Are you certain?"

"Absolutely," Jennifer said firmly. "They are all signed with the initial C. I don't know who Diana was having an affair with, but—"

"Carey," Catherine said. "Carey O'Neill."

It was Jennifer's turn to look surprised. "Do you really think so? I never told you this, but I knew Carey when I lived in Princess Anne County. He was always very kind to me, the only man I ever thought of as a friend. I can scarcely believe he was the type to carry on an affair with a married woman. And the affair did go on after she was married, I am certain of that. Besides, he was only sixteen at the time."

"Who else could it have been?" Catherine said reasonably. "At any rate, I saw Carey kissing Diana once, in the arbor. In fact . . ." She paused thoughtfully. "It was the day Diana was murdered."

Jennifer nodded slowly. It did seem to make sense.

"This explains everything," Catherine said. "I could never understand why Grey murdered her. He loved her so much. But if she was having an affair, and he found out, he would have felt terribly betrayed. Perhaps he saw them kissing in the arbor, too. Little wonder, then, that he killed her. And it would also explain why he instantly assumed your child was not his. Perhaps he thought—"

"Actually," Jennifer broke in, "I don't think he ever knew about Diana's affair." She remembered the desperate, thwarted longing in Grey's voice as he spoke to his dead wife's portrait, begging with her to come back, and she shook her head firmly. "No, I really can't believe he ever knew."

"He must have," Catherine objected. "Why else would he have killed her?"

"I have no idea," Jennifer said honestly.

"Perhaps," Catherine said slowly, "we should confront him. Show him the letters, and ask—"

"No."

"But, Jennifer—"

"No," Jennifer repeated firmly. "If he never knew about Diana, I won't be the one who hurts him by telling him. Grey has suffered enough, Catherine. He's punished himself long enough for whatever happened between them. I won't cause him more pain. I *won't*."

A child. He was going to have a child.

Grey sat slouched in his leather-upholstered easy chair in the study the day after his confrontation with Jennifer, morosely sipping a glass of apple brandy. He had descended into the depths of a gloom darker than any he had

known since he had met Jennifer. Since her arrival at Greyhaven, he had been fascinated by her unsuspected intellect
and aroused by her unimaginable beauty. Now, due solely
to his own stupidity, Jennifer despised him. And to make
matters worse, he had sired a child, and he could blame no
one but himself. He should have known better than to
have made love to her in Williamsburg. He should have
known better! But his emotions had gotten the better of
him, and now—

A child deserved better than an alcoholic, cold father
with no love left in his heart for anyone. He had no business siring a baby, any more than his father had. He bitterly
recalled his own childhood, his indifferent, drunken father
and his self-absorbed, shallow mother. Neither of them
should have had children. If it had not been for Catherine,
he might have gone mad. Perhaps he *had* gone mad. Certainly most people thought so.

His lonely childhood had left him able to care deeply
for only one woman, and when that woman had died, his
soul had died with her. His own child would probably suffer the same fate, becoming a man or woman unable to
love in the normal way, loving one person obsessively and
shattering into a million pieces when that person was
gone. His child would grow up to be cold, hateful, and indifferent to the world, just as his father and grandfather
had been. It was a vicious and never-ending cycle.

His child would have only one hope—Jennifer. At least
Jennifer would be able to love the baby. Grey knew all too
well that Jennifer was capable of love. He was certain that
she had loved him when they made love in Williamsburg,
despite her angry words to the contrary yesterday. She had
loved him.

Surely she had loved him.

She was warm, loving, and kind. Though she was no
longer in love with him—he had ensured that by the horrible things he had said to her—she needed someone to
love. He was certain that she would cherish her baby, even
though she despised its father.

Perhaps, with Jennifer's love, the child might break the cycle and grow up to be a happy, normal adult, capable of love and joy. It was Grey's only hope. Jennifer had transformed herself, but he could not. Even for the sake of a child, he could not change. It was impossible, he told himself. Absolutely impossible.

TWENTY

After their confrontation, Grey avoided Jennifer, going on rides early in the morning and even refusing to eat his meals in the dining room. He spent every waking hour in his study or on horseback. Jennifer did not know whether to be relieved or angered. She had no desire to speak to him again after the savagely ugly words they had exchanged, yet she was annoyed that he found it so easy to ignore her presence in the house. After a week, she concluded that Grey was simply doing what he did best—running away from reality. Thus she was surprised, a sennight after their confrontation, when he strode into the parlor where she sat reading.

During that week, she had spent a great deal of time dwelling on the story Catherine had told her. At last, after a great deal of internal turmoil, she determined that it simply was not true. She did not doubt that Catherine believed that Grey had killed Diana, but she could not believe it herself. She had read his letters and could recite every one from memory. There was nothing in those letters that suggested Grey was capable of murder. On the contrary, it was obvious he had loved Diana deeply. No, she decided, there must be more to this story than Catherine knew. This conclusion, however, did not ease her anger toward Grey. The horrid things he had said to her, the hideous things he had accused her of, were burned into her mind.

Though it was late March, there was a fine snow being

blown on the wind outside and accumulating on the ground, and forced as she was to stay inside by the weather, she had found her thoughts returning with unpleasant frequency to her argument with Grey. She had settled down to read *The Taming of the Shrew*, with William curled companionably on top of her bare feet, in the hopes of forgetting Grey's vicious words, but the memory of their confrontation still whirled sickeningly in her brain.

Despite her preoccupation, she found the play delightful. She smiled, a little bitterly, as she read Katherina's statement, "I am ashamed that women are so simple/ To offer war where they should kneel for peace." Unlike Katherina, she had been more than willing to kneel for peace, but she had found herself wed to a man who only offered war.

As if her thoughts had conjured him up, she heard Grey's voice. "Excuse me."

She looked up, startled, to see her husband standing in the doorway looking uncomfortable, and regarded him with a distinctly hostile expression. Unlike Petruchio, she thought unhappily, she had very little chance of ever taming her wayward spouse. Grey was untameable.

Grey hovered hesitantly, almost shyly, in the doorway, feeling an odd pang in the region of his heart at the charmingly domestic scene before him. Jennifer was clad in a dark blue woolen gown of simple, unadorned design that covered her arms to the wrist. Her bare feet rested on the Oriental rug, warmed by the roaring fire and William, who seemed to think he was a muff. Her long hair was unbound and fell around her face in charming disarray. She looked very young, and heartbreakingly beautiful.

Annoyed by his unwanted physical and emotional reaction to her beauty, Grey spoke coldly. "I know you don't wish to speak to me," he said curtly across the distance that separated them, "but I need to tell you something. My friend Kayne O'Neill and his family from Princess Anne County will be visiting us in a few days. They will be here a fortnight or longer. I had hoped——" He hesitated and looked at Jennifer's stony expression. "I would like them to believe that all is well with our marriage," he went on haltingly. "I would like you to treat me with—civility, while they are here. Merely for the sake of appearances, you understand."

Jennifer raised her eyes to his and stared at him as though he were hideously deformed. "May I assume that you will treat me with 'civility' as well?"

"Of course."

"That will be a welcome change."

Grey looked away from her icy green eyes, stung more than he cared to admit by her sarcasm. It was true enough that Kayne and his family were coming to visit. What he did not tell her was that he had sent a note to Kayne asking him to come.

He had not realized how important Jennifer was to him until this past week, when he had been totally deprived of her presence. Intentionally angering her was the most idiotic thing he had ever done in the course of their relationship—and God knew he had done enough idiotic things. He could not go on this way, yet he knew an apology would not be enough. Not this time. His words had been too hurtful and too vicious to simply retract.

If they had visitors, however, Jennifer would have no choice but to pretend that all was well with their marriage. If she was thrown into his company every day, he hoped, their rapport and their friendship might be reestablished.

Friendship, he had told himself firmly, was all he wanted from her. He enjoyed her company and could not seem to get through the day without it. He needed her as much as he needed alcohol, or perhaps more. Somehow she had become necessary to his very survival. His attraction to her was still present as well, but he had promised himself that he would not succumb to it again. They could be friends, nothing more. Her friendship would have to be enough.

He had hoped to use the visit as a pretext to get on speaking terms with his wife once again, but he realized with a sinking heart that she despised the idea of being forced to pretend a courtesy she did not feel. The expression on her face made that all too clear. "Jennifer," he said hesitantly, "I only want—"

"I know what you want," she interrupted with biting contempt. "Your pride makes you want to show me off for your friend, even though you cannot stand the sight of me. Very well, I'll be civil to you for the duration of their visit. I suppose I owe you that much, at least."

"Thank you." At least he would have the opportunity to speak with her and to spend time in her presence. Perhaps, he mused as he walked back to his study, he could make her see, by his words and his actions, how sorry he was for his ugly words.

Or perhaps not. Perhaps nothing could heal the rift between them. He hoped to God that would not be the case.

Another long week passed, a week in which the cold anger between Jennifer and Grey became more glacial with each passing day. Jennifer spent the time playing the harpsichord, and was annoyed with herself because, no matter what tune she started playing, she always seemed to end up playing the tune she had composed as Grey's Christmas present over and over again. She also spent hours riding in the woods, careful to choose times to ride when Grey was occupied with the running of his estates. The last thing she wanted was to encounter Grey, in the house or out of it.

Preoccupied with bitter thoughts about her life as she rode through the woods one afternoon, the devoted William trotting at the heels of her mare, she glanced up in surprise at the sound of thundering hoofbeats. Grey was riding his stallion toward her at breakneck speed. As he approached, he reined in the horse so sharply that the beast half reared as it skidded to a stop. His face was dark with rage.

"What the *hell* do you think you're doing?" he snarled between gritted teeth.

Reining in her dappled mare, Jennifer stared at him in blank surprise. She had thought herself used to his unpredictable rages by now, yet she found herself bewildered by this unexpected display of anger. After all, he had avoided her for days. Why in the world had he sought her out and chosen to fight with her this afternoon? "What—what do you mean?"

"Get off that mare," Grey thundered.

Jennifer looked at him in confusion. She was riding the same gray mare she always rode.

"Get off her now, or I will drag you from her back."

Sensing he meant it, but nevertheless completely baffled, Jennifer dismounted and stood looking up at him. "Why are you being so unreasonable?" she burst out angrily.

"*Unreasonable?*" Grey repeated scathingly. "On the contrary, I thought I was being infinitely reasonable. If I ever see you on this mare's back again while you are in this condition, I will show you what an unreasonable husband looks like."

"This—condition?"

Grey exploded, "Don't you realize that if you were to fall, you could lose the baby?"

Jennifer stared at him in shock. Such a thing had never occurred to her. She had not realized that she had been unnecessarily risking a life that had become very precious to her. The thought of losing the baby sent a cold chill down her spine. "No," she said dully. "No, I didn't realize."

"You could have lost the baby," Grey elaborated angrily, "and you yourself could have been killed. Women die of miscarriages, Jennifer! Is that what you want?"

Jennifer felt herself growing angry at his autocratic tone. She had been foolish, she realized now—but he was being so self-righteous! How dared he, after the things he had said to her when she had told him she was pregnant? "And would you have cared?" she lashed back at him. "You said you didn't want the baby, and you certainly don't want me. If I were to fall from the horse, that would end all your problems, wouldn't it?"

Grey stared at her, his features hardening into stone. "Is that what this is all about? Were you *trying* to lose the baby?"

Belatedly, Jennifer realized that it could seem that way to him. "No, of course not," she said in what she hoped was a more conciliatory tone. "I simply didn't—"

"You *were* trying to miscarry," Grey insisted, and she knew he hadn't heard a word of her protest. He had tried and convicted her on the basis of her three angry sentences. "Damn it, Jennifer, how dare you try to do such a thing?"

"I was not trying to lose the baby!" Jennifer interjected. "I simply didn't think."

Grey looked down at her, his eyes granite-gray with emotion. "Perhaps you didn't think. Or perhaps you didn't care about the baby. Either way, you won't get another chance. The slaves at the stable have been instructed not to let you ride your mare until after the baby is born. You won't be permitted on a horse—*any* horse, even the most placid nag in my stables—until then."

"How dare you—"

"I dare," Grey interrupted in a voice like steel, "because that is *my* baby, and *my* heir, that you are carrying. You have a duty to protect it. And since you seem to have abdicated that duty, through either stupidity or carelessness, I am forced to step in. Don't try to ride a horse again until the baby is born." At her mutinous expression, he added softly, but with a world of menace in his tone, "Don't defy me, Jennifer. Or you will regret it, trust me."

With that he whirled his stallion about and cantered down the path, leading the gray mare with him. Jennifer turned back to the house, fuming.

Grey, for his part, was equally disturbed. When Jennifer had first told him that she was expecting, he had been horrified at the notion of becoming a father, painfully aware that he would be a far worse father than his own had been. And yet he found that he wanted a child, a boy to carry on his name, or a girl to hold on his lap and spoil with a thousand presents. And when he had gone to the stable to ride and found that Jennifer had ridden out, had in fact been riding every day, unbeknownst to him, he had realized that the part of him that wanted a child was stronger than the part that feared parenthood. The fact that he was going to have a child meant the world to him.

And that Jennifer was going to bear his child meant even more. The thought that she could have been hurt in her condition was too painful to contemplate. He could have lost everything he held dear, the baby . . .

And his wife.

Somehow, over the past year, she had insinuated herself into his soul and become dear to him. Somehow, despite his efforts to remain remote, he had come to live for the all-too-brief moments during the day when he could spend time with her. Probably he should have told her so, that she meant something to him, that she was the reason his life had become worth living again. She was the light in the darkness, the star that lit the gloom he had lived in for so long.

He should have *told* her.

When Grey had ridden off, without so much as a goodbye, Jennifer turned back toward Greyhaven. It was a long walk, especially in her condition, but she did not care. The last thing she wanted was to return to the house and risk seeing her husband. She was so angry she might have struck him.

Struggling to calm herself, she walked slowly through the forest. The woods were starkly beautiful, the bare branches still lightly dusted with the snow that had fallen a week before. Here and there the red berries of the wild holly, or the scarlet flash of a cardinal flying through the trees, gave color to the scene.

Jennifer walked on, her mind occupied with thoughts of Grey. He had insulted her viciously, infuriated her intentionally, and yet it was all she could do not to forgive him for his heartless words. She had realized, when she first glanced up and saw him astride his bay stallion, just how much she missed him. She had seen him only twice in a fortnight, and she had to admit that she longed for his company. Her life was very lonely without him.

But she would *not* forgive him, she decided firmly. His words had been too dreadful to forget. He must never know how much she missed him. Her pride forbade it.

In fact, she told herself, she would never voluntarily speak to him again. Of course, she had agreed to behave civilly for the duration of the O'Neills' visit. But that was all she would do. She would not seek his company out. She could not. He had angered and hurt her too badly.

It was dreadful to contemplate never speaking to one's own husband again, she thought, sighing. Forever was a very long time. Something Catherine had once said came back to her. *If things continue as they are, you will grow to loathe the sight of your own husband.*

Catherine, she mused, had been right. She did loathe him. And yet she could not stop her heart from leaping whenever she saw him. . . .

William's sudden excited yapping startled Jennifer from her bleak thoughts. Turning, she saw the spaniel dancing, his stubby tail wagging furiously, at the feet of Christopher Lightfoot. "Good day," Christopher said, his dark eyes fastened on her face.

"Hello," she answered uncertainly, eyeing him with curiosity. He was not dressed as finely as he had been for the rout, but his clothes were fashionable enough. His shirt was laden with large quantities of lace at the front and on his sleeves, and he wore a dark bobwig. She noted with amusement that he was trying without much success to keep William from jumping up on him and ruining his silk stockings. William loved everyone without reservation and invariably demonstrated it by leaping against their legs.

Christopher nodded in the direction Grey had disappeared. "He's quite frightening when he's in this mood, is he not?"

"Were you spying on us?" Jennifer snapped heatedly, mortified by the realization that he had heard her quarreling with Grey.

"Spying? No, I shouldn't call it that. I watch you often as you walk through the woods, my dear. I simply happened to overhear your exchange with your husband."

The knowledge that Christopher had been watching her with his intense dark blue eyes made Jennifer uncomfortable, but she strove to conceal her unease. "This is private land," she said haughtily. "Please leave at once."

"No."

"Leave! Or I shall—"

"What shall you do, my dear?" Stepping closer to her, Christopher caught her arm and looked down into her eyes. "Report my actions to your husband? I should think you would be more frightened of him than of me. After all, he is a murderer."

"I don't believe you!" Jennifer snapped as she yanked her arm from his grasp.

"Don't you?"

Jennifer blinked as tears burned in her eyes. "I don't know what to believe," she whispered. "I really don't."

God help her, she actually was entertaining the notion that Grey could be a murderer. And what was she to think, after his most recent display of temper? The memory of Catherine's words struck her painfully, and she lowered her head. "I don't know what to believe," she murmured again.

"I'm sorry, my dear," Christopher said gently. "I hate to be so blunt, but I feel that you should be aware of the facts, unpleasant though they are. Especially since you are carrying his child. Grey is in sober truth a murderer."

"It was never proven." Her whispered protest was barely spoken aloud. "You can't be certain."

"But I am certain. And so are you."

From some inner store of strength and faith Jennifer rallied, lifting her chin and staring at him with as much hauteur as she could manage. "No," she said firmly, pushing away her doubts. "I am not certain. And I want you off Greyson land. Now."

Christopher eyed her with amusement and another emotion. Good heavens, was that lust she saw in his eyes? Perhaps that explained why he had been watching her. "I do not wish to leave," he said. "I have a proposition for you, my dear."

"A—proposition?" she repeated, uncertain as to whether she'd heard him correctly.

"Yes. I've been watching you for quite some time, and I find you extremely attractive. I would like you to give consideration to becoming my mistress."

Jennifer stared at him in mingled fury and annoyance, then turned on her heel and marched away without deigning to answer. His mocking laughter followed her.

"Just think about it," he called after her. "When you find that you can no longer bear your husband's moodiness, when you can no longer stand the loneliness and the emptiness of your life, send me a note and I will be at your disposal."

Despising the man for his arrogance, Jennifer turned back and called to William, who with the typical lack of discrimination of a spaniel was still eagerly fawning over the odious man. She directed a look of distaste at Christopher as the dog ran up to her.

"I'd sooner rot in hell than become your mistress."

Christopher laughed at her as she stalked away. "Why, Mistress Greyson," he called, "didn't you know?"

She ignored him and walked away rapidly, but she all too clearly heard his last words.

"My dear girl, you already are in hell."

The O'Neill family arrived later that afternoon, while Jennifer was sulking in her chamber and Grey sat morosely in his study. The quiet gloom that was the normal state of Greyhaven was shattered suddenly by the cheerful babble of the O'Neill clan in the entrance hall and William's excited yapping. Startled by the unusual racket, Jennifer came down the stairs at the same moment that Grey emerged from his study.

Standing on the landing next to the tall case clock, Jennifer looked down on the chaotic scene below. Kayne O'Neill, an enormous bear of a man, stood next to his stunningly beautiful wife, Sapphira, his red head bent over her dark one as he laughed in response to some comment she had made. Around them stood their three youngest children, a redheaded girl who was just developing the curves of a woman and a pair of identical, dark-haired girls perhaps eight years old, all chattering like squirrels. They were the picture of a happy family, and Jennifer felt an odd tug at her heart as her traitorous imagination painted a portrait of herself standing next to Grey, his arm protectively around her as he smiled down at her, their laughing children surrounding them.

Shaking her head to clear it of the ludicrously sentimental image, she saw Carey, standing off to the side, a little apart from his family. He was watching her with an expression of stunned interest, and as her eyes met his he smiled very slightly. Jennifer smiled back, overcome with joy to see a friendly face. It had been well over a year since she had seen him, yet she felt a wave of sisterly affection at the sight of him. Unlike Grey, she thought, Carey had always been kind to her. She started down the stairs eagerly.

Grey, who was shaking Kayne's hand, looked even more sour than usual at the arrival of this noisy clan in his quiet home. Nonetheless, he grudgingly introduced Jennifer. "This is my wife, whom you may remember from our, er, wedding. This is Kayne O'Neill, his wife, Sapphira, and Carey, their eldest son. The rest of them"—and he bent a look of disgust on the younger children that almost caused Kayne to lose his gravity—"are altogether too noisy to bother with. Good Lord, Kayne, can't you keep the brats under better control?"

"I see you're as charming as ever," Kayne said calmly, not at all offended by this slur to his offspring. "Simply because your head aches from last night's excesses—"

"My head aches from the damned noise!"

"—is no reason to shout at my daughters. You are, as always, simply looking for a reason to complain."

Grey scowled darkly. "Haven't I got a right to complain? The six of you descending on my home like a plague of locusts, utterly shattering the peace and quiet, and yelping like a pack of hounds—tell me why I shouldn't complain!"

Jennifer found that she was beginning to become embarrassed by her husband's rude behavior. Even Grey rarely became this offensive. Had she known that Grey had invited the O'Neills to visit, she would have been utterly humiliated by his rudeness. Stealing a timid glance at the O'Neills, however, she was surprised to see them all grinning. Apparently Grey was expected to grumble, but none of them took him seriously.

"However do you manage to bear living with him?" Kayne asked her, laughing and clapping Grey on the shoulder. Grey frowned, and Jennifer perceived, in a flash of insight, that he truly did resent company. The laughter and cheerful conversation forced him to smile, to forget his absorption in grief and his surly self-centeredness. And yet, she realized as Grey flashed a reluctant smile and pulled the twins' braids, that the company pleased him also. Grey, she realized, was as lonely as she was.

"I wonder if we could borrow your carriage tomorrow," Kayne was saying to Grey. The O'Neills had sailed here in a shallop, since traveling by water from Princess Anne County was far easier than traveling by horseback, as Jennifer had once found to her sorrow.

"The carriage? Certainly, but why?"

Kayne looked uncomfortable. "I know we've only just arrived, but Sapphira wants to, er, visit with Rebecca and

Trev." He flushed slightly. "We wondered if perhaps you would like to go to Williamsburg with us. We plan on staying there a couple of days. If you—"

"No," Grey said flatly.

"But Grey—"

"I said no." Realizing he had spoken rather sharply, Grey smiled apologetically. "I see what you are trying to accomplish, Kayne—or more likely, what Sapphira is trying to accomplish. But the rift between Trev and myself is one that can never be healed."

Sapphira, who had been listening intently, broke in. "Grey, I am certain that if you were simply to talk to Trev, he would forgive you. It has been so long. Surely by now—"

"Actually, I saw Trev not two months ago."

"Really?" Sapphira said, her face lighting up. "And what did he say?"

"He said very little," Grey said dryly. "He was otherwise occupied."

"Doing what?"

"Trying to break my nose."

There was an awkward silence. At last Kayne said, "Very well, Grey. We will not push you into coming with us. But we would be very grateful for the loan of your carriage."

"You can have it, and welcome," Grey said. "I can certainly understand that Sapphira would like to visit her sister. And now, let me show you to your chambers." He led the O'Neills up toward the third floor, where there were four spacious bedchambers in readiness for their guests.

Jennifer played the hostess to perfection that night at the dinner table. She and Catherine had worked hard in preparing a suitable menu. The dinner started with peanut soup and ended with slices from one of the watermelons that had been preserved throughout the winter in the dark cellar. The intermediate courses included foods such as stewed oysters, roast duck, and cinnamon-topped syllabub. With Catherine's help, Jennifer had created a traditional centerpiece of fruit in an elaborate silver epergne. The topmost tray of the epergne held a pineapple, imported from the West Indies. Catherine had explained that the pineapple was the traditional symbol of hospitality.

In honor of his guests, Grey had limited his intake of alcohol, and he was a reasonably courteous host, laughing almost amiably with Kayne over a story about a horse race in which they had both competed. Jennifer carried on a conversation with Sapphira, a discussion such as any two women of their class might have, about the new fashions from London, and about the correct way of producing linen from flax. Only once did she stumble.

Sapphira had a disconcerting habit of turning her head when people spoke to her and looking very nearly right at them. It was easy to forget she was blind. Jennifer noticed that she was eating her food very neatly from her plate. Forgetting everything Catherine had ever drilled into her, she blurted out, "How do you know where your food is?"

Catherine shot her a quelling look, and Jennifer nearly clapped her hand over her mouth in horror at her tactlessness, but Sapphira did not appear to mind. She smiled gently. "Kayne tells me where it is at the beginning of the meal," she explained. "We pretend that the plate is a clock face. He told me that the duck was at twelve o'clock, the ham at four o'clock, and the corn at eight o'clock. When other courses are served he tells me where the food is as well. All I have to do is remember."

"I see," Jennifer said, too fascinated to curb her curiosity. "Is that how you get around the house so well, too? He tells you where the furniture is, and you remember?"

"Actually," Sapphira said, laughing, "I have to find out where the furniture is myself, the hard way. After I've stubbed my toes a few times, though, I remember easily enough." She smiled in Jennifer's direction. "I imagine that remembering the placement of furniture is far easier than everything you've had to remember since coming here, my dear."

"Oh, I don't know about that," Jennifer said in confusion, alarmed at the sudden change of topic.

"I'm certain it hasn't been easy for you," Sapphira persisted gently. "After all, there are so many things that the planter class take for granted. Even the simplest thing can be difficult for those of us with a handicap, such as holding a fork correctly. There are different kinds of impairments, Jennifer. I have one kind. You have another. But we've both learned to overcome them."

In that moment Jennifer knew that Sapphira accepted her as she was and knew the struggles she had suffered in becoming a lady as no one else in the aristocracy ever could. "Thank you," she said humbly. "I think—I think you see a great deal more than I realized."

Across the table, Grey watched Jennifer covertly. He was pleased to see that she was playing the attentive wife, engaging the women in conversation and making certain that everyone's plates were kept full. It was a cozy domestic scene, and it caused an odd ache in Grey's heart—or, he thought sardonically, the place where his heart ought to be. This was how he had once envisioned his life, with a lovely woman presiding over the dinner table, filling his home with laughter and conversation. Greyhaven seemed like a home tonight, lit by Jennifer as much as by the myriad candles that blazed from the chandelier and the silver candlesticks scattered around the chamber. But it was only an illusion. Greyhaven was merely a house, not a home—the cold mausoleum it always had been.

"Don't you think I'm right, Grey?"

Startled by the sound of his name, Grey turned his attention back to Kayne, realizing he had not heard a word his friend had said. "Oh, yes, of course," he agreed fervently, hoping that Kayne would not realize his attention had wandered.

Kayne raised an eyebrow sardonically. "So you do agree I am ten times the horseman you are?"

"What?"

"Ah! So you admit you weren't listening to me," Kayne said triumphantly.

Grey glared at his friend. "I was distracted."

"So I noticed," Kayne said with a knowing grin.

Tactful man and good friend that he was, Kayne said nothing more about Grey's "distraction" until they were seated in the study, enjoying port and pipes full of good sweet-scented Virginia tobacco from the engraved silver box that always sat atop Grey's secretary. The women had gathered in the parlor for further feminine conversation. Carey had been invited to join the men in the study but had curtly declined. Neither man was surprised, since Carey had never made a secret of his distaste for Grey.

"So," Kayne said as he puffed meditatively on his clay pipe, an especially fine one with a design of tobacco leaves pressed into the bowl. "How is it that you were so distracted during dinner?"

"I don't know what you mean," Grey said sullenly.

"Oh, of course you do," Kayne returned. "You had eyes for no one but your wife. A year ago you told me you had no interest in her. Now it is more than apparent that you do. I congratulate you, Grey. She is a lovely girl. I must admit, you were right to marry her."

"I was a goddamned bastard to marry her!" Grey exploded suddenly.

Kayne lifted his eyebrows in surprise, realizing that there was more here than met the eye. Well, that was generally the case with Grey. His friend was an unusually complex man. "I don't understand you, Grey. It's all too obvious that you are fond of her. She seems fond of you. What is the difficulty?"

To his complete shock, Grey dropped his head into his hands in an attitude of despair. "She hates me," he said in a muffled voice. "She has barely acknowledged my existence these past weeks. I asked you and your family to visit so that she would have no choice but to be thrown into my presence on a daily basis, and then I asked her to pretend that she can bear my company, and she has done so. I hoped that our relationship would improve if we spent more time together, but the fact is that she despises me. And it's my fault. It's *all* my fault."

He lifted his head and stared at Kayne with wide, vulnerable eyes. "I've done everything I could to make her hate me. I forcibly took her virginity without any regard for her pleasure. Later I humiliated her in public. Then, after she'd told me she loved me, I took advantage of her feelings for me and seduced her, and the next morning I told her she wasn't worldly and experienced enough for my sophisticated tastes. And still she didn't hate me. And then—then I accused her of being pregnant with another man's child. And finally she learned to hate me."

"She's pregnant?"

"Yes," Grey said miserably. "She's going to have my child, and she can barely stand to be in the same chamber with me. And she has every reason to despise me. After everything I've done—"

"What made you do these things to her?" Kayne thundered. "You've insulted her, humiliated her, treated her like a tavern wench—good God, man, what were you thinking? She is your wife."

Grey sighed. "I wanted her to stay away from me. I *wanted* her to hate me. I was afraid that . . ." He blinked rapidly and dropped his eyes to avoid Kayne's piercing gaze. "I was afraid that she would come to mean too much to me."

Kayne remembered the lovely young lady who had presided over the dinner table, smiling and keeping up a lively conversation, and the longing way Grey had watched her. The pain and confusion on Grey's face were all too obvious. "But it's too late," he said slowly. "She already has come to mean something to you."

"Yes," Grey admitted wretchedly. "She already has."

Despite her lack of vision, Sapphira saw more than did her husband. As soon as she was comfortably ensconced in the parlor with Catherine and Jennifer, she asked gently, "You are not happy, are you, my dear?"

Judging from the silence that Jennifer was looking at

her with surprise, she went on, "Oh, come now. I have some idea of what your life was like in that wretched tavern. I was there when you were married, after all. And I know Grey. Despite the fact that you are far more intelligent and kind than he could have hoped for, despite the fact that you are a wonderful wife for him, he has no doubt managed to ruin your relationship. Am I correct?"

"I have no relationship with Grey," Jennifer said icily.

"Oh, nonsense," Sapphira returned, sipping at her toddy, which was considered a suitable drink for women. "He is your husband. Like it or not, you have a very permanent relationship with him. Also, he is the father of your child."

Jennifer lifted her head abruptly and stared at Sapphira. "How in the world did you know that?" she demanded. "Even if you could see, you wouldn't be able to tell. I haven't begun to show yet."

"I heard the longing in your voice when we talked about my children," Sapphira explained. "I guessed perhaps you were with child. Or perhaps you only wanted children. But I gather from your response that you are going to have a baby."

"Yes."

"Is Grey happy?"

"Is Grey ever happy?" Jennifer retorted icily. "Of course not. He accused me of having another man's child."

"He didn't mean it, surely."

"I don't know," Jennifer replied slowly. "He has been so hateful these last few weeks, even more hateful than he was when we first married."

"Being hateful is an area in which he excels," Sapphira said dryly.

"But Sapphira, he's grown worse," Catherine said, entering the conversation for the first time. "You don't know the horrid things he's said to her. Truly, I've begun to wonder if he hasn't gone insane."

Sapphira did not answer for a moment. Then she said, "My husband tells me that Jennifer is very lovely."

"She is," affirmed Catherine.

"That is a matter of opinion," Jennifer interjected.

Sapphira smiled. "Yes. But Grey's opinion is the only one that matters. I've known Grey for a long time. I am certain he is not insane, and I am equally certain he is terribly confused."

Jennifer frowned. "I don't understand."

"Consider it from his perspective, Jennifer," Sapphira suggested. "Why did he marry you?"

"To irritate Catherine."

"Yes," Sapphira agreed, "although I wonder if Grey was completely honest with himself when he married you. I suspect he married you at least partially for chivalrous reasons. He knew how dreadful your life at the tavern was."

"He cared nothing about that," Jennifer said sharply.

"I wonder. At any rate, he wed a tavern wench. Then he found himself married to a lovely young lady. Is it any wonder he's confused? I think he loves you, my dear."

Jennifer stared at her as though she were mad. "Love?" she repeated, choking back a hysterical giggle as she thought of their last conversation. "No, Sapphira, he loves Diana."

"Diana has been dead for many years."

"But he still loves her!"

Sapphira smiled slightly. "Men are such idiots, are they not? Yes, he believes himself to be in love with Diana. But let me tell you something, Jennifer. Diana was a beautiful girl and I loved her dearly—she was my niece, you know—but she was shallow and heartless. Not unlike my sister, her mother, in her younger days. Had Grey remained married to her for very many years he would have realized that she did not love him."

"What?" Jennifer said faintly. She and Catherine exchanged glances. Did Sapphira know that Diana had loved another man?

"Well, it was all too obvious," Sapphira explained. "Every time she came to visit us at Windward, she talked about the enormous house Grey was building for her, and how he was having the *best* furniture made by the *best* local artisans and importing the *best* silver from England. It was really quite wearying to hear her talk about it. She never talked about Grey, just about this pile of bricks. It was painfully obvious that she loved the money rather than the man."

Jennifer assimilated this information silently. Poor Grey, she thought. He had learned from his parents to purchase the love of those he cared about. Unfortunately for him, he had not managed to buy Diana's love—just her hand in marriage.

It appeared that Diana had never loved Grey at all.

The next afternoon, as Jennifer took her customary stroll on the meandering path that ran through the woods, she was arrested by the sound of running feet on the thick carpet of pine straw behind her. Morbidly certain that Christopher Lightfoot had returned to pester her with his revolting proposition, she began to walk faster.

"Jenny!"

At the sound of her name—a name that no one used anymore—she turned and, to her relief, saw Carey. He slid to a halt, dark auburn hair disheveled, and stared at her with undisguised admiration.

"I thought you were going to Williamsburg this morning," she said in surprise.

Carey shook his head. "The rest of my family took the carriage, but I chose to stay here. I've scarcely had an opportunity to speak to you since we arrived yesterday," he said, panting. "I wanted to talk to you. How have you been?"

Jennifer regarded him thoughtfully. He was tall, a trait he had inherited from both parents, and undeniably handsome, despite the wide nose and jutting chin he had inherited from his father. Although he was a very attractive man, she could not help thinking that she preferred Grey's dark, brooding beauty. Where Grey was powerful and strongly masculine, Carey seemed almost weak in comparison, despite his broad shoulders and muscular body.

She shook herself mentally. Must she compare every man she knew to Grey? And why must they all pale by comparison? She forced her attention back to the young man who stood before her. Carey's gentle blue eyes shone with concern as he looked down at her.

"Have you been well?" he asked.

He had been so kind to her at the ordinary, her only friend, really, even though he had been a customer. Her heart warmed to the idea that he had not forgotten about her, that he had worried about her. His first thoughts had been for her happiness. It was nice to know that somewhere in the world, someone cared about her well-being. "Quite well," she said softly, smiling at him. "And you?"

Carey shrugged, as though he was of no consequence whatsoever. "I've thought about you endlessly," he said earnestly, studying her features. "I had never expected to see you so—changed."

Jennifer recalled the look of stunned admiration on his face when he had first seen her on the staircase yesterday, and a feeling of pride, of pure vanity, rose within her. Even now he was watching her with an intensity that made her feel very feminine indeed. "I have worked hard to become a lady," she admitted proudly.

"I scarcely knew you. Everything about you—your voice, your gown, your hair—"

Absurdly pleased that he was so impressed by her altered appearance, Jennifer shrugged. "It never could have happened if it had not been for Grey."

Carey's face underwent a startling transformation at the mention of her husband. He looked suddenly furious. "It was not what he meant to happen," he said coldly.

Jennifer stared at him uncomprehendingly for a long moment, then an expression of stark anger started to dawn over her features as well. "You knew," she breathed. "You *knew.*"

"Knew what?"

"You know Grey," Jennifer went on. Although her voice was soft, there was steel beneath the surface of the words. "You told me you had known him for years. You knew how he felt about Diana, and you must have known—you knew that he never intended for me to live as his wife." Her voice was calm, as always, yet the sense of betrayal she felt was evident in her tone. "Why didn't you warn me?"

Carey swallowed nervously. "I tried to tell you—"

"You told me that he was a murderer, which I did not believe then and do not now. But you never told me that he—" She broke off, then burst out, "He wanted me to live in the stables and work in the cookhouse. He would have clothed me more poorly than the slaves. And you *knew*, damn you!"

"Why should I have warned you of that?" Carey demanded. "What did you expect of him? After all, you were only—"

He paused, suddenly embarrassed at the insulting nature of what he had been about to say. Jennifer looked up at him, and the anger on her features was vivid and unmistakable. "I was only a tavern wench," she said softly, savagely. "All I deserved was to wash linens and serve drinks for the rest of my life, and eventually serve men's baser needs as well. Is that what you were going to say?"

Carey said nothing, but a muscle twitched in his cheek.

"And I thought you were different," she spat. "I thought you were my friend."

"Jenny, you're not being fair," Carey objected. "I was always kind to you at the tavern, even though I was a planter and you were a tavern wench. I always tried to treat you as though class made no difference. But you know that it *does* make a difference. You were fortunate that Greyson married you at all. What more could you have asked for? You were illiterate, untutored—"

"Grey offered me more than you planned to," Jennifer went on slowly, thoughtfully. "You didn't want me to leave, because you planned to offer me a proposition. Not marriage—you couldn't offer what Grey did, no planter in his right mind could. You were going to ask me to be your mistress. And *that* was why you told me he was a murderer, to prevent me from leaving with him."

"Jenny, I cared about you, I swear I did. But you know as well as I do that I could never have married you, even if I had loved you. What would my parents have thought? But you are right, I did intend to—to—"

"To make me your mistress," Jenny finished, remembering the odd expression in his eyes the last few months before she'd left Princess Anne County forever. She had seen that same expression in Grey's eyes too many times now not to recognize it. It was nothing more than lust.

Carey had wanted her to be his mistress. Now she understood why he had taught her to use the knife and been so intent about protecting her virginity. Now she understood why her uncle had permitted her to talk with him, had even encouraged their friendship. There had been some sort of understanding between the two men—an understanding that her uncle had apparently reneged on.

"Yes, when you turned eighteen." He scowled, adding defensively, "There was nothing else I could have given you."

Jennifer looked up at him, some of her initial anger fading. Of course Carey had comported himself exactly as a gentleman should. Gentlemen married planters' daughters and bedded tavern wenches. Grey was the one whose behavior had been ungentlemanly. "No," she agreed tautly. "Of course not."

Sensing the lightening of her mood, Carey swiftly attacked. "But now that you are married—"

Jennifer gave him a disbelieving stare. "What could you offer me now? An illicit affair? Brief moments stolen in the woods? And why would you want me? Carey, you should be looking for a suitable young lady to marry, not wasting your time with a woman who is already spoken for."

"I don't want anyone else," Carey said with great intensity. "I want you. Jenny, I always knew you were beautiful under the dirt and that absurd mob cap. Unlike that fool you married, I can see what is before my face. But now—Jenny, you're so much more beautiful than I could have imagined. . . ."

He stepped forward, caught her in his arms, and pressed his lips to hers. Caught off guard, Jennifer did not resist. He kissed her with the expertise of a man who has had a great deal of practice, yet the feel of his lips moving over hers filled her with none of the soaring emotions she had experienced the night Grey had made love to her. When she had believed that he loved her, she had felt fierce joy, primitive lust, overpowering love, a wondrous burst of emotions. In Carey's embrace she felt very little. And yet it was pleasant to know that someone in the world found her desirable. She was so starved for affection, so desperate for love, that she would have responded to any man's lovemaking.

As that thought surfaced she broke away, eluding his arms when he would have caught her again. She was not so pitiful that she would succumb to any man who found her attractive, simply because she could not have the one she wanted. "No," she protested. "This is wrong."

"How can it be wrong?" Carey demanded angrily. Her lips had been sweet, soft, and gentle, and he wanted to kiss her again. He wanted to loose the pins from her silken hair and see it tumbling around her in wanton abandon. He wanted to tear off her sky blue, low-cut gown and kiss the golden skin it concealed. He wanted all of her. His body ached with unfulfilled desire despite the briefness of their embrace.

"Adultery is never right."

"Adultery," Carey repeated scathingly. "I'm not certain you could even call it that. Why the hell should you remain loyal to a man who cares nothing at all for you? Does he even share your bed?"

His words shattered her heart, and she looked as anguished and confused as she felt. "No, I sleep alone," she confessed in a suffocated voice. "I know I'm a fool. Grey would probably tell me to take what you are offering—it is more than I will ever get from him. But I can't. Carey, I love him."

"Oh, God," Carey said in disgust. "Trust a woman to fancy herself in love with the worst possible person. Jenny, how in the world can you believe that you love that self-centered, vicious bastard?"

The ugly words, so unexpected from this gentle man, brought her back to reality with a jolt. She drew herself up proudly and addressed him sternly. "I will not permit you to speak ill of my husband," she warned.

"Your *husband*," Carey retorted, mocking her angrily, "wed you under false pretenses, permitting you to believe that he was some sort of hero. You have endured this mockery of a marriage for over a year, and now you claim to *love* him? Please, Jenny, think about what you are saying. Why are you defending him? You should be his worst enemy."

"Be quiet," Jennifer snapped, and when he would have spoken again, "*Quiet!* You don't know him at all. He's a wonderful, gentle man, everything I ever wanted or dreamed of—it's only that he's in a great deal of pain. He's so unhappy—"

"And bent on making everyone he comes into contact with miserable as well," Carey concluded. "No, Jenny, you're the one who doesn't know him at all. Wonderful? Gentle? Good God, I scarcely thought you were the type to indulge in romantic fantasies. Don't you know what he did to his first wife?"

Jennifer paused. She remembered Catherine's story all too clearly. It occurred to her that the more versions of the tale she got from witnesses, the more likely she was to be able to piece together what had actually happened. "I've heard rumors," she said cautiously. "But you were actually there, weren't you?"

"Yes. I found—I found her body."

"She was your cousin," Jennifer prompted gently when he paused.

Carey took a deep breath and forged onward with his

story. "Yes. We were visiting. Grey and Diana had been married six months before. The day we arrived, they had a tremendous fight."

"About what?" Jennifer asked, though she thought she knew the answer.

"I don't know. But I think—I think it was about me."

"Why do you believe that?"

Carey turned scarlet and did not answer.

"Carey," Jennifer said gently, "did you love your cousin?"

He nodded. "She was beautiful. I was only sixteen, you understand, but I thought she was the most wonderful creature in the world. She was more like a sister to me than a cousin."

"And did you have an affair with her?"

Carey's reaction was immediate and indignant. "Of course not!" he exploded. "How could you even ask such a thing?"

"I thought—" Jennifer paused. His appalled shock at her question appeared genuine. She could not believe that he was lying. She decided to hear the entire story from him first before telling him what she knew. "Never mind. I take it you did not?"

"No. But—" He paused and drew a hand over his eyes. "It was all my fault," he said dully. "Grey and Diana would never have quarreled if it had not been for me. And if they had not quarreled—"

"What happened?"

"Diana and I were walking in the formal garden on the house's river side. We stopped in the arbor—you know the one I mean?"

Jennifer nodded. She was familiar with the arbor, over-hung heavily with scuppernong grapes.

"I told her how happy I was for her, how glad I was that she had such a wonderful place to live, and I kissed her cheek. That's all I did, I swear it. But an hour later, when we returned to the house, she and Grey got into a tremendous argument."

"And you think the argument was about you."

Carey nodded. "He must have seen us in the arbor from the house. I couldn't hear what they were arguing about, but they were so angry—I just know it was my fault."

"Then what happened?"

"In the morning we found that they were missing. We went out to search, and I found her body." He swallowed audibly. "It still makes me ill to think about it."

"I don't blame you," Jennifer said swiftly, remembering Grey's vivid description of Diana's body. "But how do you know Grey killed her?"

"He was missing, too. Catherine swore he was in the stable all night. But I know for a fact he wasn't. I searched the stable myself, and he wasn't there. Also, he had some bruises and scratches on his face that Catherine insisted were from riding. I think Diana scratched him while trying to defend herself. Jenny, earlier you accused me of telling you Grey was a murderer just so you would stay in Princess Anne County—just so I could have you for myself. And I must admit, perhaps that was my motivation for telling you. But I swear to you that I firmly believe that he murdered Diana."

"If you knew he wasn't in the stable, then how did it happen that he wasn't hanged?"

"It was my word against Catherine's. In the end, everyone chose to believe her."

Suddenly Jennifer had a realization. "Even your father."

"Even my father," he agreed tightly. "My father all but called me a liar—he was so certain Greyson could never do such a thing. Damn Greyson to hell. My relationship with my father was a good one until—" He blinked rapidly and said in a hoarse voice, "Sometimes I think my father cares more for that bastard than he does for me."

Jennifer took his hand gently. "You don't really believe that," she said softly.

"I don't know what to believe."

Jennifer did not know what to believe either. Everyone seemed convinced her husband was a murderer. All the evidence pointed to Grey. She had to get to the bottom of this affair before she went mad. "Carey," she said quietly, "thank you for telling me everything you know. Now I'm going to tell you what I know.

"I found love letters to Diana in her desk upstairs."

"Letters from Grey, no doubt," Carey said dully. "He used to write her constantly."

"Yes. Letters from Grey. And from someone else."

Carey's head snapped around sharply. "From whom?"

"I don't know. I thought it was you. He signed all the letters C. But if it wasn't you—well, Diana was having an affair. With whom, I'm not certain. And judging from the dates on those letters, it went on *after* they were married."

Carey was silent for a moment while he considered this. "I can't believe it."

"I could show you the letters."

"No. No, I believe you." It was painfully difficult to believe the beautiful cousin he had adored could have had an affair, but Carey knew Jennifer too well to believe that she would lie about such a thing. He frowned in concentration as he considered her information.

"Could it have been Catherine?"

Jennifer stared at him blankly. "I beg your pardon?"

Carey reddened slightly but pushed on with his thought. "The person Diana was having an affair with. Perhaps you're not aware of this, but sometimes women, er . . . that is, they occasionally . . ."

"I take your meaning," Jennifer interrupted his stammered explanation, taking pity on his obvious embarrassment. She knew that women sometimes took other women as lovers. She had heard about such things in vulgar conversations at the ordinary.

"Is it possible?"

Jennifer frowned thoughtfully. "I don't believe so," she said at last. "The letters I found were written in a very masculine hand. At any rate, I am familiar with Catherine's handwriting. This was different. No, I believe it was a man."

Carey shrugged. "We may never know who it was, then. But simply because Diana was having an affair does not justify the fact that he murdered her."

"I'm not convinced he did," Jennifer said. She decided it was best not to volunteer the details of the story Catherine had told her, knowing as she did how Carey felt about Grey. Despite the incriminating nature of the story Catherine had told and despite the fact that Carey's story dovetailed all too well with Catherine's, she had a conviction that there were facts she had not uncovered. Perhaps it was simply that she could not believe the man she loved was capable of murder. Perhaps she was deluding herself. Or perhaps her heart knew something her mind did not.

And of course, it was entirely possible that Carey was lying. He was definitely still a suspect, and she did not want to tell him too much. He had loved Diana, and he might well have been jealous when she wed Grey.

But jealous enough to kill?

At last she made a decision. She was going to have to confront Grey, despite their differences, and demand his version of the story. If she ever hoped to understand exactly what had happened, she had to ask Grey. She hated to bring up the subject again, recalling as she did how much pain it had caused the last time they discussed it, but she really had no choice. *She had to know.*

"I just can't believe he killed Diana, Carey," she whispered. "I can't believe it. He's no murderer, of that I am certain. I love him."

"I've known Grey a long time," Carey said slowly, looking at her with sympathy, "and I can tell you that every shred of humanity he had disappeared on the day Diana died. After that he didn't care anymore, for anything or anyone. Regardless of whether or not he killed her, he'll never care for you, Jennifer. He *can't.*"

Jennifer swallowed hard and looked up at him earnestly. "I know that. But I can't help caring for him."

The powerful emotions she felt shone clearly on her face, illuminating it to such a degree that Carey felt his heart melt. He had never seen her face lit by that indescribable mixture of love and longing, joy and torment. For the first time he admitted to himself that she meant something to him. She was more than a beautiful face and a shapely figure.

She was an extraordinary woman.

"And I can't help caring for you," he said gently. "I think we're both hopeless romantics."

Jennifer smiled, a little sadly, it seemed to him. "I'd like to think," she said softly, "that nothing is hopeless."

TWENTY-ONE

Grey did not turn at the sound of his study door opening. In his conversation with Kayne yesterday, he had finally admitted, both to Kayne and to himself, just how desolate he was without Jennifer. He was wretched, and he did not want to talk to anyone. He simply wanted to be left alone.

"Grey?"

At the sound of Jennifer's voice his head snapped around. Silver eyes filled with empty misery stared at her in shocked surprise, their expression rapidly metamorphosing into one of hope. After two weeks of loneliness and despair, Jennifer had finally sought him out. Perhaps she wanted to speak to him. Perhaps she would accept an apology. Perhaps she did not despise him after all. A hundred hopeful scenarios filled his mind.

"I need to talk to you," she announced.

Grey rose to his feet and gestured politely to a chair. "Please sit down."

Jennifer sat, wondering at Grey's courtesy. He had never come to his feet when she walked into a chamber before. Never before had he made the simplest gesture to suggest he considered her a lady, worthy of his respect. He settled back down in his chair and fixed her with an oddly hopeful gaze. "What may I do for you?"

"I need to talk to you about Diana."

The hope drained out of his eyes. "Diana?" he repeated in a dull voice. "What about her?"

"I need to know how she died."

"I already told you," Grey said a little too quickly, remembering her sympathy in Williamsburg, remembering how she had held his hand and told him that he was incapable of murder. Remembering how her misplaced faith in him had touched his heart. Remembering how they had made love.

"This time I want to know the truth."

Grey stared at her steadily for a long time. "You've been talking to Catherine," he said at last.

Jennifer nodded.

"Very well." He spread his hands in a gesture of defeat. "I'll tell you the truth.

"I killed Diana."

The admission struck her like a fist in the stomach. Despite everything she had learned from Catherine and Carey, she had simply not been able to believe that Grey was a murderer. And yet it explained so much—the relentless, unbreakable, inescapable prison of grief and guilt he had built for himself, his erratically vicious behavior, his violent self-loathing. "Why?"

"We had an argument," Grey said softly. His voice was very calm, as though he was discussing the weather. "She—she told me she was with child. And she told me that since she would be presenting me with an heir in seven months, she would no longer be sharing my bed . . . that she would never share it again."

There was a world of hurt in his tone. She could imagine how much that rejection, from the woman he loved so dearly, had injured him.

"I was taken completely by surprise," Grey went on in the same level, quiet voice. "I knew that she did not enjoy lovemaking as much as I did, but I had never imagined that she intended to shut me out of her bed completely. We quarreled. And when she left my study, I—I got drunk."

Jennifer noted that his explanation of their fight involved no mention of another man. Evidently Carey's chaste kiss had had nothing to do with it. Nor did Grey have any idea that Diana had been cuckolding him. Well, she certainly wasn't going to be the one to tell him. It was just as well he had never known about it. But the fact that he had no notion of Diana's illicit affair, she reasoned, meant that he had had very little motive for killing her. An argument over conjugal rights was hardly likely to drive a man to murder.

"And then what?"

"And then—I have no idea," Grey said unhappily. "I can't remember what happened. Damn it! If I could only remember—"

"If you can't remember," Jennifer asked reasonably, "then how do you know you killed her?"

"Catherine found me, not ten feet from her body, scratched and bruised. She told me that I said over again that I had killed her, that it was my fault. I have no memory of anything but seeing her body. I—"

He broke off with an anguished expression on his face. Jennifer, recalling his vivid description of Diana's mangled body, was sorry that she had had to force him to relive those painful memories a second time. But she went on doggedly with her questions.

"So you have no proof that you killed her except Catherine's word?"

His head jerked up abruptly, and he looked at her oddly. "Are you suggesting that Catherine may have been *lying*?"

"Yes. That is exactly what I am suggesting."

"Why in the world would she have done that?"

"To protect someone else, perhaps." She paused significantly. "Or even herself."

Grey thought about her statement for several seconds. "I take it you're suggesting Catherine killed Diana. Ridiculous. They were not the best of friends, I'll grant you, but Catherine had no motivation to kill Diana whatsoever."

"On the contrary, she did." Jennifer briefly sketched out the tale Catherine had told her about how her leg had been broken. "So, you see," she finished, "Catherine hated Diana far more than she ever let you know." When Grey still looked skeptical, she said strenuously, "Grey, it's the only explanation that makes any sense! You didn't kill Diana, I *know* you didn't! Catherine had motivation, and she lied about it to you to divert suspicion from herself."

Grey leaned back in his chair and steepled his fingers thoughtfully. "Your theory has several holes in it, Jen," he pointed out. "If I didn't kill Diana, then why was I in the woods a mere ten feet from her body?"

Jennifer paused, and her face showed her dismay. "I didn't think of that," she admitted slowly. "Could Catherine have taken you there in order to make it appear that you were guilty?"

"It was a long way from the house. She certainly couldn't have dragged me out there. Nor could she have gotten me up onto a horse. She was still recovering from a broken leg, remember. No, Jennifer, I must have gotten there by myself."

"You were terribly drunk," Jennifer countered. "It would have been simple enough for her to lead you into the woods, or anywhere else she wanted you to go, for that matter."

"Perhaps. But you're forgetting that Catherine lied to everyone about my whereabouts that night. If she was trying to set me up as the murder suspect, why would she tell everyone I spent the night in the stable?"

"I don't believe she was trying to set you up as the suspect. I think she wanted you to believe you killed Diana so that you would not suspect that she did it. After all, you loved Diana so much that if you did suspect Catherine, she might have feared for her life. As for why she lied to everyone else . . . she was dependent on you, Grey. You were her guardian. If you had been hanged, what would have become of her?"

"Good point. But you've forgotten one important fact. Diana was beaten and raped as well as having her throat cut. A *man* killed Diana. There can be no question."

"You're right," Jennifer said glumly. "Catherine couldn't possibly be the murderer." Though she was distressed at her failure to clear Grey, she was immensely relieved that Catherine was not the culprit. After all, Catherine had been her best friend for many months now. She could no more imagine Catherine as a murderer than Grey.

She was no closer to a solution to the mystery than she had ever been. And yet . . .

Grey looked at her, his features harsh with mingled self-hatred and sorrow. "I'm a murderer, Jennifer. I'm sorry that you know it, for it means that there can be no hope for us, but even sorrier that I lied to you in Williamsburg. I cannot tell you what it meant to me that you believed in me. If only I had been worthy of your trust. I wish—" He stopped abruptly and turned away. "Never mind. What I wish for doesn't matter. If I weren't such a damned coward, I'd have dangled at the end of a rope long since. You deserve better than someone like me." He sighed and finished in a harsh near whisper. "It's too late for us."

Jennifer scarcely heard him. In her haste to solve the mystery of Diana's death and clear Grey, in her certainty that she had found a suspect with motive, she had forgotten the last piece of the puzzle. Grey's words, resounding in her brain, filled her with a sudden insight.

A man killed Diana.

A man.

A man.

At last she knew who had killed Diana.

She did not tell Grey of her suspicion, deciding that she had made enough unfounded accusations for one day. This time she would have absolute proof of who the murderer was before telling Grey her suspicions. But her intuition told her she was correct.

She needed no proof to be certain that Grey had not killed Diana.

She stood up suddenly, filled with resolve, and crossed the chamber, settling down on the arm of his easy chair. "I still don't believe you killed Diana," she said with soft sincerity. "Despite all evidence to the contrary, I simply don't believe it. I love you." She took his hand and held it tightly. "It's not too late, Grey."

Grey's eyes met hers, and in them she saw the wounded

vulnerability he ordinarily took such pains to conceal. Then his expression became shuttered. "I told you before," he said coldly, "that I was not interested in unskilled, inexperienced women."

To his surprise, Jennifer only smiled. "It isn't going to work, Grey," she murmured, stroking his onyx-black hair. "I know what you are trying to do."

Grey tried to ignore his overpowering reaction to her caressing hand. "I don't know what you mean," he ground out, wondering how her briefest touch could ignite surging desire in him so rapidly.

I understand you at last, she thought as she caressed his hair. *I understand why you couldn't let me love you.* She remembered his words, spoken with such bitter self-loathing: *You deserve better than someone like me.* Finally, she understood why he had held her at such a distance, and why he had attacked her so viciously every time she had managed to slip under his guard. "You're trying to drive me away again," she whispered, bending over and kissing his ear. "It won't work."

At the touch of her lips on his ear, Grey went rigid. "Jennifer—" he gasped, catching her hands and trying to push her away. "You don't understand."

"I do understand."

"No, you don't," he protested, trying very hard to ignore the fact that she was now kissing his throat. It was painfully difficult to ignore. "I'm a murderer and a drunkard and a self-absorbed bastard, Jennifer. You deserve better. You're a lovely young woman, and I am only—"

"The man I love," Jennifer finished. She straightened up and held out her hand. "Come upstairs, Edward."

At the sound of his given name, Grey looked up at her, studying her features as if trying to convince himself that she really wanted him. Everything she felt for him was clearly written on her face. There could be no doubt that she loved him. And he knew it was far more than he deserved.

He could fight against her love no longer.

He took her hand.

•   •   •

The house was quiet and they encountered no one as
they made their way up the stairs. Jennifer led him to her
chamber, dark but for the moonlight that streamed in
through the wooden slats of the venetian blinds. Closing
the heavy door behind her, she started to lead him across
the chamber through the moon-streaked darkness, but he
resisted.

"Are you certain you want to do this, Jennifer?"

His expression was very serious. She nodded. "Absolutely." Standing on tiptoe, she brushed her lips across his
chin. He stood, rigid and unyielding, for a moment. Then
his arms came around her and she knew that she had won.

"Please kiss me," she whispered.

His lips met hers hungrily. Torrential passion poured
through him like whitewater at the touch of her lips, and
he picked her up easily in his arms and carried her across
to the bed, laying her on the coverlet as carefully as though
she were a child, or an infinitely precious treasure. He
stared down at her for a long moment, devouring her
beauty with his eyes, and then sat next to her and bent over
to kiss her again.

As their lips met she ran her hands caressingly through
his hair until the ribbon that secured it fell away. His long
black hair swept forward, mingling with hers. Her hand
slid beneath the heavy, wavy mass of his hair, caressing the
nape of his neck, sliding across his linen-clad shoulders,
and she felt his powerful muscles jump beneath her caressing fingers.

It was all he could do to pause. With a giant effort of will
he pulled his mouth from hers. Cupping her face in his
hands he studied her features admiringly. "You are so
beautiful . . ." he whispered hoarsely.

"Not as beautiful as you are."

Her words struck him like a physical blow, affecting
him even more powerfully than her caresses. No one had

ever called him beautiful before. He lowered his head and met her lips in a ravishing kiss, then pulled away again.

"I don't want to frighten you," he breathed in her ear, thinking that she had every reason to be afraid of him. But she only smiled and kissed his cheek in a whisper-soft caress.

"I'm not frightened of you. I love you, Edward. I've loved you longer than you would believe."

She was not frightened. It was all he needed to know. Propping himself up on his arms so as not to crush her, his lips began a leisurely exploration of her throat, then slid down toward the expanse of skin exposed by her low-cut blue gown. Her skin smelled of lavender. He kissed the top of her breasts, then kissed her nipple, hidden though it was beneath the blue fabric.

"Edward?"

Grey lifted his head slowly, sure that she'd been frightened by his ardor, painfully certain she was going to ask him to stop. "Yes?" he rasped.

"It seems to me that our clothing has become something of an impediment."

Her husband stared at her for a moment in the moonlight, then let out his breath and whooped with sudden laughter. "Yes," he agreed when he'd stopped laughing. "I find that I must agree with you."

"Will you unhook my gown?" she asked, sitting up and presenting her back to him.

"I would be more than happy to assist you, madam," Grey replied with mock formality, then found that he was laughing too hard to manage the hooks. He managed to suppress his laughter by leaning forward and kissing the nape of her neck. That seemed to take his mind off laughing rather rapidly. He found himself unhooking her gown at breakneck speed.

"Careful," she whispered chidingly. "Don't tear the fabric."

"I'll buy you a hundred gowns just like it if I do," Grey promised huskily.

Somehow he managed to get her out of her clothing without doing any of it permanent damage. After he had unhooked her dress he unlaced her stays, then removed her boned canvas hoops. At last he untied her embroidered garters and pulled the silk stockings from her legs. He left her barely translucent linen shift on, assuming that her modesty might be offended if he took it off. To his surprise, she stood up and slid the shift over her head, then stood naked in front of him.

She smiled at his stunned expression. "I don't want any impediments between us, Edward."

"Evidently not," he said hoarsely. It was her turn to laugh.

"And now," she said when she had recovered her composure, and he had stared long enough, "I will take off your clothes." She leaned forward and began to unhook his breeches.

"Don't you want to take off my shirt first?" Grey inquired dryly.

She grinned cheekily. "Why? It's not in the way."

Once she had taken off his breeches and peeled off his stockings, Grey unbuttoned his shirt and threw it aside. "I don't want any impediments between us," he said softly, echoing her earlier words. "Nothing is going to come between us ever again, Jennifer."

He caught her by the waist and pressed her back into the softness of the feather mattress, imprisoning her between his powerful arms. His lips sought hers hungrily. The last time they had made love, he had taken care to be gentle. This time he could not restrain himself. She was too beautiful, too sensual, too desirable for him to maintain any sort of self-possession.

He felt like a flame, burning out of control.

She did nothing to quench the flames.

His hands were everywhere, exploring her silken skin, caressing the taut flesh that was so unlike that of any other woman he had ever known. She was fragile yet strong, delicate yet powerful. Finding her small, firm breasts, he rolled the nipples between his fingers and she writhed and cried out, clutching at his back.

Grey stiffened at the feel of her hands against his bare skin. "Jennifer," he whispered harshly. "Touch me. Please."

Her eyes flew open and she looked at him with surprise. "Do you like to be touched?" she asked softly, kneading his shoulders, which were rigid and damp with sweat. She had never imagined that he might enjoy being caressed as much as she herself did.

Grey closed his eyes and nodded, unable to speak, as she shyly stroked his back.

"Where?"

"Everywhere," Grey grated. "Anywhere." It occurred to him that he was virtually begging for her favors, like a clumsy teenage boy with his first woman, but he could not help himself. The touch of her hands was painful ecstasy to him, driving away all rational thought.

Shyly, her hands slipped lower, exploring the strongly contoured muscles of his lower back, sliding over his buttocks, caressing his thighs. "There?" she asked softly.

"Yes," he whispered between gritted teeth. "Yes. And . . . *there.*"

He moved her hand. Jennifer hesitated a moment, then took him in her hand. Hearing his explosively indrawn breath, and realizing the ecstasy she seemed to be giving him, she stroked him delicately, taking pleasure in his soft groans. At last he caught at her hand, stilling it.

"Did I hurt you?" she asked, a little anxiously.

"Hardly." His voice was little more than a harsh rasp.

"Don't you want me to touch you anymore?"

"No."

"Why not?"

"Because," Grey ground out, "you are driving me insane."

Jennifer looked at his face in the moonlight. His face was dark with desire and tense with the effort of controlling himself. "I believe," she said, reaching for him again and caressing him boldly, "that is the idea."

At the renewed touch of her hands Grey could control

himself no longer. He slid between her thighs and plunged into her with a savage hunger, thrusting fiercely. She cried out with pleasure. An agonized groan tore from his chest.

The flames consumed them.

Grey did not get up and return to his chamber after they had made love. Nothing could have moved him from her side. He held her against his chest, his chin resting atop her head, and felt utterly content.

He thought of what he had said to her: *Nothing is going to come between us ever again.* It wasn't true, of course. The knowledge that he was a murderer still stood between them. Nothing could ever change that. But he would do what he could.

He had made his decision. Tomorrow he would go to Williamsburg and confess that he had killed Diana. He would hang, of course, but it was no more than he deserved.

For the first time in a very long time, he felt at peace.

When Grey's soft, even breathing told her that he had fallen asleep, Jennifer propped her head on an arm and studied her husband.

Though she had lived with him for more than a year, she had rarely dared to look overmuch at his face, for fear of betraying what she felt for him too plainly. But he had always seemed to look older than his years, his face lined and weary. In the aftermath of their lovemaking, and in the peace of sleep, however, his face looked startlingly young. Perhaps, she mused, the impression of age on his face was due to his habitual embittered expression, rather than his features.

For his features were lovely, she thought, studying his hooked nose, the forceful lines of his black brows, the finely sculptured lips. No—"lovely" was the wrong word; there was nothing feminine about his strong face. On the contrary, he was powerfully masculine. "Handsome" was not the right word, either; it conveyed a certain bland conventionality Grey was entirely lacking.

He was beautiful, just as she had blurted out during their lovemaking. It was the only word she could think of that could describe him adequately.

She stared at him for a long time, mesmerized by the man she had fallen in love with so long ago, who had at last demonstrated that he cared for her as well.

There was no doubt in her mind that he did care for her. Perhaps he did not love her yet, but he would come to love her. She would see to that. She would prove to him that he was no murderer, and then he would feel free to return her affection.

The happiness of their union still filled her, for although of course that peak of ecstasy she had experienced could not be sustained for more than a breathless, joyous moment, the intimacy of it could not be forgotten. Her happiness was so sharp that she could not sleep. Her eyes remained stubbornly open, drawn irresistibly to her husband's beauty.

At last, when she had admired him to her heart's content, as she had never dared to do before, and was just about to drop off into peaceful slumber, she was startled by the sound of the door to her chamber opening. Ordinarily she would have sat up in fright, but Grey's presence gave her courage. She lay quietly, listening.

In the moonlight she could see a figure moving stealthily across the chamber. It stopped near her bed. "Jenny?"

"Carey?" she whispered in surprise. She would have recognized his soft tenor voice anywhere, even had he not addressed her by that old name that no one else used anymore.

"Jenny, I must talk with you."

"Go away!" she hissed.

"I've tried to stay away," Carey whispered, "but I can't. Please listen to me. I want you. I've wanted you since we first met in Princess Anne County. It's simply not fair that you should be tied down to a man incapable of satisfying you when you're capable of so much passion. When you kissed me today—"

"Shh!" Jennifer hissed indignantly, hoping against hope that Grey did not awaken. She thought of sliding from the bed and discussing Carey's unfortunate lack of timing with him elsewhere—anywhere but here—but she recalled suddenly that she was naked beneath the linens. Getting out of bed was clearly not her best option.

"When you kissed me today," Carey went on more strongly, "I realized just how much passion you have to give. I can't offer you much, Jenny, but if only you would agree to share my bed—"

"I am afraid," a sardonic male voice drawled, "that the lady's bed is already occupied."

Jennifer felt her heart lurch to a painful stop in her chest. Grey was awake. How much had he heard? What conclusions had he drawn? Silently she cursed Carey for bringing up the subject a second time. Damn it, she had told him forcibly enough this afternoon that she had no interest in being his mistress. Couldn't the man accept a refusal gracefully?

There was a sudden, horrified silence, and then Carey said in an accusing tone, "You told me you always slept alone, Jenny."

"I—" Jennifer began, then fell silent, aware that anything she said might be misconstrued by her husband. What would Grey think of the fact that they had been discussing her sleeping habits? Being Grey, he was bound to put the worst possible interpretation on Carey's statement.

"Your earlier words were correct, Mr. O'Neill," Grey rumbled, a sneer in his voice. "The lady indeed has a great deal of passion. However, I am quite comfortable where I am, and I have no intentions of vacating this warm bed so that *you* can enjoy her charms as well."

"But—"

"Get out," Grey snarled in tones of loathing and fury so intense that Carey fled without further argument.

When he had gone, Jennifer reached out and placed a trembling hand on her husband's arm. "Grey," she began.

Grey yanked his arm away as if she had burned him, sitting up. "So," he said contemptuously. "You met Carey in the forest today, did you? When you invited me to your bed, did it somehow slip your mind that you'd already invited your lover?"

"He isn't my lover!" Jennifer protested heatedly as she sat up, facing him.

"Oh, come now, my dear," Grey said in a silky voice. The flame was gone, replaced by glacial ice. "Surely you don't expect me to believe that your bed was empty last night. A woman with such a *passionate* nature could hardly be expected to sleep alone, could she? And it's evident you've known Carey for a long time—and that you have been meeting him for trysts for all those years."

Jennifer stared at him as though he were mad. "You know I was a virgin when we married!" she objected hotly.

"Indeed you were," Grey agreed, "but there are other ways a woman can please a man. I would never settle for less than all of you—but I suspect that milksop might."

He stared at her, seeing her face in shadow, surrounded by the moonlit halo of her hair. Her naked body was slim and shapely, and he thought that she looked like an angel—a fallen one, perhaps.

Even through his anger, he could feel his body responding, aching, his pulse leaping at the sight of her lithe figure, and he bit back a curse. She was a witch, not an angel. Only a witch could make his body ache like this. Only a witch could make him forget his fury in the power of a more elemental emotion.

His hand reached out to caress her cheek, stroking her high cheekbones. Unable to see his face in the shadows, Jennifer could not discern what was going through his mind. She was bewildered and frightened by his quicksilver changes in mood, but she resisted the urge to pull away.

It seemed to her that the world stood between them.

Only their passion bound them together. Perhaps, if she made love to him, if she demonstrated once again just how much he meant to her, he would listen to her explanations.

And then she gasped as he caught her in an embrace, and savagely covered her mouth with his own.

Jennifer's soft whimper of protest was smothered by the crushing weight of his lips. This kiss was nothing like the ones they had shared earlier in the evening. It was bruising and punishing. In the long habit of years, Jennifer did nothing to protect herself despite her fear, only remained quiet and passive. But then she yanked herself away from him in sudden hurt and anger.

"What's wrong, *Jenny*?" Grey jeered. She did not fail to notice the mocking use of her old name. "Don't you like my kisses as well as you like O'Neill's?"

Jennifer said nothing, only ground her teeth together in anger. She knew him well enough to hear the agonized hurt he was concealing beneath his hostile tone, and she did not want to hurt him further. He had every reason to be angry, she thought, for what conclusions could he have been expected to draw from Carey's words? But if only he was not so easily hurt! He seemed so powerful, so strong, and yet he was so vulnerable. . . .

"Answer me," Grey growled. "Does Carey kiss better than I do? You seemed to like my kisses earlier."

"Earlier it was different," Jennifer whispered, feeling horribly exposed as her nipples went rigid in the cool air. She knew the moonlight shimmered on every curve of her body, producing an effect more erotic than simple nudity could ever be. And she became terribly ashamed and horribly wounded.

"Ah, yes," he murmured, "Because earlier I did not know of your affections for another man. I thought that you were what you pretended to be—a woman in love with her husband. The more fool I!"

"That is exactly what I am!" Jennifer retorted proudly, wishing that a cloud would cover the brilliant sphere of the moon to shield her from his hungry gaze. "A woman in love with her husband." And—" She hesitated, then finished quietly, "And I do love you, Edward."

She could not see his eyes, for his eyelids were lowered as his gaze raked over her body. "Indeed," he said mockingly, but she heard the pain in his voice. The raw anguish of it tore at her heart like broken glass. "You have a curious way of showing it, mistress. Bedding another man—"

"I did not share Carey O'Neill's bed," Jennifer interrupted, her voice rising in desperation. "And *he* kissed *me*!"

Grey broke from the bed and Jennifer abruptly. He had had enough. His heart was broken and he needed to escape.

And having tried, judged, and condemned her without another word, he gathered his clothes and strode from the chamber wordlessly, leaving Jennifer humiliated and angry and shockingly hurt.

She would have been less furious had she known that Grey, like herself, ached with unfulfilled passion. But she could not know that. All she knew as she sobbed into the pillow was that Grey did not believe that she loved him.

And he did not love her.

Grey lay sleepless in his oak-paneled chamber. He simply could not believe the depths of Jennifer's perfidy. She had made love to him with all the passion and gentle affection a man could desire; she had made him happier than he had been in many long years; and then she had lain awake, waiting for her lover.

He remembered her soft voice whispering "I love you" in the darkness, and the memory struck him painfully, like a whip across his back. It was unbearable that the light in the darkness should be so suddenly extinguished. It was unbearable that the fragile bond that had formed between them, anchoring him to reality, should be snapped so suddenly, leaving him adrift on his dreams.

His dreams were simply not enough to sustain him anymore. He knew that now. Once upon a time they had been enough. He had been perversely content to live in misery;

he had even found his happiness in the reliving of his sorrow—until Jennifer's arrival. Damn her!

For a few moments he entertained the thought that if Jennifer had sought affection elsewhere, he might have borne at least part of the blame, morose and distant as he had been. But the thought that he himself was responsible for the intolerable situation he now found himself trapped in was too painful.

After a long, lonely night spent tossing and turning, when the first dim golden rays of sunshine drifted into his chamber, reminding him inevitably of her long silken hair, he admitted that sleep was going to elude him. Angrily he threw on clothing, utterly careless of his appearance, and stalked to the stables, where he demanded that the bay stallion be saddled. The dangerous expression on his face sent slaves hurrying to obey.

Moments later, he and the thoroughbred were galloping headlong through the woods. For the time being, he forgot about justice, forgot about going to Williamsburg. No, he wanted to ride merely so he could be alone. He could not bear to look at her face over the breakfast table. Even the memory of her beauty was acid eating into his heart.

More dreams, he thought bitterly, urging the great stallion to an even more reckless pace. But the memories of the previous night could not be left behind so easily.

"Where the hell is my wife?"

Catherine resisted the very strong urge to cringe before the fury in Grey's voice. There was something in his face other than his usual bad temper that frightened her, something coldly vindictive and brutally savage. Only with difficulty did she keep her voice level.

"I believe she went out to sit by the river this morning," she said evenly, adding, "She seemed—upset."

Grey scowled so blackly at this comment that she added

hastily, "Did you need to see her? I can send one of the slaves down for her if you wish."

Grey did want to see her, to ask her why she had not found him to be enough, to ask her why she had made love to him as if she cared for him . . . to beg her for explanations. After everything they had shared last night, why had he not been enough for her? But he shook his head slowly.

"No," he said. "No, I have something else to do." And turning he made his way up the staircase. In his wife's chamber, he slammed the door behind him and walked slowly across to the desk.

His rage of the night before had blinded him to all logic. But this morning, as he rode, he had calmed down enough to think rationally. And something had been puzzling him. He knew that she had been a virgin when he had married her. Carey had implied they had kissed in the woods, but perhaps they had not shared any real intimacies.

Then again, for all he knew Carey had been coming to Williamsburg and meeting Jennifer somewhere on the grounds of the plantation. If that was the case, he must have written her notes, in order to arrange their trysts, and perhaps Jennifer had been foolish enough to save them. Slamming the door of her desk down, he began yanking letters from the pigeonholes.

Most of the letters were written in his own bold hand. Love letters of his youth, from himself to Diana. These he replaced carefully, with all the reverence he had felt for his dead wife. She had never disappointed him like this. A few were in Diana's graceful handwriting—unfinished letters to him.

Finally, after some minutes of searching, he found a letter written in a faltering, uneven hand. Jennifer's writing, of course. And the blotchy, awkward shape of the letters suggested it had been written quite some time ago. The date at the top confirmed this suspicion. He seized it, certain that this was the clue he sought.

But to his surprise, the letter was addressed to himself.

"My dearest Edward," it began:

"I wish I cud" (this had been scratched through and replaced with "cood") "begin to tell you ov my lov. You canot begin to gess wot you mean to me, and I grately fear that if you did, you woud not care."

Grey scowled, puzzled as he deciphered the appallingly bad handwriting. Why in the world had she addressed him as Edward in the letter? It had taken her many months to work up the courage merely to address him as Grey. Never had she called him by his given name until last night.

And had she really loved him so long ago? He remembered something she had said last night. "I've loved you longer than you would believe," she had whispered in his ear. He had not thought she meant it so sincerely. How the hell could she have loved him, self-centered and surly bastard that he had been?

The ice in his heart began slowly to melt.

After a few more flattering inanities, the letter ended midsentence. Perhaps the writer had found her limited vocabulary inadequate to express her feelings. But in another pigeonhole he found a second letter, written in a hand which, if not precisely graceful, was at least legible. He read:

"Beloved Edward,

"It breaks my heart when you scowl at me as you did today. Sometimes, when your face is cold and shuttered, I feel I cannot bear to remain in your presence. Sometimes I wish I could run from Greyhaven and never look back. But oh, Edward, how I would miss you. Curious, isn't it, how my love for you frightens me so?"

Grey read on, fascinated by the glimpse into her heart that her words provided. She had painted a portrait of him with her words, a portrait at once unflattering and tender. She spoke of his soul, the "true Edward" that she was in love with, and closed the note by writing sadly that she wished the sentiments enclosed in the desk had been directed at her rather than at Diana.

When he had read the note twice through, he leaned back and stared blankly into space. This at least explained why Jennifer loved him—she had read his letters to Diana, and they had touched her somehow. It seemed that she had fallen in love with the man he had been eight years before. Moreover, she seemed to believe that man still existed.

Strangely, he felt flattered, rather than violated, by the knowledge that she had struggled, barely literate as she had been, to read the letters in the desk in an effort to know him better. But having read her note to him, it was difficult to believe that she had sought a lover elsewhere. Whatever else she was, she was no liar. She had told him she loved him, and she had meant it sincerely. Her letter was proof of that.

Could he have been wrong?

It occurred to him belatedly that Carey might have been in pursuit of her. Perhaps he had asked her to be his mistress and she had declined. Even if she had bedded Carey, as the scene in her chamber last night had convinced him, perhaps it was not entirely her fault. It could be that she had been so lonely that she had filled the void in her life as best she could, much as Grey himself had done. Perhaps the pain of unrequited love had driven her to seek comfort elsewhere.

Slowly he was coming to see her side of the situation, and he admitted unhappily that he had not been entirely fair.

There were other letters, scattered here and there throughout the pigeonholes, the hopeless letters of a woman in love with a man who had long ago ceased to be lovable. Reading through them, Grey felt his throat tighten in sympathy at her obvious pain and grief.

But still he found no letters from Carey. Puzzled, and more than half ready to concede she had never bedded anyone but himself, he sat back and wondered: where would she have hidden letters from a lover?

His eyes fell upon the burled walnut prospect door in the center of the desk. *Of course!* Any letters she wanted to hide would be concealed behind that door. After a brief search, he found the key on the twilight and opened the door.

What he found there stunned and lacerated him.

Jennifer found him there, half an hour later, sobbing.

"Edward," she whispered, frightened by his desperate tears and at a loss to know what could have caused him such anguish. "What is wrong?"

Her husband lifted his head, and what she saw in his face frightened her more. He was not drunk. These were the tears of a sober man whose world has been ripped asunder.

"Tell me," he grated, red-rimmed eyes staring into hers. "Did you know?"

"Know what?" Jennifer began in honest puzzlement, and then she saw the open prospect door and the letters spread across the desk, and she understood. Grey had found the letters another man had written Diana. The letters that proved all too clearly that she had made love to another man. "Oh, God," she whispered. "I knew I should have burned those letters. Edward, I'm so sorry."

"You—you have nothing to be sorry about," Grey said brokenly. "I thought—I believed that she—" He shook his head and tried unsuccessfully to suppress a sob. "I was a fool," he bit out.

Jennifer stepped toward him, instinctively seeking to comfort him, to drive away the agony that quivered in his voice, but he raised both hands as if to ward her off. "No." His voice was stronger. "Keep away from me. I can't—I can't think clearly."

He stood up and brushed past her, stumbling blindly down the stairs. His shoulders were bent in an attitude of utter defeat, and watching him, Jennifer felt a wave of pity and grief for him, which evaporated instantaneously into fury as she heard his study door slam.

He had gone to drink himself into a stupor again, she realized angrily.

Didn't the fool realize that drinking wouldn't solve anything?

"Damn you, Grey," she said to the empty chamber. "Damn you to hell."

•   •   •

"I need to talk to you."

Carey, idly puffing at a pipe as he sat in the parlor, looked up in surprise. "Oh. Good afternoon, Catherine. How can I help you?"

Catherine limped into the chamber and sat down on the leather-upholstered settee in front of the blazing fire. It was still cold outside, despite the fact that it was nearly spring. "I'm worried about Jennifer," she said without preamble.

So am I, Carey thought. *Worried because she fancies herself in love with a lunatic. I should have stopped her from marrying him last year. I could have made her my mistress. I could have offered her uncle more money. I could have—*

He cut off that line of thought, aware that it was unproductive. Jennifer *was* married, and she was in love with Grey. And there was nothing to be done about it now, nothing at all. "Why?"

"Grey is very angry with her," Catherine said haltingly. "I don't really know what happened, but—"

Carey lifted a russet eyebrow. "Are you afraid he might murder her?" he said cruelly.

Catherine said nothing, but he saw her pale slightly.

"I know you lied all those years ago. You told everyone that Grey was in the stable all night, when in fact he killed Diana. Didn't you?"

When she stubbornly said nothing, he shrugged, feeling a reluctant stab of admiration for her obstinate, if misguided, loyalty. "Very well. Let's table that for now. Tell me exactly what has you concerned."

"He's been in his study all afternoon," Catherine said. "He was so angry this morning that I was frightened. I don't know what happened, but I know Jennifer had something to do with it." She hesitated, then looked at him squarely. "Please, Carey. You have to watch Jennifer to make certain—to make certain nothing happens to her."

Carey drew a mouthful of smoke into his lungs

thoughtfully. He knew what had caused the discord between Grey and Jennifer, even if Catherine did not. It was his fault. Damned blundering fool that he was, he had unwittingly caused another argument, just as he believed he had caused the quarrel between Grey and Diana that led to her death.

This argument might lead to Jennifer's death. He could not permit that to happen.

"Very well," he agreed tightly. "I will keep an eye on Jennifer tonight. I promise. And Catherine . . ."

"Yes?"

"Don't worry. I'll take good care of her. I promise."

Jennifer did not see Grey again that afternoon. Distressed as she was over the situation with her husband, she was grateful for the absence of the O'Neills. In a way she was even grateful for Grey's refusal to leave the study. She was not certain she wanted to see him in this mood. Surely, in his current vitriolic and angry state, he would be infuriated if he knew of her plans.

She was not required to entertain anyone at dinner tonight. Catherine and Carey ate in the dining chamber, and Grey did not eat at all. She supposed he was still trying to numb the pain of his discovery by drinking. Jennifer ate nothing at all, though a slave brought food to her chamber. She was too nervous to eat. She could do nothing but wait.

Since she did not have to play the hostess tonight, she spent the early part of the evening sitting anxiously in her chamber with no company other than William. Earlier she had sent a note, which said only, "I have reconsidered your proposition. Please meet me at nine o'clock at the wharf to discuss."

She did not pause to consider that her plan was dangerous. She was determined to establish, once and for all, that Grey was no murderer.

At eight-thirty she left the house.

Though she left as quietly as possible, Grey heard the soft tapping of her shoes on the planks of the hall floor. Arising from his easy chair, he strode from his study and followed her.

In his hand he carried a pistol.

TWENTY-TWO

Jennifer walked across the wide, moonlit lawn that sloped
down to the river. Despite her determination to get to the
bottom of this matter, her mind was not on the task at
hand. All she could think about—all she had thought
about all day—was the tender way Grey had made love to
her last night. He had been so gentle, so kind—

And then everything had been shattered because he had
thought that she had been unfaithful.

She remembered his grief at the discovery that Diana
had lain with another, and she felt a brief spurt of annoyance. He had been angry and wounded when he thought
Jennifer had sought affection elsewhere, but the discovery
that his long-dead wife had loved another had hit him far
harder. It was a painful reminder that Diana meant more
to him than Jennifer could ever hope to.

Or was it?

Thoughtfully, she considered the situation. Grey had
been distraught because he had somehow, over the course
of many years, come to believe that Diana was more than
human. He had canonized her in his mind and was understandably horrified when he discovered that she was no
saint, but only a very fallible woman.

Perhaps the fact that he knew Jennifer was merely a
woman, a human being with myriad faults and flaws,
worked to her advantage.

She did not want to be placed on a pedestal; she only wanted to be loved.

Grey strode swiftly down the front stairs of Greyhaven and stepped quietly onto the grass, following the small figure of his wife. He was halted abruptly by a voice behind him.

"Stop right there, Greyson. Turn around. Slowly."

At the menacing voice, Grey turned. Behind him stood Carey O'Neill, his face dark with anger. His blue eyes blazed from above a dueling pistol—a duplicate of the pistol Grey held in his hand.

The pistol was pointed straight at Grey's heart.

Diana was no longer a factor, Jennifer reasoned as she picked her way across the grass. Whatever Grey had felt for his first wife had surely been smashed into a million pieces by his discovery that she had loved another man.

But Grey felt something for Jennifer. She was certain of it. The passionate way he had made love to her last night demonstrated all too clearly that he cared for her.

The only thing that stood between them, then, was Grey's belief that he was a murderer. If she could prove that someone else had murdered Diana, then the last barrier would fall.

And she planned on proving it tonight.

"Drop the pistol, Greyson."

Grey cursed mentally. He had taken the dueling pistol he held from his case, carelessly leaving the box open on his desk. Obviously Carey had found the open case and taken the matching pistol. "Carey—" he began placatingly.

"*Drop it.*"

Recognizing the menace in the other's tone, Grey

dropped the pistol. Whatever else he might be, he was no fool.

"Now," Carey said. The pistol did not waver. "Suppose you tell me what you are doing out here."

"Carey, I really haven't the time—"

"Tell me why you were following Jennifer with a pistol," Carey said. The expression on his face was deadly.

Grey sighed. Damn the young fool's ridiculous attraction to Jennifer. Damn him to hell for interfering.

"I was following her," he said briefly, "because she's going to meet another man."

Jennifer reached the wharf at the bottom of the lawn, glancing around. There was no one here. Well, she was early. She pulled her cloak around her, feeling the cold more intensely here near the river.

Now all she had to do was wait.

"You idiot!" Carey exploded. "I know you think she's been unfaithful to you, but you couldn't be more wrong. Damn it, I asked her to be my mistress and she declined. She loves you—God only knows why."

"She kissed you," Grey pointed out mildly.

"*I* kissed *her*!"

Grey felt a wave of relief. After a long day spent reflecting on everything he knew of Jennifer, he had come to suspect as much. Nonetheless, it was a relief to know for certain that his efforts to hold her at a distance had not forced her into the arms of another lover.

"You're so jealous you can't see what's right in front of you," Carey growled. "She loves you, and you're too damned suspicious and surly to love her back. She isn't going to meet another man, you fool. There is no one for her but you."

Grey did not answer. His eyes were fixed on something over Carey's left shoulder. "My God," he whispered.

Carey glanced around, and Grey leaped on him like a panther. The full impact of his weight knocked the younger man to the ground, slamming the pistol from his grasp and sending it flying harmlessly into the grass. Grey caught the younger man by the throat and held him pinned helplessly to the ground despite Carey's impotent struggles.

"Now," he said in a conversational tone, "we will talk. We don't have much time. Unless I am greatly mistaken, Jennifer is in very real danger."

"Hello, Jennifer."
Jennifer turned around and forced a smile to her lips.
"Hello, Christopher."

"Jennifer sent a note to Christopher Lightfoot this morning," Grey explained, in much the same tone he would have used had they been sitting in the parlor companionably smoking pipes. He ignored Carey's expression, which promised death. "Unfortunately for her, she asked old Moses to take it over to the Cove. What she didn't realize is that Moses, unlike most of our slaves, can read. He looked over the message, thought I should see it, and brought it to me this afternoon. It said, "I have reconsidered your proposition. Meet me at the wharf to discuss. Jennifer.' "

"I don't believe it," Carey growled. He was still annoyed by his ineptitude in allowing himself to be bested by Grey. Damned idiot that he was, he had been taken in by the oldest trick in existence. "I just finished telling you that she loves you."

"She isn't meeting Lightfoot for a tryst, damn it!" Grey took a deep breath and finished, "She thinks he killed Diana."

·   ·   ·

"You look lovely," Christopher Lightfoot breathed admiringly, taking Jennifer's hand. She smiled at him in a way that she hoped was flirtatious and batted her long eyelashes. She had practiced fluttering her eyelashes in front of the looking glass for a full hour today. She thought she looked like a fool, but men seemed to like that sort of thing.

She dropped the concealing cloak to the ground and his eyes widened. His gaze seemed irresistibly drawn to the expanse of flesh that swelled above the neckline of her gown. In the hopes of putting him off his guard, she had worn the lowest-cut gown she owned, displaying a shockingly immodest amount of her small but firm breasts. The peach-colored silk set off her golden coloring well. Atop her carefully coiffed hair she wore a small, frilly confection of peach silk and lace known as a butterfly cap. She looked lovely, young, and entirely defenseless.

In a pocket beneath her overskirt she carried her knife.

"She may think Lightfoot murdered Diana," Carey said sneeringly, "but we know better, don't we?"

Grey's silver eyes, unreadable in the dim light, bored into his. At last he said, "I've already admitted to her that I killed Diana. But she—"

"Bastard!" Carey exploded. "I knew it was you! I *knew* it!" Enraged by the other man's admission, he began to struggle violently, and one of his fists struck Grey in the mouth, splitting his lip. Cursing in annoyance, he struck Carey hard. Carey grunted and lay still, the wind driven out of him.

"Yes, damn it, it was me," Grey snarled. "I don't remember killing her, but I know I did it. Catherine said—"

"Catherine? But she said you were in the stables all night!"

"She lied," Grey said shortly. "Carey, I told Jennifer I was the murderer, but she simply won't believe me. As you said, she loves me, and she's blind where I'm concerned. She's gone to confront Lightfoot. She doesn't realize that he's a very dangerous man. The bastard wouldn't object to raping her if he thinks he can get away with it."

"Why the hell does she think Lightfoot murdered Diana?"

"I told you, I don't remember killing Diana. I don't remember anything except finding her body, damn it. I was dead drunk. Catherine found me, and she told me I said I killed Diana over and over again—so obviously I'm the murderer. If only I could remember—" Grey broke off. "The reason Jennifer thinks Lightfoot killed her," he went on, more calmly, "is because he was having an affair with Diana."

"I'm so glad you came," Jennifer exclaimed, batting her eyelashes coyly. "It's been so lonely for me in that great big house, with no one for company except Grey—and he's scarcely any company at all."

"Is that the reason you've suddenly decided to have an affair with me?" Christopher inquired. "Because you're lonely?"

Beneath his polite tone Jennifer detected a hint of menace. There was definitely more to Christopher Lightfoot than met the eye, she decided. He seemed like a harmless dandy on the surface, kind and very handsome, but the dark blue eyes hid something that Jennifer did not care for at all. Perhaps, she reasoned, he was suspicious of her sudden capitulation.

"Oh, it was hardly a sudden decision," she said airily, aware that in the cold air her nipples were hardening under her gown. Christopher's avid stare made her realize that the thin silk of the gown did not hide that fact at all. "I've always thought you were terribly attractive. But I've been afraid. Afraid of Grey." She paused, then added, "So many people seem to believe he is a murderer."

• • •

Carey did not look as surprised as Grey had expected. "Yes, Jennifer said Diana was having an affair with someone whose initial was C. I suppose it could have been Christopher Lightfoot as well as anyone."

"It was, I'm certain of that. I recognized his handwriting on the letters he wrote to Diana. And Jennifer must have realized that he was the one having an affair with Diana as well. But somehow, from that, I think she has made the improbable deduction that he was the one who murdered Diana. That's why I was going after her." When Carey only looked at him skeptically, Grey explained further in a rush of words. "I've known Christopher Lightfoot as long as I can remember. All through our boyhood we were friends. But when we were young men I caught him in several cruelties—I don't have time to describe them now. Suffice it to say that he is dangerous. Jennifer may have trouble with him."

"If that's the case, why didn't you simply stop her from going to talk with him?"

"Jennifer is stubborn," Grey said, unaware that the affection he felt for his wife was clear in his tone. "She would have tried again. And I might not be able to stop her next time. Carey, I'm going to Williamsburg tomorrow. I'm going to turn myself in."

Carey looked at him blankly. "You mean that you are going to admit that you murdered Diana? After all this time?"

Grey nodded.

"They'll hang you," Carey predicted with grim satisfaction.

"Very probably. A murderer deserves no less." He took a deep breath. "Carey, I swear to you on my honor that I was following Jennifer, not to injure her, but to protect her. I have to get down to the wharf and make certain Lightfoot does her no harm. Will you let me go?"

Carey stared at him for a long moment. Finally he said grudgingly, "Only if you let me go with you."

"Very well," Grey replied, coming easily to his feet and helping Carey to his as though they had not earlier been at each other's throats. He bent and picked up one of the pistols, handing it butt first to Carey, who looked surprised.

"You do realize," Carey said slowly, accepting the pistol, "that you will have a ball between your ribs if I have any reason to believe that you intend to hurt Jennifer?"

Grey grinned at him, the honest smile that he reserved for close friends. "You are your father's son," he said, picking up his pistol. "I expected no less."

He turned and strode toward the river. Carey followed, bewildered by the friendly note he had heard in the other man's voice. It was as though Grey had finally accepted him as an equal. He felt oddly disarmed by the implied compliment.

But of course, he was dealing with a criminal, a man who had killed his wife in the most horrible of ways. He could not forget that, even for a second.

If he had not forcibly reminded himself that Grey was a murderer, however, he would have found himself liking the man.

The two men crept toward the river, concealing themselves in the brush that grew down to the beach. Jennifer and Christopher stood near the wharf, conversing intently, and Grey's chin dropped as he saw the gown she was wearing, and the charms it amply displayed. *Good God,* he thought in astonishment, *I was right to worry about her.*

"And what do you think?" Lightfoot was inquiring. "Do you believe he is a murderer?"

Jennifer shuddered delicately. "I simply don't know what to believe," she declared. "Grey is always so cold, so remote." *Except last night, when he made love to me for hours,* she amended mentally. "But I know he loved his first wife very much. I find it terribly difficult to believe he killed her. And it's not surprising he worshipped her so. She was so very beautiful."

Christopher's eyes narrowed suddenly, and she was chillingly aware that she had not brought up the subject of Diana with a great deal of subtlety. "Indeed," he said softly. "But of course, I did not know Diana well."

Cursing her lack of finesse, and frightened by the ugly expression that had entered his eyes, Jennifer took a deep breath and forced her pounding heart to slow. "Really?" she said, her eyes widening innocently. "I had been told you knew her well. *Quite* well, in fact."

Christopher caught her arm and yanked her up against him. Looking up into his face, she quailed. His dark blue eyes no longer seemed friendly. They were like chips of ice—brittle and very, very cold. The eyes of a murderer.

In the brush, Carey started to jump to his feet, but Grey's hand on his arm restrained him. "Wait," he barely whispered.

"But he's—"

"Wait a moment," Grey repeated in a low voice.

If it became necessary, he himself would defend his wife, not Carey. He had no intentions of letting Lightfoot manhandle Jennifer—he would strangle the man if he so much as bruised her, damn it—but he wanted desperately to know the details of Lightfoot's relationship with Diana. He *had* to know. How long had it gone on? When had it started?

And, God help him, had it begun while he still considered Christopher his best friend?

"You know about Diana," Christopher said, reading the fear written on the delicate planes of her face as easily as he might read a printed page. "You know that we had an affair. That's what this is all about. You don't want me at all. You simply want to know more about Diana."

Despite her paralyzing fear, Jennifer forced herself to nod.

He shoved her away with such force that she stumbled and fell to the ground. His action was all too reminiscent of her uncle's abuse, reminding her painfully of her life in the tavern. Suddenly the last year fell away. She was no longer the self-confident, silk-clad lady she had become through painful effort and study. She was merely a defenseless tavern wench, cringing in fear of a blow from an angry man's fists. She could not have done anything to save herself if her life depended on it. Anticipating a blow, she lowered her head.

But Christopher did not strike her. He knelt on the ground in front of her, holding her arms in a painful grip, and stared coldly, angrily into her eyes. "I loved Diana," he gritted out between his teeth, "ever since I laid eyes on her. I went to Williamsburg with Grey to meet her and I fell in love with her. But she had already agreed to marry him when I presented my suit. She told me that she loved me, but her parents were happy with the match and she would not break it off. Besides, Grey was building her a mansion, the finest one in the colony. I couldn't afford to give her so much—I couldn't afford to give her what she deserved. My holdings are far less extensive than Grey's.

"We met in Williamsburg as often as possible without raising her parents' suspicions, and when she came to Greyhaven we started meeting in the woods. She loved me, I know she did. But then—"

Jennifer managed to fight off some of her paralysis. "She broke off your affair?" she hazarded.

"No." Christopher's eyes were filled with cold rage. "She told me she was going to have a baby. She didn't know for certain—but she thought it was my child. I couldn't stand to see her raise my child as Grey's. I couldn't stand it."

"So you killed her?"

Christopher said nothing. His eyes blazed with fury.

Jennifer felt a constricting knot of horror in her throat. Despite everything she had done, Diana had not deserved such a fate. Certainly her unborn child had deserved better. Hoarsely, she said, "But it might have been your child! How could you kill her? How could you kill her baby?"

"It might have been my child. It might not have been." Christopher stared into her face, and she shuddered at the slightly vacant expression in the dark blue eyes. For the first time she fully understood that he was not sane. "Don't you understand? Grey already had *everything*. He had a house that was the envy of the colony, he had Diana, and he was going to have the child. A child that was very probably mine. He was going to claim my child as his own, just as he had claimed my beloved as his own. Grey had everything and I had nothing. I could not bear it. I *had* to kill her, don't you understand?"

Hidden in the brush, Grey felt a wave of nausea overcome him. He felt the overpowering urge to double over and vomit, and he fought frantically against it. Memories, excruciatingly painful memories, surfaced, assailing him and all but driving him insane with agony and horror.

It was all my fault. . . .

He did not want to remember.

But he had no choice.

Grey had never before been as drunk as he was this night. Earlier, he and his young wife had fought bitterly, and he had drunk to forget the ugly things she had said to him. Yet despite the quantity of brandy he had imbibed, he could not seem to forget. How could he forget that the woman he loved no longer wanted to share his bed? The pain of that knowledge was still as sharp as a sword edge, lacerating his pride as well as his feelings.

Slumped in his chair, his head in his hands, he heard stealthy steps tiptoeing past his study. Diana. Lurching to his feet, he staggered across the chamber, which for some reason seemed unusually large. After some effort, he found the door and made his way out into the hall.

Catherine, emerging from the parlor, saw him stumble from the study. She hobbled across to him. "Grey," she protested, "let her go. She's not worth the effort."

Grey tried to focus on her, but there seemed to be four of her. "She doesn' love me anymore," he said blearily. "I wanna know why."

"Grey!"

She tried to restrain him, to hold his arm, but even drunk, Grey was stronger by far. He wrenched his arm free and staggered out the door after his wife.

Somehow he mostly kept on his feet as he trailed her through the woods. Once he fell down, scraping and bruising his face badly against the rough bark of a fallen log, but he struggled to his feet and kept following her like a hound on the trail of a fox. Lost in thought, she did not appear to be aware of him trailing her.

At last he halted at a clearing. Leaning wearily against a tree, his head whirling, he saw that his wife was talking with a man. A man who had formerly been his friend—Christopher Lightfoot. He watched in drunken bewilderment. Their voices were too low for him to overhear, but it was clear they were arguing about something.

Slowly the brandy he had consumed began to overpower him. He sank to the ground, still leaning against the tree trunk, barely upright as he watched the drama in the clearing unfold. His eyelids were beginning to close despite himself.

Suddenly, through half-open eyes, he saw Christopher Lightfoot strike his wife. Horrified, he tried to stand up, only to find that the brandy he had consumed had done its work too well. He was too drunk to stand. Another blow snapped Diana's head back and she fell to the ground, unconscious.

Barely conscious himself, Grey struggled to crawl across to his wife, to save her from the man who was now viciously raping her unconscious body, but he could not move. He could only watch in stunned horror as her throat was cut.

He could not so much as crawl over to her body as he wept helplessly.

It was all his fault.

His wife had been beaten, raped, and killed, and he had been utterly powerless to help her. He might as well have killed her himself.

It was all his fault.

He had killed her.

That was his last thought before unconsciousness finally claimed him.

"Bastard," Grey growled beneath his breath. His earlier warnings to Carey forgotten, he leaped from the brush. "You bastard!"

Jennifer, who of course had no idea that he had followed her, blinked at him in shocked surprise. Then she yelped in terror as Christopher, with the speed of a striking snake, jumped to his feet, pulling her up against him. The savagely sharp edge of a knife was pressed against her throat.

She had not realized he had been holding a knife in his hand.

For the first time she realized that Christopher had planned to kill her, just as he had killed Diana.

"Drop it, Grey," Christopher spat.

She saw the pistol in Grey's hand. For a long space of time Grey said nothing, stared at his opponent with eyes like molten steel. The knife pressed more tightly against her skin.

"Drop it. Or I will cut her throat, just as I did Diana's."

Grey dropped the pistol.

"That's better." Christopher smiled. "Of course, I always planned on slashing her throat anyway, eventually."

Jennifer saw Grey's eyes drop to the knife at her throat, saw him swallow. It was the only evidence that he gave of his nervousness as he said coolly, "You must hate me a great deal, Chris. Why?"

"Why?" Christopher repeated. "Why? You ruined my life. You stole Diana from me, you son of a bitch."

Grey refrained from retorting that Christopher had stolen Diana from him, not the other way around. The man was clearly not rational. "But that wasn't all," he speculated idly in a calm voice, fighting to keep his gaze from straying to the knife at Jennifer's throat. His opponent must not know how frightened he was.

"No. That wasn't all. You nearly cost me my inheritance, damn you."

Grey blinked. "Do you mean that business about the slave girl?"

"That's exactly what I mean," Christopher growled. "You told my father that you caught me lying with one of your slaves—"

"You were raping her, damn it!"

"What of it? She was nothing but a slave. You told my father, and he began to worry that I was too irresponsible to run a plantation. Just the week before I had run his prize stallion into the ground. And we had been fighting about my gambling. He was going to disinherit me, to leave everything to my younger brother. If he hadn't fortunately eaten something that disagreed with him and passed away that very week, I wouldn't have gotten the Cove. I would have gotten nothing at all."

"You killed your own father," Grey said slowly. He remembered the way the elder Lightfoot had died, the horrible stomach pains and retching, and he stared at Christopher with wide eyes that clearly expressed his revulsion and horror. This man had once been his best friend, but Grey had ended their friendship abruptly, refusing to have anything further to do with him, after he had caught him raping a terrified slave girl—a girl who was only thirteen or so.

He had not realized, even then, how badly twisted Christopher was.

"I had to," Christopher said sullenly. "It was your fault."

Grey bit back an angry retort. There was no use in arguing

with someone so demented. His eyes rested briefly on the knife that rested against Jennifer's throat, then moved up. Jennifer's gaze met his own. She looked frightened, as any sane person would, but the blank hopelessness he'd seen earlier was gone. He was relieved by the spirit he saw shimmering in her eyes.

The submissive tavern wench was gone forever. She would not submit tamely to her fate.

"Tell me," he said slowly, trying to keep Christopher talking, playing for time. As long as the man was talking, he wasn't killing. Also, he was mindful of Carey, still hidden in the brush, and hoped he might manage to get a clear shot off at Lightfoot. Unfortunately, Lightfoot was not very tall, and Jennifer provided a good shield. "If you've planned to kill Jennifer all this time, why haven't you killed her before now? Surely you've had the opportunity. She walks in the woods by herself quite often."

"There was no point in killing her until she meant something to you," Christopher said. "I wasn't certain that you cared anything for her at all, but I see now that you do. You can't keep your eyes off my knife, no matter how hard you try. You care for her, and for the babe she carries." He moved the knife slowly, and a thin line of blood appeared, black in the moonlight. Grey blanched despite himself.

"At any rate," Christopher added carelessly, "I wanted you to see her death. Just as you saw Diana's."

Grey's head snapped up in surprise, and he stared in shock at the other man. "You knew I was there?"

"Of course. You were drunk. You moved like an ox through the trees. Diana thought a large animal was following her, but I knew better. And then I saw you leaning against a tree, watching us. You saw everything, everything I did to her, but you were too drunk to stop me. You poor drunken sot."

It was my fault. All my fault.
Oh, God, I killed her.

With an enormous mental effort, Grey pushed back the horror and the sickening feeling of helplessness that threatened to overwhelm him. He had been too drunk to save his first wife from a horrible death at the hands of this man, and he had punished himself endlessly for his mistake. But he was not drunk this time. He was not going to fail Jennifer the way he had failed Diana. Somehow, he was going to get her out of Christopher's clutches. He toyed with the notion of charging them, but discarded it. Jennifer's throat might be slashed if he so much as moved. And Christopher's arm was very firmly around her waist.

"Why didn't you kill me afterwards?" he asked in a reasonable tone. "After all, as a witness I might have been able to have you hanged."

Christopher gave a ghastly smile. "I was willing to risk it. I wanted to punish you for everything you'd done to me. I wanted you to live with the memories."

And he had. For eight long years he had lived with the memory of Diana's battered body, and with the memories of her death that he had repressed so completely.

He could not bear to live with Jennifer's death as well.

"Of course," Christopher added, "I didn't know you'd be here tonight. I hoped I could get Jennifer to become my mistress if I told her the rumors about you. Eventually, I knew, you would find out she was my mistress. And then you would follow her into the woods when she came to meet me, and I would—"

As he rambled on, his arm around Jennifer's waist loosened slightly. Seeing her opportunity, Jennifer suddenly brought her foot down with all her strength onto Lightfoot's toes. He yelped and cursed as she twisted away from his suddenly loosened grasp and fell to her knees on the ground. Without pausing to realize that Carey now had a clear shot at Christopher, Grey charged the other man, striking him in the chest with a massive shoulder, and they struck the ground in a tumbling heap.

Grey's fists were everywhere, beating his opponent into

a bloody pulp. He fought viciously, savagely, the image of the knife at Jennifer's throat still haunting him. So enraged was he that he barely noticed the other man's blows.

And in his fury, he had entirely forgotten Christopher's knife.

With a sudden, violent effort, Christopher shoved him, hard. Grey tumbled backward, striking his head painfully against the ground. He lay momentarily stunned, temporarily unable to struggle to his feet. Christopher knelt next to him and raised his knife.

At that moment a shot rang out.

Christopher fell to the ground, dead.

Jennifer, kneeling on the ground with her knife at the ready, looked around in surprise and relief as Carey stepped from the brush. He grinned at her, as casually as if nothing at all out of the ordinary had happened, and offered Grey a hand, helping him up as Grey had helped him to his feet half an hour before.

"About bloody time you fired that thing," Grey grumbled, becoming painfully aware of his bloodied lip and several other bruises he was sporting.

"I couldn't very well take a chance on hitting you or Jennifer, could I? At any rate," Carey said, still grinning, "you were doing all right by yourself."

Grey shrugged. He knew very well that the other man's timely intervention had saved his life. Then his eyes fell upon Jennifer, and he saw the knife she was clutching as she stumbled to her feet. An overpowering wave of love broke over him. If Carey had not saved him, he was certain Jennifer would have.

"Are you all right?" he asked her.

Jennifer nodded, eyeing him uncertainly. There were yards of distance separating them, and he did not seem at all inclined to sweep her into his arms and kiss her. She glanced down self-consciously at her excessively low-cut gown, realizing exactly what was probably going through Grey's mind. "You may be wondering," she began tentatively, "exactly why I met Christopher out here, dressed this way. It's not—"

"It's not what I think, I suppose."

"No. It's not."

"Are you certain?"

Beneath his impassive expression she could have sworn she saw a hint of laughter. "I don't know," she said suspiciously. "What *do* you think?"

Grey quirked an eyebrow. "I think," he said softly, "that you are an amazing, brave, extraordinary, and beautiful young woman."

"Oh," Jennifer said in confusion.

"Did I leave anything out?"

"I think that about covers it," Carey said. "Except perhaps 'foolish.' Jenny, why did you risk confronting Lightfoot by yourself? Are you mad?"

Grey gave him a dire look, recalling that just last night this man had been asking Jennifer to be his mistress. "Go back to the house," he commanded shortly. "We'll be up in a few minutes."

His shoulders shaking with laughter at Grey's all too obvious jealousy, Carey started up the hill, only to be nearly bowled over by Catherine, who was hobbling down the lawn as quickly as she was able. She grasped his arms and stared up at him anxiously, her normal hauteur entirely evaporated. "My God! Carey, what happened? I heard—"

"I'll explain everything," Carey said gently, taking her arm and helping her back toward the house.

When they had gone, Jennifer walked slowly over to Christopher's body and stood staring down at him. "Poor Melissa," she whispered. "She really loved him, you know."

Grey found it odd that her first thoughts were for his erstwhile mistress. She certainly had a forgiving nature. "I know," he replied. His thoughts toward Melissa were not as charitable. He now realized she had known about Diana's affair with Christopher. All these years she had been bedding

Grey in a futile effort to avenge herself on her husband. She had known that Diana had been having an affair, and she had never told him. He felt oddly disappointed in her.

The more fool he, to have expected honesty from his mistress.

Worried by his long silence, Jennifer put a tentative hand on Grey's arm. "Edward," she whispered, "I'm so sorry about—"

"Shh," Grey interrupted, putting a finger on her lips. "We're not going to concern ourselves with what happened in the past anymore. We're starting over, Jennifer. From now on, nothing matters but the future." He stared down at her, his face very solemn as he realized he could have lost her forever. "And if you ever risk your life in this way again," he murmured gently, "I'll lock you away in your chamber forever."

Putting his arms around her, he held her close. Jennifer buried her face against his chest. "Edward," she murmured. "I love you."

His arms tightened around her. But he said nothing.

Nothing at all.

"Are you busy?"

Grey looked up from the papers on his desk to see Jennifer standing in the doorway to his study, looking uncomfortable. He smiled. "No. Come in."

"I wanted to show you something." She waved him over to the window. Quizzically, he stared out through the wavy glass.

Carey and Catherine were walking together through the sun-drenched formal garden, engaged in an animated conversation. Her hand rested on his arm, and she looked up at him with an admiring expression.

"Well, well," Grey said softly. "Look at that. At long last, she has a suitor."

"I hope so," Jennifer said sincerely.

Grey grinned down at her. "So do I. I much prefer that he court my sister rather than my wife."

"Grey," she began chidingly.

"I am only joking," he assured her. "He's a good man. I like him."

"You really do, don't you?"

Grey nodded. "There's more of his father in him than I thought."

"I'm glad. He was so kind to me at the ordinary. Even though he had an ulterior motive, I still think of him as a friend. He means a lot to me." She smiled out the window, seeing Carey laugh at something Catherine had said. "It would mean a great deal to me if he was part of the family."

"We'll see," Grey said. He hadn't seen Catherine smile so much in a long time. He added, "Carey and I will be riding to Williamsburg tomorrow. We need to visit Trev Lancaster and tell him what really happened to Diana."

As he said the words he realized how fortunate he was. He had been planning to go to Williamsburg to turn himself in. He would have been in gaol until he was tried, and then he would have dangled at the end of a rope. Now, thanks to Jennifer, he was a free man, and at long last he knew he was not a murderer. Thanks to Jennifer, and her stubborn belief in his innocence.

At his words, Jennifer had turned slightly and glanced toward the portrait of Diana. He saw the shock on her face as she realized the portrait was gone.

"I took it down yesterday," he said by way of explanation.

Jennifer looked stunned. "You must have felt very disillusioned when you realized she'd loved another man," she said softly.

"I did," Grey admitted, "but that wasn't the reason I took it down. I don't hate Diana for what she did. She was only human, as capable of making mistakes as anyone, and God knows she paid a horrible price for her infidelity. No, I took it down because I finally realized it was time to stop living in the past. Diana is no longer part of my life, Jennifer." He paused. "You are my life now."

"You built Greyhaven for her," Jennifer whispered.

"Does that bother you? If you prefer, we can live on

another one of my quarters. I could build another house. I will, if you like."

Jennifer stared thoughtfully out the window, seeing the boxwood hedges lining the oyster-shell-strewn paths in the formal garden, the wide lawn, and the blue waters of the James River. "I don't think so," she said at last. "I like it here."

"So do I," Grey admitted. "There are a great many bad memories here for me—but there are a great many good ones as well." He smiled, remembering the day he had brought her to Greyhaven, the day he had brought her into his life, never imagining that the dust-covered tavern wench would become a lady. No doubt that day, when Jennifer fell from her horse and sat forlornly in the dust, was not something she liked to recall—but it was one of his most cherished memories.

"Jennifer," he said slowly. "I think I should tell you . . ."

His wife glanced around. "Yes?"

He saw the hope in her eyes. Last night, he had taken her to his bed, and they had made love for hours. She had whispered to him of her love, and he had held her close.

She was going to bear his child, and she meant everything to him. But he had not been able to tell her he loved her. The words simply would not come.

"Never mind," he said. "It wasn't important."

Jennifer lifted her chin slightly. "I see," she said chillingly. "In that case, I will leave you alone now." She started to walk from the chamber, then turned and looked back over her shoulder. "If you *do* think of anything you want to tell me," she said in her most regal voice, "I shall be in the garden."

It seemed quiet once she had left the house. It *was* quiet; Catherine, Carey, and Jennifer were in the garden, and the other O'Neills were still in Williamsburg. Grey was alone. In the long habit of years, he found himself picking up a goblet and a decanter of Madeira. He stared at them thoughtfully.

He knew why he had been unable to tell Jennifer that he loved her.

He might not be a murderer, but he was not worthy of her love.

He wanted her love, but he wanted her respect and admiration as well, and he could not hope to win them as he was—a self-absorbed drunkard. In the cold sunlight streaming in through the window, he at last saw himself as others saw him, and he despised what he saw.

He had been hiding here in his study for far too long.

His eyes drifted back down to the decanter in his hands. "Damn it, no," he whispered, and hurled it away from himself. It exploded against the wall in a spray of dark amber liquid and shattered glass.

He smiled then, and thought, *My life is not over yet*.

On the contrary, his life had just begun. Feeling in control of his own destiny for the first time in too many years, he strode from the study to find Jennifer and tell her how much he loved her.

He walked out into the sunshine.

ABOUT THE AUTHOR

Ellen Fisher is a native Virginian and a fourth-generation writer who received her B.A. in history from the College of William and Mary in Williamsburg, Virginia. She has wanted to be a writer since she was three years old, watching her mother type newspaper articles on an old Royal manual typewriter. She is married to her high school sweetheart, Don, a true romantic hero cleverly disguised as a mild-mannered programmer analyst, and has a three-year-old daughter who watches *her* write . . . thankfully, on a computer rather than a manual typewriter.

Bestselling Historical Women's Fiction

✳ AMANDA QUICK ✳

____28354-5 SEDUCTION ...$6.50/$8.99 Canada

____28932-2 SCANDAL ....$6.50/$8.99

____28594-7 SURRENDER ....$6.50/$8.99

____29325-7 RENDEZVOUS ....$6.50/$8.99

____29315-X RECKLESS ....$6.50/$8.99

____29316-8 RAVISHED ....$6.50/$8.99

____29317-6 DANGEROUS ....$6.50/$8.99

____56506-0 DECEPTION ....$6.50/$8.99

____56153-7 DESIRE ....$6.50/$8.99

____56940-6 MISTRESS ....$6.50/$8.99

____57159-1 MYSTIQUE ....$6.50/$8.99

____57190-7 MISCHIEF ....$6.50/$8.99

____57407-8 AFFAIR ....$6.99/$8.99

✳ IRIS JOHANSEN ✳

____29871-2 LAST BRIDGE HOME ...$5.50/$7.50

____29604-3 THE GOLDEN

BARBARIAN ....$6.99/$8.99

____29244-7 REAP THE WIND ......$5.99/$7.50

____29032-0 STORM WINDS ....$6.99/$8.99

Bestselling Historical Women's Fiction

❧ IRIS JOHANSEN ❧

____28855-5 THE WIND DANCER . . .$5.99/$6.99

____29968-9 THE TIGER PRINCE . . .$6.99/$8.99

____29944-1 THE MAGNIFICENT
              ROGUE . . . .$6.99/$8.99

____29945-X BELOVED SCOUNDREL .$6.99/$8.99

____29946-8 MIDNIGHT WARRIOR . .$6.99/$8.99

____29947-6 DARK RIDER . . . .$6.99/$8.99

____56990-2 LION'S BRIDE . . . .$6.99/$8.99

____56991-0 THE UGLY DUCKLING. . .$6.99/$8.99

____57181-8 LONG AFTER MIDNIGHT.$6.99/$8.99

____57998-3 AND THEN YOU DIE.... $6.99/$8.99

❧ TERESA MEDEIROS ❧

____29407-5 HEATHER AND VELVET .$5.99/$7.50

____29409-1 ONCE AN ANGEL . . . . .$5.99/$7.99

____29408-3 A WHISPER OF ROSES . .$5.99/$7.99

____56332-7 THIEF OF HEARTS . . . . .$5.50/$6.99

____56333-5 FAIREST OF THEM ALL .$5.99/$7.50

____56334-3 BREATH OF MAGIC . . . .$5.99/$7.99

____57623-2 SHADOWS AND LACE . . .$5.99/$7.99

____57500-7 TOUCH OF ENCHANTMENT. .$5.99/$7.99

____57501-5 NOBODY'S DARLING . . .$5.99/$7.99

- -

Ask for these books at your local bookstore or use this page to order.

Please send me the books I have checked above. I am enclosing $____ (add $2.50 to cover postage and handling). Send check or money order, no cash or C.O.D.'s, please.

Name _____

Address _____

City/State/Zip _____

Send order to: Bantam Books, Dept. FN 16, 2451 S. Wolf Rd., Des Plaines, IL 60018
Allow four to six weeks for delivery.
Prices and availability subject to change without notice.   FN 16 9/98